Bedlam

The Further Secret Adventures of
Charlotte Brontë

Bedlam

THE FURTHER SECRET ADVENTURES
OF CHARLOTTE BRONTË

Laura Joh Rowland

THE OVERLOOK PRESS
New York

This edition first published in the United States in 2010 by
The Overlook Press, Peter Mayer Publishers, Inc.
New York & London

NEW YORK:
141 Wooster Street
New York, NY 10012

Cataloging-in-Publication Data is available from the Library of Congress

Book design and type formatting by Bernard Schleifer
Manufactured in the United States of America
ISBN 978-1-59020-271-5
10 9 8 7 6 5 4 3 2 1

To Juliet Grames, my editor.
Thank you for daring to take a chance.

Bedlam

The Further Secret Adventures of
Charlotte Brontë

PROLOGUE

*B*EFORE I LEFT MY BED IN THE MORNING, LITTLE ADELE CAME *running to tell me that the great horse-chestnut at the bottom of the orchard had been struck by lightning in the night, and half of it split away.*

Reader, that sentence is from a novel I wrote. It ends the scene in which Mr. Rochester proposes marriage to Jane Eyre, she accepts, and a fierce storm rages over Thornfield Manor. The lightning symbolized the earth-shattering event in Jane's life; the split chestnut tree, the lovers soon to be torn asunder. When I wrote the sentence, little did I suspect that I had prophesized my own future.

In the summer of 1848, lightning struck me when I was plunged into an adventure the like of which I had never believed possible. I journeyed far beyond my wildest imaginings; I experienced momentous events now cloaked in secrecy. If I now say that my actions influenced the fate of nations, please forgive me the appearance of immodesty: I only speak the truth.

During my adventures, I found the man of my dreams. His name is John Slade; he is a spy for the British Crown. We shared the love that I had hoped for all my life but despaired of ever knowing. But we were too soon torn apart. My heart was rent as severely as the poor chestnut tree. The similarity between my situation and Jane's did not escape me; nor did the fact that the division between fantasy and life is sometimes akin to a line drawn in sand blown by the wind. While I mourned the loss of adventure as well as love, I had no intimation that what happens once can happen again.

In 1851, adventure came calling once more. The circumstances were different, but the second adventure had an important aspect in common with the first. Both involved John Slade. The first adventure led me to him, then took him away. The second brought him back.

Nearly three years had passed, time during which many changes transformed my life. But I never ceased to remember those events of 1848, nor to yearn for the happiness that had departed when he left. And I never suspected that far away, in the country to which he had gone, events were building into a tide of peril that would sweep me along in its current.

These events I did not witness, but the mind of an author can travel to places where she cannot. Her imagination substitutes for actual experience. Fiction built upon facts creates a semblance of the truth. I will now, to the best of my ability, reconstruct the events in question.

1851 January. The city of Moscow lay beneath a heavy fall of snow. Its rooftops glittered white in the light of the moon and stars that sparkled in a sky as dark as obsidian. Near the city gate loomed Butyrka, the dreaded prison built in the eighteenth century during the reign of Catherine the Great. Snow frosted the crenellated towers, blanketed the tops of the high stone walls, and covered the prison compound. The scene was as bright as day, but devoid of color, painted in stark shades of white and black.

The ironclad portals opened, and three men stumbled out. Blindfolds hid their eyes. Ropes bound their wrists behind their backs. They wore only shirts and trousers; their feet were bare. Prodded by three guards armed with rifles, they limped and staggered. Cuts, bruises, and gashes marked their faces and bodies. They shivered in the bitter cold as the guards, joking among themselves, lined them up against the wall. Their breath crystallized in the air. They trembled so hard they could barely stand as the guards aimed the rifles at them, but they were too weak to protest. Without ceremony, the guards fired.

The men uttered agonized cries; their bodies jerked. Blood spattered the wall and flooded the snow, wet and black and steaming. Gunshots blared until the prisoners fell. Three corpses lay on the ground. Cruel justice was served.

The echoes of the gunshots faded as they reached the heart of town. There, bonfires burned on the banks of the frozen Moscow River. Skaters glided over the ice, in rhythm to gay music from an orchestra. High above the river rose the Kremlin. The turrets, domes, and spires of its palaces and cathedrals soared to the heavens. The Grand Kremlin Palace was a magnificent Byzantine structure of white stone, lavishly gilded. Tiers of arched windows shone, the rooms within lit by crystal chandeliers. From one window, a man gazed down at the skating party. A high, intelligent forehead crowned his eyes, which drooped at the corners. His mustache curled up at the ends, but his mouth did not. His posture was proud, his expression humorless and calculating.

He was Nicholas Pavlovich, Tsar of Russia.

In the chamber where he stood, a lofty, vaulted ceiling arched from carved columns encrusted with gold. An entourage of soldiers, courtiers, and servants awaited his orders. Footsteps rang on the mosaic floor, and a man joined the Tsar. He was a Prussian, whose face had a Germanic cast laid upon pale eyes with heavily hooded lids and a long nose whose end overlapped the upper lip of a cruel, sensual mouth. His close-cropped silver hair gleamed. The Tsar waved his hand, dismissing his attendants. They discreetly faded away.

The only person who remained was a man who had secreted himself behind a column, from where the faintest word spoken in the chamber could be heard.

"What have you to report?" the Tsar asked.

"The agents from England have been put to death," the Prussian said.

"All of them?"

". . . Yes, Your Highness." The Tsar didn't notice that a heartbeat had passed before the Prussian answered.

Troubles weighed visibly upon Tsar Nicholas. "More will come. The British are determined to extend their control over the world and diminish mine. They have allied with France, Spain, and Portugal for the sole purpose of keeping me in check. But they are not content to stop at mere political maneuvering. They send their agents to spy on my regime, to foment insurrection among my people, to weaken my empire from within." His eyes burned with the reflections of the bonfires on the river. "It is just a matter of time before our hostilities culminate in war. If only there were a way to guarantee a victory for Russia."

"There may be."

The Tsar turned to his companion. "Oh?" His eyes narrowed. His court was full of men who placated him with false assurances. "Have you a new idea?"

"I do. It arose from a message I've just received from our agents in London." The Prussian related the contents of the message and told the Tsar how the information could be used to Russia's advantage.

The hidden listener overheard everything. He knew he should make his escape before the men discovered him, but he lingered, rapt with horror. The details provided in the message were sketchy, but the Prussian built upon them a scenario of a battlefield that spread east as far as China, west over Europe and across the English Channel, of countries laid to waste and carnage on a scale greater than ever known in history. Yet the listener had more immediate, personal concerns: his own days were numbered.

All of this I learned about much later. By then I was already embroiled in the adventure, and it was too late to turn back. By then I had learned a lesson.

Lightning does strike twice.

Reader, I am proof.

Herein is my story.

CHARLOTTE BRONTË
Haworth, England, 1852 June

1

WHEN I WAS YOUNG, I WISHED FOR ADVENTURE AND ROMANCE, for travel to exciting locales far from Haworth, the tiny village where I have lived most of my life. I wished for success as an author, to be famous and sought after, to leave my mark on the world. Outrageous ambitions these were for the daughter of a Yorkshire parson! Little did I realize that when I achieved my ambitions, the reality would bear scant resemblance to the dream. Nor did I realize that I should have been careful what I wished for because I might get it.

These thoughts were much on my mind on the Thursday evening of 29 May 1851.

Arm in arm with my publisher, George Smith, I strolled into Almack's Assembly Rooms in London. We entered the salon, where a chattering crowd of society folk occupied rows of damask-covered benches. Light from gas chandeliers gleamed on the women's silk gowns, upswept hair, white bosoms, and glittering jewelry. The scene dazzled my nearsighted eyes as I peered through my spectacles. Miserably destitute of self-possession, I hesitated.

"Have courage, my dear Charlotte," George Smith said. Tall and youthful, he had brown eyes and smooth brown hair; he looked elegant in formal evening dress. He was as perceptive as he was handsome, and he knew about my shyness. "Everyone is positively dying to meet you."

"That's what I'm afraid of." This was my fourth trip to London, but my dread of appearing in public had never diminished. Before leaving home I'd been so plagued by nerves that I had suffered one of my bilious attacks. I was still weak, my stomach still queasy.

George Smith laughed and patted my hand. "Fear not. I'll protect you."

Four years ago, I'd sent the manuscript of my novel to him. Smith, Elder and Company had published *Jane Eyre*, and it had become a famous bestseller. When we had first met in 1848, I had become briefly infatuated with George. We had since become friends—indeed, very intimate friends. Flirtation pervaded our letters and our talk. Three years ago I could not have anticipated such a turn of events. Nor would I have believed that if one of us fell in love with the other, it would not be me.

As we walked through the salon, faces turned in my direction. I felt dowdy in my black silk frock. Having a bestselling novel to my name did not quell my lifelong fear of what other people thought of how I looked. When I'd dared to imagine myself famous, I'd always imagined myself transformed into a beauty. Would that all dreams could come true! Yet, even though I remained as small and plain as ever, excited murmurs arose. Before the publication of *Jane Eyre*, no one had ever heard of Charlotte Brontë. Now, it seemed everybody had. Once I could have walked as if invisible among these folk, but no more: I was an object of curiosity and speculation. That I had never expected.

George's mother, walking on my other side, said, "Miss Brontë, if you're uncomfortable, we'll be glad to send you home."

Mrs. Smith was a portly, dark-haired woman, still attractive despite her age, and she did not like me any more than I liked her. Despite her solicitous tone, I knew she wished I would go back to the Smith family house, where I was staying, so she could enjoy the evening with her son. That was something else about fame that I hadn't expected—that I would make enemies.

When George had first introduced her to me three years ago, he had not told her that I was the author of *Jane Eyre*; for reasons I will not detail here, it had been published under my pseudonym, Currer Bell, and I had wanted my true identity kept confidential.

When my identity was finally revealed, Mrs. Smith was furious at the deception. She was also mortified that I—whom she'd treated as a poor, dull nobody—was responsible for earning a fortune for her son's publishing company. And she feared that I had designs of a matrimonial nature on George.

Mrs. Smith didn't know that my heart belonged to another man, whom I would most probably never see again this side of Heaven.

"Thank you, but I don't want to go home," I said, hiding my antipathy behind politeness. "I would not want to miss hearing Mr. Thackeray."

The great author William Makepeace Thackeray had lately embarked upon a series of lectures, The English Humorists of the 18th Century, which were all the rage with the fashionable literary set. This was the kind of event I had once dreamed of attending.

"Be careful not to steal his thunder," George said playfully.

"I could never," I said, aghast at the idea.

At the front of the room, surrounded by fawning ladies and gentlemen, stood the author of the famous novel, *Vanity Fair*. He was above six feet tall, with a mane of gray hair, and quite ugly, his expression at once stern and satirical. His sharp gaze homed in on me through the spectacles perched on his nose. He smiled, and I smiled back. I was proud to count him among the friends I'd made since the publication of *Jane Eyre*. I was glad he had noticed me, but the glint in his eyes should have warned me to expect mischief.

He left his admirers, drawing one of the women with him, a fine old lady with snow-white hair. They approached me, and Mr. Thackeray said loudly to her, "Mother, allow me to introduce you to Jane Eyre."

The room fell silent. Everyone stared at me. Mr. Thackeray smiled as if he'd done me a favor by identifying me as the heroine of my novel and making me the center of attention. But I was mortified. Blushing furiously, I wished a hole would open in the floor and swallow me. Mr. Thackeray was waiting for my reply, but I was so upset, and so angry at him, that I could think of none.

Mrs. Smith said, "Come, Miss Brontë." She drew me away to a

vacant bench near the wall. I knew she resented any attention paid to me, but I was thankful that she'd separated me from Mr. Thackeray before I did something regrettable. As she and George sat on either side of me, I heard murmurs in the crowd.

"Miss Brontë dedicated the second edition of *Jane Eyre* to Mr. Thackeray, didn't she?"

"Do you know that his wife is mad and she had to be put in an insane asylum?"

"They say that his wife was the model for the madwoman in *Jane Eyre*."

"Yes, and I heard that Miss Brontë was once a governess in Mr. Thackeray's house. I wouldn't be surprised if they'd had inappropriate intimacies. Remember, Becky Sharp and Jane Eyre were both governesses who married their employers."

What a scandal had my innocent gesture of admiration caused! Alas, no one had told me about Mr. Thackeray's insane wife until too late. Many readers now thought my novel was autobiographical and Mr. Thackeray and I were the hero and heroine, even though it was patently untrue: Although I had been a governess, I had never worked for Mr. Thackeray. We had not met until after I became a published authoress. Mr. Thackeray had been kind about my blunder, and if his prank were his only retribution, I should be glad.

More whispers reached my ears: "Miss Brontë and her publisher seem on very intimate terms." "Yes, even though she is his elder." George Smith was twenty-nine years of age, a most eligible bachelor, and I thirty-five, a spinster long past my prime. "I wonder if we'll soon hear wedding bells."

George smiled and pretended nothing had happened. His mother fumed. By this time I should have gotten accustomed to being the subject of rumors, but I had not.

At long last, the audience was seated. The room quieted as Mr. Thackeray took his place behind the lectern. He spoke with simplicity and ease. Humor and force enlivened everything he said. The audience responded with laughter and approval. I would have enjoyed it completely, had I not felt the glances upon me, as intrusive as the unwanted touch of hands. The evening had just begun, and there was worse to come.

When the lecture ended, the people in the audience arranged themselves in two lines along the aisle. Mr. Thackeray walked down the aisle, shaking hands, accepting compliments, exchanging quips. When he reached the door, the people did not follow him out; they remained.

"They're waiting for you," George gently informed me.

Shrinking between him and his mother, I walked the gauntlet. It was an endless tunnel of faces that smiled too close to me, warm, moist hands that pressed mine, and cultured voices making enthusiastic remarks. I smiled, murmured polite replies, and tried not to faint from embarrassment. When we entered another room, in which refreshments were served, I became separated from the Smiths and cornered by a formidable group of my admirers.

"I simply loved *Jane Eyre*," exclaimed the Duchess of Sutherland. "When will your next book be published?"

"I'm afraid I can't say," I replied unhappily.

It had been nearly four years since the publication of *Jane Eyre*, and going on two since my second novel, *Shirley*, had appeared. The second had not been received as well as the first. Hence, I felt considerable pressure to produce a new work that would live up to *Jane Eyre*.

"At least tell us what the book is about," came the outcry.

I only wished I knew. I had been unable to settle upon a subject for my next book. Thus far my publisher had been understanding and patient, but I couldn't expect him—or the public—to wait forever. "I'm sorry," was all I could think to say.

I escaped, only to be accosted by other folk asking the same questions. Once I would have given my life for such avid interest in my literary works. Now I only wanted to hide. Once I could have comforted myself with the knowledge that when I went home I would describe this evening to those I loved most. But they were gone.

My brother Branwell had died first, in 1848 September, of consumption. Too soon afterward, in December, did my sister Emily die of the same disease. I prayed to God that He would spare my youngest sister, Anne, but in the New Year she became ill with consumption. By 1849 May, she, too, was dead.

In our youth my siblings and I had encouraged one another in our artistic pursuits, and I'd believed that we would share a brilliant future together. My prediction came partially true when Emily and Anne and I all published novels. But Emily's *Wuthering Heights* and Anne's *Agnes Grey* and *The Tenant of Wildfell Hall* were not favored by the critics or the public. And never did I suspect that I would be the only one of us to achieve any fame and financial success, or that I would be left to experience it alone. Their deaths still haunt me; my grief is still raw. I am thankful that I still have my father, but the one other person who could have alleviated my sorrow is far away.

That person is, of course, John Slade, the spy with whom I fell in love during my adventures in 1848. He asked me to marry him, but I refused because he was due to leave for an assignment in Russia, and we could not count on seeing each other again. I love him yet, even though I have not heard from him in all these years and do not know whether he still loves me—or even if he is still alive.

The matter of what to call John Slade, in my mind as well as in this narrative, has required some thought. "Mr. Slade" would be most proper, but in view of our relations it seems too formal. "John" seems too familiar because we didn't know each other long enough to progress to first names. Therefore, I think of him as "Slade," a compromise. But no matter how I refer to him, he is always in my heart. I miss him daily, keenly.

My longing for my lost loved ones still overcomes me at unpredictable, inconvenient times. Now, in the midst of gay society, I felt tears sting my eyes. Groping toward the door, I bumped smack into a gentleman.

"Miss Brontë," he said. "May I be of service?"

His voice had a calming quality; it soothed my nerves so unexpectedly that I looked up at him instead of continuing on my way. He was not above average height, with not more than average good looks. His graying hair receded from his high forehead, and his somber air made him seem less superficial than the rest of the crowd. Concern showed in his hazel eyes. He procured a glass of wine from a nearby table and gave it to me.

"Drink this," he said with a quiet authority hard to resist.

I drank, and my spirits rose somewhat. I felt oddly safer, as if the crowds around us would not trouble me while I was in his presence. "Thank you, Mr. . . . ?"

"Dr. John Forbes," he said. "We've never met, but we've corresponded. Perhaps you remember?"

"Yes, of course. I wrote to you concerning my sister's illness." Dr. Forbes was one of Britain's foremost experts on consumptive disease. He was also a personal friend of George Smith, who had suggested I consult him about Anne during her illness. "Please allow me to thank you in person for replying so quickly."

"You're quite welcome." Dr. Forbes's somber air deepened. "I was sorry to hear that your sister did not recover. Please accept my condolences."

I did, with heartfelt gratitude. Usually, when someone mentions my sisters, I break down, but his presence was so steadying that this time I remained composed.

"How are you?" he said. "I hope that your writing has been a comfort to you?"

I told him that I had not been able to write. "If only I could manage to find a subject that was fascinating enough." Then I inquired about his work.

"I have been treating consumptive patients at Bedlam," Dr. Forbes said.

Bedlam. Hearing the popular name for the Bethlem Royal Hospital caused me a shiver of morbid curiosity: London's insane asylum was notorious. But I had more than a prurient interest in madness. I had firsthand experience with it, and I eagerly questioned Dr. Forbes about the patients he treated.

"They suffer from delusions, paranoia, mania, and dementia, among other things," he said, and described a few cases.

I recognized symptoms exhibited by my brother Branwell, and

by a murderous villain I'd encountered during my adventures of 1848. "What causes these conditions?"

"Most experts say they're a result of physical defects or spiritual disturbances," Dr. Forbes said. "But there is a new school of thought which suggests that madness originates from experiences in early life."

I expressed such fascination that he said, "Would you like to visit Bedlam? I'd be glad to escort you. Perhaps it would furnish a subject for your new book."

"Yes, I would like that very much," I said, so eager that I forgot to be shy.

George Smith and his mother came hurrying up to us. "Ah, Charlotte," he said. "I see you've met my friend Forbes." He and the doctor greeted one another.

"We were just leaving," Mrs. Smith said, tired of having so much fuss made over me in public. She turned to me and said, "It's time to go home."

"I've just invited Miss Brontë to visit Bedlam with me," said Dr. Forbes, "and she has accepted."

"Visit Bedlam?" As George looked from Dr. Forbes to me, concern flickered over his smooth features. "But you might see disturbing things."

"Miss Brontë has a taste for disturbing things," Mrs. Smith said. "Her novels are full of them." She smiled kindly at me.

I seethed, but I could not retort: she was my hostess, and I owed her courtesy even if she didn't deserve it. "I daresay I can cope."

"I won't show Miss Brontë the parts of the asylum that an outsider shouldn't see," Dr. Forbes promised.

"I still think it's unwise," George said with a frown.

"I agree," his mother said. "Miss Brontë, it might be construed as unseemly for a lady to visit such a place." Her tone hinted that I was no lady. Her smile remained bright and kind.

"Ladies visit Bedlam every day," Dr. Forbes said. "The public is always welcome."

Mrs. Smith pretended not to hear. "If you don't care about yourself, at least have a thought for my poor son. What if it were to distress you so much that you became unable to write your next book?"

She wanted me to think that my next book, and not me, was all George cared about. George exclaimed, "Never mind the book, Charlotte." His mother winced. She disliked that he and I were on first-name terms. "My fear is that you'll be attacked by a lunatic."

"That might please some people," I couldn't resist saying.

Before his mother could think of a rejoinder, Dr. Forbes assured George, "Patients who are dangerous are kept away from the public. And I promise to protect Miss Brontë. But of course," he said to me, "if you would like to change your mind . . . ?"

Once I would have bowed to the will of the people to whom I felt obligated. But I am stubborn by nature, and another unexpected thing that my fame had brought me was the backbone to resist coercion.

"I am determined to visit Bedlam," I said. "Shall I meet you there at ten o'clock tomorrow morning?"

"That would be fine," Dr. Forbes said.

George Smith looked resigned, his mother distinctly put out. None of us knew at the time that my innocent trip to the insane asylum would ultimately bring peril to us all.

2

LIFE ABOUNDS WITH CHANCE ENCOUNTERS. MOST LEAVE NO residue, but some have consequences that are serious and far-reaching. Such was my encounter with a woman named Isabel White, whom I met during the summer of 1848. Such was my meeting with Dr. John Forbes. Chance encounters such as these send us down one path instead of another, and we cannot know until much later that they have changed the course of our lives.

However, I had no intimation of this on the morning I was engaged to visit Bedlam. As I sat in the parlor of the Smiths' house at Number 76 Gloucester Terrace in Hyde Park Gardens and waited for the carriage, I thought only of the interesting material for my long-overdue book.

I heard wheels rattle and horses' hooves clop outside. I hurried to the door and opened it. In the sun-drenched street between the rows of elegant houses was a carriage, but not the one hired for me. Down its steps clambered Mr. Thackeray.

"Good morning, Miss Brontë," he said, all sardonic smiles. "I've come to pay you a social call."

Although furious at him for what he'd done to me last night, I had no choice but to usher him to the parlor.

"How is Jane Eyre today?" His eyes twinkled mischievously behind his spectacles.

My eyes saw red. "How dare you! After introducing me as 'Jane

Eyre' and making a public fool of me yesterday, you mock me again!"

Mr. Thackeray took an involuntary step backward. Astonishment raised his bushy eyebrows. "Why, Miss Brontë, were you offended by what I said?"

"I was and am offended."

"I meant you no harm," Mr. Thackeray said, stung by my criticism. His manner turned patronizing. "You are too sensitive. If you intend to survive in the cutthroat world of literary society, you must grow a thicker skin."

"People who think other people are too sensitive are usually as insensitive as a rhinoceros themselves," I retorted.

Mr. Thackeray glared indignantly; then he remembered his manners. "All right. If your feelings were hurt, I apologize."

"What kind of apology is that? I could just as well call you a cad and then say I'm sorry you are one!"

"You've already called me a rhinoceros," Mr. Thackeray said, nettled yet amused.

"Only because you deserved it."

Baffled now, Mr. Thackeray said, "I don't understand what all this fuss is about. What I said was just idle, harmless teasing."

"No, sir!" I exclaimed with a passion. "It was in poor taste at best, and cruel at worst!"

We faced off, I all in rage and Mr. Thackeray all haughty resentment. My fists were clenched, and I know not what I would have done if George Smith hadn't heard us arguing and rushed in from his breakfast.

"Charlotte, you have every right to be upset," he said, "but I'm sure that Mr. Thackeray truly didn't mean to cause you pain. Do give him a chance to apologize properly."

These reasonable words served to dash cold water onto the heat of battle. "I am sorry for offending you," Mr. Thackeray said with genuine contrition. "Will you please forgive me?"

"Yes, of course." I didn't quite trust him, but felt better now that we'd had it out.

"I'd like to make it up to you," Mr. Thackeray said. "Please allow me to take you and a party of friends to the theater. You may choose the play."

The idea of another social occasion made my nerves quail, but I accepted rather than have him think me still angry. We made a date for the next evening. Then my carriage arrived, and I set out for Bedlam.

As the carriage bore me away from the decorous streets of Hyde Park Gardens, I began to have misgivings. St. George's Fields, in which Bedlam was located, contained some of London's worst slums. Deteriorating tenements lined dirty, narrow streets filled with the poorest, most downtrodden of humanity. The stench of garbage and cesspits was sickening. But of course the city authorities would not have situated an insane asylum in a finer district.

Bedlam was an imposing edifice, three stories high, crowned by a huge dome, with a classical portico and columns at the entrance, surrounded by a stone wall. Stately as a temple, it dominated the wide boulevard. Dr. Forbes was waiting for me at the gate. We exchanged pleasantries and he led me inside. A lawn bordered with flowering shrubs and shaded by tall trees seemed out of place amid the squalid slum. So did the folks who accompanied us up the wide staircase in an excited, chattering horde. Many were fashionable ladies and gentlemen, such as one might see in Pall Mall.

"Who are all these people?" I asked.

"Visitors," replied Dr. Forbes. "Some are here to see family members who are patients. Most have come to tour the asylum."

To view the inmates as if they were wild animals in the zoo, I thought. I felt ashamed of my own curiosity, until Dr. Forbes pointed out a booth at the entrance, where an attendant was taking admission fees, and said, "The money paid by the visitors helps to defray the cost of caring for the patients."

Inside, the visitors' footsteps and chatter echoed in a vast hall with high ceilings, lit by sunlight from many windows. So far Bedlam seemed a respectable institution, not the gloomy dungeon I'd imagined. It did not even smell any worse than other buildings in London, whose sewers taint the air everywhere. Dr. Forbes escorted me through a chapel, then the basement, which contained the kitchens, pantry, and laundry. There labored people I first took for servants.

"The patients who are well enough work to earn their keep," Dr. Forbes said.

I took a second look at the men cutting vegetables with sharp knives and the women pressing sheets with hot irons. I was glad to see attendants standing watch over them, for I'd not forgotten George Smith's warning about dangerous lunatics. We inspected the kitchen gardens, where patients watered neat rows of plants, and the recreation grounds where they strolled. Dr. Forbes talked about the therapeutic benefits of fresh air and exercise. The crowds of visitors lent the place a holiday air. I could almost have thought myself on tour of some great country manor, if not for the howls and shrieks that periodically emanated from the asylum.

"Shall we proceed to the wards?" Dr. Forbes asked.

I eagerly agreed. We went up a spacious staircase. The women's ward had sunny corridors furnished with carpets, comfortable chairs, oil paintings, marble busts, and baskets of flowering plants. Matrons in white caps and aprons supervised the patients. These were young women and old, modestly dressed and clean. Some wandered aimlessly. One muttered to herself as she passed us; one followed us, plucking at my sleeve. Other patients welcomed visitors to a table that displayed knitted mittens, lace collars, pincushions, small baskets, and other hand-made articles.

"They're allowed to sell the things they make," Dr. Forbes said.

I purchased a lace collar for my friend Ellen, and a wool muffler for John Slade. I know it is strange to buy something for a man I might never see again, but I have stockpiled a collection of small gifts, in case he should return.

So far the gifts were all I'd found to take with me from Bedlam. Where were the dramatic sights that would inspire a new novel? Mrs. Smith had said I have a taste for disturbing things, and I suppose she was right. Alas, my taste would not be satisfied here.

Then Dr. Forbes said, "I can show you some things that the general public is not allowed to see, but they're not for the fainthearted."

Various experiences had toughened my heart to the consistency of leather. I assured Dr. Forbes that I was ready for my tour behind the scenes at Bedlam. We watched doctors set leeches on inmates who were sick with physical as well as mental ailments, and apply hot, pungent, medicinal compresses on the shaved scalps of patients who moaned and resisted.

"It removes turbulent spirits that are thought to disrupt the brain," Dr. Forbes explained.

We saw patients sitting in bathtubs of cold water, metal lids locked over their bodies, only their heads showing. Dr. Forbes said it calmed them, and indeed they seemed calm to the point of insensibility. In one room a man wearing a gag lay trussed in a "blanket gown"—a garment wrapped and tied tightly around him so that he could not move.

"The blanket gown keeps him from hurting himself or anyone else," Dr. Forbes said.

I thought of Branwell, who'd suffered from violent fits due to drink and drugs. A blanket gown would have come in handy for him. The memory of him saddened me. Indeed, I found the patients more saddening than inspiring, and they were hardly a suitable subject for a novel. Critics had called *Jane Eyre* coarse, shocking, and vulgar. God help me if I set my next book in Bedlam!

Leaving the treatment rooms, we met two physicians who asked Dr. Forbes for his advice about a patient. As he spoke with them, I looked around a corner and saw, at the far end of a passage, a door that was open just enough for me to see darkness on the other side. The darkness called to that which is dark in me. I approached the door, which was made of iron and had a large keyhole. I wondered why a door so obviously meant to be locked was not. What lay beyond?

Reaching the door, I peered around it. Into my face blew a cold draft that smelled of urine and lye soap. I saw a dim, dismal corridor with an arched ceiling, its only light from a barred window at the end; I heard wails and gibbering. A not entirely disagreeable fear shivered through me. I had a premonition that the corridor led to something I should not see but must. My heartbeat quickened with anticipation; I looked over my shoulder. No one was about. No one saw me step through the door.

The wails and gibbering echoed around me as I tiptoed down the passage; they sounded like utterances from Hell. On either side of the passage were doors, each with a window covered by metal grating set at eye level. I peeked through these. In one locked cell after another, through a maze of corridors, I saw a man or woman imprisoned. Some crouched in corners like animals in pens, but others were in wrist and ankle cuffs, chained to beds. How they struggled and moaned! These were scenes from a medieval torture chamber. I'd stumbled upon the dark heart of Bedlam.

I was headed back the way I'd come when I felt a touch on my shoulder. My heart vaulted up into my throat with a mighty thump. Gasping, I whirled. Before me stood a young woman, small and thin and pale. She wore a plain gray frock and a white shawl. A white bonnet framed brown, curling hair and delicate features. Violet-gray eyes too large for her face calmly met my gaze. Shock paralyzed me, and not just because she'd crept up on me so unexpectedly.

I am haunted by those I have loved and lost. Although they are dust in their graves, I encounter them time and again in persons I meet. This woman was my sister Anne in every lineament.

"Excuse me, madam," she said, and her voice was Anne's, sweet and gentle.

The terrible memory of Anne's passing swept over me like a black wave. Anne had meekly accepted every remedy we pressed upon her; foul medicines and painful blisters added to her suffering, but she patiently endured. I took her to the seaside for a change of air, a last-resort treatment recommended by her doctor. Alas, it didn't work. Anne died at the age of twenty-eight, in Scarborough. She was buried there, on a headland overlooking the sea she always loved. But here, with me, was her ghost.

"Who are you?" was all I could think to say.

"I'm Julia Garrs," she said, and curtsied. "What's your name?"

"Charlotte Brontë." Now reason overpowered fancy. I saw that she was not my sister reincarnated. She was some ten years younger than Anne had lived to be, and prettier; she had a full bosom, Cupid's bow lips, and thick, black eyelashes. She was a stranger.

Relief flooded me as I said, "What do you want?"

"I'm lost," she said. "Will you help me get home? My baby is there. He needs me."

I deduced that she was a visitor who'd wandered here by chance just as I had. "Certainly."

She smiled, and as I escorted her along the passage, she took my hand. Her fingers were cold and frail, and I shivered: it seemed that Anne had reached from her grave to touch me. I lost my sense of direction and could not find the door. We turned corner after corner until we came upon a matron. She was a heavy woman with a coarse, red, common face. "Julia!" she said. "What do you think you're doing?"

Julia shrank behind me. I wondered how the matron knew her name and why she was frightened. "We're visiting the asylum. We got lost," I explained.

The matron sneered. "You may be a visitor, mum, but she ain't. She's an inmate."

I was shocked. "But—"

"But she looks so normal." The matron laughed. "I know. All the visitors think so. You're not the first one she's tried to fool into helping her escape. She charms the attendants into letting her out of her cell." The matron's tone hinted at the sort of wiles Julia employed. "Then she goes looking for her next mark."

"Is this true?" I asked Julia.

She clung to my hand but averted her eyes from mine.

"Oh, it's true, all right," the matron said. "She's in Bedlam 'cause she killed her own baby. Born out of wedlock, it was. She drowned it in the bath. Afterwards, she went mad. Thinks it's still alive."

I stared at Julia in horror. The matron yanked her away from me and said, "Come on, then, girl. You're going back to your cell."

As she led the reluctant but meek Julia down the corridor, she said to me, "You hadn't ought to be here, mum. This wing's not on the public tour. It's for the criminal lunatics."

Stunned by fresh shock, I said, "How do I get out?"

The matron pointed. "The door's that way."

I gladly went in the direction she'd indicated. Then I heard a loud rattling of wheels. I saw, down the passage, four male nurses pushing a cart on which lay a patient wrapped in a blanket gown. He bucked and writhed; he grunted through the gag in his mouth. The sounds caused my own mouth to drop. My heart began a thunderous pounding.

The unintelligible noises that a human makes are as individual and distinctive as his voice speaking words. A sigh, cough, or groan can reveal identity. Every fiber of my being told me who that madman was, even though reason said he could not be.

The nurses pushed the cart into a room; the door slammed behind them. Torn between disbelief and fearful hope, I hurried to the door. I peered through the grated window and saw the nurses wrestling with the madman, removing the blanket gown. He was tall and thin, with sinewy muscles, clothed in a torn white shirt and black trousers. I strained to see his face, which was hidden by the gag and his disheveled black hair. A white-coated doctor with a tonsure of gray hair and a bland, bespectacled face tinkered with a strange apparatus—a clutch of squat black cylinders connected to a machine. Long wires protruded from metal posts at their ends. Nearby stood a wooden table fitted with leather straps with buckles and a set of clamps at the end. I watched the nurses heave the madman onto the table. They tried to buckle the straps over him. As he thrashed and struck out at them, his face turned toward me.

It was lean and swarthy, dripping with sweat, the nose like a falcon's beak. His mouth was an agonized grimace around the gag. His eyes were a rare, brilliant, crystalline gray. I saw them in my dreams every night. He did not see me now. I clapped my hand over my mouth to stifle a cry of horror mixed with recognition.

My first, visceral impression had proved true: the madman was John Slade.

3

✦✦

HOW HAD SLADE, THE MAN I LOVED, COME TO BE HERE IN BEDLAM?

Almost three years ago he had told me he was going to Russia. I had thought him still there. I'd had no reason to believe otherwise.

What was happening to him, and why?

I saw a door at the back of the room open. Through it stepped a man whose narrow figure wore a dark coat and trousers of a distinctly foreign cut. He had Germanic features—pale, hooded eyes behind gold-rimmed spectacles, a long nose, a cruel mouth. His hair was close-cropped and silvery, his bearing imperious.

Reader, you will recognize him as the Prussian who conspired with the Tsar against England. At that time I had no knowledge of the man.

He strode toward Slade. An object glittered in his hand. It was a glass cylinder with a plunger, attached to a long, sharp needle. While the nurses struggled to hold Slade still, the man jabbed the needle into Slade's arm. He worked the plunger. Slade jerked as the liquid contents of the cylinder ran into his body. His struggles weakened. His eyes closed. The nurses adjusted the clamps around his head. The doctor gathered up the wires connected to the strange apparatus. Each had a small metal disc at its end. He affixed these discs to Slade's temples and forehead. He turned a crank on the machine.

Lights on its surface blinked. I heard a crackling sound. Slade stiffened as if from a convulsion. The foreigner moved to his side, whispered in his ear. I did not know what these men were doing to Slade, but it could not be good. I tried to open the door; it was locked. I beat my fists against it and cried, "Stop!"

The doctor, the nurses, and the foreigner looked in my direction. At the same instant I heard someone call my name. Dr. Forbes hurried toward me, saying, "There you are, thank heaven." He seized my arm and propelled me away from the door, out of the dungeon. Soon we were in the ward where I'd left him, amid the staff, the visitors, and blessed normalcy.

"That was the criminal lunatics' ward," Dr. Forbes said. "I shouldn't have let you wander in there."

"In there—I saw—they—" With an effort, I composed myself. I stammered a description of what I'd seen.

"It's a treatment called galvanism," Dr. Forbes explained. "An electrical charge is administered to the patient's head. It cures melancholia, hypochondria, mania, and dementia. It's perfectly safe. Don't be upset."

"The patient. I know him. He—"

Dr. Forbes frowned. He led me down the staircase, toward the main door. "You should go home. Your experience has distressed you so much that you're confused. You couldn't possibly know that patient. He's a lunatic who was arrested and brought to Bedlam by the police. He's the suspect in a crime."

I was sure a mistake had been made. John Slade a lunatic and a criminal? It was impossible!

He was a graduate of Cambridge, a former clergyman. He spoke at least four languages besides English. He'd been a soldier in the army of the East India Company, had served in the Middle East, and later joined the British intelligence service. Moreover, he was a hero who'd risked his life in the line of duty.

Now I told Dr. Forbes that I must save Slade; I begged him to stop the torture. Perhaps if I had behaved calmly and rationally he would have complied, but I was so agitated that I raved as if I were mad myself.

"Miss Brontë, you must leave at once," Dr. Forbes said. "People are staring."

That brought me to my senses. If the gossips should hear about this episode, what hay they would make of it! *Famous authoress Currer Bell goes insane in Bedlam*, the newspaper headlines would read. I had to let Dr. Forbes escort me out.

"This is my fault. I shouldn't have let you come," he said regretfully as he put me into a carriage. "I must apologize." He added, "I am leaving in two days for a holiday in Ambleside in the Lake District, but if you should need my assistance, please let me know."

Alone in my carriage on my way back to Gloucester Terrace, I conjectured that Slade must have gotten himself into trouble which had led to his arrest and incarceration. But what kind of trouble? I wondered if Dr. Forbes had sent me away from Bedlam because he was a party to Slade's persecution and he didn't want me to see it. But I could not persuade myself of that. He must truly believe Slade was a criminal lunatic and I had mistaken his identity.

When I arrived at the Smiths' house, I would have liked to sit alone in my room and decide what to do, but George greeted me at the door and said, "I'm glad you're back early. We're going to the Great Exhibition."

The Great Exhibition was a huge museum, opened just this month, that contained some one hundred thousand mechanical devices and works of art from many different countries. It had been conceived by Prince Albert, with the mission of advancing humanity and celebrating the progress achieved in the modern age. Although the Great Exhibition was the talk of England, I didn't want to go because I was so distressed. Still, I could not refuse George. After a quick luncheon I found myself riding in a carriage with him, his mother, and his two younger sisters. They talked excitedly about the things we would see. Nobody noticed that I sat brooding in silence.

Why had Slade returned to England? Why hadn't he let me

know? I thought of the three lonely years I'd spent without him. I alternated between hurt feelings, fear for Slade, and the first pangs of doubt about what I'd seen at Bedlam. Was that inmate really Slade? How could Slade have become a criminal lunatic? My mind refused to believe he had, for I thought him to be a thoroughly sane, honorable man. But what else could explain his incarceration in the asylum, if indeed the man I'd seen was Slade?

The popularity of the Great Exhibition became evident long before we got there. Our progress slowed behind a crush of carriages and omnibuses. Pedestrians crowded the sidewalks. Eventually we reached a long avenue that led through Hyde Park, where merrymakers lounged on grass shaded by trees. It was such a bright, gay scene that my experience at Bedlam seemed unreal. Perhaps Dr. Forbes was right, and the man I'd seen wasn't Slade. I'd mistaken Julia Garrs for my sister Anne; why might I not have made another mistake?

"Look!" Mrs. Smith pointed out the carriage window. "There is the Crystal Palace!"

The "Crystal Palace," the popular name for the building that housed the Great Exhibition, was an enormous glass shell supported by a skeleton of iron, like a gigantic conservatory, more than a hundred feet high. The newspapers had proclaimed it "The Tenth Wonder of the World." We disembarked from the carriage and joined the queue at the entrance. What a varied company we were in! Clergymen from the countryside shepherded flocks of parishioners; teachers presided over groups of barefoot schoolchildren; rich ladies and gentlemen waited amid soldiers in uniform. I heard foreign languages spoken by visitors from abroad.

As his mother and sisters chattered, George Smith leaned close to me and said, "You're awfully quiet. Is something wrong?"

"No, I'm fine." I couldn't talk about what had happened at Bedlam; I didn't want to worry him, especially if it had been a case of mistaken identity. Perhaps I'd wanted so much to see Slade that I had superimposed his face upon a stranger.

We entered the Crystal Palace. Its interior resembled a vast cathedral. Awestruck, carried by the tide of the crowd, the Smiths and I moved down a long transept roofed with a glass barrel vault. Iron posts, wrought to resemble classical columns, supported upper galleries on either side of a wide main thoroughfare.

"It's over eighteen hundred feet long and four hundred fifty feet wide," George said. "It covers nineteen square acres."

"There are trees indoors," his sister Eliza marveled.

I, too, was amazed by the live, full-sized elms that rose within the transept.

"The transept was offset to accommodate the trees that were on the site," George explained. "The building isn't completely symmetrical."

I was so impressed by the Crystal Palace that I almost forgot about Slade. Sunshine poured through the glass ceiling and walls onto potted shrubs, flowering plants, and palmettos set along the main thoroughfare. White marble statuary gleamed. The voices of the spectators and their footsteps on the wooden floor blended into a deep hum, like the sound of the sea. Above it I heard the tinkle of falling water. We joined a crowd that was gathered around a huge crystal fountain.

"It's twenty-seven feet high and weighs four tons," George said.

At the center, a column like a splinter from an iceberg glittered with rainbow iridescence. Water cascaded into an enormous, overflowing crystal basin. As we moved on, George said to me, "Queen Victoria and Prince Albert held a grand opening ceremony for the Great Exhibition. I wish you could have come to that. But maybe you'll see them here some other time. I hear they plan to make frequent appearances."

I did not tell him that I was acquainted with the royal couple. They had played a part in my secret adventures of 1848.

The Smiths and I explored the displays arranged in courts beneath the upper galleries. Each was dedicated to a particular nation or subject. We saw silk carpets, shawls, and a model of a snake charmer in the Indian Pavilion. The United States Pavilion contained a nude statue of a Greek slave that caused much furor. In the Medieval Court we inspected an altar, vestments, candelabra, and chalices. We wandered among railway locomotives, hydraulic presses, farm and mill machinery, and a zinc Amazon on horse-back. We saw vases made of human hair and of mutton fat. The grandeur of the Great Exhibition did not lie in one thing, but in the unique assemblage of all things, arranged with colorful, marvelous power of effect.

"What do you think?" George asked me as we listened to a bellows that played "God Save the Queen."

"It's very fine, gorgeous, animated, and bewildering," I said.

He smiled and agreed. "They say that thirty thousand people visit every day. Some come back again and again."

One would have to, in order to see everything. Three hours later, we had barely scratched the Great Exhibition's surface. Everything began to blur together. The only thing that stood out in my mind was a model of a steam-powered airship—a hot air balloon combined with a boiler, engine, and propeller. Overwhelmed and fatigued by so much ingenuity, I was glad to sit in the refreshment court and eat strawberry ice. Even gladder was I to visit what I considered the most wonderful attraction of all—the "retiring rooms," the first public conveniences in Britain. A penny bought me a clean seat in a water closet, a towel, a comb, and a shoeshine.

I was also glad for a few moments alone, to think. Perhaps it was too big a coincidence that Slade should have been in Bedlam on the day I happened by. Perhaps the man I'd seen wasn't he. But I firmly believe that coincidences do occur. One could call them fate. It was fate when Jane Eyre was rescued by her long-lost cousins after she ran away from Mr. Rochester. Fate had brought Slade and me together the first time. I realized then that I could not help believing that the madman in Bedlam was Slade, and that fate had brought us together again.

As I walked through the park to meet the Smiths, I heard someone call, "Miss Brontë!" It was a man perhaps twenty-eight years old, brown-haired, dressed in a brown coat and trousers. He hurried up to me, smiling radiantly.

"It is Miss Charlotte Brontë, the authoress, isn't it?" he said.

"It is," I said warily. I was often recognized by strangers who'd read *Jane Eyre*, but it usually happened at literary gatherings or in

Yorkshire, where everyone knew everyone else. It had never happened in a public place in London. "Have we met?"

"We shook hands after Mr. Thackeray's lecture last night."

I took a closer look at him. He had pink, boyish features, a slight build, and a habit of tilting his head. His eyes were large, brown, protuberant, and shining with earnestness. His clothing was neat and clean, but frayed at the collar and cuffs, his shoes polished but worn. He didn't look familiar, but there had been such a big crowd at the salon, I could easily have forgotten him. "Well, it's a pleasure to see you again, Mr. . . . ?"

"Oliver Heald." Seizing my hand in both of his, he pumped it vigorously. His hands were warm and moist. "I'm so glad we ran into each other! I've been so wanting a chance to talk to you. I love *Jane Eyre*. I've read it ten times. It's my favorite book."

He held my hand too long. He stood too close, leaning toward me, his earnest brown eyes gazing into my face. As I stammered my thanks, I backed away, but he followed.

"I can't wait to tell everyone at school that I met you." Mr. Heald added, "I teach geography." That he was a teacher didn't surprise me. His diction was that of an educated man, and I could imagine him with a class of boys who did mocking imitations of him. "I heard that you were once a teacher, too. Is it so?"

"Yes."

"But you went on to become a famous authoress." He confided, "I write a little, too. Were you also a governess?" When I admitted as much, he seemed gratified. "I hope you'll pardon me for saying that you are exactly as I pictured Jane Eyre."

Too many people have likened me to her. Although I am aware of the resemblances, it embarrasses me. I made polite, modest disclaimers as I sought a chance to escape.

"You are unmarried?" Mr. Heald inquired.

I owned that I was, although my spinsterhood is a tender subject that I don't care to discuss. People assume that it is due to my plain appearance. They don't know that I have turned down four marriage proposals, including Slade's. I was beginning to be annoyed by Mr. Heald.

He greeted my admission with delight. "I, too, am unattached."

This conversation was going in a direction that I did not like. "Sir, it's been a pleasure speaking with you, but my friends are waiting for me. I must go now."

When I joined the Smiths at our carriage, I forgot Mr. Heald. He was a chance encounter of no significance—or so I believed at the time. My thoughts returned to John Slade.

I knew I must go back to Bedlam, for another look at that lunatic.

4

As I write my story, I become ever more aware that there is much more to it than what I personally experienced. The whole of it includes crucial dimensions that I can never know as intimately as do the people who shaped them. I can only conjecture at the scenery, sensations, and emotions involved. That is the limitation of writing from the first-person point of view, as I did when I wrote *Jane Eyre*. The characters other than Jane, the narrator, could be portrayed only as she saw them. They depended on her to bear witness to their actions and feelings and bring them to life. I faced the same problem when I penned the story of my adventures of 1848. Many things important to understanding the big picture happened to people besides myself; yet I am the sole narrator. My solution was to recreate the story's hidden dimensions using my imagination, my knowledge of the facts, and my skill as an author. I will employ the same strategy now.

Reader, forgive me if I take liberties with the details. Be assured that my narrative captures the essential truth. Here I will begin with the story of the man around whom my story revolves.

THE SECRET ADVENTURES OF JOHN SLADE

1848 December. A blizzard assailed Moscow. Its rooftops, domes, turrets, and spires disappeared into the swirling white sky. Snow from earlier falls mounded the walls of the buildings, lay piled along every street. Sleighs zoomed through the city, their runners creaking, their harnesses jingling, their horses blowing jets of vapor out of ice-caked nostrils.

John Slade leaned into the wind that blew cold, stinging snowflakes against his face as he strode along Tverskaya Street. After two months in Moscow, he blended perfectly with the Russians. He appeared to be one among hundreds of men muffled in fur-lined greatcoat, hat, and boots. No one could tell he was English. After days spent exploring the city and striking up conversations with strangers, he had learned where to find the people he wanted to meet.

He turned onto a side street lined with restaurants and taverns. Lights burned in windows fogged with steam. He entered the Café Philipov. Heat from a blazing fire and the sweet, Oriental-smelling smoke from Russian cigarettes engulfed him. Young men, engaged in loud, fervent conversation, crowded around the tables. Waiters served tea from samovars. Slade sat in a corner by himself. He shed his outdoor garments, lit a cigarette, and ordered tea. Listening to the other men nearest him, he learned their names and occupations.

"Damn the censors!" said one unkempt, shaggy-haired fellow named Fyodor, a writer for a progressive journal. "They suppress all my articles!"

"The Tsar doesn't want ideas about freedom to spread from the West to the populace," said Alexander, dignified and bespectacled, who taught philosophy at Moscow University.

Their companion was a burly, bearded poet named Peter; he thumped the table with his fist. "Revolution is coming, whether His Royal Highness wants it or not!"

Slade hitched his chair up to their table. "Revolution has already come to most of Europe, and often failed, thanks to the Tsar. He has sent his army to crush rebellions wherever he could. He is determined to keep revolution from spreading here. No wonder he's known as the Policeman of Europe. If you want things to change, you'll have to do more than talk."

The men turned to Slade. "And who are you?" Fyodor asked.

"Ivan Zubov," Slade said. "I'm a journalist from St. Petersburg."

He spoke Russian perfectly, a result of his natural aptitude for languages and intensive study with native experts. For months before he'd come to Moscow, he'd lived in St. Petersburg, where the experts had drilled, coached, and groomed him. He'd practiced in that city until he was confident that he had mastered the role he'd chosen as his disguise. But the men regarded him with suspicion: they couldn't afford to trust any stranger who wandered into their haunt. As Slade prepared to convince them that he was a fellow radical, the door burst open. In rushed a dozen big, stern-faced men wearing gray greatcoats and hoods, armed with clubs and pistols. Someone exclaimed, "It's the Third Section!"

Slade knew that the Third Section was the Tsar's secret service, the branch of the government charged with maintaining surveillance on the citizens, censoring publications, and uncovering plots against the Tsar and his regime. It employed many police, spies, informants, and agents provocateur, and had arrested hundreds of intellectuals who embraced Western notions of government reform. It had evidently learned that these intellectuals liked to gather at the Café Philipov.

Customers jumped up from the tables and rushed toward the back door. Slade didn't want to be arrested any more than his new acquaintances did. He followed them. The Third Section policemen lunged after the departing horde. They attacked men too drunk or too slow to run. As they wielded their clubs, Slade heard bones crack and cries of pain. He evaded the policemen who grabbed at him, but Alexander the professor wasn't so agile. A policeman caught him. He called for help. Peter and Fyodor hurried to his rescue, but Slade shouted, "Go! I'll save your friend!"

He seized the policeman who had begun beating Alexander. The policeman rounded on Slade, club swinging. Slade ducked. He rammed his fist into the policeman's stomach. The policeman grunted and doubled over. Slade wrested the club from his hand, then smote him on his head. He fell, unconscious. While Slade hurried Alexander to the door, the other police fired their pistols. Gunshots erupted behind Slade. Bullets struck walls, shattered windows. Slade and Alexander tumbled outside, into the blizzard.

Peter and Fyodor were waiting. "Hurry!" they cried. Supporting Alexander, whose leg was hurt, they led Slade through the maze of alleys. Behind them, rapid footsteps broke the snow and screams blared as the police pursued other men who'd escaped from the café. More gunshots exploded. Slade and his group tumbled down a flight of icy stairs to the cellar of a tavern. They crouched, coatless and shivering, until the night was quiet.

"Thank you," Alexander said to Slade. "If not for you, I would be dead now."

The other men nodded. The suspicion in their eyes had given way to respect. Peter said, "You may be a stranger in town, but you are our comrade."

As Slade shook hands with his new friends, he felt a mixture of satisfaction and sadness. He liked these men, and he sympathized with their cause, but he was duty-bound to exploit them. He regretted that the friendships he cultivated in the course of his work often turned out badly, for both sides.

5

I FELT BETTER AFTER MAKING THE DECISION TO RETURN TO Bedlam, but I couldn't go alone, and I knew Dr. Forbes would be unwilling to escort me. During breakfast at Number 76 Gloucester Terrace the next morning, I told George Smith what had happened the previous day and tried to press him into service. He said, "I'm sorry, Charlotte, but I think Dr. Forbes is right. You must have made a mistake. It would be best to forget the whole business."

"Surely, *Miss Brontë*, you wouldn't drag George into it?" his mother was quick to object. "Not on his Saturday off." She sounded as much aggrieved because I dared make work for him as appalled that I'd gotten mixed up in sordid doings.

I said, "I am afraid that until I discover the true identity of the lunatic, I won't be able to concentrate on my writing."

This was sheer blackmail. Mrs. Smith bit back a retort: she knew how much the fortunes of Smith, Elder and Company depended on me. George protested that another trip to Bedlam would only worsen my state of mind, but in the end he capitulated.

While we drove through London, rain began to fall. We hurried up the steps of Bedlam, got drenched in the downpour, and paid our admission fees. As I hurried George through the wards, I noticed matrons and attendants standing in huddles, conversing in low, nervous voices. Patients roved, more agitated than they'd been the day before. Upon reaching the door to the criminal lunatics' wing, we found a uniformed police constable standing guard.

"What's going on?" George asked.

The constable was young, as fresh-faced as a farm boy, and clearly distressed. "There's been a murder."

The word struck a mighty throb of alarm through me. My fears for Slade surged higher.

"Who's been killed?" George asked.

"I'm not at liberty to say," the constable said. When I threw myself at the door, he held me off. "Sorry, mum, you can't go in there."

George read the name on the constable's badge and said, "Look here, Constable Ryan—I'm George Smith of Smith, Elder and Company, and the police commissioner is a friend of mine." It was true; George had many friends in many places. "Let me in, or the next time I see him, I'll mention that you were uncooperative."

Constable Ryan hesitated, torn between his duty and his fear that George could put him in bad odor with his superior. He opened the door and stood aside.

"I'll see what's happened," George told me. "You stay here."

"No! I'm going with you!"

I spoke with such determination that his will gave way to mine. Together we entered the criminal lunatics' wing. The stench and the inmates' howls greeted us.

"Good Lord," George muttered.

Blind instinct guided my steps through the dungeon. As I broke into a run, I chastised myself for allowing Dr. Forbes to rush me away from Bedlam yesterday, and for my doubt that the lunatic was Slade. Was he dead? Might I have saved him? Winded and panting, I arrived at the cell in which I'd seen Slade. Voices issued from the open door. Inside, two police constables were milling around, examining the table with the straps, the weird apparatus. Two more, and a man who wore a black raincoat, stood gazing down at something at their feet. I perceived an odor at once sweet and salty, metallic and raw.

The odor of blood.

It seemed to leap through my nostrils and claw at some deep, vulnerable place in me. The blood was wet and fresh and shockingly red, pooled on the floor, smeared where feet had skidded in it. A frantic cry burst from me: "Slade! No!"

The men turned. As they stared at me, they shifted position, and I saw what they'd been looking at. Two men lay on the floor. They were dressed in plain cotton trousers and smocks. One was crumpled on his side. A gory halo of blood surrounded his head. The other man sprawled on his back, arms flung out. From his left eye protruded a slim glass cylinder equipped with a plunger, such as the one I'd seen used by the foreigner yesterday. Its needle had penetrated deep into the man's brain.

I experienced an onslaught of relief, confusion, and astonishment. Neither dead man was Slade.

I fell into the arms of George Smith. He beheld the scene inside the room and said, "Good Lord!" He turned me so that my face was against his chest and I could see no more.

I managed not to faint; my adventures of 1848 had given me a reserve of stamina. But I was so breathless that I couldn't walk. George carried me out of the lunatics' wing, shouting for help. I was put in a wheelchair and conveyed to a chamber used for conferences. A doctor administered smelling salts. A matron fetched me a cup of hot tea. I drank the tea and revived somewhat. George sat at the table with me; he wiped his forehead with a handkerchief.

"That was the most awful sight I've ever seen. I'm just glad it wasn't your friend who was murdered." He paused, then said, "Who exactly is this John Slade?"

I hadn't told him that Slade was a spy for the Crown. None but a few privileged persons were supposed to know. "He's a clergyman from Canterbury." That was a false identity Slade had once used. It would have to do.

"How did you come to know him?"

I'd been sworn to secrecy about the circumstances under which I'd known Slade. "We had a mutual acquaintance." It was Isabel White, the woman whose murder had launched me on my adventure of 1848.

George stroked his chin; he seemed to debate with himself on the wisdom of pursuing the subject. "May I ask exactly how well you know Mr. Slade?"

He didn't want to hear that Slade had been my suitor, I could tell. He most certainly didn't want his company's famous authoress to have romantic connections with a mental patient. What an ado the newspapers would make about that! And I couldn't tell him anything of what had passed between Slade and me.

"Mr. Slade is a good friend, but no more," I settled for saying.

George scrutinized me closely, and I averted my eyes from the suspicion in his. Fortunately, we were interrupted by the arrival of the man in the black raincoat and a middle-aged woman dressed in a gray frock, a white apron, and a white cap. She had a prim mouth, sharp eyes and nose, and cheeks as rosy, mottled, and hard as crabapples.

"I'm Henrietta Hunter, matron of Bethlem Hospital," she said. "Are you feeling better?"

I said I was. The black-coated man said, "Good, because I want a few words with you." His high, stooped shoulders, black garments, and long face gave him the look of a vulture. His greenish eyes flicked over me as if I were a carcass he was wondering whether to eat. "I'm Detective Inspector Hart, from the Metropolitan Police."

George rose and demanded, "What is going on here? Who were those men that were killed? Who killed them, and how did it happen?"

"Mr. Smith, is it?" D. I. Hart said with a humorless smile. "You bullied my constable into letting you into the crime scene. You hadn't ought to have done that. He's in trouble, and so will you be, unless you sit down and keep quiet."

George reluctantly obeyed.

"That's better." D. I. Hart pulled up a chair next to mine, turned it to face me, and sat. Matron Hunter remained standing near me, like a jailer. He asked my name, and after I gave it, said, "What do you know about this, Miss Brontë?"

My status as a famous authoress gave me the confidence to stand up to him instead of meekly surrendering. "I refuse to say until you answer Mr. Smith's questions."

D. I. Hart looked surprised and vexed. I folded my arms. He put on a condescending expression and said, "The murder victims were nurses. It was an inmate who killed them."

I had been so relieved to discover that Slade wasn't the victim, but now I felt a cold, ominous touch of dread.

"As far as I can deduce, they were removing him from the treatment table," D. I. Hart said. "They thought he was unconscious, but he was faking. When they undid the straps, he attacked them. He hit one nurse on the head with a truncheon. He fought with the other, grabbed a hypodermic syringe, and stabbed him through the eye."

George Smith shook his head in disapproving wonder. I could hardly bear to ask whether Slade was the murderer, but I had to know. "Was the inmate a tall, thin man with shaggy black hair and gray eyes, about forty years old?"

Interest kindled in D. I. Hart's gaze. He looked even more carnivorous than before. "So I'm told. How did you know?"

It was as I'd feared: the police thought Slade was the murderer.

"A nurse reported that a lady visitor had wandered into the criminal lunatics' wing yesterday." Matron Hunter bent a speculative stare on me. "Was that you, Miss Brontë? Did you see the inmate then?"

"It was, and I did," I said. "But he didn't kill those men!"

"What makes you so sure?" D. I. Hart said. "Do you know him?"

"Yes," I said with passionate conviction, "and I know that John Slade is innocent."

"It appears you don't know the man at all," D. I. Hart said with a smug, unpleasant smile. "His name isn't John Slade. It's Josef

Typinski. And it's highly unlikely that you've ever met him. He's a refugee from Poland."

At first I was shocked by this news, and jarred out of my certainty that the man I'd seen was Slade.

"It's just as I suggested," George said gently. "You made a mistake."

Then I recalled that his work often required Slade to use aliases. Adept at foreign accents and languages, he could easily have styled himself as a Polish refugee. But I couldn't tell the detective inspector any of this, for I was sworn to secrecy.

"I want to see him," I said. "Where is he?"

"I'd like to see him, too, but that's not possible at the moment," D. I. Hart said. "He's escaped."

Relief vied with fresh horror in me. Slade wasn't under arrest, but he was a wanted man, a fugitive.

"Why was this Josef Typinski committed to Bedlam in the first place?" George asked.

"I'm not allowed to say," Matron Hunter answered. "Information about the inmates is confidential."

I had to find Slade. I had to hear, from him, the truth about the murders. "Where might he have gone?"

D. I. Hart's eyes narrowed. "You wouldn't be thinking of looking for him yourself, now would you?" He rose from his seat and stepped back from me, as if he'd finished picking my carcass down to bare bones. "Information concerning police investigations is confidential. You'd better go home and stay out of this, for your own sake."

Walking through the asylum with me, George said, "I didn't care for the detective inspector, but he's right. I'll take you home. You can rest and forget this whole business."

"No! I can't!" As I resisted the pressure George applied to my arm, I saw some hospital staff members standing idle, watching me. One of them was the foreigner. I pointed and said, "That's the man I told you about—the one I saw with Mr. Slade!"

The foreigner met my gaze. His gaze was as pale as if bleached by lye, and menacing. I felt a chill, like a cold draft from a distant climate. Intuition warned me that I should avoid this man's attention, but it was too late, and he had knowledge I wanted.

"I must ask him what he was doing to Mr. Slade yesterday," I said. "Maybe he knows what's become of Mr. Slade and who really killed those nurses."

The foreigner turned and disappeared around a corner.

"What man?" George craned his neck, saw no one, and shook his head in confusion. "Charlotte, we must go."

As we passed down a corridor in the women's ward, I heard a soft voice call, "Charlotte."

I saw Julia Garrs peeking out of a doorway. She beckoned me. Today she didn't resemble Anne as much as I'd thought; today I knew she was a murderess who'd killed her own baby. But I pitied her because she was so young and apparently doomed to spend the rest of her life searching for the baby and incarcerated in Bedlam.

"Please excuse me a moment," I said to George. I hurried to Julia. "Hadn't you better go back to your room before you get in trouble?"

Julia put her finger to her lips and pulled me into a closet that contained a washbasin, brooms, mops, and buckets. She shut the door and smiled her sweet smile. "You were so kind yesterday. I wanted to thank you." She added wistfully, "I like you. I wish we could be friends. Nobody ever comes to visit me."

Probably her friends and family had disowned her. As a parson's daughter I felt a duty to comfort the unfortunate, but I was nervous being alone with Julia. "How did you get out?"

"A madman has escaped. There was so much confusion, someone left the door unlocked." Julia studied me, her gaze frankly curious. "You're interested in the madman, aren't you, Charlotte?"

"Yes, but how did you know?"

A hint of slyness crept into her smile. "People talk. I listen."

Gossip must have traveled through Bedlam even faster than it

did through literary society. "What do you know about him?"
I asked urgently.

"I saw the police bring him in. They said he'd done terrible
things."

"What kind of things?" I dreaded to hear, but I had to know.

"They didn't say. But they did say where they'd arrested him."

My heart leapt at this meager clue. "Where?"

"At Number Eighteen Thrawl Street," Julia said. "In Whitechapel."

6

>≺

S ATURDAY IS MARKET DAY IN
WHITECHAPEL, AND DESPITE THE
rain, the East End of London was jammed with wagons and
omnibuses. The crowds in the high street slowed the carriage in
which I rode with George Smith. Piles of fruits and vegetables
spilled from storefronts in tall buildings with slate roofs and smoking chimneys. Housewives bargained with vendors at stalls that
sold toys, carpets, fish, crockery, furniture, hairbrushes, flowers,
and all manner of other goods. In the meat market, hundreds of
carcasses hung. I smelled cesspools and rotting garbage; I saw itinerant peddlers, legless beggars, organ grinders accompanied by
monkeys, and women selling fortunes. This was not the elegant
London of the fashionable literary set, but it had a raw, invigor-
ating vitality.

George hadn't wanted to come. The madman was better left to
the police, he'd said. But I'd argued just as strenuously that I would
not be able to rest until I'd done all I could to learn more about the
madman I still believed was John Slade. In the end George had
given in.

Our carriage turned off the high street, and we left the bright
market-day bustle. The back streets of Whitechapel were narrow,
the gray day darkened by buildings that towered and leaned. The
odors strengthened into a powerful stench. This was London at its
poorest and most squalid. Dank passages, doorways, and staircases

swarmed with children. Women called out windows, speaking in languages I couldn't identify. Stores displayed sausages and peculiar foodstuffs in windows labeled in Hebrew script. Immigrants from the Continent loitered, smoking pipes by a tavern. They eyed George and me with suspicion as we disembarked from our carriage outside Thrawl Street.

"I don't like this," George said.

Thrawl Street was a particularly malodorous, dim alley. Number Eighteen was one in a row of soot-stained tenements. A sign that said Rooms to Let hung by its doorway. A line of people extended along the sidewalk and up the stairs. The people included women with babes in arms, surly youths, and a dark, muscular man in a butcher's bloodstained apron. When George and I attempted to climb the stairs, the butcher blocked our way.

"You wait your turn." He spoke with a rough, foreign accent.

"Our turn for what?" George asked.

"To see the murderer's room."

A bad feeling crept into my heart. "What murderer?"

"The Pole," said one of the mothers, a London Cockney holding a little boy. "Josef Typinski. The one what killed those three women. Mary Chandler, Catherine Meadows, and Jane Anderson."

"Stabbed 'em and cut out their innards," a youth said with relish.

George questioned these folk; I was too upset to speak. We learned that the three victims had been women of the street. They'd been killed in alleys late at night and found there in the morning, lying in pools of blood, their female organs missing. Rumors of a monster on the loose had spread through Whitechapel. A witness—nobody knew who—had seen Josef Typinski near the scene of the latest crime, which had taken place last summer. The woman with the little boy had seen the police drag Typinski out of his lodgings in Number Eighteen.

"He were in handcuffs," she said. "They threw him in their wagon and took him away."

"Well," George said to me, "that explains why he was in the criminal lunatics' wing in Bedlam. He's not only a multiple murderer—he must be insane, to do such horrific things."

"The landlady is giving a look at his room for a penny," said the youth.

Londoners must be the most avid curiosity seekers in the world, I thought. They flocked to the Great Exhibition, to Bedlam, and to the lodgings of a murderer. "But maybe he didn't do it," I protested. "The witness only saw him near the scene. There's nobody who saw him kill those women, is there?"

Heads shook, but an old man with a cane said, "He must have done it. Otherwise, he wouldn't have been arrested."

His statement was met with general agreement. George said, "Charlotte, we've learned enough."

"No." Although sickened by what I'd heard, I walked to the end of the line and stood there. "I want to see."

George sighed in exasperation as he joined me. "You need to consider the possibility that even if this Josef Typinski is your friend John Slade, he's not the man you knew."

I wondered if something had happened to Slade, had changed him from a sane man of honor into a crazed murderer. As to what it might be, I couldn't imagine. I had to know the truth, and Josef Typinski's lodgings seemed the only source of clues.

We waited an hour, inching up a foul staircase so narrow that people coming down had to squeeze past us. Finally we reached the head of the line, outside a door on the second floor. There the landlady stood, like Cerberus guarding the gates to Hades. Indeed, she resembled a small, fierce bulldog. A neat black frock and white cap gave her a veneer of respectability, which was compromised by the tobacco pipe gripped between her sharp yellow teeth.

"That'll be a tuppence," she said. George paid. "You've got five minutes."

We stepped into the room. The landlady hovered inside the door, to make sure we didn't steal anything. The room was a tiny cell, its window so begrimed that little light came through, furnished with an iron bed and a washbasin on a stand. A travel-worn black valise stood in a corner. I breathed a scent that brought forth a flood of memories.

Scent is a time machine that can instantly transport one to places and people long lost. My surroundings faded. I lay in a forest with Slade, his arms around me, our mouths locked in a kiss. It was Slade's scent—masculine, faintly salty with sweat, but fresh despite the squalid conditions in which he apparently now lived. The sensations of nostalgia and yearning were so powerful that tears sprang to my eyes.

"There's not much here." George Smith's voice snapped me back to the present.

He was examining clothes strewn upon the unmade bed. I surreptitiously wiped my eyes before I joined him. The clothes were such as a poor European immigrant might own—worn trousers, shirt, undergarments, coat, a pair of socks. I didn't think Slade would have left his possessions in such disorder. He had once stayed at my home for a while, and he'd been a tidy, self-contained guest.

George opened the valise. "This is empty."

I eyed the landlady. She must have put all of Slade's things out, the better for curiosity seekers to gawk at. I wanted to snatch up the shirt, bury my face in it, and inhale the vestiges of Slade's presence, but I didn't want to betray my feelings. The washstand held a towel, comb, soap, cup, and shaving brush. I saw a black hair tangled in the comb. My hand made an involuntary movement toward it, but the landlady snapped, "Don't touch." I snatched my hand back. She added, "The police took away his razor. They figured he used it on those women."

I couldn't control the shudder that passed through me. George said, "Even if he isn't the killer, let us hope that your friend John Slade is not the same man as Josef Typinski. That he would use an alias is extremely shady."

However, I could think of a legitimate reason why Slade would pose as an immigrant Pole. Maybe he was on a secret assignment for the Foreign Office, the branch of the British government that employed him. Maybe Slade hadn't contacted me because he couldn't risk breaking his disguise. But I couldn't tell this to George. Not only was I sworn to secrecy; he would never believe me.

"Time's up," the landlady said.

"Not yet!" I couldn't bear to leave without the answers to my questions, and here I felt close to Slade. I cast a frantic gaze around the room and saw, under one leg of the washstand, a folded piece of paper. It must have been put there to prevent the washstand from rocking. I bent and picked up the paper. The landlady was instantly at my side.

"What's that?" she said.

I unfolded the paper. It was a handbill printed on cheap paper, which read, "The Royal Pavilion Theater Presents Katerina the Great in *The Wildwood Affair*." A crude illustration showed a dark-haired woman with haunted eyes.

"Give me that." The landlady snatched the handbill from me. She laid it on the bed with the clothing, for the next gawkers to view.

George shot me a look that said he knew what I was thinking. "No, Charlotte. I would do just about anything for you, but I am not taking you to see *The Wildwood Affair*."

"That's quite all right," I said. "You needn't."

I had a better idea.

7

THAT EVENING, IN MY ROOM AT THE SMITHS' HOUSE, I PUT ON my best gown. My hands trembled as I smoothed the folds of gray satin that glowed with an emerald sheen. I supposed that other women all over London were preparing for a night out, but I felt none of the frivolous gaiety that they must have felt. I donned the gown as if it were armor for a battle.

I arranged my hair in a simple knot. The face in the mirror was as plain as ever. Once my plainness had caused me much grief, but these days I liked my visage better: it belonged to Currer Bell, the author who'd fulfilled my childhood dreams. And the dress brought back happy memories of the first time I'd worn it, three years ago, the first and only time John Slade and I had danced together. His admiration had made me feel beautiful. I saw my eyes shine with tears. Had I lost him forever? Or would I find him tonight?

I went downstairs and met Mr. Thackeray and two ladies, one buxom and willowy and fair, the other slight and dark, both dressed in silk gowns and glittering gems. "Good evening, Jane—er, Miss Brontë," said Mr. Thackeray. "Please allow me to present two dear friends of mine." He introduced the slight, dark lady. "This is Mrs. Crowe, your fellow authoress."

Mrs. Crowe had huge, intense, unblinking eyes. She might have been pretty were she not so thin. "It's a privilege to meet you," she said in a hushed voice. "I so admire your work. Perhaps you've heard of mine?"

"Yes." I understood that she wrote about mediums, séances, and the spirits on the Other Side. I thought it utter claptrap, but I said, "I look forward to reading your books."

"And this is Mrs. Brookfield," Mr. Thackeray said.

Smiling, conspiratorial glances passed between him and the fair woman, a rich society hostess. Although not young, she was beautiful. She was also Mr. Thackeray's paramour. "I'm glad to make your acquaintance," she said in a friendly fashion. I took an immediate dislike to her. Mr. Thackeray was himself a married man, and I could not condone adultery.

"You look splendid tonight," Mr. Thackeray said to me with such sincere admiration that I forgave him his sins. "Are you ready for our expedition to the theater?"

Here I must describe other events that occurred outside my view. The details, based on facts I later learned, are as accurate as I can make them. Reader, you will see that when I went to the theater that night with Mr. Thackeray and his friends, I was in grave danger.

As our carriage rattled down the road, the street seemed deserted; the pools of light beneath the lamps were empty. A warm hush enveloped Hyde Park Gardens. I didn't notice the figure standing in the shadow under a tree near the house I'd just left. It was the foreigner I had seen in Bedlam, the Tsar's Prussian conspirator. He had followed George and me from the asylum to Whitechapel, and from Whitechapel to the Smith house. Now he watched the house until a maid stepped out the front door, on her way home for the night.

"Excuse me," he said.

She gasped and paused. "Lord, you gave me a scare."

"Who is the master of this house?"

"Mr. George Smith," the maid blurted.

"Who was the lady that left in the carriage?"

"Which lady?" The maid stepped back from him, wary of strangers, sensing that he was more dangerous than most.

"The small, plain one."

"None of your business, I'm sure." Offended by his impertinence, she was haughty as well as frightened.

He took a sovereign from his pocket and offered it to her. Her eyes bulged with greed. She accepted the coin. "The lady's Charlotte Brontë, also known as Currer Bell. The famous authoress."

"Does she reside in the house?"

"No. She's just visiting."

"Where does she reside?"

"Haworth. In Yorkshire." The maid slid a nervous glance toward the house. "I can't talk anymore. The mistress doesn't like us to gossip." She hurried away.

The Prussian walked around the corner, to a waiting carriage. He climbed in and sat opposite the two men already inside. Their names were Friedrich and Wagner. They sat rigidly upright, foreign soldiers in British civilian garb. Friedrich was a fine specimen of strong manhood; Wagner his lanky, puffy-faced, distorted reflection.

"Did you find out what you wanted to know, sir?" Friedrich asked.

"Yes." The Prussian relayed the intelligence gleaned from the maid.

Wagner said, "Sir, is this Charlotte Brontë a problem?"

"Obviously. She witnessed our operation in Bedlam. If she tells the police what she saw, they may investigate because she is a woman of position. And we do not want the police snooping in our business."

Wagner frowned. "She could make trouble for us in Bedlam."

"Also in more important spheres," the Prussian said grimly. "She is acquainted with John Slade. Maybe they spoke before we got to him. Maybe he told her something."

"What should we do, sir?" Friedrich asked.

"For now we'll watch her," the Prussian said. "If she appears to know too much—" He removed from his pocket a long, slender knife and slid it out of its leather sheath. The sharp blade reflected his pale eyes, which were devoid of mercy. "We follow standard procedure."

As we rode through Hyde Park Gardens, Mr. Thackeray said, "Which play have you chosen for our enjoyment, Miss Brontë?"

"*The Wildwood Affair*," I said.

"I've not heard of that one," Mrs. Brookfield said.

"At which theater is it playing?" Mrs. Crowe asked.

"The Royal Pavilion," I said.

Mrs. Brookfield said, "Where, pray tell, is that?"

"In Whitechapel." I could tell that neither Mrs. Brookfield nor Mrs. Crowe wanted to attend a play not endorsed by the critics, in a poor part of town. I confess that I was a little amused by their discomfiture. They turned entreatingly to Mr. Thackeray.

Mr. Thackeray said, "I told Miss Brontë that she could choose the play, and a man must keep his promises."

The ladies conceded with good grace. They chatted politely with me until we reached Whitechapel. The bright Saturday afternoon bustle was gone. Harlots posed under the flickering gas lamps along the high street and called to passing men. Drunkards filled gin palaces, from which spilled rowdy laughter and discordant music. The crowds were still thick around the stalls, but new attractions had sprung up, like plants that only bloom at night. Curtained enclosures housed a freak show, whose signs advertised hairy men and hairless dogs, gorillas and giants, Aztecs and bearded women. Excitement and danger laced the foul, smoky air. The back streets were dark, fearsome tunnels.

It wasn't hard to believe that a murderer had stabbed and mutilated his victims there.

Mrs. Brookfield murmured, "My heavens." Mrs. Crowe's huge eyes grew huger with fright. Even Mr. Thackeray looked uncertain.

The carriage stopped outside the Royal Pavilion Theater. With its Grecian columns and dingy white plaster façade, it resembled a ruined classical temple. The people who poured in through the door hailed from the lower classes, the men in laborers' clothes, the women in cheap finery. When we alit from the carriage, a crowd gathered to watch. We were ridiculously overdressed. Boys jeered and whistled at us. We walked toward the theater, surrounded by coarse, staring faces, jostled by the other patrons. Mr. Thackeray nodded, smiled, and bowed as if making an appearance at Buckingham Palace. Mrs. Brookfield and Mrs. Crowe cringed. I searched the crowd for Slade, but in vain.

At the ticket booth, Mr. Thackeray bought four seats in front boxes. Inside, the shabby auditorium was dimly lit by guttering lamps around the stage. Our shoes stuck to the floor as we walked down the aisle. Most of the seats were already filled. A roar of conversation and laughter resounded up to the galleries. The air smelled of gas, tobacco smoke, urine, and the crowd's breath, which reeked of beer, onions, and bad teeth. People stared and pointed at us as we took our seats. We were the center of attention until the play started.

The first scene featured a miserly old man who owned a mill in a fictional town called Wildwood. Sporting a black mustache and hat, he cut the wages of his workers; he strutted, sneered, and counted piles of cash. He was a ludicrous caricature, whom the audience booed with great gusto. Mr. Thackeray chuckled tolerantly. Mrs. Brookfield and Mrs. Crowe looked bored.

When the mill owner called for his wife, an expectant hush settled over the audience. A young woman walked out onto the stage. She was as slim as a wraith, dressed in a white, diaphanous gown that clung to her full breasts. Black, curling hair streamed down her back. Her features were distinctly Slavic, her deep-set eyes aglow with passion. The portrait on the playbill had not done her beauty justice. All gazes were riveted on her. Whispers of "Katerina the Great" swept the audience. Someone murmured, "A Jewess from Russia." I'd never seen her before, but I was so shocked by recognition that I uttered a cry I couldn't stifle. For the second time since

I'd arrived in London, the dead had been resurrected. Katerina the Great was my sister Emily.

She did not resemble Emily in physical appearance, but rather in spirit. She burned with the same inner fire. She looked as I imagine Emily would have, had she traveled to Heaven and Hell and returned.

Katerina spoke her first line: "Here I am, Husband."

They were ordinary words, not the stuff of great playwriting, but Katerina imbued them with her vibrant spirit. Her deep voice, free of any foreign accent, filled the theater. Such power had Emily's voice possessed. Emily rarely spoke, but when she did, one was compelled to listen. Now the audience listened, with all ears. We watched with fascination and horror as the mill owner made Katerina wait on him at dinner as if she were a slave. When she accidentally spilled the soup, he threw the bowl at her. Because the roast was overcooked, he slapped her face. Then he embraced her with cruel, wanton lust. Katerina endured her humiliation with the dignity of a saint. Alone at night, she sang a lament that would break the hardest heart. I could feel the audience's sympathy toward her and its hatred of her husband. But my emotions were aroused for another reason.

Thus had Emily endured the trials of her life. She had been happy only at home, and the occasions she'd been compelled to leave Haworth had caused her much anguish. When she'd accompanied me to school in Belgium, when she'd ventured out into the world to assist me during the course of my adventures of 1848, she had displayed the same courage as Katerina did now. I could hardly bear to watch and remember.

The story took a dramatic turn when the mill owner's son, a handsome young soldier named Richard, arrived home from the war against Napoleon. Richard and Katerina fell in love and wanted to marry; but they could not, as long as the mill owner was alive. Hence, they began plotting his murder. The story owed something to the Greek myth of Phaedra, and more to the tales in the newspapers that sold for a penny. The actor who played Richard was a rank amateur, but Katerina's acting raised the cheap, sordid drama to the very level of Shakespeare. One moment she was as pure and selfless as a nun, resisting temptation; the next, a brazen seductress. She enchanted.

"Not bad at all," was Mr. Thackeray's muttered opinion.

Mrs. Brookfield sniffed. "I think her exceedingly vulgar."

Mrs. Crowe beheld Katerina with terrified awe. "I can sense the spirit in her, and an evil spirit it is," she whispered. "It's the very Devil!"

I sat on the edge of my seat as Richard shot the mill owner. Having stolen the dead man's money, the lovers fled. The police discovered them hiding at an inn. Richard was killed while attempting to escape. Katerina was arrested and tried for her husband's murder. During the trial, the audience hissed at every witness who testified against Katerina. They booed the jury that found her guilty. When the judge sentenced Katerina to death, they hurled beer bottles. Standing on the gallows, Katerina said her final lines.

"I confess that I murdered my husband." Her voice was tuned to a note of torment. "I am guilty in deed, but not in spirit. Evil must be repaid by evil, an eye exacted for an eye. So says the Bible." Katerina's face contorted into a demonic mask. "Vengeance is mine."

Her words sent shivers through me: she was hate and madness incarnate. Katerina said, "God is my ultimate judge." Her expression altered; she looked as holy as an angel. "I shall go to meet Him with the courage of the innocent."

The hangman placed the noose around her neck. An awful thump echoed in the theater. By some magic of stagecraft, Katerina hung from the rope, her limp body supported by no means I could see. The curtain fell. The audience rose up from its seats in a frenzy of applause. I was on my feet, with tears running down my face, clapping so hard that my hands hurt. The spell Katerina had cast was shattered, and the effect was almost unbearably cathartic. The curtain rose. The actors marched out to take their bows. When Katerina appeared, the audience went wilder. Mr. Thackeray yelled, "Brava! Brava!"

Mrs. Crowe cried, "I feel the spirits!" and fainted in Mrs. Brookfield's arms.

Mrs. Brookfield looked shaken in spite of herself. "Take us out of here, William," she begged Mr. Thackeray.

The house lights came on; the audience headed for the exit. I swam against the tide, fighting my way toward the stage: I must speak to Katerina. I went through a door that led backstage and found myself in a dim passage. Light from a room near the end beckoned me. I walked to the threshold. Inside the room, Katerina sat at her dressing table. Her back was to me, but I could see her reflection in the mirror. She was wiping the makeup off her face. I realized that she was older than I'd thought—perhaps my own age.

Her deep, black eyes blazed as she saw me. "No one is allowed to disturb me after a performance. Get out." I heard in her voice the Russian accent she'd suppressed while on stage. When I didn't move, she demanded, "Who are you?"

I could still see a shade of Emily in her. "My name is Charlotte Brontë," I stammered.

"What do you want?"

"I'm looking for someone," I said. "A mutual friend, I believe."

Katerina turned and regarded me with surprise, as if she thought the likes of me couldn't possibly have any acquaintances in common with the likes of her. "Who is it?"

"His name is John Slade. But he may also call himself Josef Typinski."

"I don't know anyone by either of those names." Katerina spoke indifferently, but I had seen what a talented actress she was. "What makes you think I know your friend?"

"He had a playbill with your picture on it in his room."

"Those playbills are scattered all over London. Many men keep them because they admire me. It doesn't mean I know them."

"But you are from Russia," I persisted. "John Slade went to Russia three years ago. Perhaps you met him there?"

Her eyes darkened at the mention of her native country. "I came to England ten years ago, to escape the persecution of the Jews," she said coldly. "I sang on the streets for a living, until I was discovered by the director of the Royal Pavilion Theater. I have never been back to Russia. I have wiped its dirt off my feet. I don't know John Slade. If you don't leave this instant, I'll have you thrown out."

There seemed no point in staying. I apologized for bothering Katerina, then exited the theater by a back door. I trudged up an alley to the high street, where I found Mr. Thackeray and his friends.

"Ah, Miss Brontë," he said. "I thought we'd lost you."

Mrs. Brookfield supported the pale, quaking Mrs. Crowe. "If only we could get a carriage."

That proved difficult. Carriages for hire were snapped up by other folk in the crowd. We waited for half an hour, my companions impatient and I depressed because my search for Slade was at a dead end. Then I heard someone shout, "Here comes Katerina the Great!"

Out of the alley emerged Katerina, with a man at her side. She wore a crimson, hooded cloak. She walked down a path lined by gawkers, as regally poised as if she were the Queen. But I hardly noticed her. The man captured all my attention.

It was Slade.

Dressed in an elegant black evening suit, brilliant white shirt, and black top hat, he appeared miraculously restored to sanity. His face was clean-shaven, his hair neatly trimmed and combed; his gray eyes were as clear as when I'd said goodbye to him three years ago. My breath came hard and fast and my heart clamored as I gazed upon my long-lost love. My emotions skyrocketed from misery to joy.

"John Slade!" I called.

He didn't react. I hurried forward and stood before him and Katerina. They stopped. Both eyed me, she with annoyance, he with mild puzzlement.

"I beg your pardon, madam?" he said politely.

His accent was as Russian as Katerina's. That didn't surprise me; in order to spy in Russia, he would have had to learn the language. What surprised me was the lack of recognition he showed toward me.

"It's Charlotte Brontë," I said.

He flicked his gaze over my person. His eyes showed no recollection of me, or of the fact that three years ago he'd asked me to marry him. As I stood stunned, he said, "Madam, I'm afraid you've mistaken me for someone else."

He led Katerina to a carriage, helped her in, then sat beside her. As the carriage moved off, I caught a last glimpse of them through the window. Slade turned away from me, toward Katerina. He put his arm around her and kissed her passionately.

Then the carriage was gone, and I was left alone with my companions. Mr. Thackeray said, "What was that all about?"

8

✤

THE SECRET ADVENTURES OF
JOHN SLADE

1849 March. Winter gradually released its frosty grip on
Moscow. Snow fouled by ashes and manure gradually thawed.
People filled the city streets, basking in the weak sunlight. They
savored the warming air and dreamed of the long-awaited
spring.

In the Presnya quarter, wagons laden with coal rattled past
factories whose machinery clanged, pounded, and roared inces-
santly. Smoke and steam issued from a bathhouse near the workers' barracks. John Slade entered, stripped off his clothes in the
changing room, then lay on a marble table in a bath chamber.
An attendant sprinkled him with boiling water, lathered him
with soap, and scrubbed him down. Slade endured a vigorous
massage, then a whipping with a broom made of twigs, to stim-
ulate blood circulation. He rinsed himself in a pool of ice-cold
water, then went to the steam room. He sat on a bench, one
towel draped over his lap, another over his head and shoulders
to protect him from hot clouds of steam, and he waited.

The three Russian intellectuals joined him, one at a time.
These days they were careful not to be seen together in public.
They met at different places where nobody knew them. When
they were all seated, Peter the poet said, "Bad news, comrades.

There was a raid on a meeting last night. Sasha, Ilya, and Boris were arrested."

Fyodor the journalist cursed. Alexander the professor shook his head. Arrests were ever more frequent; the Third Section had intensified surveillance on the dissidents. Slade himself had had a policeman following him around since January, when he'd published an article in a magazine that advocated revolution. He had easily spotted his shadow, and he easily managed to shake it off when he wanted. The rest of the time he led the policeman around town, pretending not to know he was there, keeping him on the string for future use.

"I had a visit from the Third Section last week," Fyodor said, pale despite the heat. "Three of them came to my rooms. They offered me a job writing propaganda for the Tsar. They said that if I refuse, I'll be sent to Siberia."

Banishment to that cold, remote wasteland was a common punishment for opposing the Tsar's regime. Wagons full of exiles departed from Moscow daily.

"I have bad news, too," Alexander said. "Today I lost my post at the university. The Third Section convinced the administration that I am a bad influence on my students."

He removed his spectacles and wiped sweat, or tears, from his eyes. Peter said, "They're eliminating us one after another! We have to do something!"

"We'll call a special meeting," Fyodor said. "We'll talk about the problem."

Peter jeered. "Talk has gotten us nowhere."

"He's right." Slade hid his reluctance to speak behind the fiery passion for revolt that was part of his disguise. "It's time to take action."

Peter eagerly took the bait. "Yes! We must strike back!" He pounded his fist into his palm. "We must fight fire with fire!"

"But we swore that we would never resort to violence," Fyodor said. "To do so would make us no better than our enemies." But Slade could see that he was ready to be persuaded.

"They've given us no choice!" Peter persisted.

"This is war," Slade said. "In war, no holds are barred."

Even as Fyodor nodded, Alexander said, "How can we fight a war against the Tsar's regime? It is too strong. We are so few, so weak, and so unorganized. Besides, we don't have enough guns."

Here it was, the opportunity for which Slade had been laying the groundwork ever since he'd met Peter, Fyodor, and Alexander. Here the Russians were, at the point toward which Slade had been covertly, carefully urging them. Triumph excited him at the same time he felt ashamed of how easy it had been. Manipulation was one of his best talents as a spy, one reason he'd drawn this assignment. But never had he been so loath to use it on trusting, unsuspecting subjects.

Slade spoke quickly before his companions, or he himself, could lose heart. "There are acts of war that can be carried out by a few men. And I own a gun. All we need is one."

Understanding dawned on the Russians' faces. "You mean assassination," Fyodor said.

Slade held up his empty palms: *What else is left?*

"I'm all for it," Peter declared.

Shocked by the turn the conversation had taken, Alexander said, "If you're thinking of assassinating the Tsar, that's impossible. We can't get to him in the Kremlin."

"Not the Tsar," Slade said. "Someone who is not so well guarded but just as much our enemy. Someone whose murder would strike terror into the heart of the regime and inspire the intellectuals, the workers, and the peasants to unite and rise up against the Tsar."

"Prince Alexis Orlov," Fyodor suggested. "The Chief of the Third Section."

Orlov was widely feared and hated. He was exactly the target Slade had in mind.

Fyodor and Peter, excited by their own audacity, set out to convince Alexander that they must assassinate the prince. After much argument, he gave in. "But how should we go about it? We are inexperienced in these matters."

The three Russians looked to Slade. He felt his heart sink under a guilt as heavy and cold as the snow that had buried Moscow all winter. He reminded himself that his loyalty was not to his Russian friends; his duty lay elsewhere.

"I have a plan," Slade said. "Listen."

9

A RECURRING NIGHTMARE OFTEN DISTURBS MY SLEEP. I DREAM that I encounter persons who are dear to me, only to have them greet me with cold indifference. Often they are my two elder sisters, Maria and Elizabeth, who died twenty-five years ago. In that version of the dream, I am at the boarding school where they both fell fatally ill with consumption. The headmistress informs me that I have visitors. When I go to the drawing room, I find Maria and Elizabeth. How overjoyed I am to discover that they are alive! But Maria and Elizabeth are much altered from how I remember them. They are elegant and haughty. They have forgotten everything that once mattered to us. I am crushed. I awaken relieved that it was only a dream.

Alas, my encounter with Slade was no nightmare: it was miserably real. Once he had loved me, but at the theater he had turned coldly from me.

When I left the theater, I could hardly restrain my tears during the trip back to Gloucester Terrace. There I spent a sleepless, terrible night. Alone and devastated, I wept. But hope is stubborn, and the mind interprets facts according to what it wishes rather than what is logical. The dawn of a new day infuses strength into the most broken heart. When the sun's first rays crept in my window, I sat up in bed and took a fresh view of last night's events.

The man I'd met was Slade; I had no doubt. Perhaps he'd only been pretending not to recognize me, for some reason related to his work as a secret agent. Perhaps he was in disguise and mustn't reveal his true identity to anyone. But what about Katerina the Great? Unable to ignore her, I speculated that she was a part of whatever mission he'd undertaken. Slade wouldn't be so inconstant, so callous.

Or would he?

Three years had passed, during which I myself had aged and changed. Slade's life during those years must have been much more eventful than mine; he would have changed even more than I. And I couldn't deny the fact that he'd been a patient in the criminal lunatic wing of Bedlam, accused of multiple, savage murders. Had something disastrous happened to Slade? Had it transformed him from an honorable man to a monster?

I could draw no definite conclusions. I saw no course of action except to pursue the truth about Slade, and the morning brought new inspiration as to how I could. I rose, washed myself, and dressed. A few years earlier I would have hesitated to go out by myself, but my adventures had given me a certain independence of spirit. I left the house so early that the Smiths were still abed, and I hailed a carriage. I rode through a city that looked as lonely as I felt. It was Sunday, and London was quiet; few other people were about. Yellowish smoke from the factories hung in air that was already warm and sultry at seven o'clock. By the time I arrived in Downing Street, church bells had begun to ring, dull as lead. I climbed out of the carriage, paid the driver, and hesitated outside a row of grimy brick buildings.

These comprised the seat of the Foreign Office, which managed Britain's affairs abroad. Here Slade's employers had their headquarters. If anyone knew what was happening with Slade, they surely did. I'd had doubts as to whether they would be here on a Sunday morning, but I saw lights in some windows. I took a deep breath and went inside. A dapper official was stationed at a desk in the foyer. He said, "May I be of service, madam?"

"I'd like to see Lord Eastbourne."

That gentleman was Slade's immediate superior. For three

years I'd searched the newspapers for items relating to Slade, and I'd spotted a notice to the effect that Lord Eastbourne had taken the place vacated by Slade's former superior, Lord Unwin. The sly, selfish, and incompetent Lord Unwin had sabotaged Slade's efforts, and mine, to save the Royal Family from a madman. The Foreign Secretary had punished Lord Unwin by assigning him to a post in India. He'd died there, of cholera, six months ago; I'd seen his obituary. Now I hoped that Lord Eastbourne was in, and that he could shed some light on Slade's current situation.

"Lord Eastbourne can't be disturbed," the official said. "Come back another time."

"Tell him it is Charlotte Brontë. Tell him I must speak with him about John Slade."

I didn't know which name had changed his attitude, but the official said, "One moment." He left, then soon returned. "Follow me."

He escorted me through a series of ill-lit passages and left me in an office. Lord Eastbourne rose from his chair. He was a tall, robust man who had the appearance of a country solicitor. Ruddy skin complemented features that were blunt and strong. He would have looked as much at ease walking the moors as he did behind his massive desk, which was covered with letters and documents written in a bold, slanted, masculine hand. On first glance he was a big improvement over Lord Unwin, but I cautioned myself that appearances were often deceiving.

"Miss Brontë," he said, coming out from behind his desk to shake my hand. "It's an honor to meet you. I've been briefed on the good work you did for us."

I was glad he knew who I was. It saved me the trouble of convincing him that I'd helped Slade save the British Empire.

Lord Eastbourne seated me on a divan and himself in an armchair opposite me. "Whatever I can I do for you, just ask."

His brown eyes were shrewd and intelligent but not unkind. I poured out the story of how I'd come upon Slade in Bedlam and everything that had happened since. Lord Eastbourne listened with close attention. When I'd finished, I said, "I need to know what has happened to Slade. I came to you because I had nowhere else to turn."

Concern appeared in Lord Eastbourne's expression. "You've posed me a bit of a dilemma. Information about our agents is strictly confidential."

My heart sank.

"But I have a certain amount of discretion. And considering the fact that you risked your life for the sake of our kingdom, I owe you an explanation."

Hope resurged. I eagerly leaned forward. "Where is Slade?"

"Before we discuss John Slade, I should give you a little background on the assignment he undertook for us three years ago," Lord Eastbourne said.

I tried to quell my fear that he was postponing bad news.

"Slade was posted to Russia," Lord Eastbourne began.

"I'm aware of that. He told me before he left."

"What do you know about Russia?"

"I know that Russia is a land where Europe blends with Asia." Since Slade had left for Russia, I had read up on it. "It covers millions of square miles, and its population includes Mongols, Slavs, Turks, and Tatars. Their written language is the Cyrillic alphabet. The state religion is the Orthodox Christian Church, which I understand combines Roman Catholicism with pagan rituals."

"Those are some basic facts," Lord Eastbourne said in the condescending tone that a schoolmaster uses toward a clever little girl. "Allow me to tell you a little more. Russia began, during the ninth century, as a handful of principalities in the Ukraine, controlled by tribal chiefs. It was invaded in the thirteenth century by Mongols. Russia was united under Prince Ivan the Great, who drove out the Mongols in the fifteenth century. He arrested, imprisoned, tortured, and executed anyone who opposed his rule. When he died, there ensued a period of uprisings and civil wars that lasted into the seventeenth century. A new dynasty, the Romanov, took over, and still reigns today."

"I know. I have studied Russia's recent history." My habit of pride in my education compelled me to demonstrate my knowledge to Lord Eastbourne, and I hoped I could speed up this lesson on Russia so we could proceed to the matter of John Slade. "During the last two centuries, Russia has won multiple wars against Turkey and Persia. The result is that Russia captured the Crimea and gained other territory, along the Black Sea coast, the Bosporus, and the mouth of the Danube. It has incorporated Georgia and Finland, part of Armenia, and expanded westward into Poland and Lithuania. When Napoleon invaded it in 1812, Russia fought back so fiercely that he was forced to retreat. Russia became a major world power, an empire that extends from Poland to the Pacific Ocean, and the Arctic Ocean to the Persian Gulf. Today, Russia is Britain's rival for control of the Middle Eastern territories. Its influence in those parts is a threat to Britain's Indian Empire."

"You are well informed," Lord Eastbourne said, surprised into respect. "But please allow me to broaden your understanding. Russia is a backward, primitive country controlled by the present Tsar, Nicholas Pavlovich. He is a tyrant who has absolute power over his subjects. They have none of the rights or freedoms that make our own country great."

He swelled with patriotic pride; then he turned grim. "Our relationship with Tsar Nicholas is complicated. On one hand, we are thankful to him for maintaining order in Europe. He has vigorously acted to crush revolutions and preserve the ruling monarchies. In 1849, for example, when Polish citizens of the Austrian Empire rose up in support of Hungarian rebels, he sent Russian troops to help Emperor Franz Josef put down the insurrection. On the other hand, we consider Russia a threat because the Tsar is bent on enlarging his domain. His army is almost a million men strong. India is a sitting target, its wealth ripe for plunder. Britain must prevent Russia from invading India and maintain her own influence in the Middle East."

I knew all this, but I forced myself to listen politely.

"Fortunately for us, the Tsar has problems at home, which have checked his ambitions. There is much civil unrest. The Russian leaders fear that subversive ideas from the West will bring about a cataclysmic revolution within Russia's own borders. In order to control their own people, they created a secret police force known as the Third Section. The Third Section maintains surveillance on Russian citizens suspected of revolutionary activity. Its agents censor material printed in the press. They investigate crimes against the state, such as sabotage and political assassinations. They often provoke revolutionaries to commit those crimes, then imprison them or exile them without a trial."

"This is all very interesting," I said, "but how does it concern Slade?"

"Slade's purpose in Russia was twofold," Lord Eastbourne said. "He went there to establish contact with Russian revolutionaries, supply them with money, and do whatever he could to further their cause and weaken the Tsar's regime. That he did, while posing as a Russian scholar and journalist. Second, he was supposed to put himself in a position to learn what the Tsar's plans are regarding action against Britain. He achieved both purposes, although the details as to how are unclear."

For three years I'd wondered what Slade was doing in Russia; now I knew, but I had yet to learn anything that pertained to the present.

"Slade managed to infiltrate the Kremlin—the Tsar's palace," Lord Eastbourne said. "He was our best agent in Moscow. He smuggled messages to us, reporting secrets from the highest echelon of the Russian government. But in January of this year, his messages stopped. So did the flow of all other intelligence from Moscow. We heard nothing until February, when one of our Russian informants showed up in London. He told us that Slade had turned traitor."

My mouth dropped. Shock delivered after too many previous shocks rendered me speechless.

"Apparently, Slade had given the Third Section the names of his three fellow British agents," Lord Eastbourne said. "The Third Section arrested and murdered all of them. Our informant said that Slade had begun working for the Tsar, as an expert on British espionage, foreign policy, and military strategy."

I found my voice. "That can't be! Slade would never betray his country or his comrades!"

"Our source is reliable," Lord Eastbourne countered, "and his statement was corroborated by the team of agents we sent to investigate."

"I refuse to believe it!" My whole body was shaking, so agitated was I. "Where is Slade? I must hear his side of the story!"

Lord Eastbourne regarded me with a sympathy that I found more ominous than reassuring. He took my hand and held it between his own, which were warm, dry, and strong. The intimate gesture filled me with dread, for I had often seen clergymen extend it to the newly bereaved. "Miss Brontë, I know you think highly of John Slade. I regret to inform you that Slade was executed for treason. Our team of agents ambushed him in Moscow and shot him."

Even as I went faint with horror, disbelief and anger flooded me. I wrenched my hand out of Lord Eastbourne's. "Slade is alive! I saw him last night! I just told you so!"

The sympathy in Lord Eastbourne's eyes turned to pity. "Whoever you saw, it couldn't have been him. Whether or not you believe he was a traitor, you must face this fact: John Slade has been dead for four months now."

10

WHEN I RETURNED TO GLOUCES-
TER TERRACE, ALL I WANTED
to do was avoid everyone, shut myself in my room, think on what
I'd learned at the Foreign Office, and try to recover from my shock.
But George Smith met me at the foot of the stairs. "Where have you
been?" He was clearly relieved to see me, but vexed by my absence.

"I had business to attend to." I couldn't tell him what business.

Mrs. Smith joined us, happy that I'd displeased George. "Miss
Brontë might have told us she was going out. But she is a secretive,
stealthy sort of houseguest."

"Our appointment with Dr. Browne, the phrenologist, is at
nine o'clock," George said. "I was worried that you wouldn't come
back in time. Had you forgotten?"

"Oh, dear. I am sorry." I had indeed forgotten that we'd
arranged to meet with Dr. Browne, who examined the skulls of his
clients in order to assess their characters. Phrenology was all the
rage, and Dr. Browne so popular that this Sunday morning was the
only time during my stay in London that he could see us.

"You evidently don't appreciate the trouble my son takes to
entertain you." Mrs. Smith addressed me but caught George's eye.

"Well, no matter, Charlotte," he said, looking uncomfortable. I
could see he'd begun to sense that his mother didn't care for me.
"You're here now. Shall we be on our way? I thought we could visit
the zoo afterward."

"Yes, but first I must go up to my room." I desperately needed some time alone before facing the rest of the day.

As I ran up the stairs, I heard Mrs. Smith say, "Miss Brontë looks ill. Her constitution is delicate." *Too delicate for her to make you a good wife*, her tone implied. "Perhaps she should go home."

I wouldn't give Mrs. Smith the satisfaction; and I couldn't leave London now, when momentous events were happening one after another with no resolution in sight. In my room I drew deep breaths to calm myself, then splashed cold water on my face. Soon I was in a carriage with George, riding along Bayswater Road.

"How was the play last night?" he asked.

"Good enough," I said in a tone meant to discourage further questions.

"Oh." He felt snubbed, I could tell. But George is so good-natured that he seldom takes offense for long. He began to point out interesting sights and talk about them, although I barely listened. My mind dwelled on my conversation with Lord Eastbourne. He had kindly but firmly insisted that I must accept the truth and forget John Slade, for my own good. I'd left the Foreign Office upset because the authorities would not help me find Slade. They believed he was dead. They would not change their minds on the word of a hysterical woman. Perhaps that was for the best, since they were no longer his friends. But now I began to question my own credibility. Maybe the man I'd seen really wasn't Slade. Maybe my nearsightedness was getting worse.

Dr. Browne had his consultancy in a row of townhouses near the Strand, that great thoroughfare that skirts the bank of the Thames from the West End to the city proper. When George rang the bell, a butler answered and said, "Mr. and Miss Fraser, I presume?"

Those were the names under which George had booked our appointment. We'd decided to pose as brother and sister and not reveal our true names, in case Dr. Browne had heard of us—foreknowledge might compromise his analysis. The butler sat George in the waiting room and ushered me to Dr. Browne's office.

A slender man of perhaps fifty years, Dr. Browne had a long face with drooping jowls and pink cheeks. He was so clean that he smelled of soap and everything about him shone—his rimless spectacles, his long white coat, the gray hair combed over his bald pate, and his toothy, ingratiating smile. On the wall hung a phrenology chart—drawings of a head in front, back, top, and side views, with areas divided by dotted lines and labeled. He seated me by the window, in a chair with a cushioned seat and low back. I noticed a display of framed portraits of well-known people.

"Those are clients," Dr. Browne said proudly.

I thought it a good thing that I'd used an alias. I wouldn't care to have my portrait hung in his office and the results of his examination of Currer Bell publicized.

"Please allow me to explain the theory of phrenology," Dr. Browne said. "The mind has different mental faculties, which reside in different organs within the brain. Bumps on the skull reflect the size of the underlying organs. I can therefore measure a person's capacity for a particular mental faculty by measuring that bump."

He took up a set of calipers. "First, I shall take some overall measurements of your skull. Hold still, please." I obeyed while he fitted the calipers to my head, front to back, then sideways, and read off the numbers. "Ah! Your head is quite large."

I wondered if the numerous folks who thought phrenology was quackery were right. I hardly needed Dr. Browne to tell me what anyone could see—that my head was too big for my body. "Is it?" I said, ever self-conscious about my awkward proportions.

"Indeed. It's remarkable for its intellectual development. You have a large forehead, which signifies deep thoughtfulness and comprehensive understanding."

That consoled me somewhat. Dr. Browne set aside his calipers, worked his fingertips gently but firmly over my scalp, and felt the bumps and indentations. "You have a fine organ of language. I deduce that you can express your sentiments with clearness, precision, and force."

Perhaps there was merit to phrenology.

"You are very sensitive, with a nervous temperament, an exalted sense of the beautiful and ideal, and a gloomy view of the world. Although you are anxious to succeed in your undertakings, you are not so sanguine as to the probability of success."

I winced, for he'd hit the target smack in the bull's-eye.

His fingers expertly probed my skull. "You form strong, enduring attachments."

I thought of Monsieur Constantin Heger, the Belgian professor I'd loved unrequitedly for three years. I realized that I had loved Slade for the same length of time. I blinked away tears.

"You also have a very strong sense of justice," Dr. Browne said.

Even though Slade had repudiated me, I didn't want him labeled a murder and traitor if he was not.

"I also detect a dedication to the truth," Dr. Browne said.

And I still wanted to know whether Slade was guilty as charged.

"That concludes my examination." Dr. Browne stepped back, clasped his hands, and smiled. "Have you any questions?"

"Yes," I said. "Is it possible for the organs in a man's brain to change? Can that turn him into someone else, even a criminal?"

"It's entirely possible, and not uncommon. I've examined convicted murderers, and quite a few of them had suffered injuries to their heads. I remember one case—a boxer. He'd been knocked out many times, and he'd changed from a nice chap to a violent brute."

I wondered if something similar had befallen Slade in Russia. Maybe his organ of memory had been so damaged that he'd forgotten me. But there occurred to me another, even more disturbing idea. Maybe Slade wasn't the person whose mental faculties were impaired.

"Doctor, may I ask—" I had to swallow fear before I could continue. "Did you detect any damage to the organs in my brain?"

My brother Branwell had been a lunatic. Seeing things that didn't exist was a symptom of his madness, and perhaps madness ran in our family.

"None at all," Dr. Browne said reassuringly. "In my opinion, you're completely sane."

I thanked Dr. Browne and sat in the waiting room while George

Smith had his consultation. I occupied myself with wondering about Slade.

George returned, unusually pensive. As we rode away in our carriage, I asked, "What's wrong?"

"Dr. Browne said I have an affectionate, friendly disposition. I am strongly attached to my home and family, and I am an admirer of the fair sex. I am active and practical, but not hustling or contentious."

I laughed despite my worried mood. "But that's not unflattering. And it's you exactly! Why don't you like it?"

He looked annoyed by my mirth and stung because I agreed with Dr. Browne. "It makes me sound so shallow. What did he say about you?"

When I told him, it was his turn to laugh at the justice of Dr. Browne's observations. Cross with each other, we traveled in silence to the London Zoo.

The zoo occupied a spacious green park on the north side of Regent's Park. The animals were housed in fanciful Gothic palaces. The many visitors included a preponderance of children. The sun had come out, brightening the colorful scene. Roars from the lions and screeches from monkeys and exotic birds made the zoo seem a tropical outpost of the British Empire. George and I marched along without speaking. He was still out of sorts. He darted glances at me, and I feared he would ask questions that I would rather not answer. When we reached the pond in which ducks, geese, egrets, and flamingos were gathered, I said, "I would like to walk by myself awhile. Shall we meet here in an hour?"

"Very well," George said, although he didn't look pleased.

I ambled through the zoo, hardly cognizant of where I went. My mind was so tired of wondering about Slade that I decided to give it a rest. I watched giraffes, camels, and zebras, whose comical faces made me smile. The barnyard smells reminded me of Haworth; they soothed rather than offended me. I viewed the hippopotamus, submerged in his tub, only his eyes above the water; he resembled a fat black hog in a farm wallow. The herd of elephants included a baby—a darling creature. I went into the house where

lions and tigers prowled in cages. I listened to them roar and the
children shriek in fright. By the time I entered the aviary, I was
more at peace than I'd been since my visit to Bedlam, even though
I knew not what my next course of action should be.

Brightly colored birds flitted between the palm trees under the
glass roof. As I listened to parrots squawk and watched plumed
cranes strut, I felt a sudden prickling sensation. I knew that sensation from my years as a schoolteacher. I'd felt it whenever I'd
turned my back to my pupils. It was the feeling of unfriendly eyes
on me. I turned and saw a man holding his little boy up to feed a
macaw perched on a branch. A group of people admired a peacock
spreading his brilliant tail feathers. Two women laughed as they
wiped bird dung off the head of a bald man. No one appeared to
be watching me, but my pulse quickened. I knew the scent of danger. I smelled it now.

I fled the aviary and mingled with a crowd gathered around a
lemonade stand. Here I was safe among numbers, but I could not
shed the certainty that someone was following me, someone with
malice in mind. As to who, I knew not. As to why, I could only spec-
ulate that the reason must involve Slade and our past relationship.

"Miss Brontë," said a voice startlingly close to me.

I yelped and almost jumped out of my shoes. I whirled to face
the young man who'd spoken. He smiled an earnest smile, his protuberant brown eyes shining. His pink, boyish face was familiar,
although I couldn't place him. He said, "It's Oliver Heald."

He was the man who had made me so uncomfortable at the
Great Exhibition with his questions about my marital status. I said,
"You frightened me half to death!"

His smile faltered; he tilted his head, a habit I recognized. "I'm
terribly sorry."

"What are you doing here?" I said, forgetting that he had as
much right to be at the zoo as I did.

"I—I was hoping you would inscribe your book for me," he
said, disconcerted by my harsh manner. He held out a copy of *Jane
Eyre*.

I stared at the book, then at his nervous, blushing face. How odd that Mr. Heald should happen to have the book with him at the same moment we ran into each other! It seemed too much of a coincidence. "Have you been following me?" I demanded.

"Well, yes," he admitted sheepishly. "I saw you, and I remembered how gracious you were the last time we met, and I thought, 'Here's a once-in-a-lifetime chance to get my favorite author's signature.'"

I ignored his compliments. My temper, already strained by the events of the past two days, found in him a handy target. "How dare you intrude on my privacy?"

"I'm sorry," Mr. Heald said, alarmed by his own breach of manners, hurt by my reaction. "Will you please forgive me?"

"Go away." I shooed him as if he were a buzzing fly. "Leave me alone!"

"Yes, Miss Brontë. I'm sorry." Mr. Heald turned and ran, holding *Jane Eyre* against his heart.

I belatedly felt relieved that my pursuer had turned out to be the innocuous Mr. Heald. I also calmed down enough to regret how cruelly I'd treated him. "Wait, Mr. Heald," I called, "I would be honored to sign your book."

He'd gone into a wooded area that bordered the zoo. So guilty did I feel toward him, and so eager to make amends, that I didn't stop to think about the possible danger of following a man I barely knew into what looked to be an isolated area. Instead, I did what every witless heroine in every second-rate romance novel would have done: I hastened after Mr. Heald, following a trail under a canopy of trees. Their leaves filtered the sunlight into a cool, green shade. The voices, the children's laughter, and the animals' cries sounded far away. I saw no one. Pausing, I called, "Mr. Heald?"

There was no answer. Leafy branches rustled behind me. I turned, glimpsed movement among the trees. Mr. Heald didn't appear. Another rustle came, then soft footsteps. I felt a spurt of irritation. Was he teasing me? "Come out. Don't play games," I ordered.

A figure materialized behind a screen of foliage. That it belonged to a man was all I could discern, but his silhouette radiated menace.

Fear shot through me. I began to run. I tried to steer a course toward the open, populated area of the zoo, but every time I turned in that direction, I saw the man's shadow moving through the trees, between me and safety.

"Help!" I cried.

If he was Mr. Heald, would he hurt me? If he wasn't, then who was he? A criminal who preyed on women he happened to meet? I thought of the women killed in Whitechapel. Fighting my way past low branches, I felt like a deer stalked by a tiger in a jungle. I panicked as I heard his footsteps moving faster, coming closer. I grew certain that this was no random encounter.

Somehow I had once again stumbled into bad business that involved John Slade. I acknowledged the terrifying possibility that it was he—lunatic, traitor, and murderer—who pursued me. If he caught me, what would he do?

I came abruptly upon a brick wall. From its other side I heard carriage wheels racketing and horses' hooves plodding. This was the wall that separated the zoo from the street. It was too high for me to climb. I sought but found no gate. My back pressed against the wall, I watched with terror as swaying branches and rustling leaves heralded the arrival of my stalker.

11

I HEARD A SUDDEN CRASH. A WILD THRASHING AND SCUF-fling ensued. It was the sound of men fighting. They flailed behind the bushes. Grunts punctuated thuds as blows landed. I could have taken the opportunity to escape, but I had to see who the men were. I crept toward them, but before I could gain a clear view, one jumped up and ran away. The other clambered to his feet. I tore through dangling vines and burst upon him. It was Slade.

He stood, brushed dirt off his black coat and trousers, and faced me. I realized that I did not know who had stalked me and who had rescued me, Slade or the other man. My heart drummed a cadence of fear and desire.

His expression was as distant as when I'd confronted him outside the Royal Pavilion Theater. "Go home, madam," he said in the same Russian accent he'd used then. "From now on, do not wander by yourself. It is dangerous."

He turned to leave. I was suddenly furious. Whether he remembered me or not, I had gone to much trouble to help him whether he deserved it or not. And I knew this was Slade, no matter what he or anyone else said. His were the eyes that had once looked deep into mine; his the lips I had kissed; his the hands that had caressed me in places touched by no other man. The least I deserved from him was an explanation.

"Don't you walk away!" I shouted.

I seized his arm. He stared at me, surprised by my temerity. He looked at my hand that clutched him, and I felt his tough, strong muscles stiffen in resistance. I also felt the warmth of his skin through his coat sleeve. A torrent of emotion weakened me. For three years I'd longed to touch Slade. Now I was touching him, but this was not how I'd wanted it to be. I'd yearned to have his arms around me, our bodies united in love. But he wrenched free of my grasp, as callously as if throwing off a stranger who'd begged him for a penny. Anger overrode my hurt feelings and restored my strength.

"What are you doing here?" I demanded.

"I see you go in woods and man follow." Slade's face had an impassivity that was as foreign as his accent. "I think he mean to hurt you. So I catch him, chase him away."

"Stop pretending!" I was so incensed that I didn't care whether what he'd said was true. "You're not Russian." My voice rose. "You're as British as I, Mr. John Slade!"

The sound of his name uttered so loudly alarmed him. "For God's sake, keep your voice down!" he said in a furious whisper. The Russian accent was gone.

"Aha!" I said. "You admit you are John Slade. What took you so long?"

He made shushing motions while he looked around to see if anyone was listening. "Be quiet! You don't know what you've gotten yourself into!"

"You're right, John Slade, I don't. Until I do, I won't be quiet. Now tell me, why were you in Bedlam? Did you murder the nurses? Or those women in Whitechapel? Why did you come back to England? Do you remember who I am?"

When he frowned and didn't reply, I shouted, "Tell me, John Slade!"

Repeating his name was like chanting a magic spell that gave me power over him. Annoyed resignation settled over his features. I'd seen that same look in the past, whenever I'd determined upon doing things he thought I shouldn't. "All right," he said, but in a manner so cold that it was like an icicle driven into my heart. "Yes,

I remember you, Miss Charlotte Brontë." He spoke my name as formally as if we were little more than strangers. "I'll tell you everything, on one condition—that you never breathe a word of it to anyone."

I glared and kept silent, letting him think I agreed to his bargain; later, I would decide whether to renege. Eyeing me cautiously, he began his story: "The Foreign Office sent me to Russia. My mission was to aid and abet Russian intellectuals who are trying to bring about a revolution, and to discover what actions the Tsar plans to take against Britain."

That corresponded to what Lord Eastbourne had told me. "Go on." Although I began to relax because I could believe Slade so far, I warned myself against taking him at his word: deception was his trade, and I had good reason for doubt.

"While I was there, I infiltrated the Tsar's court. The Tsar anticipates a war with Britain in the near future," Slade said. "He's been searching for a way to ensure his victory, and he thinks he's found it at last."

Here, Slade's story departed from Lord Eastbourne's. I listened with suspicion.

"His spies abroad learned of a scientist named Niall Kavanagh, a British citizen, Irish by birth. Dr. Kavanagh has apparently invented a device that could give its possessor a crucial advantage in a war. He is currently building a model of his device for the British government, which is keeping him hidden. The Tsar means to have the device."

"How do you know this?" I asked.

"From eavesdropping on the Tsar's private conversations in the Kremlin," Slade said. "The Tsar has sent his favorite spy to fetch Dr. Kavanagh to Moscow. The spy is a man named Wilhelm Stieber." Darkness pooled in the depths of Slade's crystalline gray eyes. "Wilhelm Stieber also serves as chief spy to the King of Prussia. He is an expert at espionage, with his own agents all over Europe." His tone indicated a strong personal dislike for Stieber, and perhaps a rivalry between two expert spies pitted against each other in a deadly game. "I came back to England to find Kavanagh before

Stieber does and keep him out of the Tsar's hands."

I wished to believe Slade. How I wished it with all my heart! But his story about the scientist and the secret device seemed fantastic, and I had no corroboration for it. "How does this explain why you were arrested for murder and committed to Bedlam?"

"Stieber employs agents among the staff at Bedlam. He has turned the asylum to his own purposes. He kidnaps political refugees, smuggles them into Bedlam, and tortures them to extract information about anti-Tsarist plots among the immigrant community. He has begun using the same tactics on British officials, trying to learn where Niall Kavanagh is."

Such audacious behavior by a foreign mastermind was credible to me. I'd gained intimate knowledge of another foreign mastermind, in 1848. But my distrust of Slade deepened: perhaps he'd invented the story because he thought I would believe it based on our past experiences. "You didn't answer my question."

Slade narrowed his eyes; he knew I suspected he was lying. "I'm getting to that. When I arrived in England, I searched for Kavanagh. I tapped all my usual sources, but it was as if he'd dropped off the earth. I wondered if Stieber had already spirited him out of England. I went to Whitechapel to get news of Stieber from the European refugees there. They pass around news about their homelands and the authorities who drove them out. I posed as Josef Typinski, a Polish immigrant. I heard that Stieber had been seen at Bedlam. I obtained a position as a janitor there. I watched for Stieber, and when he showed up, I spied on him."

"You weren't spying or working as a janitor when I saw you," I said. "You were an inmate in the criminal lunatics' ward. Explain that."

Memory and anger suffused Slade's expression, all the while he watched me, trying to predict what I might do next. "Stieber found me out. I don't know how. He must have tipped the police onto me. One minute I was asleep in bed; the next, I was locked up in Bedlam for the murders of three women I'd never heard of, that I didn't commit. Two nurses in the criminal lunatics' ward were in Stieber's pay. So was the doctor. He and Stieber tortured me in an attempt to learn what I was up to and what I knew about Niall Kavanagh."

This was the scene I had witnessed. Wilhelm Stieber was the sinister, foreign-looking man who'd presided over Slade's torture. Or so Slade said. "Did you kill the nurses?"

"I had to." Slade spoke with a combination of guilt and defiance. "Stieber was going to kill me. It was the only way I could escape."

He'd explained everything logically, but not to my satisfaction. "I don't believe you." I was all the angrier because he'd tried to dupe me.

"Why not? It's the truth." His gaze steadfastly held mine.

I fired the shot that would pierce his tissue of lies: "Because you're not on a mission for the Foreign Office. You're no longer in their employ. You're a traitor!"

He blinked. "Where did you get that idea?"

"From Lord Eastbourne."

"You spoke with Lord Eastbourne?" Alarm resonated in Slade's voice.

"This very morning. After I saw you last night." *With Katerina.* I bit my tongue before I could utter the words. My pride refused to let Slade know that his unfaithfulness had hurt me more than his betrayal of our country.

"What else did Lord Eastbourne tell you?" Slade asked.

"That you were executed for treason. He thinks you're dead."

"Well, that's obviously not the case." Slade spread his hands. "Here I am."

"Are you?" My voice and my heart filled with raw anguish. "Are you the John Slade I used to know?"

He brushed off my words with an impatient gesture. "I am not a traitor. The fact that I'm not dead should convince you that Lord Eastbourne is wrong." He began to pace, and I sensed his thoughts speeding through his mind. "Did you tell Lord Eastbourne you saw me?"

"Yes," I admitted.

Slade grimaced in displeasure. He ran his hand through his

unruly black hair. I remembered the feel of its silky tangles. My heart clenched painfully. "What did Lord Eastbourne say?" Slade asked.

"He didn't believe me. He said I was mistaken. He advised me to forget you."

"Have you told anyone else anything about me?"

"I told Dr. Forbes, my acquaintance who showed me round Bedlam the day I saw you. And George Smith, my publisher. He accompanied me to Whitechapel to look for you. Your landlady gave us a tour of your lodgings. I found a playbill for the Royal Pavilion Theater. That's how I happened to be there last night."

"Damnation!" Slade said. "You always were an obstinate, inquisitive woman who went places where she had no business!"

This was the first sign of personal emotion Slade had expressed toward me. These were his first words that revealed he knew me better than he purported. Although they weren't flattering, my heart leapt. "So you do remember me! You haven't forgotten!"

I was too proud to beg him to say he recalled wanting to marry me. Instead, I willed him to remember what we'd once been to each other. I extended my hand in a mute plea.

Slade backed away as if my touch were poison. His hands went up, perhaps in denial, perhaps in self-defense. "Lord Eastbourne was right. You must forget you ever saw me, ever knew me. Never think of me again."

Then he turned, ran into the forest, and vanished.

12

"WHERE WERE YOU?" GEORGE SMITH SAID WHEN I MET him at the pond. He was flushed with sunburn and annoyance. "I've been waiting half an hour."

I swayed, on the verge of fainting. The bright scene of children, ducks, geese, and water shimmered before my eyes. George's annoyance turned to alarm. "What's wrong?"

I began to cry so hard I couldn't speak.

"Come on," George said, "I'll take you home."

After escorting me out of the zoo, he bundled me into a carriage. I tried to calm myself but could not. I had finally seen Slade, but even if I could have believed his story, the happy reunion I'd desired was never to be. How disappointed, broken, and wretched was I!

"Please tell me what the matter is," George said anxiously. "I want to help."

Nothing could relieve my sorrow; not even God could change what had happened. I offered the first excuse I could think of: "I've a terrible headache."

The excuse immediately came true. A crushing pain gripped my head. The illness that emotional strain invariably causes me now struck with full force. Almost insensible from the pain, wracked by nausea, I shut my eyes and hoped I wouldn't be sick.

George hesitantly stroked my hair. "I do wish you would confide in me. It hurts me to see you in such distress." He added, in a tone much less self-assured than usual, "You have become very dear to me, Charlotte."

Here was a hint of what I'd feared to hear from him. Once, during my brief infatuation with George, I'd hoped we could be more than friends, but now I wept harder and felt worse. If only he were Slade!

Fortunately, he realized that I was too upset to talk, and he said no more. Back at Gloucester Terrace, I lay in bed, tormented by physical and mental agony. I'd forgotten that George had arranged a dinner party of famous literary critics for me to meet. When the doorbell rang, it was too late to cancel the party, and I had the further discomfort of listening to the guests talking and laughing, probably about me. After some hours my headache and nausea lessened enough that I thought I should make an appearance at the party. I got up and tidied myself, but facing a pack of critics was the last thing I wanted to do.

What I wanted, in spite of all that had happened, was to see Slade again. If he didn't love me anymore, I needed him to tell me so. Maybe then could I forget him, pick up the pieces of my heart, and go on with my life.

I sneaked down the back stairs. George and his guests in the parlor didn't notice. The clock struck ten o'clock as I slipped out the door. The night was warm; smoke and clouds in the sky glowed like brimstone in the light from the city below. I walked to Bayswater Road and hired a carriage. I alit outside the Royal Pavilion Theater, only to find it dark and quiet, as was the whole Whitechapel high street. The only person I saw was a beggar seated in the doorway.

His body looked oddly truncated. Eyes as bright and unblinking as an owl's gleamed in his bearded, grimy face. "Lookin' for somethin', mum?"

"I wanted to see Katerina the Great." I noticed with a shock that he had no legs. His trousers were pinned up, covering the stumps. "Do you know where she lives?"

"Maybe." The beggar held out his tin cup. I tossed in a coin. "Come on. I'll show you."

We made an odd pair—he racing along the pavement on his hands, I trotting to keep up. The streets along which he led me were devoid of gas lamps. Tenements rose into the sky's acid-yellow glow. Most of the buildings were dark except for the cellars, through whose windows I could see people sewing, making baskets, or doing other piecework. The beggar turned so many corners so fast that I lost my sense of direction. I felt like a lost soul being led through Purgatory by a guide not quite human.

We stopped in an enclave of tall, thin, terraced houses built of brick, crowned by steeply pitched slate roofs. My guide jerked his chin at the one in front of us. "There."

As he pattered away, I looked up and down the street. Not a hint of life was evident. The only sounds I heard were clangs from distant factories. A shiver of fear and desolation crept up my spine. I looked at the house that the beggar had indicated was Katerina's. I'd thought she would live in a residence as glamorous as she; then I recalled that she was but a foreign actress at a seedy theater. Dim light leaked around the curtains in the windows. Was Slade visiting his mistress tonight?

I almost quailed at the idea of meeting him in Katerina's presence. Steeling myself, I walked up the steps. My heart raced; my head still throbbed. The door was ajar. A strange, ruddy light glowed within. Eager for a confrontation yet dreading it, I pushed the door open further and peered inside. To my right was a parlor. Crimson and gold wallpaper and tapestries decorated the walls. Burgundy velvet sofas and chairs stood on a patterned red Turkey carpet. A carved table held a brass samovar. Red candles burned on the mantel over the fireplace. The profusion of color seemed to bleed outward and engulf me. I smelled coffee and exotic perfume. Timid yet curious, I stepped inside the house.

To my left, a flight of carpeted stairs led upward. I heard a woman moaning, and a masculine voice, low and urgent. Although I am no expert on such matters, I recognized the sounds of a couple making love. Slade was with Katerina. Anguish lacerated my heart. I had hoped to find Slade here, but I'd refused to think that I might find him thus engaged. But I started up the stairs, as furtive as a thief. I was more determined than ever to confront Slade, even though it meant witnessing things that would only cause me more pain.

Katerina's moans turned to cries; the man's utterances grew more insistent. They were nearing the climax of their pleasure. I knew how that pleasure felt. I had experienced it once with Slade, and, I confess, many times thereafter, alone in my bed; yet I was a virgin still. I had never experienced the ultimate fulfillment that Katerina was experiencing. Choking on rage, jealousy, and tears, I was halfway up the stairs when she began to scream.

Her screams were piercing, shrill, loud enough to hurt my ears. I realized then that my perceptions had been distorted by my jealousy, that those screams expressed not rapture but terror and agony. These were not the sounds of a couple enjoying an amorous encounter. Rather, they conveyed the impression of a woman being tortured. I was so startled that I tripped on the stairs. I fell hard on my knee, with a resounding, painful thud. I exclaimed before I could stop myself. Then I heard rapid footsteps pounding down another set of stairs at the back of the house. A door slammed. The man must have left; I could no longer hear his voice. Katerina shouted words in Russian between her screams, calling for help.

Should I go to her aid and expose myself as a trespasser, or steal away and avoid trouble?

The daughter of a parson cannot turn her back on someone in need. I rushed up the stairs, to a chamber at the top, and almost fell across the threshold. A bizarre sight greeted my eyes. I thought it was a Crucifixion from a medieval painting. A naked figure lay on a background of gold, arms spread out and legs extended, like Jesus Christ on the cross. Sheer white fabric twisted around its groin. Its limbs and torso were marked with red gashes that oozed blood.

As I squinted through my spectacles, trying to make sense of what I saw, the figure groaned and writhed. Its chest heaved, and there I saw female breasts. It was Katerina, on a bed covered by a gold quilt. Her wrists and ankles were tied with ropes to the wrought-iron bedstead. Her head tossed. Her dark eyes were huge with fright.

She saw me and gasped out inarticulate pleas. I rushed to her and tried to untie the ropes that restrained her hands. She struggled so frantically that the knots tightened. "Be still," I said.

But she fought like a trussed wild beast. I looked around the room for something to cut her bonds, and noticed a knife on the rug. Its black handle and long, narrow steel blade were smeared with blood. It was the weapon used to wound Katerina. The thought of touching it made me ill, but I snatched it up; I cut the ropes. Katerina moaned, her hands clutching her deepest wound— a cut across her abdomen.

"I'll fetch help," I said.

She reached out and grabbed my wrist. "No! Don't leave me!"

Her grip was as strong as a bear trap. I tried to break free but could not. I tried to convince her that she needed a physician.

"It's no use," Katerina said. "I am dying." She breathed in short, uneven gasps. "Please stay with me. I do not want to die alone."

I snatched up a white shawl that lay upon a chair and pressed it to the wound on her stomach. As I desperately tried to stanch the bleeding, I saw that so much blood had already flowed that the bed was drenched. I noticed that Katerina was also bleeding from between her legs. Although suffering twisted her face, she tried to maintain her self-control. I stared at her, stricken. When I had seen her on stage, she had reminded me of my sister Emily, and now the resemblance was stronger than ever. When Emily took ill with consumption, she never uttered a complaint. She insisted upon going about her business despite the pain in her chest, the violent coughs, and the crippling shortness of breath. She fought for life until the end, when bodily weakness triumphed over her strong spirit; then she faced death with dignity.

As I stood beside Katerina and held her hand, I saw Emily lying on the sofa in the parsonage. I remembered watching helplessly as she declined. Katerina coughed; blood spilled from her mouth. That had happened to Emily, her lungs ravaged by the disease.

Now I wept for her all over again. But I was not so lost in memory or grief that I forgot why I'd come. I did not overlook the possibility that Katerina might have information that I wanted.

"Who did this to you?" I asked.

Her lips moved, but no sound came out.

I thought of the women mutilated and murdered in Whitechapel. "Was it John Slade?"

A word emerged from Katerina in a fit of coughing. "Stieber . . ."

That was the name Slade had mentioned. "Wilhelm Stieber? The Tsar's spy?" When Katerina nodded feebly, I said, "Why did he do it?"

Katerina mumbled in Russian. Had she forgotten how to speak English? I tried another question: "How do you know Stieber?"

She moaned; her eyes rolled. She brought to mind a horse I'd once seen on a farm outside Haworth. It had fallen and shattered its leg. Its eyes had rolled just like Katerina's just before the farmer shot it. "I work for him."

"Doing what?"

"I go with men . . . I . . ." Katerina lapsed into Russian again, words that smacked of vulgarity. ". . . They tell me secrets."

I pieced together a story influenced by what I'd learned from Slade. "Russian men? You seduce them? And they tell you secrets about plots against the tsar?"

Her head tossed. "Not just Russian. English. Stieber want to find man." In her agony, her English had deteriorated.

Excitement quickened my pulse. "Is it Niall Kavanagh?"

Katerina gripped my hand harder. I winced. She said, "Man . . . have gun. Stieber want."

The scientist's invention was a gun, I deduced. It must be unique in design, and so powerful that it could guarantee Russia a victory in a war with England. Wilhelm Stieber meant to obtain it for the Tsar. Wilhelm Stieber had ordered Katerina to use her charms on British men who might know where Kavanagh was. And if I could believe Slade, he meant to stop Stieber and keep the gun out of Russian hands.

"Did Stieber find Niall Kavanagh?" I asked. "What about the gun?"

Katerina didn't seem to hear me. Her face was pale and waxen; she gasped out bloody saliva. When repeated attempts failed to elicit the answers, I reverted to my previous question: "Why did Stieber do this to you?"

She spoke in a whisper so faint that I had to lean close to hear. "Because I betray him."

"You betrayed him? How?"

". . . I told . . ."

Urgency agitated me, for her strength was fading. "Told whom?"

She sighed, her breath moist and feverish against my ear. "Josef."

That was the Polish name Slade had been using. Katerina appeared to have been his informant as well as Wilhelm Stieber's. It must have been she who had told Slade about Stieber's comings and goings at Bedlam. Yet these explanations didn't tell me whether that was all there had been to Slade and Katerina's relations. That they had also been lovers was not my only horrific thought. If she had betrayed Stieber in the service of Slade, she might also have betrayed Slade to Stieber, and Slade might have retaliated by torturing and stabbing her. Perhaps I had misinterpreted a garbled story from a mortally injured woman. So many people had lately expressed doubts about my mental capacities; I had begun to doubt them myself.

Katerina muttered something that I hopefully took for, "Stieber say I must die."

"But why torture you?" Why not just kill Katerina rather than make her suffer? I couldn't believe that even a spy for the Tsar would be so cruel. Maybe the torturer was Slade, a homicidal lunatic according to the police.

". . . want know . . ."

"Know what?" I demanded, avid for information that would exonerate Slade.

She whispered, "Where is Josef."

I surmised that Stieber was on a hunt for Slade and meant to do to him what I believed he'd done to Katerina. "Did you tell him?" I cried. "Where is he?"

Her body began trembling violently; her grasp on my wrist broke. Gurgles and moans erupted from her. Her long-lashed eyelids fluttered.

"Katerina!"

Her trembling and utterances rapidly diminished until she lay still, her eyes half-closed. She could tell me no more. I could not save her. She was dead.

So stunned by shock, disbelief, and horror that I hardly knew what to do, I heard noises inside the house. They were footsteps, coming stealthily up the stairs.

13

My heart gave a mighty lurch and my breath caught as the footsteps mounted higher up the stairs. Katerina's killer was coming back. Whoever he was, he meant to make sure that Katerina was dead or finish her off if she wasn't. If I let him find me here, he would surely kill me, too.

The stairs creaked. Light crept into the hall. I was trapped. Panic spurred me to action. I bent and snatched up the knife from the floor where I'd dropped it. I gripped it in both hands, prepared to fight for my life.

The lantern appeared in the doorway. I saw the man who held the lantern aloft, and another man beside him. They wore tall helmets decorated with metal badges: they were police constables. Exclamations burst from them: "What in the devil?" "Holy Mother of God!"

The one holding the lantern was a young man so fair that his eyelashes were white; the other a rugged, older fellow. As their gazes took in Katerina's bloody corpse, then moved to me, their faces wore identical expressions of shock.

"Put down that knife," the older constable ordered me. "You're under arrest for murder."

I gaped, stunned. They thought I'd killed Katerina! "But I didn't—"

He advanced cautiously into the room, his hand raised to ward off an attack and admonish me. "Put it down and come along peacefully, miss."

The younger constable beheld me with horrified awe. "Is she the Whitechapel Ripper?"

"Looks like it," said his comrade.

"A woman! Blimey! And we thought this was just another domestic disturbance."

I realized what must have happened: The neighbors had heard Katerina screaming and fetched the police. Now the police thought me responsible for the murders of which Slade had been accused!

"No," I said, even as I looked down at myself and saw what they saw. My hands were red with blood, clutching the bloodstained murder weapon. My clothes were also smeared with Katerina's blood. I looked every bit the murderess. "She'd been stabbed before I got here. I found her. The murderer ran away. I tried to save her."

The older constable lunged, wrenched the knife from my hands, and twisted my arm behind my back. I cried out in protest and pain.

"This is a mistake!" I wailed as he marched me down the stairs. "I'm innocent!"

He laughed. "That's what they all say."

The constables took me to a dingy local police station and locked me in a small room. During an endless night, police officials interrogated me, badgered me, threatened me, and ordered me to confess. I grew so exhausted that I felt tempted to comply, if only they would stop. But I managed to continue proclaiming my innocence. After a while, they left me alone. I thanked God for the silver lining in the cloud: When I'd given them my name, they hadn't recognized it. They didn't know that Charlotte Brontë was Currer Bell, the famous authoress. I shuddered to think of what would have happened if they did. "Currer Bell arrested for murder!" the headlines of every newspaper would read. "Is Currer Bell the Whitechapel Ripper?"

Near dawn, a Roman Catholic priest came to me. He brought a blanket to cover my bloodstained clothes, and he invited me to talk. Although I was raised to distrust Romans and I wondered if he'd been sent by the police to extract an admission of guilt from me, I was thankful for his company. His was the only kind face I'd seen since I'd been arrested, and when I told him what had happened at Katerina's house, he said he believed me.

"Have you a friend who might help you?" he asked.

"Yes. His name is George Smith. He lives at Number 76 Gloucester Terrace."

"I'll go to him and tell him what's happened," the priest promised.

In the morning, the police put me in a prison van—a long, covered carriage drawn by black horses. My fellow passengers were seven ladies of the street. Our ankles were chained to prevent us from escaping. As we rode through London, they sang obscene songs and yelled bawdy invitations to men we passed. I was so mortified that I wanted to die.

How I regretted going to see Katerina! I was glad to have the information she'd provided, but what a price I'd paid! I was too upset to determine whether it could exonerate Slade, and I wondered whether it would do me any good now.

We arrived at Newgate Prison, a massive brick edifice near the Old Bailey. Fear sickened me, for I had heard tales of how evil a place it was, filled with depraved, dangerous criminals. Its reputation attracted gawkers, who were gathered outside. They jeered at us while we clambered out of the van, hobbled by our chains. My companions jeered back, but I hung my head, as ashamed as if I were guilty.

Two guards led us through the gate, to a courtyard surrounded by high walls with barred windows. The guards removed our chains and handed us over to three female warders, who ordered us to strip naked. Disrobing in front of strangers of my own sex was enough of an affront to my modesty, but I could see men leering from the windows. Although glad to shed my bloodstained clothes, I wept from embarrassment.

The warders confiscated my pocketbook and some knives carried by the other prisoners. They made us line up at a water pump and wash ourselves. We had to share towels; there weren't enough to go around. My skin crawled as I wondered what vermin I was picking up from the other prisoners. The warders gave us uniforms to wear—blue gowns, blue-and-white-checked aprons, and white muslin caps. After we dressed, they led us inside the jail.

Galleries of cells rose three stories high, to a glass roof. They stank of privies. My throat closed up, my stomach turned, and I tried not to breathe. All around me echoed the deafening chatter and noise of hundreds of women who milled about a large room below the galleries. As we were brought into their midst, the inmates stared at us. Some were mere girls; others tough, hardened crones. Many called out lewd greetings or insults. The warders herded everyone into a line for breakfast. When I got to the front, I received a piece of bread and a bowl of gruel. The food was meager in portion, grayish and sour. Outrage rose up through my misery. I was a law-abiding citizen, a bestselling authoress. I didn't deserve to be treated thus!

But railing at my fate would do me no good; I must endure until rescue came. Walking to the tables where the women sat on benches to eat, I saw a vacant place. I started to set my food on the table, but one of the women said, "That place's taken." When I tried other tables, the women said, "You can't sit there." They were subjecting me to the sort of treatment that bullies at school inflicted on new girls. Soon I was the only person without a seat. I stood alone in the middle of the room, holding my food, all eyes on me.

"Sit here." The woman who'd spoken patted the place next to her on the bench. She had a dumpy figure and the face of a prizefighter who'd lost too many matches. Her nose looked as if it had been broken and healed crookedly. Her eyes were shrewd in a broad face marked by a hint of a mustache.

I was afraid of her, but I sat. "Thank you," I said politely.

The women smirked and repeated my words, mimicking my accent. With my first utterance I'd established myself as a member of a different class, an outsider.

"My name's Poll," said the prizefighter. "What's yours?"

"Charlotte," I said.

"If you aren't going to eat your food, Charlotte, I'll take it," said a young blonde girl who sat on Poll's other side. She would have been pretty if not for the permanent sneer that twisted her mouth. Her hand shot across Poll to snatch my bread.

Poll slapped her and said, "Not now, Maisie." She seemed to be the leader of this set of women. "What're you in for?" Poll asked me.

"I haven't done anything wrong," I said. "I really shouldn't be here."

The group hooted with laughter. "Neither have we," Poll said, "but here we are, and so are you. Now, what're you in for?"

"Murder," I reluctantly admitted.

"Really?" Maisie said. She and the other women stared at me in respectful awe.

A scowl turned Poll's face even more menacing. "You ain't no murderess. I am." Her hand thumped her ample breast. "I knifed that son-of-a-bitch slave driver who beat me when I was workin' in the poorhouse. After I'm tried and convicted, I'll hang." She apparently enjoyed special status in the prison because she'd committed the most violent, serious crime, and she didn't want someone else overtaking her. "You're lyin'."

"Who'd you kill?" Maisie asked me.

"A Russian actress named Katerina was stabbed to death," I said, "but I didn't—"

"You're havin' one on us," Poll said, her ugly face turning crimson with rage. "You never killed no one."

How I wished the police were as convinced of my innocence as she was! "That's what I'm trying to tell you."

"I'll teach you to play jokes on me!" Poll hauled back her fist.

I lurched sideways, dodged the blow, and toppled off the bench. Poll lunged after me and bumped another inmate, a woman with wild red hair and a stevedore's build, who happened to walk past at that moment.

"Hey! Watch what yer doin'!" The other woman shoved Poll.

They began to fight. Suddenly, all the pent-up energy in the prison was let loose. I watched with amazement as women jumped up from the tables. They egged on Poll and her opponent. Fights broke out among them. They slapped and kicked and clawed and screamed; they hurled bowls. Gruel splattered me as I crawled, frantically seeking safety. Male warders plunged into the chaos, yanking combatants apart. Soon they had restored order. As they dragged Poll away, she pointed at me and yelled, "She started it!"

A warder grabbed me. "It wasn't my fault," I protested.

"It's the dark cells for you both," he said.

"Not the dark cells!" Poll cried, her tough bravado turning to fright. She struggled as the men marched us down a corridor. "Please! No!"

I went without resisting. I couldn't imagine what place could be worse than the one I had just left. My escort opened a door and pushed me in. I saw a tiny, windowless cell, a wooden bench, a tin chamber pot. Then the door slammed, shutting me in complete darkness and silence. The room was soundproofed; not a noise could I hear from outside. I groped over to the bench and sat. For a time this punishment seemed mild. I was thankful to be away from the women who'd mocked and abused me, glad to be alone with my thoughts. By now the priest should have arrived in Gloucester Terrace with the news of my arrest. George Smith would obtain me a solicitor, who would persuade the court to drop the charge against me. Soon George would come to take me home. All I needed to do was wait patiently.

But as time went on, I noticed the discomforts of my cell. It was dank, too warm, and smelled of stale urine. I had to use the chamber pot, which added to the unsavory atmosphere. The bench was hard, and the eerie silence gave me a frightening sense that the world outside had ceased to exist. While the hours passed—I knew not how many—my hopes of rescue ebbed. I felt as if the darkness were preying on me, dissolving my body. I touched my arms, legs, and head, trying to make sure that they were still there. Because I could not see myself, I felt like a wraith. I began to think I would die.

Ridden by fear, I closed my eyes in an attempt to shut out the darkness. But the darkness behind my eyelids was the same as in this black tomb. I tried to envision the moors that surround Haworth, their grasses waving in the fresh wind, their purple heather blooming, the wide blue sky. But instead I saw a large, stately chamber, its walls colored a soft, pinkish fawn hue. On a crimson carpet stood a bed piled high with mattresses beneath a snowy white counterpane, supported on massive mahogany pillars, hung with curtains of deep red. Blinds covered windows festooned with red damask drapery. It was the Red Room at Gateshead Hall, where Jane Eyre had been sent by Mrs. Reed as punishment for disobedience.

I opened my eyes, but the vision persisted. It appeared utterly real, perfect in every detail, no matter that Jane Eyre, Gateshead Hall, and Mrs. Reed were pure fantasy that I had created myself. The darkness, the silence, and my fear pushed me across the magic threshold between fact and fiction. I became the ten-year-old Jane Eyre, seated on her ottoman by the chimneypiece in the Red Room. I saw her small, forlorn figure—mine—reflected in the great looking glass. I raged against the injustice that had been done to her, to me.

What a consternation of soul was mine! How all my brain was in tumult, all my heart in insurrection!

The same, irrational terror that had afflicted Jane now took hold of me, for I saw a gleam of light glide up the wall to the ceiling and quiver over my head. It was the ghost of Mr. Reed, who had died in the Red Room. Seized by panic, I would have jumped up, rushed to the door as Jane had, and pounded on it until my hands bled, had I not been too scared to move. My body shook so hard that the bench rattled. I couldn't breathe. I was going to die. Hiding my face against my knees, I prayed for deliverance.

Much later, a key rattled in the lock. I sat up and wept with relief as the door opened and blessed light fell over me. A warder stood at the threshold. "Come out," he said. "You've got a visitor."

14

THE WARDER LED ME OUT OF THE BUILDING. I WAS BLINDED BY sunlight and assailed by noise in the yard where the prisoners took their daily exercise. The women strolled and chattered together. Although it had seemed that I'd spent an eternity in the dark cell, the sun was still high in the sky; the time was not long past noon. The warder led me to a long, narrow cage that spanned the yard. A man stood waiting inside. The cage was the place where people came to visit the inmates; the bars protected them and kept the prisoners from escaping. George Smith had finally come! I ran to him, then stopped short.

The man wasn't my publisher. He was Lord Eastbourne.

His air of affluence and elegant suit bespoke the sane, comfortable, normal world outside the prison. His blunt, strong face looked even ruddier in the sunlight than it had at the Foreign Office. He seemed as at ease within the cage as he had in his own chamber.

"Good day, Miss Brontë," he said.

I was so surprised that I forgot my manners. "What are you doing here?"

"I just heard you'd been arrested." Lord Eastbourne's shrewd brown eyes regarded me with concern and sympathy. "I came to help you."

"Thank you, my lord," I said, tearful with gratitude.

Lord Eastbourne nodded, then said, "You must tell me everything that happened."

I told him how I'd gone to see Katerina and found her tied up, wounded, and dying. "I didn't kill her!" I finished, desperate for him to believe me.

"Of course you didn't," he said, so adamant that I wept with relief. "But unfortunately the police think otherwise. I've spoken to them. They doubt that you just happened to arrive on the scene at the same moment that someone else was torturing Katerina."

"But it's the truth!"

"Perhaps the police would be more likely to believe your story if you could explain why you were there." He clearly thought that a lady of my class, alone at that hour of the night in that neighborhood, must have looked extremely suspicious.

I knew he wouldn't like the reason, and I had an instinct to keep my business to myself because I didn't know whether to trust Lord Eastbourne; but if I held anything back from him, he might realize it and change his mind about helping me. "Katerina was with John Slade at the Royal Pavilion Theater the night before last. I saw them together. I went to her house to ask her where Mr. Slade is."

Lord Eastbourne frowned. "I told you yesterday that John Slade is dead."

"Yes, but I didn't want to believe it. I couldn't stop trying to find him. Katerina was my last hope." Now my hunt for Slade had reached a dead end, and my liberty and life were at stake. I felt a spark of anger toward Slade. Although I still loved him, I realized that if not for him, I wouldn't be in this predicament.

Lord Eastbourne didn't move except to stroke his chin; but he seemed to withdraw from me. He contemplated the other visitors who'd entered the cage, and the prisoners who flocked to see their families and friends. Hands were pressed together and kisses were exchanged through the fence. I feared that my obstinacy had angered Lord Eastbourne and he'd turned against me. The warm day seemed suddenly chilly.

"Did you tell the police why you went to see Katerina?" Even though Lord Eastbourne met my gaze, the distance between us remained.

"Yes," I said.

"That's unfortunate. Most certainly they think you were in love with Slade, you found out that Katerina was his mistress, and you tortured her and killed her in a jealous rage."

"That's not how it was!" Had I found Slade making love to Katerina, I might have been angry enough to kill him, but I wouldn't have hurt her. Or would I have lashed out at both of them? I was horrified to realize that I could have. I have always been sedate and disciplined in my physical actions, but I couldn't deny the emotions that had assailed me while I was inside Katerina's house. The impulse to violence exists in all of us, and it could very well have overpowered me, with fatal results.

Lord Eastbourne shook his head regretfully. "Appearances often count more than facts do. In a court of law, a prosecutor would cast you as a woman scorned and out for revenge. The jury might well find you guilty."

My legs went weak at the thought of myself on the gibbet and crowds lining up to see Currer Bell hang. I grasped the bars of the cage for support. My future was looking bleaker by the moment.

Lord Eastbourne lapsed into another thoughtful silence; he watched arguments break out between prisoners and men who'd come to see them. Warders patrolled, keeping order. "Did you tell the police who John Slade was and how you knew him?"

"No," I said, offended by the suggestion that I would talk about the events of 1848 after I'd been sworn to secrecy. "I've kept my promise."

"Good," Lord Eastbourne said. "If the police question you about Slade, say you never heard of him. Pretend you've forgotten you said anything about him. Say you went to see Katerina because you admired her acting."

Consternation filled me. "I can't lie. They'll know."

"You must. Changing your story will serve you better than sticking to the truth."

I wondered whether changing my story would serve others

better than it would myself. Lord Eastbourne and I had conflicting aims. I wanted to be exonerated; he wanted secret affairs of state kept secret. Even if he owed me a favor in exchange for my service to the government, how could I trust him? Alas, I could not.

"You could also help yourself by providing evidence that someone other than you killed Katerina," Lord Eastbourne said. "Have you any?"

"I heard a man in her house. He was talking to Katerina."

"Did you see him?"

"No. He ran down the back stairs and out the door."

"That's unfortunate," Lord Eastbourne said. "The police questioned the neighbors, but no one else seems to have observed a man at Katerina's house. There are, however, witnesses who saw you going in. You are the obvious culprit."

My spirits sank deeper. "But I have Katerina's own last statement, which says otherwise."

Suddenly alert, Lord Eastbourne moved closer to the fence. "Did she say something before she died?"

This subject was dangerous territory; I knew even before my mind had time to articulate the reasons. I felt as though a field of traps and sinkholes had opened up before me. What should I tell Lord Eastbourne, and what must I not?

"She said it was a man named Wilhelm Stieber who tortured her and left her to die." That was what I'd thought I understood Katerina to say, and it would now be my story. I needed to incriminate someone other than myself and didn't want to point the finger at Slade, in spite of everything.

"Wilhelm Stieber." Lord Eastbourne repeated the name as if he'd never heard it before and wanted to commit it to memory.

But I am adept at detecting faint signs of emotion, even in those well trained at masking them. I learned my skill while I was a charity pupil and later while a governess in the house of wealthy employers. It is the skill of the weak and downtrodden, whose survival depends on the ability to read their masters, the better to avoid punishment. When I'd said "Wilhelm Stieber," I'd seen a brief but definite flare of recognition in Lord Eastbourne's eyes.

"Did Katerina say who he is?" Lord Eastbourne asked.

He already knew; I could tell. That gave credence to Slade's story and justified my tendency to believe Slade had been telling the truth. "She said Stieber is a spy for the Tsar of Russia."

"Indeed," Lord Eastbourne said, as if impressed and interested. "Did she also say what her relationship was with Stieber?"

"She worked for him as an informant." Although I distrusted Lord Eastbourne more than ever, and I didn't like to release the information, my hope of freedom hinged on him. I could not evade his questions and risk offending him. "She consorted with Russian immigrants. She learned about plots against the Tsar and reported them to Stieber."

Skepticism crossed Lord Eastbourne's face. "Then why did he torture her?"

"She said she had crossed him."

"How?"

"I don't know," I said, compelled by my instinct to conceal the details and protect Slade. If Lord Eastbourne learned that Katerina had named Slade as a party involved in her death, it might convince him that Slade was alive, even though my sightings of Slade had not. Lord Eastbourne already thought Slade was a traitor; he surely wouldn't hesitate to deem him a murderer as well. I imagined Lord Eastbourne launching a manhunt for Slade, and myself forced to participate. I didn't want Slade persecuted for yet another crime—at least not until I discovered whether he was guilty. "Katerina was dying, she was growing incoherent, babbling in Russian." I decided to test Slade's story. "But she did say that Stieber was looking for someone. A scientist named Kavanagh. She said he'd invented a device that the Tsar wants."

Lord Eastbourne listened without visible emotion, but I sensed excitement rising in him. "What kind of device?"

"A new kind of gun. She indicated that the Tsar wants to use it against England." Here I blended Katerina's statement with Slade's. "Stieber thought she knew where to find the scientist. That's the other reason he tortured Katerina."

"Well." Lord Eastbourne pondered, then said in an offhand

manner, "Anything that has to do with Russia is of interest to the Foreign Office. Did Katerina tell you Niall Kavanagh's whereabouts?"

My heart beat faster. I hadn't mentioned Kavanagh's Christian name. Lord Eastbourne knew it, and he'd let the fact slip.

"No," I said. "She died."

Kavanagh existed, and so, presumably, did his invention. What Slade had said was true—but perhaps only in part. I didn't yet know which side Slade was on—England's or Russia's—or whether he was guilty of murder. Perhaps he'd mixed truth with lies. Still, I was glad I hadn't spilled everything to Lord Eastbourne. He'd deceived me by concealing the fact that he knew about Wilhelm Stieber, Niall Kavanagh, and the secret invention. Maybe he'd done so to protect state secrets, but maybe he had other, baser motives. If my experiences during the summer of 1848 had taught me anything, it was that men in positions of authority weren't always honorable.

Another thought occurred to me. Slade had told me that the British government had Kavanagh hidden, but Lord Eastbourne had asked where Niall Kavanagh was. Did that mean the government didn't know? If Stieber didn't have him, then who did?

"Have you had any further contact with the man you thought was John Slade?" Lord Eastbourne asked.

I experienced a cold, sick sensation of dismay, for I could tell that Lord Eastbourne had revised his opinion concerning Slade: he was no longer certain Slade was dead. I had tried so hard to convince him that Slade was alive that I had gone too far toward succeeding. Probably he would send more agents to hunt down Slade, execute him, and make sure he was really dead this time. And I could not forsake my loyalty to Slade, even though he'd treated me badly.

"No," I said, "I haven't."

Although I trembled with nerves, I looked Lord Eastbourne straight in the eye. I watched him try to discern whether I was lying. I saw that he was undecided, but I could tell he knew I'd withheld information.

"I must go now, Miss Brontë," he said.

Panic struck. "Please don't leave me here!" I thrust my hand through the bars of the cage to prevent him from going.

Lord Eastbourne patted my fingers, barely touching them, and smiled. "Don't worry. I'll pull some strings and have you free in no time."

"Are you ready to be good?" the warder asked me.

Eager to avoid another stint in the dark cell, I said I was. He took me to the dayroom where I'd had my altercation with Poll. The women pretended I wasn't there, except for Maisie. She sidled up to me during dinner, which was greasy mutton stew.

"When Poll gets out of the dark cell, she'll have your hide," she whispered.

I prayed that I would be gone before then. In the evening, the warders marched us to our cells. These measured some thirteen feet by seven; each had iron bars and an iron gate across the front, a barred window, and a stone floor. Amenities consisted of a table and some stools, a copper basin with a water tap, shelves of bedding, and a water closet. A gas lamp with a tin shade burned dimly on the wall. My cellmates were three streetwalkers, two drunks who reeked of liquor, and two pickpockets. Our beds were mats that we spread on the floor. I wanted to lie down and drift into the blessed oblivion of sleep, but sleep proved to be impossible.

The other prisoners regaled one another with stories about the crimes for which they'd been arrested, the men who'd done them wrong, and their hard lives. The galleries rang with chatter and laughter. Even after the lights went out, the noise continued. My cellmates said to me, "It's your turn. Tell us a story!"

Fearing what they would do to me if I refused, I began to recite an abridged version of *Jane Eyre*. None of them had heard of the book, let alone read it. They loved the tale of Jane's suffering at the hands of the Reed family, her imprisonment in the Red Room, and her experiences at the dreadful Lowood School. They hung on every word. Women in nearby cells quieted down to listen. Those farther away shouted for me to speak up.

Everyone wept when Jane's friend, Helen Burns, died.

I remembered my childhood, when the pupils at the Clergy Daughters' School had thought me the best storyteller among them. Now my audience of criminals wouldn't let me stop, even though my voice grew hoarse. I told my tale until what must have been midnight, when a warder appeared outside my cell and unlocked its gate. Two men were with her, dressed in white coats, their faces in shadow.

"Charlotte Brontë, get up," she said. "You're leaving."

An outcry arose from the prisoners: "She can't leave! We want to know what happens to Jane Eyre!"

Gladness filled me as I sprang up from my mat. I didn't know that I was bound for somewhere much worse than Newgate Prison.

15

> > ← <

THE SECRET ADVENTURES OF
JOHN SLADE

Easter 1849. After midnight mass, a huge crowd filled Red
Square, a vast open expanse within the walls that enclosed the
Kremlin. Domes glittered in the damp, fecund spring air. St. Basil's
Cathedral loomed above the crowd, as brightly colored and patterned as Christmas candy. Everyone carried candles. Thousands of
faces lit by the flames glowed like medieval icons. The doors of all
the churches in the Kremlin opened. Light from within flooded the
square. Out marched parades of priests wearing golden vestments
and swinging censers, followed by congregations bearing banners
and lit tapers. Singing from choirs rose to heaven.

John Slade stood among the crowd. He saw a familiar figure—
the Third Section agent who'd been watching him for four months.
The agent was a common Russian type, a slim man with a pale,
melancholy face and a dark mustache. Slade noticed something different about his shadow tonight. The man hovered closer than
usual. For the first time he met Slade's gaze. Slade sensed that the
opportunity he'd been waiting for was at hand. He moved slowly
out of the crowd, allowing his shadow to keep up with him. When
he reached the bank of the river, he stopped. It was dark beneath
the trees, and quiet. The lights in Red Square shimmered in the distance. Slade didn't have long to wait. His shadow joined him and
said, "Happy Easter, Mr. Ivan Zubov."

"The same to you, Mr. Andrei Plekhanov. And to your colleagues in the Third Section."

The man's dark eyes widened. "How do you know who I am?"

Slade had done a little spying on his spy. He had followed Plekhanov to his lodgings and obtained the information from another tenant. Plekhanov hadn't noticed that Slade had turned the tables on him. Now Slade said, "I borrowed a leaf from your book."

Plekhanov smiled tensely. "You're an unusual dissident, Mr. Zubov. Your friends—Peter, Alexander, and Fyodor—would never have spotted me, let alone managed to discover my name. But they are too preoccupied with plotting against the government, aren't they?"

Slade knew he was supposed to be upset by the news that the Third Section knew who and what his friends were. He arranged his features into the proper expression of alarm and fright. Plekhanov's smile relaxed.

"So you see, we know what you are up to," Plekhanov said.

"I'm not up to anything," Slade said, deliberately speaking with a tremor in his voice, avoiding the other man's gaze, and signaling a lie. "I'm not a dissident."

"Oh? What about the articles you write for the radical journals?"

"I write for anybody who will pay me. I'm just a poor author trying to make a living."

Plekhanov laughed. "You are poor, that's true enough. Your landlord says you're behind on your rent. You also owe money at all the shops and taverns in the neighborhood." Slade had deliberately created his reputation as a debtor, and Plekhanov had swallowed the bait. "But never fear. I have a proposition to make you. Should you accept, it will solve your financial problems."

Slade combined hope with wariness in his expression. "What sort of proposition?"

"You work for me as an informant. You report on your friends, and I pay you enough to cover your debts and put vodka in your cup."

"I can't betray my friends," Slade said, aghast.

Plekhanov's melancholy face turned cruel. "If you refuse my proposition, I will have you sent back to St. Petersburg. I happen to know you're wanted by the police there."

Slade himself had spread the rumor that he'd committed petty crimes in St. Petersburg and he was a fugitive from the law. That story had led Plekhanov to believe he had power over Slade, just as Slade had intended. Slade let his shoulders sag in defeat. He nodded.

"You're a wise man." Plekhanov clapped Slade on the back. "Now that we've settled our bargain—are your friends up to anything the Third Section would like to know about?"

Slade thought of their conspiracy to assassinate its chief. They'd been spying on Prince Orlov, and their plans were almost set. Slade felt guilt descend upon him like the blade of a guillotine. Duty required him to deliver his friends to their enemies.

"Yes," he said with genuine reluctance, "there is."

16

∻∻

I WALKED OUT A FREE WOMAN, ALBEIT STILL DRESSED IN PRISON clothes. Incredulous and joyful, I offered my fervent thanks to the two white-coated men who had procured my release. They didn't speak. Escorting me down the gallery, they looked straight ahead; they walked in step, as if in a military parade. Both were tall, both some thirty years old; but the man on my right had the strong musculature and carved features of a Greek athlete, while his comrade on my left was thin and lanky, with puffy lips and eyes that bespoke sensuality and dissipation.

"Were you sent by Lord Eastbourne?" I asked.

They didn't even acknowledge that I'd spoken. But who except Lord Eastbourne could have sent them to get me out of prison? Neither of the men showed any interest in me, but I was too grateful to care about their behavior. Outside the prison, gaslights burned dimly up and down Newgate Street. It must have been two or three o'clock in the morning. Smoke drifted across the sky, which glowed orange over a foundry, like a false dawn. I didn't see a soul. How was I to get home? I doubted I could find a carriage for hire, and I was afraid to walk. London teemed with cutthroats.

To my relief, a carriage drawn by two horses emerged from the darkness between the lampposts. My escort who looked like a Greek athlete climbed onto the box with the driver. The other man opened the door for me.

"Please take me to Number Seventy-Six Gloucester Terrace," I said.

Riding in the carriage, I looked forward to a good meal, a hot bath, and the company of friends. I peered out the window to see how close to home I was, and saw an unfamiliar street. I called to my escorts, "Excuse me—is this the way to Gloucester Terrace?" They didn't answer. I had a distinct, uneasy feeling that they were taking me in the wrong direction on purpose. "I'll get out here, if you don't mind."

The carriage didn't stop. I tried the door. It was locked from the outside. Fear washed through me in a cold wave. "Let me out!" Beating on the door, I called out the window, "Help!"

There was no one to come to my aid. The window was too small for me to jump out. The carriage moved faster, racketing through the deserted streets, veering around corners. When it finally slowed, the sight of our destination filled me with horror. Bedlam loomed black against the fire-glow in the sky, like a haunt of demons. Gaslights burned at the portals. A guard opened the back gate.

"No!" I cried as the carriage rolled in. It stopped; the door opened. My escorts reached in and seized me. I resisted, but they dragged me out.

Two attendants brought a litter whose metal frame had leather straps attached to it and wheels on the bottom. My escorts flung me onto the litter. As I kicked and screamed, they held me down. The attendants buckled the straps across my body and wheeled me into the asylum. My escorts followed us through the dim wards.

"Help me!" I called to the nurses we passed. "I've been kidnapped! Please get me out!"

No one paid me any notice. Madwomen resisting incarceration must be a common sight in Bedlam. The attendants carried me up the stairs. I knew where we were going before I saw the heavy iron door.

"No!" I pleaded.

We entered the criminal lunatics' ward. As we moved down the corridor, I saw Julia Garrs peering at me from a window in a cell door. My captors wheeled me into the room that contained the table with the straps and the machine with the wires—the room where Slade had been tortured and the two nurses murdered.

I strained against my bonds; I shrieked; I tossed my head. A man leaned over me. He was the doctor with the white coat, the spectacles, and the gray tonsure of hair. I struggled harder, shrieked louder. He regarded me with detachment, his eyes as cool as gray pebbles. I might have been an insect under a magnifying glass.

"Lift her head," the doctor ordered the attendants.

They obeyed. He put a glass beaker to my mouth. I tried to turn my head away, but the attendants held it tightly. I clamped my lips shut, but the doctor pinched my nose. Unable to breathe, I had to open my mouth. He poured in bitter-tasting liquid, and although I spat and coughed, much of it ran down my throat. My captors gathered around me. They watched me closely as I continued to struggle, scream, and beg them to let me go. The drug burned inside my stomach, then seemed to spread outward in warm waves. I lost the strength to scream anymore. My limbs felt too heavy to move; my struggles ceased. The men's faces wavered in my vision, and the gas lamps behind them grew large, blurred halos. An unnatural calm spread through my body even as my mind reeled with terror.

"Don't be afraid." The doctor spoke in a soft monotone. "Just relax."

My will bent to his command. A sense of detachment came over me. My thoughts were clear, and my powers of observation intact, but I felt as if I were inside an invisible glass bell, sealed off from my emotions. My terror didn't abate, but it existed apart from me. The thundering of my heart quieted.

"Is she unconscious?" a voice said, outside my field of view. It was inflected by a foreign accent that I'd heard before, in Belgium. There I'd met some Prussians who spoke German. The man had the same accent as theirs.

"No," the doctor said, "she's quite alert."

"Good," the Prussian said. "Will you use the galvanometer?"

"That wouldn't be advisable," the doctor said. "She's too small and delicate. The galvanometer could damage her brain before she can tell you what you want to know."

I remembered seeing Slade hooked up to the machine that delivered jolts of electricity to his brain. I value my own brain above all else that I possess, and I should have felt relief at escaping from harm to it, but at that moment I did not care. I should have been worried about what these people were going to do to me, but the glass bell kept my anxiety at bay.

"We'll use a technique called mesmerism." The doctor placed flat, heavy metal plates on my chest and stomach.

"What are those?" the Prussian asked.

"Magnets. According to the great Dr. Mesmer, they enhance the flow of the magnetic fluids within the body and render the mind susceptible to manipulation."

Their cold weight crushed my breasts and my ribs. The drug didn't take away the pain, but rendered me as impervious to it as to fear. The doctor bent over me and said, "You will not move or speak unless I tell you to. You are under my power."

A spark of rebellion flared in me, for I detest being told what to do, but it quickly faded, as if the glass bell that enclosed me lacked enough air to sustain fire.

"Can she speak?" the Prussian asked.

The doctor said to me, "State your name."

"Charlotte Brontë." The name issued from me against my will.

He unbuckled the straps that bound me to the litter. Here was my chance to flee, but my body lay inert, uncooperative.

"Raise your right arm, Miss Brontë," the doctor ordered.

My arm rose, of its own, eerie volition.

"Drop it."

My arm hit the litter with a thud.

"She's ready," the doctor said.

The Prussian joined the doctor in my field of vision. I recognized him as the foreigner I'd seen on my previous visits to Bedlam. His face was pitted by old scars, healed over with tight, shiny skin. His eyes were the palest blue I'd ever seen. They reminded me of windows reflecting the sky at an angle, deflecting all the light. It was as if he could see out of them, but no one could see inside to his soul.

"My colleague is going to ask you some questions," the doctor informed me. "You will answer truthfully."

I deduced that the Prussian was Wilhelm Stieber, spy for the Tsar. He had indeed turned Bedlam to his own, criminal purposes. Everything Slade had told me was true. I should never have doubted him. I should have forgotten Slade as he had ordered me to do, should have ceased following his trail. I'd thought he was spurning me, but he'd been protecting me from Stieber. Now I was under Stieber's power.

"Why did you go to see Katerina Ivanova?" Stieber asked.

He meant Katerina the Great, I realized. He'd somehow learned that I'd been caught at the scene of her murder and arrested. "I was looking for John Slade," I said, even though I knew I must keep silent to protect Slade, and myself. "I thought Katerina might know where he was."

Stieber regarded me with the interest of a hunter examining an animal caught in a trap he'd set. Important human traits such as kindness and humor appeared to have been left out of his nature. He seemed a man composed entirely of intellect, discipline, and purpose. "Why were you looking for John Slade?"

"Because I'm in love with him." The words I'd never spoken aloud to a soul slipped out of my mouth.

"How do you know Slade?"

I didn't mean to tell, but the drug and the magnetic forces had broken my inhibitions. The whole story spilled out of me. I told Stieber about my adventures in 1848 and described how Slade and I had foiled an attack on the British Empire. Not only did I violate my oath of secrecy, I gave up my own most personal secrets. I told Stieber how Slade and I had fallen in love, while shame and guilt assailed the glass bell like pounding fists.

When I had finished, Stieber wore an expression that I had often seen on the faces of people to whom I'd just been introduced. They could hardly believe that my small, plain self was the famous Currer Bell. Now Stieber couldn't believe that I had collaborated with a secret agent for the Crown and together we had saved the Royal Family.

"Can she be telling the truth?" he asked the doctor.

"Either she is or she thinks she is. In her condition, she cannot lie."

Stieber shook his head, as nonplussed as the fashionable literary set meeting Currer Bell for the first time. "Did you find Slade?"

Even as I prayed for the strength to protect Slade from his enemy, I answered, "Yes."

"Where?"

"At the zoo."

"When?"

"On Sunday afternoon."

Stieber's pale eyes gleamed with satisfaction. Helpless misery joined the league of emotions trying in vain to inhibit my speech. I had made Stieber aware that Slade had still been in London as recently as two days ago.

"What did Slade tell you?" Stieber asked.

Out came everything Slade had said at the zoo, plus that which I'd learned from Lord Eastbourne. I told Stieber that the Foreign Office had sent Slade to aid Russian revolutionaries in their uprising against the Tsar and find out what the Tsar was plotting against Britain. I did not neglect to mention the reason Slade had returned to England. "You're trying to find Niall Kavanagh and his invention," I told Stieber. "Slade followed you in order to stop you." I could no more stanch the flow of my words than I could have halted a flood from a broken dam.

Shock quenched the gleam of satisfaction in Stieber's eyes. Apparently Slade had managed to keep his intentions secret during his torture. Now, thanks to me, Stieber knew. But I didn't realize just how much I had compromised both Slade and myself until Stieber spoke.

"You said that *I* am trying to find Niall Kavanagh and his invention." He leaned closer, his gaze boring into me. I could see smaller pits within the pits that marred his face. Breathing the air around him, I made an unsettling discovery: he had no odor. "So you know who I am?"

"Yes." Common sense blared a distant warning that I was unable to heed.

"What is my name?"

"Wilhelm Stieber," I said. "You're the Tsar's favorite spy."

He drew back, the instinctive reaction of a man who travels in disguise and hears his true identity suddenly proclaimed. "What else do you know about me?"

I perceived a chasm yawning before me. The drug and the magnetic forces banished my instinct for self-preservation. I stepped right over the edge. "You killed Katerina."

"How do you know this?" Stieber spoke in a level yet menacing tone.

"Katerina told me. Before she died."

Stieber turned away. I could surmise what he was thinking: my story would sound preposterous to most everyone, were I just an ordinary woman, but I was not. My service to the Crown had gained me the confidence of people in high places, and if I told them about Stieber, they might believe me. Stieber didn't know I had already passed on much of the information to Lord Eastbourne and been rebuffed. He only understood that I knew far too much.

The doctor put a stethoscope to my chest and listened to my heart. "She can't withstand the magnetic forces any longer. Are you finished?"

"Oh, yes," Stieber said.

"Your men can take her back to Newgate." The doctor lifted the magnets from my chest. I was vaguely conscious of physical relief, but doom vibrated like thunder outside the bell jar.

"No," Stieber said.

Confusion wrinkled the doctor's smooth brow. "What am I supposed to do with her?"

"Dispose of her," Stieber said. This was my death sentence, uttered in the perfunctory tone of a man ordering a servant to clean up a mess his dog had made.

"Do you mean . . . ?" As the doctor turned to Stieber, dismay broke the monotone of his voice; its pitch rose high with fright. "No. I can't."

"You will." Stieber's voice was flat, authoritative.

"But I've never killed anyone before." The doctor's protest was the bleat of a coward. If only his fear of taking my life were stronger than his fear of displeasing Stieber! "It's against my principles."

"Your principles didn't prevent you from accepting money for torturing people," Stieber said.

"That wasn't torture, it was medical research!"

Stieber made a moue of contempt, then said, "She can't be allowed to live."

"But how will I dispose of her body?" The doctor had given in to Stieber; only the practicalities of killing me were in question. My hope of a reprieve faded. "What if I'm caught?" My last chance rested on his fear of the consequences. "Even if I can convince my superiors that her death was accidental, they'll put a stop to my research. I'll lose my position!"

"You'll lose more than that unless you do as I say."

The doctor wiped sweat off his upper lip with his finger. "Very well."

He stepped out of my view for a moment. When he reappeared, he held a glass cylinder with a plunger at one end and a long needle at the other. It was the same kind of instrument that I'd seen him use on Slade, and that Slade had driven through the eye of the nurse. The doctor pushed up my sleeve; his fingers probed my arm. I should have bolted for the door, but I could not overcome my lethargy. My gaze fixed on the instrument. The colorless poison inside vibrated; the doctor's hands were shaking. Stieber looked on, impassive. I knew he wouldn't leave an important task in the sole care of a less capable subordinate. He'd killed Katerina himself, no matter the risk, no matter that it was dirty work unfit for the Tsar's chief spy.

How strange that I should spend my last moments on earth analyzing my murderer. But I am an indefatigable observer of human nature, and the spell that the doctor had worked on me had detached me from the terrible fact of my own impending death.

The doctor found a vein in my arm. He positioned his instrument. I waited for the lethal prick of the needle.

The door burst open.

He lost his grip on the instrument. It fell to the floor; the glass cylinder shattered. Three men surrounded me. They wore British army uniforms—red coats decorated with gold epaulets and shiny buttons, and black caps, trousers, and boots—and they carried rifles.

"What is the meaning of this?" Stieber said, all surprise and fury.

"We have orders to take custody of this woman," said one of the officers, the sort of ordinary, stolid man who'd helped win many wars for Britain.

"I won't permit it," Stieber said. "She's seriously insane. She needs treatment that can only be provided here."

The officer glanced at the doctor, who shrank against the wall, then regarded Stieber with the suspicion and distrust of a proud Englishman toward a foreigner. "And who might you be?"

"Dr. Richard Albert, chief physician of the criminal lunatics wing," Stieber lied smoothly. "I'm responsible for her care."

"Not anymore," the officer said. "She's coming with us."

His comrades wheeled my litter out the door. Stieber stood with his hands clenched at his sides, containing his rage: he dared not oppose the troops; he could not afford to be arrested. As the soldiers rolled me down the corridor, we passed Julia Garrs. She waved to me and smiled. I realized that however the army had learned that I was in Bedlam, once the soldiers had arrived it was she who had guided them to me. She clearly thought she'd done me a good turn.

I only wished I could be so certain.

17

✣

THE SECRET ADVENTURES OF
JOHN SLADE

1849 June. Summer in Moscow flares briefly, like a fever before
the chills of winter return. In the alleys around Trubnaya Square,
northeast of the Kremlin, red lights burned above the doors of
squalid brothels. Cheap prostitutes in tawdry finery called invitations to men who passed. Some of the men stopped to banter, bargain, and take their pleasure. But Peter, Fyodor, Alexander, and
Slade ignored the women. Furtive and solemn, they hurried along.
The Russians sweated in the coats they wore despite the hot night.
Peter the poet carried Slade's pistol hidden under his coat. He had
volunteered to do the shooting. Although Peter had been eager and
confident when they'd planned the assassination, Slade could see
his bravado wane. By the time they reached Tsvetnoy Boulevard,
Peter was trembling with nerves.

"Don't worry," Fyodor said. "It will be over soon. Then we can
go have a drink."

Peter responded with a sickly smile. Slade felt no less ill: he
knew the Russians would never drink together again.

Elegant mansions inhabited by expensive courtesans lined the
boulevard. Inside, chandeliers sparkled behind velvet drapes. Piano
music and laughter tinkled from open windows, but the street was
empty. Slade and his friends slipped through the gate of one small,
exclusive establishment and hid in the shrubbery in the garden. The

air was heavy with the odors of garbage and flowers, perfume and latrines. They waited for Prince Orlov. Their spying had produced the information that he spent every Wednesday night in this brothel, with his favorite courtesan.

The revelry ended. Silence engulfed the street as the women entertained clients in their boudoirs. Hours passed. The street slumbered. Slade watched the Russians grow more nervous by the moment. Near two o'clock, they tensed and became alert. The Prince always left the brothel at that hour. Slade and the other men riveted their gazes on the door. Peter drew the pistol in his shaking hand and took aim.

A carriage rumbled up the street. Plekhanov and six other policemen from the Third Section jumped out of the vehicle and charged into the garden. They assailed Slade and the Russians in a welter of punches, kicks, and shouts. The Russians screamed and struggled as the police wrested the gun away from Peter and pinned them on the ground. Slade fought valiantly. The police singled him out for a particularly rough beating before they finally overcame him. They put iron shackles on him and his friends.

"You're under arrest for conspiracy to commit assassination," Plekhanov said.

"How did they know we were here?" Peter asked as the police dragged him and the others to the carriage.

"Someone must have talked." Fyodor regarded Slade and his friends with suspicion. "Have we a traitor among us?"

"It's not me," Peter and Alexander hastened to say.

"Nor me." Slade's nose was bleeding, his mouth swollen. "We weren't careful enough. We must have been overheard by a spy."

"That's enough babbling," Plekhanov said.

As he and his men pushed the prisoners into the carriage, Slade looked toward the mansion. In the doorway stood Prince Orlov. His body was thick with fat and muscle. His bald head resembled a bullet, hard and shiny as steel, rising from a thick neck to a rounded point at the top. He studied his four would-be assassins through the monocle that glinted in his right eye. His unsmiling gaze lingered on Slade.

A hot, sultry morning suffocated Moscow. Slade stood in Prince Orlov's office inside the Kremlin. His shirt was stained with blood; bruises marked his face. Orlov studied Slade from behind a carved mahogany desk the size of Red Square.

"I owe you my thanks." Contempt inflected his rough voice. He didn't like rats, even though he employed hundreds of them. But his contempt was nothing compared to that which Slade felt for himself. He had just sent three hapless men to their death.

The Prince looked over Slade's injuries. "I am sorry about your face." He didn't sound sorry. "It was necessary, you understand."

Slade nodded. The police hadn't wanted to favor him and expose him as the man who'd betrayed Peter, Alexander, and Fyodor. The three Russians would "disappear," but Slade would be freed to continue working for the Third Section. The bruises and scars from a beating by the police would give him extra cachet with the other secret societies that he'd already infiltrated. Now he tasted his own blood; he welcomed the pain. A beating was far less punishment than he deserved.

"You have proved to be worth ten other informants," Orlov said with grudging respect. "I can use a man of your skills. From now on, you work directly for me."

Slade felt no triumph, even though he'd achieved his goal of penetrating the Tsar's inner court. He was as happy as a man can be when he stands before the gates of hell and watches them open.

18

WHENEVER I EMBARK UPON A JOURNEY, I HAVE MIXED FEELINGS. Excitement about encountering fresh vistas and new people vies with anxiety about travel arrangements, the strain on my health, and uncertainty about what awaits me at my destination. Even in cases of journeys that I undertake reluctantly, I can look forward to getting them over with. But my journey from Bedlam was different. I felt unadulterated dread.

Day broke as the soldiers lifted me into a carriage outside the asylum. The rising sun shimmered dull orange behind a haze of smoke and heat. The effects of the drug and the magnetic forces had begun to weaken and my free will to revive.

"Let me go," I said. But the lethargy still possessed me, and I slumped in the seat, as limp and heavy as a rag doll stuffed with sand. "Where are you taking me?"

The soldiers climbed into the carriage with me. The commanding officer said, "There's nothing to be afraid of. Just relax."

We rode through streets that came alive with people hurrying to work, shopkeepers opening their establishments, and peddlers wheeling carts. I realized the futility of calling for help. Who would take on the British army? We stopped at King's Cross Station. An animating prickle spread through my muscles; I could flex them, but when I tried to jump from the carriage and run away, I was so weak that I fell on my knees. The soldiers supported me through the station, to a train. They laid me on a berth inside a sleeping compartment.

"If there's anything you need, just ask," said the commanding officer. "I'll be right outside."

It appeared that I would be a prisoner under guard for the duration of this trip to Heaven knew where.

The whistle blew. The train rolled out of the station. As I watched London stream past the window, I experienced the aftereffects of my ordeal in Bedlam. The glass bell that had separated me from my emotions dissolved. Shame, guilt, and horror rushed upon me like horsemen of the Apocalypse. They tormented me while I faced the full extent of what had happened. I had revealed secrets and betrayed Slade, my country, and myself; I had put us all in jeopardy. Now that Wilhelm Stieber knew that Slade knew about Niall Kavanagh and the weapon, he would hunt Slade to the ends of the earth. And he could not let me go free to tell the world what I knew. He would hunt me down, too. The British army couldn't protect me forever. Furthermore, my confession had put sensitive information about Britain into the hands of a man who served its rival. What dangerous ideas might Stieber and the Tsar glean from my story? If there were a repeat of the events of 1848, I would be to blame.

I am a harsh judge of other people's faults, but no less of my own. I have always denigrated myself for lacking the beauty, intellect, competence, and moral and physical strength that I crave. But never until today had I had as much reason to hate myself. I cursed my failure to stand up to Wilhelm Stieber. There seemed no chance of rectifying the evil I'd done.

Many hours and many miles passed. I was so absorbed in my misery that I didn't know which direction I was traveling in; I didn't care. If I was to be murdered when I reached my destination, I deserved it. Finally I grew so exhausted that I fell asleep. I awakened when the soldiers came to fetch me. Stiff and dazed, I emerged at a small station, in late afternoon sun so bright that it hurt my eyes. A sign above the platform read: Southampton.

Southampton is a pretty seaside town about a hundred miles

from London. As we rode in a carriage through its streets, I was blind to its charms. Dirty and disheveled, still wearing my wrinkled jail uniform, guarded by troops, I felt like a prisoner of war being transported to the enemy stockade. My life as Currer Bell, the famous author, seemed part of a distant, glittering dream. We reached the port, where the captain on a steamboat called, "Last ferry to East Cowes! All aboard!"

The soldiers escorted me onto the ferry. We traveled down a broad watercourse, past fishing villages and piers, toward the blue, sparkling expanse of the English Channel. I love the sea, and usually the sight of it invigorates and uplifts me; but even it could not lighten my heart. I did not ask the soldiers why we were going to East Cowes. I sat mute with despair.

As we entered the Channel, the sun descended; the western sky turned a radiant pink that cast a rosy sheen upon the ocean. Ahead, some five miles distant, loomed the Isle of Wight, whose cliffs rose up out of the sea to wooded heights cloaked in dusk. We approached the shore through a flotilla of pleasure craft. Laughter, singing, and music drifted from parties aboard. The coppery sun melted into the ocean as the ferry docked at the tiny village of East Cowes. We disembarked, then climbed into a carriage that conveyed us uphill, through meadows and woods, past pretty summer houses. The cool evening breeze revived me somewhat, but I was weak from hunger; I'd not eaten all day. My head ached, and I felt dizzy and tremulous. My heart began to race because we must have been nearing the end of our journey and my reckoning with fate.

On a rise that overlooked the sea was a huge mansion that looked like a palace lifted out of the Italian Renaissance period. Its white walls, square towers, and tile roofs shone pink in the waning light of sunset. Recognition struck me. I'd seen this mansion before, in a newspaper illustration, several years ago. My lips moved in a silent exclamation: *Dear God.* I knew where I was. I knew who had summoned me here.

The carriage paused outside a gate, which two guards opened; they greeted my escorts and waved us inside. We drew up in a wide driveway. Gas lamps burned in the grand porch. As the soldiers handed me down from the carriage, the door of the mansion opened. Out stepped a small woman dressed in a pale summer frock. She was plumper than when I'd last seen her, in 1848; she'd given birth to her seventh child the previous year. Her face was rounder, her cheeks ruddier from the summer heat; but she was the same regal, imperious personage with whom I had the honor of claiming an acquaintance.

Queen Victoria glided to the head of the stairs and gazed down her long nose at me.

"Welcome to Osborne House, Miss Brontë." Her voice was tart with displeasure. "What sort of trouble have you caused us this time?"

19

>‹‹

Reader, the Queen of England did not like me. Despite the fact that I had saved the lives of her children, she bore me a grudge because she could not forget that they'd been kidnapped while in my care. Although she knew that the disastrous events of 1848 would have transpired with or without me, in her mind I was inextricably associated with them. No matter that she had pronounced herself forever in my debt; she couldn't forgive me. Perhaps she couldn't forgive me because she was in my debt. Her Majesty did not like being in anyone's debt, let alone that of someone she considered a common little upstart.

She instructed the soldiers to take me to the back terrace, then turned and went back inside the mansion. The terrace was enclosed by stone balustrades and decorated with statuary and potted plants. In the daytime it would command a fine view of the ocean. White ironwork chairs surrounded a table on which a lamp burned. Sitting alone, I gazed up at the stars that began to appear in the sky, then down upon the garden, whose flowers exhaled sweet perfume. I gasped with shock because I had traveled from murder scene to jail to insane asylum to the royal retreat in the space of twenty-four hours.

Children's laughter tinkled in the garden. A fair-haired girl in a pink frock ran up onto the terrace, chased by a boy who yipped like a wild Indian. Four younger children followed on their heels. They all saw me and skidded to a halt.

"Who are you?" the eldest boy demanded.

He and the girl in pink were taller than when I'd rescued them from their kidnapper—he would be ten now, she eleven. She was Princess Vicky. He was Albert Edward, called Bertie, Prince of Wales and heir to the throne. I am not fond of children, but I'd developed an affection for these two. As courtesy brought me to my feet, I resisted the urge to hug Bertie and Vicky.

"Hello," I said. "Don't you remember me?"

"It's Miss Brontë!" Vicky exclaimed. "How nice to see you." She was still the perfect little princess, all gracious manners. She introduced the younger children. "These are Alice, Alfred, Helena, and Louise."

"Miss Brontë and I defeated the evil Chinaman and his army," Bertie told them. "Like this!" He grabbed his little brother Alfred. They began tussling and yelling.

Vicky said, "Stop that before someone gets hurt!" Neither her nature nor Bertie's had changed: he was still naughty and heedless; she, the big sister who tried to maintain order.

"That's enough, children." Their mother spoke kindly but firmly from the doorway. Beside her stood her husband Albert, Prince Consort. "Go inside now. It's late."

She gave me a look that said she wanted her precious offspring nowhere near me. As they marched into the house, Vicky called, "Good night, Miss Brontë." The Queen came out to the terrace, responded to my curtsy with an indifferent nod, and plopped herself down in a chair.

"Please sit down, Miss Brontë," said Prince Albert. I obeyed. "How glad I am to see you again. I am sorry that it must be under such circumstances." He spoke in the same formal, ponderous manner that I remembered, but he shook my hand with genuine friendliness. His face was pale, moist with sweat, and tired; his figure had grown paunchy, and he seemed older than his thirty-two years. His health had been poor when I'd first met him, and perhaps three more years with the Queen had taken its toll. "I regret that you suffered in Newgate Prison and Bethlem Hospital for so long."

"It wasn't that long." The Queen clearly thought he was making too big a fuss over me.

"We sent for you as soon as we heard what had happened," Prince Albert said.

It seemed a miracle that they had come to my aid. "How did you hear, may I ask?"

"We have ears everywhere," said a man who joined us on the terrace.

Surprise followed surprises. "Lord Palmerston," I blurted.

"None other." Henry Temple, or Lord Palmerston, the Foreign Secretary, bowed with a flourish. "Good evening, Miss Brontë." He lifted my hand, kissed it, smiled into my eyes, and said, "You're looking lovely, as usual."

We both knew better. He was still the jaunty, handsome flirt who'd earned himself the nickname "Cupid." His eyes still glinted with the wits that had masterminded the Queen's cooperation in Slade's and my plot to capture the villain who'd tried to bring down the British Empire. But he was thinner, his curly hair grayer; his sixty-seven years showed.

I had developed an avid interest in these three august personages whose paths had briefly crossed mine in 1848. I had read everything about them that I could find in the newspapers, and I therefore knew that Lord Palmerston's career had recently hit some rough patches. One of these was the Don Pacifico Affair. In 1850, rioters in Athens burned down the house of a merchant named Pacifico. Pacifico, a British subject, appealed to London for help. Lord Palmerston sent a fleet to seize Greek ships worth enough to compensate Don Pacifico. An international uproar brought England to the brink of war with France and Russia, which disapproved of Lord Palmerston's actions, and the British government to the brink of dissolution. Lord Palmerston had made a speech in Parliament, claiming that British citizens everywhere in the world were entitled to protection from the British government. He'd saved the government and his own career, but he'd created much bad feeling.

The Queen couldn't condone what Palmerston had done without her blessing, and she'd threatened to dismiss him. He'd promised never to behave so high-handedly again, and so gained a reprieve. But I could feel the tension between them as he took the chair next to mine.

"A network of informants maintains a watch on persons of interest," Lord Palmerston explained. "It helps keep the British Empire in power. And you, Miss Brontë, have been a person of interest since the events of 1848. You also merit attention due to your status as a literary figure." He added gallantly, "I read *Jane Eyre*, by the way. I found it quite entertaining."

"So did I," the Queen admitted. "I couldn't put it down."

That was high praise from her. "Many thanks, Your Majesty."

"Word of your arrest filtered up to me from the police department," Lord Palmerston told me. "Had I been in town, I would have sent someone to fetch you sooner. Unfortunately, I was here on the Isle of Wight, conducting business with Her Majesty. By the time I received the news, you had been taken to Bedlam. I sincerely apologize for the delay."

"I sincerely thank you for rescuing me," I said.

Lord Palmerston smiled. "It was the least I could do. After the service you rendered our nation, we owed you a favor."

"Consider it a favor repaid," the Queen said grumpily. "But do not consider yourself a free woman, Miss Brontë. You are still facing a charge of murder. Did you kill that actress?"

"Of course she didn't," Lord Palmerston said.

Prince Albert said, "Miss Brontë is incapable of doing such a thing."

"Stay out of this," the Queen snapped at them. "Let Miss Brontë answer, and let me draw the conclusions."

"Yes, dearest," said Prince Albert.

"Excuse me, Your Majesty," said Lord Palmerston.

The Queen's round, protuberant eyes fixed me with a suspicious stare. "I want to know what in Heaven is going on. Did you kill that woman, or did you not?"

"I did not kill Katerina," I said with all the force of the truth.

She looked askance at me. "I understand that you were caught standing over her dead body with the murder weapon in your hands. How do you explain that?"

"Katerina had been tortured and stabbed before I arrived," I said. "I found her. Then I heard someone coming. I thought it was the murderer, and I picked up the knife in order to defend myself."

The Queen harrumphed, although the men seemed satisfied by my explanation. "If you didn't kill her, then who did?"

"It was Wilhelm Stieber," I said.

"He is a spy for the Tsar," Lord Palmerston interjected.

"I know who he is," the Queen said, peeved. Lord Palmerston had educated her about foreign politics, and she chafed at her role as his pupil.

Lord Palmerston leaned toward me, chin in hand. "I've heard reports that Stieber has been sighted in London. This is a most interesting development."

"How do you know Wilhelm Stieber killed Katerina?" the Queen asked me.

"She told me before she died."

The Queen studied me skeptically. "How convenient. Why, pray tell, would the Tsar's spy torture and kill a cheap, common actress? How did Wilhelm Stieber even know Katerina?"

"She was his informant." I explained that Katerina had apparently consorted with men, that she'd elicited from Russian immigrants their secrets about plots against the Tsar, that she'd sought from Englishmen clues to the whereabouts of Niall Kavanagh and the gun he'd invented. I mentioned that the gun could decide the outcome of a war between Russia and England, and that Wilhelm Stieber meant to obtain it for the Tsar. "But Katerina began working for a British secret agent. Stieber found out. He tortured her in an attempt to learn where the agent was, and he killed her for betraying him."

The Queen's response was a derisive snort. "Surely a woman on her deathbed would be incapable of relating such a complete, coherent, and fantastic story as that."

"She didn't," I admitted. "I deduced it by combining her last words with what the British agent had told me earlier. The agent is John Slade."

"Slade!" The Queen smiled with good humor for the first time that evening. Although Slade had been as much involved in her children's kidnapping as I had, she bore him no grudge. "That marvelously attractive spy who thwarted the attack on my kingdom!"

Lord Palmerston's expression turned grave at the mention of Slade. "That marvelously attractive spy is no more, Your Majesty. John Slade went to Moscow in the autumn of 1848. While there, he turned traitor and revealed the identities of his fellow agents to the Russian secret police. He was executed."

"My heavens." The Queen stared openmouthed at Lord Palmerston. "When was this?"

"Four months ago."

"This is the first I've heard of it. Why have you not told me until now?"

"I didn't want to upset Your Majesty," Lord Palmerston said smoothly.

Anger flushed her cheeks a brighter red; she put her fists on her hips. "I've told you time and again that I want to know everything that happens, yet you are always keeping me in the dark! I've also made it clear that all important decisions should be mine, but you make them without consulting me. Now you've gone behind my back and permitted the execution of a man I considered a friend! You are insufferable!"

"There was strong evidence against Slade," Lord Palmerston said. "We had to conclude that he'd committed treason. In a case like his, execution is standard procedure."

I was appalled to realize that Lord Palmerston had a part in Slade's troubles, even though he probably hadn't given the order of execution himself. I wanted to protest that Slade was innocent, but I did not know that for sure.

"Calm yourself, dearest," Prince Albert said. "Overexcitement will make you ill."

The Queen narrowed her eyes at him. "You knew about Slade,

didn't you?" The guilty look on her husband's face was her answer. "Ah!" she exclaimed, throwing up her hands. "You are as bad as Lord Palmerston!" She subsided into dark, ominous brooding.

Lord Palmerston said to me, "Were you in contact with Slade while he was in Russia?"

"No," I said.

"Then how could he have told you about Wilhelm Stieber or this Niall Kavanagh?"

I searched Lord Palmerston for a hint as to whether he'd heard of Kavanagh before. His smooth face gave me none. I didn't know whether to trust him, but I had nowhere else to turn. "I saw Slade in London. He was alive, at least as of Sunday."

Lord Palmerston was startled into silence. The Queen bent a distrustful look on me. Prince Albert watched her cautiously. The sounds of crickets chirping in the garden, a cool breeze stirring the trees, and the distant rush of ocean waves drifted up to the terrace. Lord Palmerston leaned toward me and clasped my hands in his. "My dear Miss Brontë," he began.

"Don't tell me it's impossible." I wrenched free of his warm, subduing grasp. "Lord Eastbourne already tried to convince me that Slade is dead. I didn't listen to him, and I won't listen to you, either. I refuse to believe what my own eyes and ears have told me is untrue!"

Lord Palmerston and the Queen sat back in their chairs, surprised by my vehemence. "I'm afraid your mind has deceived you," Lord Palmerston said regretfully.

Prince Albert said, "I deem Miss Brontë to be a levelheaded person. I do not think she would invent such a fantasy."

"She invented plenty of fantasies in her book," the Queen retorted.

"I believe that Miss Brontë knows the difference between fantasy and reality," Prince Albert said. "If she says Mr. Slade is alive, we should give her the benefit of the doubt."

The Queen seemed to realize that although she wanted to contradict her husband and claim that Slade was dead, that meant she would be agreeing with Lord Palmerston. And perhaps she liked

Slade enough to want to think he was alive. "You're right, dearest. We will operate under the assumption that Mr. Slade is alive, until evidence to the contrary presents itself." She shot a triumphant look at Lord Palmerston.

An inaudible sigh of resignation heaved Lord Palmerston's chest. I met Prince Albert's eyes and gave him a gaze filled with my gratitude for his support. He responded with a somber nod.

"Supposing that John Slade is alive, Miss Brontë," Lord Palmerston said, "what is he doing in England?"

I replied that he had come back to find Niall Kavanagh and the invention before Stieber did.

"How did you chance to see Slade?"

Alas, the answer would put Slade in a bad light; but I related the story of my first visit to Bedlam, my glimpse of Slade, the second visit, and the murdered nurses. I revealed that Slade was a fugitive known to the police as Josef Typinski, a Polish refugee. By the time I'd described the incident at the zoo, the royal couple looked incredulous and Lord Palmerston grim.

"Slade has much explaining to do," Lord Palmerston said. "I would like to know why he's not dead. What did he say about that?"

"He didn't say. But he did swear that he's not a traitor. He never stopped working for Britain." I wanted to believe it, and I had to convince Lord Palmerston. "Now he's in danger because Stieber knows he is an enemy agent who plotted against the Tsar and he is after Niall Kavanagh and the invention."

Lord Palmerston thoughtfully tapped his cheek with his finger. "How does Stieber know?"

My shame and guilt resurged. "I told him." I described how the doctor in Bedlam had drugged and mesmerized me, Stieber had interrogated me, and I had spilled the information.

"Shocking and deplorable!" The Queen was ready to believe me, if only to spite Lord Palmerston.

"I beg you to help Mr. Slade," I said with all the passionate force I could manage. "Please tell your colleagues in the government that he's not a murderer or a traitor. Please save him from Wilhelm

Stieber!" I appealed to Lord Palmerston's self-interest. "You must save England from the Tsar and Niall Kavanagh's weapon!"

Lord Palmerston was sympathetic yet still skeptical. "Let me see if I understand you correctly. You heard about the scientist, the invention, and the Tsar's plot from Slade. You believe that the man who interrogated you in Bedlam is Wilhelm Stieber, who uses the asylum as his personal prison and interrogation ward, because Slade told you as much. Slade also told you that he is innocent of all the crimes laid on him and he has been framed. Is that correct?"

Dismay crept through me because I sensed where this was going. ". . . Yes."

"In fact, all your information comes from Slade," Lord Palmerston said.

"Also from Katerina," the Queen reminded him.

"The incoherent speech of a dying woman," Palmerston said. "Your Majesty pointed that out earlier." She looked nonplussed; he'd stymied her with her own statement. "We have only Slade's word to support Miss Brontë's story, and Slade has been officially discredited." He said to me with regret, "The government cannot mount a search for a secret weapon that may not exist. Nor can it take action to protect Slade."

My heart plunged into despair. Rejected by the highest authority, at the end of my resources and strength, I wanted to put my head on the table and weep.

"The government can take action if I say so," the Queen declared. "And I say that it shall answer Miss Brontë's plea for help, rescue John Slade, and save England from a Russian attack!"

Surprise accompanied the hope that revived in me. Even though the Queen was in a contrary mood, I had not expected to find her my partisan. I'd thought she hated me too much.

"That would be most unwise, Your Majesty," Lord Palmerston said.

"Why?" The Queen was flushed and exuberant, spoiling for another clash of wills with him. Her husband laid a cautioning hand on her arm, but she shook it off. "What is so unwise about helping a friend who once rendered me a heroic service?"

"Should you come to the defense of a traitor, your reputation with the public would suffer," Lord Palmerston said.

"That is a valid point," Prince Albert said.

Now faced with two opponents, the Queen swelled with determination. "Then *you* shall act on my behalf." She pointed dramatically at Lord Palmerston.

"Me?" He flinched. "What do you expect me to do?"

"You're so clever, you'll think of something."

"But there will be objections from everyone in Parliament."

"Just run roughshod over them, like you do over me," the Queen said blithely.

Palmerston tried but failed to hide his dismay. "I don't have as much influence in Parliament as I once did." His political exploits had made him not a few enemies.

The Queen glowered at him. "Are you defying me?"

"No, but—"

"Well, it certainly seems you are. In fact, I begin to question your loyalty."

"I've always been your devoted servant," Palmerston said, but his gallantry fell flat.

"Oh?" The Queen leveled an accusatory stare on him. "You always go against my wishes when it comes to foreign policy. You supplied arms to Garibaldi and his rebels in Italy to use against King Ferdinand. You also supported the revolutionaries in Hungary against the Emperor of Austria. I begin to think this is a deliberate ploy to undermine my relations." The Queen shared bloodlines with virtually every monarch in Europe. "I wonder if you are trying to take over the world."

Palmerston laughed. "That's absurd."

But perhaps he did entertain such an ambition. I wouldn't have put it past him. The evening air was thick with sweet, floral fragrances and danger. An insinuation of treason from the Queen was no joke. I could feel Lord Palmerston's fear.

"Dearest, please don't say things you'll regret later." Prince Albert obviously dreaded the scandal that would ensue if she sent her foreign secretary to the gallows.

The Queen rose up in a magnificent fury. "Don't tell me what not to say! And don't tell me to calm down, either! You don't understand what I go through, ruling a nation while perpetuating the dynasty. Men!" She uttered the word with the same bitter exasperation as I'd heard women everywhere do. She pointed at her husband. "You enjoy yourself while I suffer!"

Lord Palmerston winced: the royal couple's argument had turned too intimate. He and the Prince seemed to realize that the conversation was headed for dangerous territory.

"I'm sorry, dearest," the Prince said contritely. "Please forgive me."

"Your wish is my pleasure to grant," Lord Palmerston said. The Queen gleamed with triumph. "However, I must warn you that there will be repercussions when this business about Slade becomes public."

"Then don't let it become public. That should be easy for you; you excel at covering things up. Work out the details with Miss Brontë. Don't tell them to me. Wouldn't you agree that it's better if I don't know?" Hinting that his actions must not be traceable to her, the Queen smiled sweetly.

"Yes, Your Majesty," Lord Palmerston said

She said to her husband, "Darling, it's time to say goodnight to the children." As she and the Prince strolled hand in hand into the house, she called, "Farewell, Miss Brontë. I trust that we need not meet again soon."

Lord Palmerston and I looked at each other in mutual flabbergasted silence. The lamp seemed dimmer, as if the Queen had taken some of its light with her. Shadows encroached on the terrace. The evening breeze had turned chilly. Then Palmerston shrugged and smiled.

"Well, that's that, as far as Her Majesty is concerned. However, there remains a problem. Whoever removed you from Newgate Prison—whether it was Wilhelm Stieber or not—did so through unofficial channels. You are out of jail illegally, which makes you a fugitive."

"But I'm innocent," I said, dismayed that he apparently did not intend to make my problems with the law go away. "I don't belong in jail."

"I know," he said with as much conviction as I could have hoped for, "but I've little influence with the police. And although I will put forth my best effort for John Slade, it may not be enough." His smile was rueful. "Slade and I may both take a fall."

My shoulders slumped as defeat crushed me. If he couldn't help Slade, who could?

"However, there is a possible solution," Lord Palmerston said.

"What?" I didn't like his dubious tone of voice.

"A certain judge owes me a favor. I'll persuade him to muddle up the records concerning your arrest. It will be a few days before the police realize you're missing from Newgate. Until then, you'll be free to help Slade. If you're lucky, you'll find evidence to support your story and prove that you're both innocent. It would certainly help your cause if the weapon does exist and you could obtain it for the British government."

The daunting weight of responsibility settled on my spirit. "And if I can't by that time?"

"I suggest that you turn yourself in, stand trial for the murder of Katerina, and trust to the mercy of the court."

I nodded, for although I knew the court had little mercy and if convicted I would be sentenced to imprisonment, committed to Bedlam, or hanged, what other choice had I?

"It's too late to do anything tonight," Lord Palmerston said. "You'll stay here and recover your strength. Tomorrow, you'll be given new clothes, money, whatever you need. My men will escort you anywhere you wish."

As a maid led me to my room, I thought back on what had been said on the terrace. I was too weary to reconstruct the whole conversation or identify all the motives beneath it, but I had a feeling that Lord Palmerston had manipulated the situation to come out exactly as he'd planned.

20

THE SECRET ADVENTURES OF JOHN SLADE

1850 July. A feverish orange sun set over Moscow. Smoke veiled the red gothic tower that rose above the Saviour Gate to the Kremlin. Inside the tower, John Slade and Prince Orlov mounted the stairs to the lookout post at the top, a small, octagonal space with open arches that provided views in all directions. Tsar Nicholas stood looking over the city toward the Presnya quarter, where radicals had incited violence among workers angered by bad conditions in the factories and peasants starved by high food prices. A riot was underway, and riots inevitably led to fires. The Tsar turned away from the distant orange glow of the flames. He faced Slade and Prince Orlov, who bowed.

"Your Highness," Orlov said. "This is Ivan Zubov, the man I mentioned."

"Ah. The informant who warned us about the riot," the Tsar said.

As he and Slade studied each other, Slade saw an intelligent man burdened by responsibility yet determined to lead his kingdom to world supremacy. He knew that the Tsar saw in him a traitor to his own cause and a useful tool for the regime. That was exactly what Slade wanted the Tsar to see. This was a moment of professional triumph for Slade: at last he had breached the strict security around the Tsar.

"Mr. Zubov spied on the radicals who planned the riot," Prince Orlov said, eager to curry the Tsar's favor. "Thanks to him, my men were able to contain it before it could spread to the rest of the city."

"Very good," the Tsar said.

"Perhaps Mr. Zubov is too good. Or perhaps not good enough." The harsh voice belonged to a man who stood in a shadowed corner of the tower.

Slade was disturbed that he hadn't noticed the man. How could he, an expert spy, fail to detect someone who was only six feet away? The man emanated none of the signals by which people reveal their presence. His breathing was silent. His body had no odor, even on this hot night. He had stood perfectly still until now, when he shifted position. The lights from the city edged his face, whose skin was pitted, whose pale eyes gleamed like mercury.

"Comrade Wilhelm Stieber," Prince Orlov said. "I didn't know you were there. What do you mean by your comment about Mr. Zubov?" He bristled at the criticism of Slade, his gift to the Tsar.

Slade recalled the information he'd read in Stieber's dossier. Stieber had been born in Prussian Saxony, had studied law at Friedrich Wilhelm University in Berlin, had worked for the Berlin police and risen to the rank of Inspector of the Criminal Division. After the revolutions of 1848, he'd been promoted to chief of police. He'd then ventured abroad and cropped up in courts all over Europe. According to his dossier, he was thirty-three years of age, but his gray hair, confident poise, and air of wisdom made him seem decades older, even though he had the vigor of youth. The dossier provided only the meager details that the Foreign Office had managed to compile. Stieber was an enigma.

Now Stieber addressed Prince Orlov but watched Slade. "Mr. Zubov has warned us about many problems. The riot in Presnya, the anti-government propaganda strewn around the city, and the secret societies recruiting members among the workers and peasants, for example."

"That's to his credit," Prince Orlov said.

"But he never warns us soon enough to prevent trouble," Stieber said. "It always happens anyway."

The Tsar frowned as he listened. He was not a rash leader who jumped into disputes and imposed his own opinion; he would rather hear all sides first. Slade hid his own consternation. Did Stieber suspect that he was deliberately delaying his reports? Instinct warned him not to speak. He'd heard that Stieber excelled at reading people. One tiny lapse in his Russian accent could give him away. If there was anyone who could discern that Slade wasn't whom he purported to be, it was Stieber.

Prince Orlov said, "Even the best informant can't always find things out as early as we would like. And if you're implying that the Third Section is at fault—well, my men react as best they can on short notice." His bald head and fleshy face glistened with sweat.

"Those are good excuses," Stieber said. "If excuses were horses, all men would ride."

"We've arrested many political enemies since Mr. Zubov began working for us." Prince Orlov glanced at the Tsar, whose frown deepened.

"Have you noticed that most of those 'political enemies' are thieves, street brawlers, confidence men, murderers, and other common criminals? They're hardly the cream of the dissident intelligentsia, the people we want to crush," Stieber said.

"The three who tried to assassinate me were," Prince Orlov retorted.

"So it would seem. Have you also noticed that since Mr. Zubov began working for you, activity among the secret societies has increased, and so has civil unrest?"

"What are you saying?" demanded Prince Orlov.

Slade wondered if Stieber suspected the truth about him. Or perhaps Stieber automatically distrusted anyone new to the Tsar's inner circle; perhaps he was jealous because he viewed Slade as a rival for influence over the Tsar. Slade waited, outwardly calm, tense inside.

"Just that Mr. Zubov bears watching," Stieber said evenly.

His gaze locked with Slade's. Antagonism sparked between the two men, hot and bright as the fires burning in the city. The figures of Prince Orlov and Tsar Nicholas seemed to waver, no more substantial than ghosts. For a moment Stieber and Slade were alone in the world. Slade realized that he'd met his match. Of the three powerful men, Stieber was the one from whom Slade—and the world—had the most to fear.

21

>＜

EVERYTHING IN THE WAY OF FOOD, CLOTHING, SHELTER, AND SERVICE was provided for me at Osborne House, but I didn't like to impose on the Queen after the last, disastrous time I'd spent under her roof in 1848. I hardly slept. The next day I traveled to London and arrived in the evening. I trudged up the steps to 76 Gloucester Terrace and found the Smiths seated inside at dinner. They beheld me with surprise.

"Charlotte," George said as he rose from his chair. "I didn't expect you back so soon."

So soon? I'd been gone for three days. I was surprised that he didn't seem worried. "I'm sorry I left without telling you."

"Never mind," George said. "You're always welcome here."

"Indeed," Mrs. Smith said, but her smile was false. "Please join us."

George pulled out a chair at the table for me and ordered the maid to set another place. "That's a pretty frock," his sister Eliza said. "Is it new?"

"Yes." The Queen's servants had obtained it for me. It was a blue-and-white striped summer frock, much more fashionable than the clothes I usually wore. They'd also provided me with new undergarments, shoes, stockings, coat, and parasol. I hardly felt like myself.

"I'm sorry you had to interrupt your visit because you'd

been called home," George said. "Is everything is all right with your family?"

I regarded him in confusion. "I wasn't called home. What gave you that idea?"

He looked to his mother. Avoiding my gaze, she said, "Why, I just assumed that was what had happened." She added, "I packed your things and sent them to Haworth."

"How kind of you." I deduced that Mrs. Smith had been glad to have me gone and persuaded George to think I'd been called home. She hadn't cared what had really become of me.

"Then what did happen?" George asked. "Where did you go?"

"I was arrested and put in Newgate Prison," I said.

Shocked gasps burst from everyone at the table. George said, "Whatever for?"

I explained that I had gone to call on Katerina and described the condition in which I'd found her. "I didn't kill her. I was wrongfully arrested." I didn't tell the Smiths what had happened afterward. If I told them where I'd been last night, they would never believe me. Indeed, there was much about me that they would never believe. But my manner must have convinced them that I was telling the truth about my arrest.

"How terrible." Mrs. Smith spoke with pity and distaste, but she couldn't hide her delight.

I suppose I should have been embarrassed about what had happened and fearful of what the Smiths would think of me; but I had other, bigger concerns.

George was aghast. "Why didn't you let me know?"

"I tried to send word." I told him about the priest at the police station. "But it seems the priest didn't bother to deliver the message."

"That's unfortunate," George said. "Had I received it, I would have hurried to your rescue at once."

Some impulse made me look at Mrs. Smith. Her expression was compounded of slyness and pleasure. George's gaze followed mine. Astonishment appeared on his face as he drew the same conclusion that I had. "The priest did come," he said. "I wasn't at home. He delivered his message to you, didn't he, Mother?"

She stammered, then said, "Well, yes."

"Why didn't you tell me?" George demanded.

Guilt flushed her cheeks. "When the priest said Miss Brontë had been arrested, I didn't believe him. I thought he was a prankster." It was obvious to me that she was lying. I could tell by their expressions that it was obvious to George and her other children as well. They all looked appalled. "I didn't want to bother you," she finished lamely.

I had turned the other cheek to her gibes, but this malicious act I could not tolerate. "You knew I was in trouble and you deliberately turned your back on me! Madam, you are a selfish, jealous, wicked woman!"

She reacted with the chagrin of someone who has been tormenting a cat and had it suddenly scratch her. I could have raged at her until Christmas, but as her family gaped in shock at both of us, I remembered that George was my publisher and refrained from telling off his mother as thoroughly as I would have liked.

"I won't inconvenience you any further," I said, icily polite now, to Mrs. Smith. Then I walked out of the room.

I heard Mrs. Smith sputter and George say to her, "You and I will talk later." He hurried after me. "Charlotte, wait!" He caught up with me outside the house. "I'm sorry. I don't know what's gotten into Mother. I thought she liked you."

Men are so thickheaded, I thought. "It's quite all right."

"No, it isn't," George said. "That my mother would do such a thing to an author of mine! And I'd hoped you and she could be friends. Because . . ." He gazed into my eyes. I was dismayed to see tenderness in his. "I'd hoped that you and I—that perhaps we could be more than author and publisher."

Once I would have thrilled to hear that. Now I had no time to let him down gently. I had only a few days of freedom, their definite number unknown. "George, I'm sorry, but what you suggest is impossible. I am not the sort of woman who could make you happy. Please say no more. Let us just continue to be friends."

George was clearly disappointed, and surprised. "Well. If that's what you wish." Few women he knew would have spurned him. Then I saw a gleam in his eyes: he was a man who relished a challenge. "Friends, then. For now."

I was glad his feelings hadn't been hurt too much, but sorry that I'd not discouraged him. I saw a carriage coming up the road, hailed it down, and climbed inside. "Goodbye."

"Are you going back to Haworth?" George called as the carriage rattled away.

"Yes." I called to the driver, "Take me to Euston Station."

Although time was short, I had to return home. There I could recover from my ordeal. Only there could I find enough peace of mind to figure out how to exonerate Slade and myself.

22

THE EXPERIENCE OF A JOURNEY between Haworth and anywhere else depends on which direction I am traveling. A trip to London takes all night, requires a four-mile walk or wagon ride to Keighley Station and a change of trains in Leeds, and severely taxes my health and nerves. Yet no matter that the return trip involves the same exertions, I feel myself rejuvenating the closer I get to Haworth. It is as if home exerts a life-giving force that heals body and soul. Although I cannot bear the isolation of Haworth for long, and I repeatedly flee from it, I am always drawn back.

Rain fell as I rode in the wagon, whose tattered canopy did little to keep me dry. The moors were sodden, the morning sky an unrelieved gray. When I reached the village of drab stone cottages, I felt like a sailor who has been lost at sea and finds himself miraculously washed up on the shore of his native land. But, even though Haworth was the same as it had been forever, my own position there had changed during recent years.

The farmers, shopkeepers, and housewives I met spoke their usual respectful greetings to me, but when I passed, I heard the buzz of conversation: "What a surprise that our Miss Brontë turned out to be the famous authoress!"

I was no longer just the spinster daughter of their parson, for my fame had spread to Yorkshire. Indeed, the local people had been the first to deduce Currer Bell's identity. The postmistress had noticed the many letters and packages I received from London, and I suspected that she'd opened my correspondence with my publisher and gossiped about it. The cat was let out of the bag when the brother of my old school friend had gone about bragging that he knew Charlotte Brontë was Currer Bell. But the fact that I was an object of gossip, stares, and criticism was my own fault. I had written fictional settings and characters that bore too strong a resemblance to those real places and people upon which they were based. Too many folks had recognized them and decided that only a local person could have written *Jane Eyre* and *Shirley*. They'd eventually tracked Currer Bell to my door.

The wagon left me at the bottom of the road that led up the hill to my house, the gray-brick parsonage. Although I was nearly ill from exhaustion, my heart was lighter than it had been since the day I'd seen Slade in Bedlam. The stimulating essence of inspiration flowed, and suddenly I knew what my next step should be.

In order to find Slade, I must first find Niall Kavanagh. In order to find Kavanagh, I must go back to the point where this whole business had started.

Unfortunately, that was not to happen without complications.

As I toiled up the hill, I met Arthur Bell Nicholls, my father's curate. He lumbered along beside me. A tall, heavily built man, he had heavy features in a square face adorned with thick black eyebrows and side-whiskers. "Back from London, are ye?" he said in his strong Irish brogue.

He often seized on opportunities to talk to me, and more often of late. I didn't understand why, since we had little in common. Mr. Nicholls was a stolid, conventional man of the cloth, while I hardly led a conventional life. I didn't much care for him, and today I was in no mood for his dull attentions.

"If I weren't back, you wouldn't be seeing me here, would you?" I said.

He laughed heartily, as though I'd made a joke. I had the grace to feel ashamed, for he was a good man, diligent in his duties and a great help to Papa, kind to everyone and loved by the villagers. My terrible experiences in London were no excuse for treating him ill.

I forced myself to smile and make polite conversation. "It's good to be home. Did anything interesting happen while I was gone?"

"I went to visit friends in Hebden Bridge," Mr. Nicholls said. "They're all reading a book called *Shirley*, by an author named Currer Bell." His eyes twinkled. He liked to pretend that Currer Bell's identity was still a secret—one that we shared. When he spoke the name, he always emphasized the word "Bell." He seemed to think it meant something special that I'd chose his middle name for my nom de plume. I'd never told him it was a joke that my sisters and I had played on him. "They had much to say about the scenes with the curates."

Everyone had too much to say about those scenes, which featured characters based on local clergymen. I'd portrayed them as fools. Some people thought my portraits were right on the mark. Others thought me disgraceful for lampooning men of God. Mr. Nicholls had found the scenes hilarious. He read them aloud to anyone who would listen.

"They especially like the character of Mr. Macarthey." That was the character based on Mr. Nicholls, who paraphrased, "'Being human, of course he had his faults; these, however, were what many would call virtues. Otherwise he was sane and rational, diligent and charitable.'"

Mr. Nicholls smiled proudly. I regretted that I'd let him off more lightly than the other clergymen. He thought it meant I liked him. When we reached the parsonage, he followed me up the stairs. "I'll just stop in for a word with your father." He added mischievously, "Ye'll find a surprise waiting for ye inside."

Having had enough surprises to last me the rest of my life, I warily opened the door. My best friend Ellen Nussey came hurrying into the hall. "Charlotte!" All smiles, dressed in a lace-trimmed green frock that complemented her blonde hair, she embraced me affectionately.

"Ellen." I was glad to see her, but she could have picked a better time. "What are you doing here?"

"I knew you were coming back from London, so I decided to

pop in." She giggled; her light blue eyes sparkled with excitement. Although thirty-four years old, Ellen often behaved like the school-girl she'd been when we'd first met. "I can't wait to hear all about your trip!"

She had been avidly interested in my literary career since she'd learned that I was Currer Bell. At first she'd been hurt because I hadn't told her earlier, but her gentle nature couldn't hold a grudge. She took vicarious pleasure from my doings, perhaps because her own life was dull. Born into a wealthy family, she'd never had to earn a living. Not having married, she occupied her-self with visiting her friends, fancy sewing, and caring for her elder-ly mother. Once I had envied her affluence; now I pitied her dependency and boredom, and I shared as much of my good for-tune with her as possible.

She noticed Arthur Nicholls standing in the doorway. "Oh, it's you. To what do we owe the pleasure of your company?"

Ellen disliked Mr. Nicholls, and not only because she found him sanctimonious. She'd always been possessive, but my fame had increased her tendency to resent other people I knew because she feared they might take her place as my best friend. I should have tried to talk her out of it ages ago, but I was reluctant to hurt her feelings. Ellen was so loyal, so ready to give of herself whenever I needed her. Ellen had helped me nurse Anne during her fatal illness and supported me during the awful time of Anne's passing. Whatever Ellen wanted in return, she deserved. If she tried to drive a wedge between me and other folk, I couldn't object, and I didn't want Mr. Nicholls around, either.

"I happened to see Miss Brontë, so I escorted her home," Mr. Nicholls said, clearly mystified as to why Ellen didn't like him. "I thought that since I was here, I might as well have a word with her father."

"By all means have one." Ellen waved him toward Papa's study. "Don't bother Charlotte anymore. She's probably exhausted from her trip. Give her some peace!" She put her arm around me. "You're just in time for breakfast. While we eat, you can tell me everything."

She took a second look at me, and her eyebrows rose. "Why, Charlotte, you've got a new frock. It's very nice." A shadow crossed her face. It wasn't that Ellen didn't like me to have new clothes; rather, she feared I would change into someone too elegant for the likes of her. "Why, I do believe you've bought a whole new outfit. Wasn't that a bit extravagant?"

I couldn't tell her that I'd paid nothing for the clothes; that would lead to questions about how I'd come by them. Ellen wasn't aware that I knew the Queen. Ellen had played a part in my adventures of 1848, but she didn't know the whole story. Fortunately, Papa emerged from his study and interrupted our conversation. "Ah, Charlotte. Welcome home."

"Hello, Papa," I said, as glad to see him as he clearly was to see me. "How are you?"

He was an imposing figure—tall and upright, with thick white hair, broad shoulders, and noble features. At the age of seventy-four, he still walked the moors every day, visiting his parishioners. "Just a touch of bronchitis," he said, fingering the white silk muffler he wore to protect his throat from drafts even in summertime. He squinted anxiously at me through his spectacles. "But what about you, Charlotte? You look thin and pale. Are you ill?"

Ever since Anne, Emily, and Branwell had died, Papa had been terrified of losing me as well. He constantly searched me for signs that I had consumption. "No, I'm fine," I said.

If I were to be tried for murder, he would have to know eventually, but I didn't want to upset him prematurely and tax his health. I was afraid of losing him, too; we were all the family that each of us had left.

"Ellen will take good care of you." Papa smiled fondly at her, then noticed Mr. Nicholls hovering by the door. "Oh, hello, Arthur. Won't you join us for breakfast?"

"Yes, thank ye."

Following us to the dining room, Arthur cast a triumphant glance at Ellen, who pouted and grabbed the chair next to mine so that he couldn't sit there. Our servant, Martha Brown, brought our oatmeal, eggs, bread, and tea. The others ate heartily, but my stomach was upset, and the tension between Ellen and Mr. Nicholls didn't help my appetite. Nonetheless, I was glad they were here. They occupied the places at the table that had once belonged to Anne and Emily. It was still hard for me to bear seeing those two vacant chairs.

"Did you meet anybody famous in London?" Ellen asked eagerly.

I told her about Mr. Thackeray and his lecture. That seemed a safe enough subject, but Ellen soon said, "How is your debonair Mr. George Smith?"

"He's not *my* Mr. Smith," I said, vexed because Ellen always teased me about him. She insisted that he had romantic feelings toward me. I had always told her not to be silly. Little had I known that he would prove her correct.

"But he is your special friend. You write to each other so often." Ellen raised her eyebrow at me and smiled at Mr. Nicholls.

I understood what she was about. She didn't want me to marry George, or anyone else, because my having a husband would leave me less time for her, but she wanted to serve notice on Mr. Nicholls that I was unavailable. She thought he was interested in me! And she was correct again. That was why he paid me such frequent attentions!

Mr. Nicholls looked startled and abashed, then mortified by the realization on my face. His face turned red. We couldn't meet each other's eyes.

"Has Mr. Smith proposed to you, Charlotte?" Papa asked anxiously. He didn't want me to marry, either. He often said that my health wasn't strong enough for marriage, and he didn't want me to go away and leave him all alone.

"No, indeed," I said. Not yet, at any rate.

"Well, I'm glad he doesn't have designs on you," Papa said, relieved.

"Maybe he doesn't," Ellen said, "but maybe someone closer to home does." She bent an accusing glare on Mr. Nicholls.

Papa froze, his teacup lifted halfway to his mouth. "Do you, Arthur?"

He stared at his curate, who sank low in his chair. I wanted to scold Ellen for stirring up trouble. I wanted to put my head on the table and groan.

"I—well, ah—" Mr. Nicholls blushed crimson all the way down to his clerical collar.

Papa set down his teacup. He rose from his chair in such a wrath that he reminded me of God expelling Adam and Eve from the Garden of Eden. Ellen looked delighted but scared. I desperately sought a way to forestall disaster. Noticing a movement outside the open window, I pointed and said, "What is that?"

Papa paused, drawing his breath. We never heard what he meant to say to his curate who'd betrayed his trust by plotting to steal his daughter. He, Ellen, and Mr. Nicholls looked toward the window. There was the head of a man, who smiled cheerily at us.

"Hey!" Mr. Nicholls said. "Who are ye?"

I'd staved off an explosion that would have rocked the parish, but dismay filled me. "Oliver Heald."

"At your service." Mr. Heald doffed his hat. "Good morning, Miss Brontë."

"Do you know this man?" Ellen asked.

"We met in London," Mr. Heald said. "I'm one of her most fervent admirers."

"What are you doing here?" I asked.

"I wanted to see where you live."

Ellen sighed in exasperation. "Not this again."

Mr. Heald wasn't the only curiosity seeker who'd ever bearded me in my den. Once, the vicar of Batley had shown up, demanded to see me, bullied Martha into letting him into the parlor, and stayed an hour before consenting to leave. Another time, some society ladies and gentlemen had dropped by. They'd included two Members of Parliament who had literary pretensions and wanted to meet Currer Bell. Their nerve had astounded me, but not as much as Oliver Heald's did.

"Mr. Heald, this is the third time you have imposed yourself upon me," I said. "Of all the inconsiderate people I have met, you take the prize! Please go away."

Mr. Heald ducked out of the window before I'd finished speaking. In a moment I heard the front door open, and Mr. Heald walked right into the dining room.

Ellen gasped. "How dare you?"

Mr. Nicholls rose and put himself between Mr. Heald and me. "Didn't you hear Miss Brontë? She doesn't want you here."

"Sir, you are trespassing," Papa said.

Mr. Heald just looked around in delight. "So this is your home." He wandered into the parlor, touching the furniture. "Oh, everything is lovely!"

We rushed after him. Ellen said, "I shall fetch the police!"

Papa hurried upstairs, then came back with the pistol he carried to protect himself when he walked the moors. He brandished it at Mr. Heald. "If you don't leave at once, I'll shoot!"

"Oh, dear." Mr. Heald looked taken aback, then smiled. "You must be the Reverend Brontë. I'm honored to make your acquaintance." He extended his hand to Papa, who was so surprised that he shook hands. "May I have the pleasure of being introduced to your friends?" He indicated Ellen and Mr. Nicholls.

I said, "No, you may not!" A sudden thought startled me out of my indignation. "How did you happen to arrive in Haworth at the same time as I? Were you on the same train?"

"Well, yes," Mr. Heald admitted.

"How did you find me? How did you follow me from London?"

"After Mr. Thackeray's lecture, I followed you to your publisher's house. I've been loitering outside it as often as I could, hoping for a glimpse of you. When I saw you come out last night—well, there you have it."

That explained how he'd found me at the zoo. I had thought myself adept at spotting people following me, but Mr. Heald had proven me wrong. I began to fear that he and his intentions were not what he purported. He'd accosted me at the zoo moments before the terrifying chase began. Now he'd turned up again, soon after the events that had stemmed from my arrest. How had Wilhelm Stieber discovered that I was in Newgate Prison? He had to have been keeping track of me through his informants. Did they include Oliver Heald? Suddenly the irksome little man didn't seem as harmless anymore.

"Who sent you?" I demanded. "Was it Wilhelm Stieber?"

"What?" His face was a picture of confusion. "Who?"

In my excitement I forgot to be discreet. "Are you working for Russia? Was it you who chased me at the zoo? Are you helping Wilhelm Stieber find Niall Kavanagh and his invention?"

"I'm afraid I don't know what you're talking about," Mr. Heald said.

Mr. Nicholls and Ellen looked at me as if I'd lost my mind. Ellen said, "My dear Charlotte, what *are* you talking about?" Papa's face showed dawning, dismayed comprehension.

"Tell me!" I shouted.

Backing away from me in fright, Mr. Heald said, "Nobody sent me. I came on my own. I only wanted to see you." He clasped his hands and extended them to me. "I swear!"

"You've upset Miss Brontë enough," Mr. Nicholls said. He seized Mr. Heald by the arm, propelled him toward the door, opened it, and shoved him out. Mr. Heald tumbled down the steps. Mr. Nicholls slammed the door. "Good riddance!"

I went to the parlor window and saw Mr. Heald limp down the hill. He cast a wistful, hurt look at me. I turned to face Papa, Ellen, and Mr. Nicholls.

Mr. Nicholls was puffed up because he'd rid us of the trespasser. "Now, Miss Brontë, would you be so good as to tell us the meaning of what you just said?"

I supposed he had the right to ask, but I couldn't tell him. "It didn't mean anything. Please just forget it. I'm so tired that I'm not making sense." Perhaps I was so tired that my suspicions about Oliver Heald were figments of my mind.

"Don't make excuses," Ellen said impatiently. "It's clear that something bad happened to you in London." Her eyes shone with excitement. "Did you stumble onto another murder?"

She knew about the murder that had plunged me into my adventures in 1848, for I'd told her about it and let her accompany me on some of my investigations.

"Are you in the sort of trouble that we had three years ago?" Papa said, concerned.

He knew the whole story. The only person present who knew nothing was Mr. Nicholls. "Murder?" All alarm, the curate looked at the rest of us. "What trouble?"

Ellen, Papa, and I exchanged looks. Theirs showed that they remembered that Mr. Nicholls wasn't in on the story. Mine warned them that they'd been sworn to secrecy.

"We will not talk about this any further," Papa said.

Mr. Nicholls bowed to Papa's authority. "Very well," he said, hurt because he'd been shut out of our circle. "But if Miss Brontë is in trouble, I want to help."

After too many people had lately refused to give me the help for which I'd asked, I liked Mr. Nicholls a little better for his willingness. "Thank you, but there's nothing you can do."

"She's right. She doesn't need you." Ellen moved to my side and put her arm through mine. "Charlotte, dear, let's go upstairs. You can tell me everything, and we'll decide what we're going to do."

"*We* aren't going to do anything." I stepped free of Ellen. "It's too dangerous for you."

She laughed airily. "That's what you said last time. And we had such fun." She gave Mr. Nicholls a pointed look. "Haven't you any duties elsewhere?"

He bristled. "As long as Miss Brontë is in danger, I'm staying."

"Stay if you like," I said, "but I must go."

How I regretted my impulse to return to Haworth! I'd found no peace, and Wilhelm Stieber must have mounted a search for me. He would track me to Haworth—sooner rather than later if Oliver Heald were indeed his spy. I had made a dire mistake by laying my trail to my home; I'd brought the danger to my people. The only way for me to guard their safety was to leave immediately.

"Go where?" Ellen said, upset because she saw that I meant to leave her behind.

Papa beckoned me, "Come into my study, Charlotte." He said to Ellen and Mr. Nicholls, "I'd like a private word with my daughter."

We went into the study. He shut the door, sat behind his desk, and motioned me into the chair opposite him. I braced myself for more questions. He thought a moment, then asked one I hadn't expected. "Do you remember the mask we had when you were a child?"

"Yes, Papa." I pictured it now—a comical paper goblin's face.

"I bade you to put it on. Then I asked, 'What do you think is the best book in the world?' and you replied . . ."

"The Bible," I said.

"I also asked your opinion on other important matters. You spoke up readily and truthfully. The mask made you feel free to speak your mind."

Not as free as he thought. I'd not forgotten that he knew it was I behind the mask, or that if I gave answers other than those he wanted, I would get a lecture.

"I wish you would speak your mind now, Charlotte." By drawing upon our history, Papa had bound me in a filial obligation tighter than the blanket gowns in Bedlam. "What on earth is going on? Does it involve John Slade?"

I couldn't deny him the truth, and I wanted at least one person who loved me and believed in me to know it. "Yes, Papa," I said, and told him everything.

He expressed all the concern, horror, and woe that I'd expected, but he didn't try to dissuade me from carrying out the plan I'd also confided to him. "You must do what you must to save Mr. Slade, yourself, and your nation." He chuckled sadly. "Of all my children, you are the most like me. You were all intelligent, and you all inherited my love of reading and writing, but only you wanted to take on the world, as I once did. A father shouldn't have a favorite among his children, but if I did, it would be you, Charlotte."

Tears stung my eyes. I'd always thought he loved Branwell best; I thought he regretted that his only surviving child was I, the least satisfactory.

"Losing you would be the death of me," Papa said. "But I will let you go on this mission of yours, with my blessing, if you will only promise me one thing."

Beware of blessings with strings attached. "What is it, Papa?"

He held up his hand. "Promise first."

Trapped by obligation and love, I said, "I promise."

Papa rose, opened the door, and summoned Ellen and Mr. Nicholls. "Pack your bags," he told them. "You are going with Charlotte. She has agreed to take you both."

I had never seen them so flabbergasted. Ellen said, "It would be most improper for Mr. Nicholls to travel with us." Mr. Nicholls looked amazed at his good fortune and stammered out his gratitude. I was horrified that Papa had saddled me with two guardians I didn't want and whose safety I feared for. I began to protest.

Papa cut us short with the stern look he gives parishioners who talk in church. "You promised, Charlotte," he said, then addressed Ellen and Mr. Nicholls: "Protect my daughter." His stare at Mr. Nicholls said he hadn't forgotten that his curate sought to woo his daughter away from him, but he would put that quarrel aside for now. "Should any harm come to her, I will hold you both responsible."

23

T HE SECRET ADVENTURES OF
JOHN SLADE

1851 January. Slade barely managed to escape the Kremlin.

The call for his blood went out minutes after he slipped away from his listening post in the Tsar's reception hall, where he'd heard the news that the British agents had been executed. As he raced through the palace, he heard the tread of boots, the soldiers searching for him. His fall from grace had been so swift that he couldn't stop to think. All he could do was run.

Emerging into the frigid night, Slade saw lit torches carried by search parties moving around the palaces and cathedrals. He shivered in the cold; he hadn't even had time to fetch his coat. Dogs barked. The army had brought out the wolfhounds to track him. The walls of the Kremlin stood between him and safety. His only hope of getting out alive was the escape route he'd installed in case of emergencies.

He headed for the strip of wooded parkland that extended alongside the wall from the Saviour Gate to the tower at the eastern corner of the Kremlin. As he neared it, he heard the cry: "There he is!"

Running footsteps clattered on the icy pavement behind him. The dogs bayed, too close. Slade leaped through the snow between the trees and fell against the wall. He ran his hands over it, searching in the dark for the iron spikes he'd driven into the mortar, one by one, during many nights. They formed a ladder up the wall. With the army thrashing through the woods in pursuit, Slade climbed.

His head cleared the trees. He pulled himself up onto the crenellated wall. Someone in the tower shouted, "He's up there!"

Gunshots cracked. Bullets pinged off the wall around Slade. He dropped into the trees on the other side. Branches battered him all the way down. A snowdrift broke his fall. He scrambled up. As he ran along the promenade that bordered the river, he dodged gunfire from other watchtowers. Bonfires on the riverbank illuminated a skating party. Above the music from an orchestra Slade heard the furious stampede of horses' hooves. Mounted soldiers rounded the corner of the Kremlin and charged toward him. He whirled. More horsemen came galloping from the other direction. He skidded down the riverbank and hid among the people gathered around a bonfire. They wore rich sable coats; they were members of the aristocracy. Up on the promenade, the troops halted, torches raised, looking for him, hesitant to fire into the crowd and risk killing somebody important. Slade waited, panting and freezing.

A group of merrymakers strolled toward a troika parked on the ice. Slade hurried along with them. When they climbed into the troika, neither they nor their driver noticed him sliding underneath. The horses pulled the troika across the ice while Slade clung to the bottom. The relief he felt was short-lived.

Nowhere in Moscow is safe for a man wanted by the Third Section.

In the morning Slade made his way through the back alleys of the city to his lodging house, only to find policemen loitering outside. He turned and hurried away. Even if the police hadn't already confiscated the money he kept in his room, he couldn't get to it without being caught. He mingled with the people who crowded the shops and outdoor markets. By sleight of hand he stole a coat, boots, and a fur hat. A loaf of bread and a string of sausages vanished under his coat. Warmly dressed, his hunger satisfied, he set out to find a way out of town.

Soldiers patrolled every road. Wilhelm Stieber had mounted a massive search for him. Slade didn't know how Stieber had discovered his true identity, but Stieber must have had surveillance on him, even though he'd never spotted it. Now, every city gate he approached was heavily guarded. Slade watched the sentries stop, inspect, and question men who fit his description. He was trapped.

24

✦

THE TOWN OF AMBLESIDE IS LOCATED IN THE LAKE DISTRICT in the far northwestern part of England, some fifty miles from Haworth. The journey was long and arduous, requiring us to change carriages three times. At first I was glad to have Ellen and Mr. Nicholls for company. If Wilhelm Stieber and his minions were following me, they would probably not attack all three of us and risk drawing attention to themselves. But Ellen made insulting comments to Mr. Nicholls, who lost his patience and snapped at her. They bickered in the station in Lancaster while we waited two hours for the train. On the train I pretended to sleep, but they argued in whispers until we alit at Windermere Station.

It was past seven o'clock in the evening. Here in these lofty altitudes, the air was thin, chilly, and moist. Breathing it cleansed my throat and lungs, which were parched by smoke and cinders from the train. The sun's silvery rays glinted through indigo and violet clouds that floated over a landscape of green hills that rose to mountainous, mist-veiled heights.

"Mr. Nicholls, go fetch our trunks," Ellen said.

He glowered because she'd spoken to him as if he were a dog, but he obeyed, and he hired a carriage for us. As we rode, Lake Windermere came into view, a long silver ribbon winding through lush woods. Here was the landscape that had inspired the great poets, Robert Southey and William Wordsworth. Lights sparkled like strewn golden beads from towns on shore. Above, flocks of geese winged, their calls plaintive and haunting.

"We'll obtain lodgings at an inn by the lake," Ellen said. "Charlotte likes the water."

"A secluded place in the hills would be safer," Mr. Nicholls said.

Ellen turned to me. "What do you think?"

I felt like a rope in a tug-of-war between two children. "By the lake." In order that Ellen and Mr. Nicholls wouldn't think I was taking sides, I added, "That's where he is likely to be."

"Where who is likely to be?" Ellen asked.

During the trip I'd refused to say why I wanted to go to the Lake District. "The man I've come to see. Dr. John Forbes. I consulted him about Anne's illness, as you may remember."

Fear showed on my companions' faces. Ellen said, "Charlotte, are you ill?"

"Are you here to seek treatment from Dr. Forbes?" Mr. Nicholls asked.

"No, I'm perfectly healthy. All I seek from Dr. Forbes is information."

My chance encounter with Dr. Forbes had led me to Bedlam and my fateful glimpse of John Slade. He had told me that he planned a holiday in Ambleside. Now I hoped he could steer my quest for the truth in the right direction.

"Information about what?" Ellen asked.

"About a private matter," I said.

She and Mr. Nicholls gave up nagging me for answers. We rode in silence into Ambleside, whose pretty stone cottages and shops lined narrow streets. Hikers equipped with knapsacks and walking sticks congregated at taverns. We chose a modest inn near the waterfront. After securing rooms for the night, we walked out down the street.

"Ambleside is a small town," I said. "It shouldn't be hard to find Dr. Forbes."

Find him we soon did, at the third inn we tried. The proprietor told us that the doctor had gone boating and should be back soon. We went down to the lake, which reflected the fading light from the sunset in a shimmery patchwork of silver, cobalt, and bronze. Swans glided on this like graceful white specters. Islands shrouded by mist rose in the distance, as mysterious as Avalon. A rowboat came skimming across the water. I heard the splash of oars; a lone man wielded them. He paddled the boat up to the dock where Ellen, Mr. Nicholls, and I stood.

"Dr. Forbes," I called.

He secured his boat, climbed onto the dock, and smiled. "Why, hello, Miss Brontë."

I introduced him to my companions. After handshakes and pleasantries, Dr. Forbes said, "What a coincidence that we should meet here. Are you on holiday, too?"

"I wish I were, and I'm afraid it's no coincidence. You once said that if I needed your assistance, I should ask. So here I am."

Alarm erased Dr. Forbes's smile. "Is it about that business at Bedlam?"

I deduced that someone there had written to him about the murders, my second visit, and the fact that the police's suspect was the inmate I'd claimed was my friend. I could tell that Dr. Forbes would rather not involve himself with a grisly crime, an escaped lunatic, or my delusions.

"No." I was becoming more adept at lying. I met his gaze, and my voice didn't waver as I said, "I need information about a scientist named Niall Kavanagh."

Dr. Forbes's eyebrows lifted. "Niall Kavanagh." He sounded relieved to learn that I wanted nothing more. "That's a name I've not heard in a while."

"But you are familiar with him?" I asked.

"Yes, indeed. What do you want to know?"

I'd gambled that the community of scientists was as small and gossipy as that of the literati. How glad I was that my gamble had paid off! "I want to know everything."

"That would take a while to tell," Dr. Forbes said with a smile. "Will you and your friends join me for dinner?"

➤✦◄

We dined at his inn. The dining room was bright with lamplight, warm from a blazing fire in the hearth, and crowded with the inn's other guests. They noisily regaled one another with stories of the adventures they'd had that day. The larger tables were all occupied, so Dr. Forbes and I sat at a table for two in a corner, my companions across the room. That suited me fine, although Ellen and Mr. Nicholls craned their necks in a futile attempt to hear what we were saying.

"At one time I knew Niall Kavanagh very well," Dr. Forbes said as we ate a simple but tasty meal of bread, cheese, meat pie, and pickles. "We were both members of the Royal Society of science. Until Kavanagh was expelled."

"Expelled for what reason?" I asked.

"For conduct unbecoming to a member. He had a great talent for science, but a greater talent for offending people." Dr. Forbes noticed my confusion and said, "I'd better start at the beginning, with the basic facts about the man.

"Niall Kavanagh is Irish by birth. His father, Sir William Kavanagh, is head of a whiskey brewery that's been in the family for more than a hundred years. The family estate is called Clare House. It's in County Wicklow. He would be about forty years old now. He came to England as a young man, to study chemistry and biology at Oxford. He was the top scholar in his class, and he cut quite a handsome figure, but the other students looked down on him because he was Irish and harassed him because he was a Roman Catholic."

My father had endured many slights when he'd come from his native Ireland to attend Cambridge, and I supposed that anti-Irish and anti-Catholic sentiment had still run high at the universities in more recent years.

"He retaliated by mixing up a foul-smelling chemical in his laboratory and pouring it under the doors of his harassers' rooms," Dr. Forbes said. "The college had to evacuate an entire building for a week."

Men at the next table were raising glasses, reciting comical poems, drinking, and cheering. Dr. Forbes said, "Kavanagh was brought before the college authorities and charged with malicious misbehavior. He freely admitted what he'd done. He also ranted about the injustices that England had perpetuated against Ireland. He was almost sent down. But one of the dons spoke up in his defense, took him under his wing, and promised to keep him in line. Kavanagh became his research assistant. The work they did on contagious diseases earned Kavanagh a membership in the Royal Society and a teaching post at Oxford. Kavanagh's future looked bright, until he published a paper about some new experiments. He gave all the credit to himself and none to his mentor, and he criticized his mentor's earlier work. They had a falling-out. Then he offended the Royal Society by airing wild scientific theories. He claimed that tiny, invisible creatures cause diseases. Can you imagine that?"

Dr. Forbes laughed, and so did I. Everyone knows that diseases are caused by bad air.

"He made himself even more unpopular by engaging in affairs with his colleagues' wives," Dr. Forbes said. "The upshot was that Kavanagh lost his place in the Society and Oxford packed him off on a research expedition to Africa. While there, he caught brain fever. When he came back to England two years later, he was drastically changed—thin, haggard, and wasted. He neglected to bathe, shave, or comb his hair. His eyes burned with a strange light, as if some African devil had taken possession of him. He locked himself inside his laboratory and worked around the clock. He wouldn't tell anyone what he was doing, but he boasted that he was on the verge of a major breakthrough that would change the world."

Had it led to the invention of the weapon sought by Wilhelm Stieber? I felt sure it must have.

"Then his students began falling ill. They claimed Kavanagh had used them as test subjects in his experiments and had poisoned them. The college investigated, but found no proof that he'd caused their illnesses. Their symptoms were different, ranging from fever and coughs to gastric upsets and eye ailments. But one of the students died, and Kavanagh already had such a bad reputation that he was dismissed from his post. That was five years ago,"

Dr. Forbes concluded. "Kavanagh left Oxford and dropped out of public life."

Niall Kavanagh sounded like a brilliant but troubled man. I reexamined what Slade had told me about Kavanagh in the new light of what Dr. Forbes had just said. Niall Kavanagh was vindictive toward people who abused him. He had a grudge against the English in general. He had no loyalty toward his mentor or his colleagues; he was self-centered, with no inhibition against doing whatever he pleased. The brain fever he'd contracted in Africa had likely worsened his natural bad tendencies. If indeed he had experimented on his students, he had no respect for human life, which he had readily endangered for the sake of science. And this was the man who, according to Slade, had invented a weapon powerful enough to win a war.

If Niall Kavanagh fell in with Wilhelm Stieber and the Tsar, woe betide England!

"Have I upset you, Miss Brontë?" Dr. Forbes said. "I am truly sorry."

"There's no need to apologize. I asked about Niall Kavanagh, you answered, and I thank you." We ate in silence for a moment; then I said, "Have you seen Dr. Kavanagh recently?"

"Not in these five years. But I've heard that he published a pamphlet advocating Catholic rights and joined a branch of the radical group, Young Ireland, that demonstrated in London during the revolutions of 1848."

"Do you know where he might be?"

Dr. Forbes hesitated. "May I ask what your interest in him is?"

"I'm afraid it's a private matter," I said.

"If you mean to go looking for Kavanagh, I must advise you against it. He is an unpleasant man at best, and a dangerous one at worst."

"I'll keep that in mind. But if I don't find him, it will be worse than if I do."

Dr. Forbes studied me, seeking the meaning in my cryptic remark. He said reluctantly, "Very well." He laid down his fork and folded his napkin. "Last November, I ran into a friend from the Royal Society. His name is Metcalf; he is a physician. He told me he was a member of a commission formed to investigate sanitary conditions in the slums of London. He went about inspecting houses and tenements. One day during the previous summer he knocked on the door of an old, decrepit house, and the man who answered was Niall Kavanagh. Dr. Metcalf was shocked by his appearance. Kavanagh was wearing dirty, torn clothes. He looked as if he hadn't slept in weeks and he smelled as if he'd been drinking heavily. Dr. Metcalf tried to speak to him, to offer help. But Kavanagh shouted at Dr. Metcalf to go away, and he slammed the door. That's the last I've heard of Kavanagh."

This sighting was a year past, but it was my only clue to Kavanagh's whereabouts. "Did Dr. Metcalf say where this house was?"

"Not the exact location," Dr. Forbes said. "But he did mention that it was a white terraced house on Flower and Dean Street. In Whitechapel."

By seeking out Dr. Forbes, I had gone back to the point where my perils had begun. Now my path lay in other familiar territory. Niall Kavanagh had been sighted in Whitechapel, the very neighborhood of London in which I had witnessed Katerina's murder; now, to Whitechapel I must return.

I parted from Dr. Forbes and joined Ellen and Mr. Nicholls. As we walked through the cold, misty night toward our inn, Ellen said, "What did you and Dr. Forbes talk about?"

"A mutual acquaintance," I said.

"Did you get what you came for?"

"More or less."

Ellen fell silent, and I felt bad because my evasiveness had hurt her feelings. Mr. Nicholls said, "What shall we do now?"

"We should retire for the night." I was exhausted.

"That suits me." Mr. Nicholls yawned, bleary-eyed and bloated from a long day and a large supper. "What about tomorrow? Are we going back to Haworth?"

"Back to Haworth! Why, we've only just gotten here!" Ellen turned her pique at me on Mr. Nicholls. "How can you even think of going home?"

To his credit, he refused to be provoked into another quarrel. "If Miss Brontë wants to go, we'll go. If not, we'll stay."

"We'll stay another day," I said. "Tomorrow we'll rent a boat and go rowing on the lake."

"That sounds capital," Mr. Nicholls said happily.

"Yes, quite." Ellen cheered up, too.

Late that night, while Ellen slept soundly in her bed in the room we shared, I wrote two notes by candlelight. The first was to Papa:

> *Forgive me for breaking my promise. I cannot allow Ellen and Mr. Nicholls to accompany me. It would put them in grave danger. Please do not blame them. Whatever happens to me is my fault. I will explain later.*

I only hoped I would live to explain. I was bound for the place where a fiend killed and mutilated women, in the city where I was wanted for murder. Would I ever see Papa again?

The second note I addressed to Ellen and Mr. Nicholls:

> *Forgive me for leaving you. It is for your own good. Where I am going next, I must go alone.*

I left the notes on the table for Ellen to find in the morning. Then I packed my things and quietly departed.

25

> ✦ ✦ <

THE SECRET ADVENTURES OF
JOHN SLADE

1851 February. That winter in Moscow was the longest and
coldest winter Slade had ever known. By day he picked pockets in
the streets and stole money from alms boxes in churches. At night
he went to ground in Kitrovka, the haunt of brigands, drunks,
itinerant laborers, artists down on their luck, and fugitives from
the law.

A permanent pall of smoke and mist hung over the market-
place in Kitrovka. Vendors sold sausages and herring from stalls set
up in the snow; toothless women kept pots of soup warm under
their skirts. Dirty, unshaven, and haggard, Slade blended in with
Kitrovka's populace. He lived in its shelters—low houses with dark,
smoky rooms that stank of boots, latrines, and cheap tobacco. The
men slept side by side on and under bunks made of boards, like
corpses dressed in rags. Fleas, lice, bedbugs, and rats abounded.
Fights broke out often. Slade never stayed in the same place two
nights in a row, because the police made the rounds of the shelters,
looking for fugitives. He caught a bad cold that developed into a
wracking cough. Still, he was thankful for the blizzards that swept
through Moscow: the police didn't like working outdoors during
them, and the manhunt for him died down after a few weeks. By
then Slade had saved up enough money for a long trip.

One frozen, gray morning he waved down a sleigh on Yauzky

Boulevard and said to the driver, "Take me to Sergeev Posad." That was a town some forty miles northeast of Moscow. Slade had a friend there who would smuggle him out of Russia.

The driver was a squat, red-nosed man with icicles in his shaggy beard. He looked Slade over and sneered. "I don't give free rides to beggars."

"I can pay. I'll give you fifty rubles now and fifty when we get to Sergeev Posad."

Greed vied with suspicion in the driver's eyes. "You must be wanted by the law. Double the price, and we have a deal." He held out his hand, and Slade dropped a hundred rubles into it. "But we can't go now. It'll be safer after dark."

Slade had no choice but to consent. "Where should we meet?"

"Behind the Ryady Bazaar. Eleven o'clock."

The night was as still as if an ice age had paralyzed the city. The smoke from thousands of chimneys rose in vertical columns. Trudging through the snow, Slade avoided the main avenues where street lamps burned, but the snow reflected light from the full moon and a million stars onto him. He felt conspicuous and vulnerable, alone in the glacial landscape. Twice he thought he heard footsteps nearby. Twice he stopped, listened, looked around, and detected no one. Ill and exhausted, desperate to leave Moscow, Slade ignored his instincts.

The four people converged upon him from different directions. They cornered him in an alley bordered by the blank walls and locked rear doors of shops. Two blocked each end of the alley. Slade cursed, angry at himself for getting trapped. He turned in a circle, viewing his captors. One was a beggar who wore layers of clothes, his feet bound in rags. The second was a hunter dressed in smelly, uncured leather and fur; the third a dumpy woman in long skirts and babushka; the fourth a slender man in the kind of cheap black coat and hat worn by many men in Moscow, including Slade himself. Slade realized that he'd seen these people before, separately, on several occasions. Maybe they were brigands who worked as a team; maybe they had marked him out as a target and had followed him in order to rob him. But Slade had an inkling that the truth was much worse.

"The great John Slade," the hunter said. His face was smeared with soot. His eyes gleamed with malice. "We meet for the first and last time."

He spoke English, his accent as British as high tea at Windsor Castle. Shock coursed through Slade as he realized who these people were and what they meant to do.

The woman reached inside her coat. Slade lunged at the same moment she pulled out a knife. He caught her wrist as she tried to stab him. She was stronger than he'd expected—she was a man in disguise. Weakened by illness and starvation, Slade could barely hold her off while she forced the blade toward his throat. Her companions drew daggers. They rushed Slade from behind.

He spun around, hauling her with him. The beggar jabbed at Slade. His weapon plunged into the fake woman's back. She howled and staggered. Slade flung her at her companions. Her body struck the three men; they fell. Slade raced out of the alley, toward the Ryady Bazaar. The streets outside its cavernous buildings were empty of the crowds that shopped inside them by day. As Slade ran, he heard the assassins galloping over the rutted, frozen snow, gaining on him. The sleigh stood outside the bazaar. He was ten paces away from it when three men leaped out of the sleigh, drew pistols on him, and fired.

Slade dropped flat on the snow. Bullets zinged over him. Screams sounded behind him, then thuds. The shots had hit his pursuers. Slade scrambled and crawled in a desperate attempt to flee. The three men from the sleigh ran toward him. One of them was Plekhanov, the man who'd recruited Slade into the Third Section. He and the other police fired again. Someone tackled Slade. Looking backward, he saw that only three of the assassins lay dead; the slender man in black hung onto his legs. Slade kicked and fought. He and the assassin rolled in the snow while they battled over the knife in the assassin's hand. The police yelled. A whip cracked. Slade heard hooves crunch on snow, the grating of the chains that towed the sleigh, and the rumble of its runners. He broke free of the assassin and ran toward the sleigh as it skimmed down the street. He jumped aboard.

The police surrounded the assassin and fired shot after shot into him. They thought he was Slade. The driver flailed his whip at Slade and cried, "Get off!"

"You sold me out to the Third Section," Slade said. Furious, he grabbed the whip, beat the driver with its butt, and pushed him off the sleigh. He seized the reins and whipped the horses. As the police discovered their mistake and came running after him, the horses sped forward in a gallop. The sleigh picked up speed; the police fell behind. Slade gasped in relief and triumph.

He was free to make his way back to England. There he would hunt down Wilhelm Stieber, who must have already gone there to further his plan for Russia to gain unrivaled power over the world. When Slade found Stieber, there would be hell to pay.

26

>‹‹‹

WHILE DESCRIBING MY RECENT EXPERIENCES, I HAVE MORE than once remarked that reality parallels fiction. Indeed, the story of Jane Eyre seems eerily prophetic in hindsight. Now, after fleeing the Lake District, I found myself living her flight from Thornfield Hall. Both of us were leaving all that was familiar, comfortable, and dear, to venture into an uncertain future.

Not a tie holds me to human society at this moment. Gentle reader, may you never feel what I then felt!

There were profound differences between her situation and mine, however. Jane had run from Mr. Rochester, in order to save him and herself from sin. I was running toward John Slade, and I must prove him and myself innocent of terrible crimes. Jane drew comfort from nature—a lovely summer day, sunshine, pastures, and streams. On that cloudy morning when I arrived in Whitechapel, I found slums, dirt, and unwashed humanity. She had lain down by the roadside to die; I followed the trail to Niall Kavanagh. Yet neither of us had second thoughts about the wisdom of our actions.

No reflection was to be allowed now: not one glance was to be cast back; not even one forward. The burden must be carried; the suffering endured; the responsibility fulfilled.

I had endowed Jane with the strength to survive. Now I drew strength from her. If she could prevail, then so could I. Furthermore, I had advantages that I'd not given Jane. Lord Palmerston had sent me off from Osborne House with a pocketbook full of money. I was able to buy a ticket for a first-class carriage on the train to London; and, when I arrived, to secure a room in a first-class hotel. I went shopping and splurged on three expensive frocks, with accessories to match. I also bought an imitation-gold wedding ring. Standing before the mirror in my room, I looked every inch the fashionable London matron. If Wilhelm Stieber and the police were looking for a bedraggled fugitive in prison uniform, they would never spot me.

The neighborhood where Dr. Forbes's friend had seen Niall Kavanagh had been affluent and respectable years ago. The white stucco building on Flower and Dean Street was part of a terrace left over from the Regency era—three row houses with ironwork balconies and curved bow windows. On the corner was a tavern where foreigners sat drinking. Across the street rose grimy, newer brick tenements. The terrace itself had fallen into disrepair. The stucco was gray with soot, the ironwork rusty. As I mounted the cracked stone steps, a man left the tavern and sauntered toward me.

"You want room?" He was stout and wore the sort of clothes common to London bankers. His hair was as sleek as mink's fur, topped by a black skullcap. "I landlord."

I halted, intimidated by his size, his foreignness, and the suspicion in his dark eyes. "No, I am not looking for a room to rent."

"Then what you want?"

"I'm looking for Dr. Niall Kavanagh. Does he live here?"

"He gone."

I was disappointed, even though I'd known it was too much to expect that I would find Dr. Kavanagh on my first try. "When did he go?"

The landlord shrugged.

"Do you know where he went?"

"No." Irritation darkened the landlord's features. "Why so many people come ask about Kavanagh?"

I shouldn't have been surprised to hear I wasn't the first. "Who else asked you?"

"A Russian. He didn't give name."

Excitement filled me. "What did he look like?"

"Why I should remember?"

I felt sure the Russian was John Slade. He must have found out about this house from one of his mysterious sources. I had picked up his trail! "When was he here?"

"Two, three months ago."

My heart sank: Slade's trail was very cold. Another troubling thought struck me: "Has anyone else asked about Dr. Kavanagh?"

"Two English policemen. They don't wear uniform, they don't say they were police, but I know police. They the same in every country."

I had expected to hear that three Prussians—Wilhelm Stieber and his two henchmen—had come. I was very glad that they hadn't. "Did they say why they wanted him?"

"No, and I don't ask. I don't trust police, I don't poke my nose in their business. I tell them same thing I tell you: I don't know where is Kavanagh. Now I am tired of talking about him. Go!"

He pointed emphatically toward the street. His belligerence and my disappointment were too much for me. Tears welled up in my eyes. "I'm sorry to have bothered you," I said humbly.

I started to tiptoe away, but the landlord underwent a sudden transformation. His anger melted; his hard gaze softened. "Please don't cry. I don't mean hurt you. I'm sorry."

It appeared that some things were the same in every culture: some men cannot bear to see a woman cry. Many women take advantage of this fact, but I had always thought myself above employing feminine weakness to get what I wanted from the stronger sex. But now my involuntary use of the tactic served me well.

"I make it up to you," the landlord said. "When Kavanagh go, he leave some things here. I show you. All right?"

My tears dried up. If Kavanagh's things should provide clues to his location, this peace offering would be a gift beyond compare. "Did you show them to the police or the Russian?"

"No. I don't go out of my way to help them. But for you,

madam—" The landlord beckoned me down a flight of steps to the cellar. "Come."

I know better than to go into cellars with strange men, but I ignored prudence. We stepped into a black cavern that smelled of damp and decay. The landlord lit a lamp and shone it around the room. The cellar looked to be a repository for items that no one wanted, that had accumulated since the house had been built. Picture frames, washboards, a laundry mangle, broken furniture, and pieces of machinery stood on the earthen floor. Wooden boxes were stacked high against the brick walls. The landlord fetched two boxes that looked newer than the rest. He set them and the lamp on a desk that was missing its drawers and said, "I wait outside."

My heart beat fast with anticipation as I opened the first box. It contained oddly shaped glassware—cylinders with measurement markings etched on them; flat, round dishes with lids; a rack of tiny tubes; a globe with a long, angled neck. If I were educated in science, they might have given me an idea as to the nature of Dr. Kavanagh's work; but alas, I have no scientific knowledge whatsoever.

The second box held dirty clothes. I wrinkled my nose as I examined them. Kavanagh had left nothing in the pockets. In the bottom of the box lay a journal bound in black leather. Under it was a mess of papers. I opened the journal. The pages were warped, some stuck together. The first bore the inscription, "N. K." The next pages contained lines of handwriting that was full of dramatic flourishes. The ink had run in many places, and even where it had not, the text was unintelligible—scientific terms, symbols, and equations. Not until I had perused the journal almost to its end did I find any entries written in plain English.

The words "Mary Chandler" leapt off the page at me. That was the name of one of the women murdered in Whitechapel! My heart began to pound as I saw two other familiar names. The entries read:

Mary Chandler. Age 28, streetwalker. Height 5 feet 1 inch. Weight 120 lbs.

21 October 1849, initial contact, St. George's Yard. 23 October 1849, 1st examination; exposed. 25 November 1849, 2nd examination; sacrificed.

Catherine Meadows. Age 19, streetwalker. Height 4 feet 11 inches. Weight 100 lbs.

2 January 1850, initial contact, Old Montague Street. 3 February 1850, 1st examination; exposed. 7 April 1850, 2nd examination; sacrificed.

Jane Anderson. Age 29, streetwalker. Height 5 feet 4 inches. Weight 131 lbs.

13 April 1850, initial contact, Commercial Road. 17 May 1850, 1st examination; exposed. 20 June 1850, 2nd examination; sacrificed.

I puzzled over these cryptic notations. It appeared that Niall Kavanagh had known all three murder victims. His notes suggested a scientific rather than a sexual interest in them. I remembered Dr. Forbes telling me about the students who'd claimed they'd been poisoned by Kavanagh. They thought he'd made them unwitting subjects in his experiments. Had he done the same with Mary Chandler, Catherine Meadows, and Jane Anderson?

The three women had belonged to the most impoverished, desperate class of humanity; their kind was at the mercy of the men they solicited. A nauseous chill crept into my stomach as I envisioned the scene that must have taken place on the dates when Niall Kavanagh had his "initial contact" with each woman: *On a dark, lonely street in Whitechapel, she stands under a gas lamp. His shadowy figure approaches her through the fog. She calls an invitation to him; he stops; they bargain. She takes his arm and walks off with him, never imagining what evil designs he has in mind.*

I gazed upon the last word of each entry: *sacrificed.* One didn't need to be a scientist to deduce what that meant. A parson's daughter understood the word in all its permutations. To sacrifice was to destroy or surrender something for the sake of something else, as Jesus had sacrificed his life on the cross. To sacrifice meant to make an offering of a human, animal, food, drink, or other valuable thing, to a deity, as Abraham had been willing to slay his son Isaac at God's bidding. *Sacrifice* had age-old associations with violence and murder. As my lips silently formed the word, I could almost taste blood. A thunderous shock reverberated through me.

Niall Kavanagh had killed those women. I'd come looking for a scientist who'd invented a gun that could change the world, and I'd discovered the identity of the Whitechapel Ripper.

27

JOHN SLADE WAS INNOCENT OF THE WHITECHAPEL MURDERS, I now knew beyond doubt.

Even as my spirits soared with elation, the weight of reason hauled them down to earth. The entries in the journal were not a confession of Niall Kavanagh's guilt. I reread them, hoping to find evidence I'd missed. What exactly had happened between Kavanagh and the women? Had he poisoned them as he'd done his students? Was that what "exposed" meant? I surmised that he'd examined the women in the manner that a physician examines his patients; but what had Kavanagh been looking to find?

Nothing in the entries answered my questions. I turned to the next page. It bore a pen-and-ink drawing of a woman, simple but skillfully done. She was naked, her fleshy body and her breasts and genitals accurately depicted; yet the drawing didn't look erotic. It reminded me of the illustrations in a medical text I'd once seen. Under the drawing was written "C. Meadows." Her curly hair and facial features were lightly sketched. The detail rendered in the heaviest line was a Y-shaped mark, its fork on her chest, its vertical line running down her stomach. A sense of dread gripped me. As I turned the page, my hand trembled.

Another drawing of the same woman appeared, but here her torso was depicted as if the skin, underlying muscles, and ribs had been cut away. I knew that scientists performed dissections in front of public audiences, but I'd never witnessed one, and I'd never seen the inside of a human body. A tube ran down the woman's throat and branched into two lobes that appeared to be her lungs. Blood vessels fed into a fist-shaped heart. Another tube extended from her throat to a curved pouch that I took for her stomach, which was connected to a mass of coiled, sausage-like bowels. I felt as fascinated and ashamed as if I were poring over indecent pictures. I remembered that the Whitechapel Ripper had mutilated his victims, and shock hit me as I comprehended what I was seeing.

Niall Kavanagh had dissected the women he'd killed, as part of his scientific experiments. Here was the evidence. The police must not have recognized what he'd done; they'd thought the murders and mutilations were sheer, meaningless carnage. A wave of nausea sloshed through me. I turned to the last page, even though I dreaded finding something worse.

It showed an enlarged view of the woman's body from waist to groin. The bowels were parted to show a pear-shaped organ attached to two thin tubes, each ending in a clot of fibers and a little round sac. At first I couldn't imagine what these organs might be. A lady is conditioned not to think of what is inside her body that cannot be mentioned in public. A detail at the side of the page showed the pear-shaped organ removed from the abdomen and cut open. Inside was nestled a creature like a salamander, with a black spot for an eye. Realization struck.

These were the female organs. The pear-shaped one was the womb, the creature inside an unborn baby. The Whitechapel Ripper's victims had been found with their female organs missing. Niall Kavanagh had removed them before he'd dumped the bodies in the streets. Catherine Meadows had been with child. How would Kavanagh have known, and how could he have drawn the child unless he'd sliced her womb and looked inside?

Although my powers of imagination serve me well when I write my stories, they were my undoing now. I pictured a nude woman laid on a table, and a knife slicing through her flesh. Hands reached inside the slit, pushed aside red, glistening bowels. They cut out the female organs and held them aloft, crimson and dripping. My mental picture was so vivid that dizziness swept over me. Black dots stippled the room and coalesced. On the brink of fainting, I grasped the desk for support. I bent my head and breathed deeply until the blackness receded. As I hastily closed the journal, I became aware of voices outside.

"Kavanagh not live here anymore," the landlord said.

Another man asked a question, too quietly for me to discern his words, but his voice was too familiar, and the last one I wanted to hear.

"I don't know," the landlord said impatiently.

The man spoke again. He was Wilhelm Stieber. He was still looking for Niall Kavanagh, and had somehow tracked him to this house.

"No, you can't look around," the landlord said.

I crouched, paralyzed by terror that Stieber wouldn't take no for an answer.

"This private property," the landlord said. "You trespassing."

I crept to the stairs and looked up them. The open door framed a rectangle of daylight. In it stood four men, my view of them limited to their trousers and shoes. The landlord's backed toward the house as those of the other men advanced on him. Stieber had brought his two henchmen. Would the landlord tell them I was here?

Looking around, I saw a door at the back of the room. I ran for it, then reversed and picked up Niall Kavanagh's journal and papers. I fled through the door just as footsteps descended toward the cellar, and I bolted up slippery stairs to a fenced yard. Racing for the gate, I dared not look behind me: if I should see Wilhelm Stieber, I would die of fright. I burst through the gate; I ran through yards behind other houses. I didn't stop until I reached the Whitechapel high street. There I stood, panting from exertion, amid the crowds.

A block away was an omnibus—a long carriage drawn by a team of horses. It stopped to let out passengers. I hurried to it, climbed aboard, paid the fare, and sat beside an old woman with a basket of smelly fish. I traveled a mile or so; the London scenery blurred past as I watched to make sure that no one was following me. Then I felt safe enough to let down my guard and attend to the prize I'd stolen. I examined the papers. Anticipation turned to disappointment: page after page was covered with equations and scientific language. I found reprints of articles from learned publications, and incomprehensible diagrams featuring lines, arrows, numbers, and geometric figures. The two sheets I could read were a grocery list and a bill from a tailor.

But I couldn't believe that a clue to the whereabouts of Niall Kavanagh was not among the material that I'd risked my life to obtain. I turned over diagrams and found one whose other side bore a note penned in a clear, bold, masculine hand. I read:

Our agreement of 20 July 1850 is hereby confirmed. A research laboratory has been procured for you. It is located at the old workhouse in Tonbridge. The facilities and equipment you requested will be delivered on 18 August. Remember to keep all matters associated with your work and our agreement strictly confidential.

The note wasn't signed; however, I'd seen that handwriting before. Its strong forward slant, high ascenders, and emphatic punctuation marks were distinctly familiar. But where had I seen it? Gazing at the note, I had a memory of a desk strewn with papers that bore the same handwriting as the note I held. A man rose from behind the desk. It was Lord Eastbourne.

So many thoughts barraged my mind that I could not immediately sort them out. The note proved that Lord Eastbourne and Niall Kavanagh had entered into a contract under which Kavanagh would receive a laboratory furnished by Lord Eastbourne. I recalled Slade telling me that Kavanagh was building a model of his invention for the British government, which was keeping him hidden. Lord Eastbourne must be the official charged with installing Kavanagh in a secret location.

So many things that I had wondered about were now explained.

Lord Eastbourne had pretended he didn't know about Kavanagh and the invention because they were a government secret that he wasn't permitted to reveal. He'd left me to languish in Newgate Prison because he couldn't let me run loose, reveal what I knew, and interfere with Foreign Office business.

Yet so many questions were still unanswered. If Lord Eastbourne was working with Kavanagh to build the secret weapon, then why would Lord Palmerston be unaware of it? After all, Lord Palmerston was Lord Eastbourne's superior. But I would swear in church that Palmerston didn't know. At Osborne House I'd seen nothing in his manner to suggest that he'd only been pretending to doubt my story about Kavanagh. I had to conclude that his ignorance was genuine, and so must be the Queen's.

And why had Lord Eastbourne asked me whether Katerina had told me Niall Kavanagh's whereabouts? He, of all people, should have known them.

More questions had to do with John Slade. Why had Lord Eastbourne seemed unappreciative of Slade's efforts to protect Kavanagh and the work he was doing for the British Empire? Why was Lord Eastbourne instead so eager to brand Slade a traitor? Why had Lord Eastbourne been unwilling to reinvestigate Slade's case, discover the truth, and help me rescue Slade?

I could not answer these questions, and now I faced the most immediate one of all: What should I do with the journal and the note?

My first impulse was to run to the police and show them the evidence that Niall Kavanagh was the Whitechapel Ripper and I was innocent. But caution forestalled me. Nothing in the journal spelled out the fact that Kavanagh had killed Mary Chandler, Jane Anderson, or Catherine Meadows. The police would think I was clutching at straws, and so might a jury. The fact that I'd left prison before being officially released wouldn't lend me credibility. Moreover, the journal and the note didn't prove that John Slade was not a traitor. If I turned myself in to the police now, they would throw me back in prison, and I would lose my chance to exonerate Slade.

As the hot, crowded omnibus carried me past the drab cityscape of Whitechapel, I realized that I must give up all hope of a quick end to my troubles with the law. There was but one feasible course of action, which required me to remain a fugitive a little longer.

28

➤⟡⟡

AFTER RETRIEVING MY POSSES-
SIONS FROM MY HOTEL AND SET-
tling the bill, I boarded a train to Tonbridge, a market town twenty-
five miles southeast of London, and I arrived just before five
o'clock. A Norman castle overlooking the River Medway attested
to the town's ancient history, as did many buildings that dated
from the Middle Ages. I engaged a room at the Rose and Crown,
a sixteenth-century Tudor coaching inn. There were few coach
travelers in these days of railways, but the inn was still very grand,
a three-story brick structure that dominated the high street. I registered as "Mrs. Charlotte Bell" and wore my fake wedding ring.
When I asked the proprietor for directions to the old workhouse,
he said, "The old workhouse is closed, madam. You'll be wanting
the new one."

He eyed me curiously: in my smart new clothes, I did not
appear to need any workhouse. Workhouses were institutions that
sheltered the poor, who labored inside them in exchange for bed
and board. The population of poor had swelled of late due to
declines in agriculture and mass unemployment. Hundreds of new
workhouses, some as large as villages, had been built all across
England. The older, smaller establishments had been demolished
or put to other use.

"No," I said, "I want the old one." Lord Eastbourne's note had
been specific.

"Suit yourself, madam." The proprietor gave me directions.

As soon as the porter had carried my trunk to my room and I had freshened myself, I set out. It was a warm, golden evening, but I carried my umbrella in case the clouds on the horizon brought rain. I didn't know what I would do when I found Dr. Kavanagh— or how to proceed from finding him to finding Slade. My quest was like a novel that I made up as I went along.

The old workhouse was located on a street aptly named Poorhouse Lane. It was a Tudor-style mansion with half-timbered walls, two stories high, its slate roof studded with chimneys, gables, and dormers, set apart from other houses in the area by extensive grounds. These were enclosed within a vine-covered brick wall. Two huge, ancient chestnut trees flanked the ironwork gate and its crumbling stone pillars. More trees loomed over outbuildings around the mansion. Nothing about its appearance struck me as unusual, but the other senses often perceive what the eye cannot. The body reacts before the mind can articulate what it thinks. I felt such an immediate, instinctive revulsion that I stopped ten paces from the gate. The house was picturesque, with its many-paned windows that reflected the golden light from the setting sun. What caused me this strong urge to flee?

I believe that places can absorb the evil that humans have done or suffered within them. Workhouses are cauldrons of misery, where men, women, and children live in squalid conditions, labor hard at tasks such as stone breaking, and are abused by cruel masters. Maybe their ghosts haunted this workhouse. Or was it Niall Kavanagh's madness I sensed?

Curiosity overrode instinct. I moved toward the gate. A breeze stirred the air; from the workhouse issued a faint stench of decay. My nose must have registered it and warned me off before my brain had. I halted at the gate, which hung open on rusty hinges. Beyond it a path of broken flagstones led between overgrown bushes. I shook my head in disappointment and vexation at myself. How rash had been my decision to come! What had I expected—that Slade would magically appear, like a pot of gold at the end of a rainbow? Alas, I had. Since he was nowhere in sight, what should I do?

I supposed I could ascertain whether Niall Kavanagh was inside, then go on from there. But I was afraid to meet the deranged scientist by myself. I looked around for support, guidance, or encouragement, but saw nothing except the empty, quiet street. The sun's dying light turned the windows of the workhouse blood-red.

A sudden loud, splintery, jangling sound of glass breaking shattered the calm.

It would have sent me running like a coward, had I not remembered my adventures of 1848. Why should I, who'd once faced death and lived to tell, be daunted by anything now? I pushed open the gate and stepped through. Raising my umbrella against foes real or imaginary, I advanced up the path.

Stairs rose to an entrance within a porch. The noise had come from my left, and I went in that direction, along another path between shrubs higher than my head. As I rounded the corner of the house, I heard scrambling noises, branches thrashing, and leaves rustling. A man perched in a tree he'd climbed up to a window. He removed his jacket, wrapped it around his fist, and used his padded fist to enlarge a jagged hole in the window, which he must have broken by throwing a rock through it. Glass tinkled, fell, and scattered. Moving closer, I saw that the burglar I'd caught in the act was John Slade.

Amazement and vindication flooded me. The trail to Niall Kavanagh had led me straight to Slade. I forgot all about danger. I started toward Slade, spoiling for the confrontation I'd long anticipated.

"Hey!" called a loud, gruff, masculine voice. "What do you think you're doing?"

I froze. A man emerged from a grove of trees. The twilight was fading, and I couldn't see much about him except that he was stocky and wore a brimmed cap. He stood no more than twenty feet from me, but it wasn't me that he'd seen: he aimed a rifle at Slade.

"Come down," he said, "or I'll shoot."

I hadn't come this far to have Slade killed before he could answer a few questions. I stepped off the path, angled through the shrubbery, and stole up behind the man with the rifle. I could see Slade clinging to the tree, staring at the weapon leveled on his heart. His face was set in hard lines that betrayed no emotion, but I read his mind: he was thinking that he'd escaped death at the hands of mighty villains all over the world, and now he was about to be brought down by a country caretaker in an English village. He couldn't bear the stupidity of it, and neither could I.

I turned my furled umbrella in my hands, grasping it near the pointed end. I crept up to the caretaker and brought the sturdy wooden handle down on the back of his head as hard as I could. He grunted, lurched, and dropped the rifle. I swung my umbrella and hit him behind his knees. He fell flat on his face. As he struggled to rise, something in me snapped. The passions and impulses I had controlled heretofore now overflowed like water over a crumbled dam. I lost all common sense, all self-restraint. I hit the caretaker again and again while he screamed. Slade jumped down from the tree and hurried toward us.

"Charlotte, stop! You'll kill him!"

I didn't care. Glorying in unholy wrath, I beat the caretaker until he lay still and moaning. Slade tore the umbrella out of my hands and flung it away. "Have you gone mad?"

Laughter burbled from me, even though I was shocked and horrified that I had attacked a man who'd never done me any wrong. "That's the pot calling the kettle black! *You're* the criminal lunatic from Bedlam!" Now I was furious. "You thought you could avoid me, but you were wrong!"

He shook his head, astounded and exasperated. "You never give up, do you? I suppose you came looking for Niall Kavanagh in an attempt to track me down, and you found his laboratory. I underestimated you." Grudging respect crept into his tone; but then he said sternly, "You should go."

"I'm not going anywhere!" I snatched up the rifle and aimed it at Slade. "Neither are you, until you've explained everything to my satisfaction!"

His hands went up. "Put the gun down. You're not going to shoot me. You don't even know how to fire a gun."

"Is that what you think?" I had gone shooting on the moors in Haworth, although I'd never managed to hit anything. How furious I was that Slade would patronize me after I had just saved his miserable life! I pulled the trigger.

The gun fired with an ear-splitting roar. The barrel jerked upward. Slade dropped to the ground. I screamed in horror because I thought I'd shot him, which I hadn't really meant to do. But the bullet hit the foliage high in the trees. Twigs and leaves rained down on him. He cautiously raised his head. We stared at each other, and the shock on his face was no greater than the shock I felt.

That we had come to this! That I had almost killed the man I loved!

I lowered the gun. When Slade jumped up and took it from me, I didn't resist. He threw the gun into the bushes. I said, "I'm sorry."

"So am I." But his manner was more impatient than conciliatory. "I can't tell you any more than I already have. Because it's not your concern."

My anger resurged. "After what I've gone through because of you, it certainly is my concern." I played a card I thought he didn't know I held. "Katerina has been killed."

"What?" Even more stunned than when I'd almost shot him, Slade demanded, "How?"

I explained that I'd gone to Katerina's house in search of him and found her tied to her bed, stabbed multiple times and bleeding to death.

"Good God!" Slade was visibly shaken.

I wondered if it was because he loved Katerina and her death grieved him. The thought fueled my rage. I told Slade I'd been caught by the police. "They think I murdered her. They sent me to Newgate Prison." I related the indignities and terrors I'd suffered there. "So don't tell me that your business is none of mine!"

Dismay appeared in his expression. "I never wanted you to be hurt."

"You have an odd way of showing it." Close to tears, I said, "That's not the worst of what happened." I described how Wilhelm Stieber had brought me to Bedlam and interrogated me. "He would have had me killed, if not for Lord Palmerston and the Queen." I told Slade they'd rescued me and granted me a limited amount of time to prove my innocence and his. "Palmerston believed you were a traitor, but I defended you, and he's giving you the benefit of doubt. Don't you think I have a right to know what's going on?"

Slade inhaled a deep breath, then slowly exhaled. "I suppose I do owe you an explanation." He looked around to see whether any-one was coming to investigate the gunfire, then moved under the shadow of the tree I'd shot, where we wouldn't be seen from the road; he beckoned me to follow him. "Whatever you want to know, just ask."

Here was my chance to learn the truth. Perhaps it was my last because I would never see Slade again. Now was not the time to beat around the bush, to hesitate because of modesty, pride, or fear that the truth would hurt.

"Do you remember that we were once in love?" I said. "Do you remember asking me to marry you?"

The speed with which Slade turned away told me that he would prefer to discuss any other topic than this. "I do." His voice was barely audible.

"Then why have you been acting as if you'd forgotten? Why have you pretended we were strangers?"

Slade shook his head, appearing helpless and ashamed, the way men often do when confronted with matters of the heart.

I whispered the question that I was most timid to ask, whose answer I was most afraid to hear. "Have your feelings toward me changed?"

He abruptly faced me and spoke with vehement passion: "My

feelings for you remain exactly the same as when I proposed to you in that dreary, remote village where you live. I loved you then. I've loved you these three years. I love you now. If you think I'm so faithless that I would change my mind, then God damn you, Charlotte Brontë!"

29

I WAS TOO THUNDERSTRUCK TO SPEAK, AS ALARMED BY HIS LAN-guage as overjoyed to hear that Slade was still in love with me.

"For three years, I've missed you and longed for you, even though I tried to put you out of my mind," he said. "One lapse of attention can be the death of a spy. Still, I kept wondering whether *your* feelings toward *me* had changed. I couldn't write to you and ask—it was dangerous to smuggle letters out of or into Russia. I decided that I would finish this one last assignment, be done with spying, then go back to England and propose to you again."

This was a more ardent affirmation of love than I'd dreamed of hearing.

"But when the time came, I couldn't just waltz back into your life. I'm not the man you loved three years ago." Slade's features hardened into stoicism. "I've done terrible things since then."

A cold shadow of dread encroached upon me. I didn't want to hear what Slade was going to say, but I'd forced him into a confession, and I must listen to it all.

"While I was in Moscow, I befriended three Russian intellectuals." Slade told me the story of Peter, Fyodor, and Alexander, which I have recorded in my tale of his adventures. "I betrayed them. I bought my way into the Tsar's court with their deaths."

I felt a revulsion so strong that I took a step backward from Slade, down the path that led away from the workhouse. His gaze showed disgust at himself and pity for me. "I tried to warn you. Now do you wish you'd stayed away from me?"

What I wished was that Slade had never gone to Russia. I hurried to defend him, even though I deplored his exploitation of harmless men who would have been content to talk about revolution rather than take action if not for him. "You were doing your duty."

Slade gave me a bitter smile; he perceived my ambivalence. "The blood of those men is still on my hands. And they aren't the only ones I've betrayed."

A cadence of foreboding drummed inside me. "The British agents? But you told me you weren't a traitor."

"I didn't give their names to the secret police, but I might as well have signed their death warrants." Slade described how he'd worked as an informant for the Third Section while spying on the Russian government. He told me the story of the men and the firing squad in Butyrka Prison. "I used to meet with them on occasion, to share news. Wilhelm Stieber must have followed me to a meeting, although I never saw him—I swear, the scoundrel has a cloak of invisibility. He must have caught one of our agents, then tortured him into admitting he was a British spy and exposing the rest of us. I didn't know what had happened until it was too late to save them. All I could do was run for my own life."

I hope my retelling of his story has conveyed what Slade had experienced. When he described the wild chase through the Kremlin and living as a fugitive in Moscow, I felt as harrowed as if I'd gone through it all myself. "How did you escape?"

"By an accident of fate." He told me how he'd been ambushed on his way out of Moscow and the four men who'd tried to murder him had been killed by the secret police. "They were British agents, my comrades, disguised as Russians. I figured that my superiors had discovered that my fellow spies had been caught. They blamed me, and they'd sent the agents to deliver me to justice. But I didn't know for sure until you told me what Lord Eastbourne said."

"Why did you let your superiors think you were dead?" I asked.

"Why didn't you tell your side of the story?"

"I did," Slade said, "after I came back to England. A friend in Russia smuggled me into Poland. The Polish people don't like Russia, which has taken over their country. Some were glad to give me food and shelter and money and teach me their language. I went on to Amsterdam, then stowed away on a ship and landed in England this past April. I wrote to Lord Palmerston at the Foreign Office, explaining what had happened. I warned him about Stieber, Kavanagh, and the invention. But I didn't trust Palmerston enough to meet him face to face or tell him where to send a reply to my letter. So I don't know whether he received it."

"I'm certain he didn't," I said, recalling our conversation at Osborne House.

"At any rate, I doubted that I could walk into the Foreign Office, turn myself in, and expect my problems to be straightened out," Slade said. "All I could do was proceed with my plan to search for Niall Kavanagh. And I wanted revenge on Wilhelm Stieber."

I'd known that Slade was a man of strong passions, but I'd never seen the full power of his hatred until now. Stieber had better pray to God that he and Slade never met again.

"My quest led me to Katerina." Slade spoke with such sorrow that I felt a stab of jealousy. "While I was in Whitechapel, looking for Stieber, I learned that she was his informant. I struck up an acquaintance with her and persuaded her to work for me."

I envisioned him using his charms on her, engaging her affections. I couldn't bear the images that my mind conjured up.

"I knew it was dangerous for her. I knew what Stieber would do to her if he found out. But I was like a speeding train that can only go in the direction that its track is laid. I killed her as surely as if I'd plunged a knife into her heart." Slade clenched his hand and pantomimed stabbing. The rage in his voice underscored the violence of his words. "Katerina's murder is another death I'm responsible for. And my actions have also put you in trouble with the law."

My emotions were in turmoil. My horror at the carnage he'd left in his wake now reverted to fury at Slade. If he wanted to add me to the list of people he'd harmed, he should accept responsibility for his most egregious crime against me. "You say you love me; you purport to be sorry I've been charged with murder. If you really care for me, then why did you take Katerina as your mistress?"

"I did not," Slade said, adamant.

"Couldn't you have obtained her cooperation without making love to her?" I was too beside myself to use politer words.

"I never made love to her," Slade insisted.

"You're forgetting that I saw you with Katerina, that night at the theater. I saw you kiss her." My voice quavered at the memory. "You didn't even care if I saw."

"I kissed Katerina precisely because I wanted you to see."

"What?" This was cruel torment. "Why?"

"To protect you." Slade rushed to explain: "When I came out of the theater with Katerina and you suddenly appeared, I wanted to rush to you, seize you in my arms, and never let you go. But I couldn't." Agony glazed his eyes. "You looked so beautiful and innocent. I couldn't touch you, lest you be contaminated."

Slade held up his hands and regarded them as if they were smeared with filth from his sins. "I had to drive you away. So I climbed in the carriage with Katerina, and even though she and I weren't on intimate terms, I kissed her." He smiled glumly; he rubbed his cheek. "You didn't see it, but she slapped me. I resisted my urge to look back at you. I couldn't bear to see the look on your face. I hated to leave you, but it was for the best."

He leaned closer, his eyes shining fiercely in the remains of the daylight. "Now I've told you everything. Now that you know the worst, do you still love me? Will you still have me?"

My heart urged me to cry, *yes*! My love for Slade was as ardent as ever. I was humbled by his belief that he no longer deserved me, and moved by his wish to protect me. But as blind as love can be, my mind couldn't ignore the fact that eight people were dead and Slade deserved at least some of the blame, no matter that he'd done everything he'd done in service to his country and I believed he was a good man at heart.

"I see you hesitate," Slade said. "At the risk of driving another nail into my coffin, I must remind you that I'm a fugitive. I can't wed you in church, lest I be caught and arrested. If you choose to be with me, it would be on the lam, without the benefit of clergy."

Once more I found myself walking the same path down which I'd sent Jane Eyre. She'd had to choose whether to live with Mr. Rochester in sin or flee and retain her honor. Now I faced my own crossroads. Slade was a criminal in the eyes of the law, and although I had stepped outside the law in order to find him, I was bound by convention. My love couldn't stand against my bred-in-the-bone belief in the sanctity of marriage. Choosing to be with Slade meant estranging myself from everyone else who mattered to me. I must renounce him or lose my family, my friends, and my virtue. My choice must be the same as I'd made for Jane.

Slade's face took on a look of triumph blended with devastation. "I see that I've succeeded in destroying whatever regard you had for me. You are offended because I made you such an insulting proposition. You despise me now."

Of course I did not! Yet I was so upset that I couldn't find words to explain my decision or lessen his guilt and misery. I could hardly believe that our positions had reversed—that I was the object of his unrequited love, or so he thought.

"You should go," Slade said. He wasn't Mr. Rochester, who'd begged Jane to stay even though it would compromise her. He was a stronger man, with higher moral standards.

I realized that my path must diverge from Jane's: running away wouldn't save me from disgrace. "I'm not leaving."

Slade looked at me as if he thought he'd heard incorrectly.

"Not until I prove I'm innocent and exonerate you," I clarified. I didn't admit that I wasn't ready for us to part even though we must. Now that I had found Slade, I could not immediately give him up, and I had ample justification for delaying. "I can't go home while I'm in as much trouble with the law as you are."

"Damn your obstinacy!" Slade burst out, venting his emotions in anger. "Just how do you intend to clear both our names?"

I was silent: I had no idea. I'd plotted my course up until this point, but no further. Alas, I was like a heroine in a novel

whose author did not know how to bring the story to a satisfy-
ing conclusion.

"Are you hoping to turn Niall Kavanagh over to the police and
say he's the Whitechapel Ripper?" Slade said, incredulous and
scornful. He was trying to offend me and thus drive me away. "And
after that, track down Wilhelm Stieber, drag him before Lord
Palmerston, and make him confess that he, not I, was responsible
for the deaths of the British agents?"

I knew how foolishly simplistic it sounded, but I supposed I had
entertained thoughts along those lines. "That would do."

Slade regarded me pityingly. "You are so naïve."

"I admit that I am," I retorted. "It takes a certain amount of
naïveté to think that one can write a novel that people will buy. It
takes even more to believe that one can foil a plot against the
British Empire. The fact that I've done both things indicates that
God rewards naïveté."

Slade groaned. "She invokes God as her accomplice!"

"Why not? I'm a parson's daughter."

Night had come; the moon had risen. The workhouse appeared
even more intimidating than ever. But I took my courage in hand,
and I moved along the path, circling the mansion.

Slade followed. "What are you doing?"

"Having a look around."

"I wish you had shot me and spared me the trouble of protecting you from yourself!"

The windows of the house were dark now that there was no
sun reflecting from them. "Is Niall Kavanagh here?"

"No," Slade said. "I've been keeping watch on the place for two
days. He's gone. Nobody in town seems to know where. That's
why I was breaking in—to see if he left any clues, or if there's any
sign of his invention inside."

I thought he would try to force me to leave, but he didn't;
perhaps he couldn't bear for us to part any more than I could.
We seemed to have come to a tacit agreement to quit the topic of
our relationship, to pretend Slade's confession hadn't happened.
We were conversing easily, but our talk felt brittle, like ice thinly

frozen over a turbulent ocean. I said, "How did you find out about Kavanagh's secret laboratory?"

"I went to his house in Whitechapel. While questioning people in the neighborhood, I found a man who used to be Kavanagh's servant. He told me where Kavanagh had moved." Slade said with abrupt suspicion, "How did you find out?"

I evaded the question in case the answer was a bargaining chip I might need later. The path veered away from the house. "What's in that building up ahead?"

The smell of decay wafted toward me as I approached it. Slade hurried in front of me to block the path. "You don't want to go in there."

"Why not?" I stepped around him. The building was a barn that had once contained animals that the workhouse residents had raised for food. The wooden doors were open; a padlock dangled from broken hinges. I entered before Slade could stop me. The foul odor was so strong that I covered my nose with my hand. On one side of the barn, sheep lay dead in pens. Flies buzzed and maggots swarmed over the rotting carcasses. On the other side were cages of small corpses with matted fur, wizened claws, and long tails—rats.

I gagged and ran out of the barn. Gulping fresher air, I said, "What was Niall Kavanagh doing with those animals?"

"I haven't the slightest idea."

"Did he kill them?"

"There are bare patches on their bodies where the hair was shaved off. I saw cuts in the skin, but not deep enough to kill. Maybe they died of neglect after Kavanagh left."

My stomach was so queasy that I feared I would vomit. I marched back along the path. "Maybe the answer is in the house."

We stopped near the window Slade had broken. The caretaker was gone; he'd regained consciousness and escaped. Slade said, "You're not going in there."

"Oh, yes, I am."

"You're leaving before the caretaker comes back with the watch. If I have to drag you away, I will." Slade advanced on me.

I stopped, but I stood my ground. My gaze dared him to make good on his threat. The air between us was charged with heat. If Slade had touched me then! But he didn't. He thought I would repulse any contact with him. His mouth twisted in frustrated despair.

"You wanted to know how I found out about the laboratory." My voice was unsteady, my heart racing. "I spoke with a friend who knows Dr. Kavanagh. He told me about the house in Whitechapel. I went there, too. The landlord let me see some things Dr. Kavanagh left behind. Among them were his journal and some papers. The location of the laboratory was there."

Slade beheld me with surprise, and heightened alertness. "What else did you find?"

"I'll tell you if you let me go in the house with you."

"That's blackmail," Slade protested.

"So be it."

"The parson's daughter should be ashamed of herself," Slade said in disgust. "All right. You win. Tell me."

"After we've had a look around the house."

Slade exclaimed, "I can take on the Tsar of Russia and his spy, but God save me from devious women!"

Grasping the tree beside the window, I started to climb, but Slade said, "Here, I'll help you up." He clasped his hands and lowered them. "After we're finished, you're going home."

"We'll see." I stepped onto his hands. He boosted me through the window.

30

I TUMBLED INTO A DARK SPACE. AS I STOOD AND DUSTED MYSELF off, Slade climbed in the window. He took matches from his pocket and lit one, illuminating an empty room with cracked plaster walls and a stone fireplace. We passed through other rooms in similar state, until we reached the kitchen. Slade lit a fresh match, and we gazed around in awe.

The kitchen was furnished like none I'd ever seen before. The worktops along the walls were black stone slabs. Below them were metal drawers and cabinets; above, a network of copper pipes. On their surfaces stood glassware such as I'd found in the Whitechapel house. Slade fiddled with lamps mounted on the walls. I heard a hissing sound and smelled gas.

Slade said, "Let there be light." He lit the lamps. "I'm surprised there's gas in a house this old. It must have been recently installed."

We explored the laboratory. The drawers contained rubber gloves, cloth masks and caps, steel knives, unidentifiable implements, and glassware: magnifying lenses; syringes like the ones used by the doctor in Bedlam; round, flat dishes with lids; long, tapered tubes connected to rubber bulbs. Cabinets held jars of powdered substances, labeled with numbers. The copper pipes were attached to spigots. When Slade turned them, water gushed from some and poured into sinks; others fed gas into burners that looked like metal candles. Glass flasks sat on stands above the burners. There were scales, and basins of water with thermometers mounted inside, an empty icebox, and a strange, clear glass case. The case had a lid sealed with a rubber gasket and two holes into which protruded a pair of rubber gloves. Beside it lay a small device comprised of two brass plates riveted together, a circle of glass set in a hole in them, a clamp holding a long, threaded bolt with a metal crosspiece, and various tiny screws.

"It's a microscope," Slade said.

I examined the stove, a cast-iron monstrosity with eight gas burners. A large pot sat on top. I lifted the lid. A horrible stench burst out from a rotten stew of meat and bones. I hastily clapped down the lid. Inspecting the pantry, we covered our noses to keep out the odor of more spoiled food. Shelves were stacked with the sort of glass dishes we'd found in the drawers. These held brown, moldy residue. Glass bell jars contained more of the same, plus burnt-out candles. On other shelves sat racks of glass tubes with cork stoppers, filled with murky liquid. Some corks had exploded out of the tubes, and the liquid had spattered the walls. On the floor stood several braziers, as if Niall Kavanagh had wanted to keep the pantry warm instead of cool.

"If this is food, Dr. Kavanagh eats a very strange diet," I said.

"It must be his experiments," Slade said, "although I can't imagine the purpose of them. I don't see any evidence that he was building a weapon."

In the dining room we did find mechanical devices—fans with blades like pinwheels, operated by cranks; a bellows attached to a bicycle. When Slade rode the bicycle around the room, the bellows pumped.

"I'm beginning to wonder if Kavanagh was a fraud," I said. "Perhaps he led the British government to believe he'd invented a new kind of gun but he really hadn't. Perhaps he fooled Wilhelm Stieber, too."

"I had the same thoughts," Slade said, "but I'm not ready to believe I've been chasing after a gun that doesn't exist."

He stalked from the room. Although I should have been relieved to think that Britain might be safe from the weapon, I couldn't forget that Katerina had been murdered because of it. Stieber believed the gun existed, and perhaps it really did. We had to keep searching.

The kitchen was the only room supplied with gas. Slade lit an oil lamp he found there, while I extinguished the gaslights. He carried the lamp and we mounted the broad staircase. The rooms on the second story were empty except one in a round tower. Here Niall Kavanagh had lived. An unmade bed with dirty linens stood amid stained clothing, empty liquor bottles, and a chamber pot that contained dried urine and feces. Dishes on the bedside table held moldy cheese and bread crusts.

I think I need not describe the smell.

Slade flung open the window. We glanced at a bookcase filled with scientific texts, then examined the desk, on which were strewn ink pots, pens, journals, and papers. The papers were covered with Niall Kavanagh's drawings and script. I riffled them while Slade perused a journal. I couldn't help being conscious of his nearness. Glancing at him, I discovered that he was looking at me. He quickly dropped his gaze. Despite the fact that we were working together and nothing more, we were bonded by love—his confessed, mine undeclared and forbidden.

He handed the journal to me. "I can't read this aloud. Words like these shouldn't be spoken to a lady." I read to myself:

I found a whore who was sick with gonorrhea. I paid her to let me scrape effluvium from her puss. I prepared a medium from sheep's blood and mutton broth boiled with horse's hooves, poured it in dishes, and let it set. I spread the effluvium on the surface of the medium, then placed the dishes in a bell jar with a lit candle. The candle burned away the air. I incubated the dishes for 3 days. A luxuriant growth of molds, slimes, and scum resulted. I separated the various kinds of growth, repeated the procedure, and obtained cultures of reasonable purity. Now I must find clean women on whom to test the cultures.

"That explains the dishes in the pantry and the sheep, but what was Kavanagh thinking?" Slade shook his head in disgust. "I'm not an expert at science, but I know that what he describes isn't accepted practice."

I barely heard Slade; I was too stunned, for I remembered the journal from the Whitechapel house. "He found them."

"What?" Slade said.

"The clean women." I told Slade about the journal, summarized the entries for him, then interpreted them. "Kavanagh picked up Mary Chandler, Catherine Meadows, and Jane Anderson on the streets of Whitechapel. He examined them to ascertain that they were clean; then he applied the 'cultures' to them." I pictured hands smearing slime on a woman's private parts, and bile rose in my throat. "He let a few weeks pass, then reexamined them to see if they had the disease. And he killed them so he could dissect them." The horror of it choked my voice. "He even made drawings."

Slade stared. "That's what you discovered in his house in Whitechapel?"

"Yes," I said. "Niall Kavanagh is the Whitechapel Ripper. The murder victims were subjects in his experiments."

"Good Lord." Slade was awed by the truth about Kavanagh and the fact that I'd discovered it. "Kavanagh wasn't inventing a gun; his work involved determining the cause of diseases. He thought it was a substance that could be taken from a sick person, grown in a laboratory, and passed to other people."

Slade leafed through the journal, frowning at the illegible, ink-blotted script. "Kavanagh must have been drunk when he wrote this. Look, there's wine spilled on these pages. 'Dutch scientists have studied samples of water, soil, and vegetable and animal material under the microscope. They have observed tiny animalcules moving therein. I have repeated the experiments and seen the animalcules myself.'" We beheld drawings of spherical, ovoid, and wormlike creatures. "'I have a theory that it is some species of these animalcules that are the cause of all contagious diseases.'"

"My friend Dr. Forbes mentioned Kavanagh's theory," I recalled. "He said it was met with ridicule and contributed to Kavanagh being expelled from the Royal Society."

"Kavanagh deserved it," Slade said. "His theory goes against hundreds of years of learning, the judgment of the best minds in the world, and all common sense. If Kavanagh believes it, he isn't just a fraud; he's mad!"

"Madman or not, he's still dangerous. He's a murderer even if he can't help Russia win a war against England." I was jarred by a sudden idea. "Perhaps we've misinterpreted Niall Kavanagh's work. Perhaps he really has invented a weapon."

"What are you talking about?"

My idea sprang full-fledged into my mind while I spoke. "We assumed the weapon was a gun. But what if it's some completely new kind of device for killing?" Slade looked puzzled, and I rushed on: "No matter that his theory is ridiculous, Niall Kavanagh demonstrated that he could cultivate a substance that causes disease and use it to make people sick. Maybe he discovered how to do those things on a larger scale, how to affect more than one person at a time."

"One couldn't apply his animalcules to enough people to make a difference in the outcome of a war. Besides, the disease he gave those women isn't fatal."

"Other diseases are," I said, convinced by my own logic. "Fevers, cholera, typhoid, consumption—they kill thousands of people. And what if Kavanagh invented another way to spread the agents that cause those diseases?"

"That's preposterous. You've been writing fiction for so long that you've started to believe—" Sudden, dismayed recollection and enlightenment stopped Slade. "The fans. The bicycle with the bellows. That's what they're for—to spread diseases through the air. Damnation. You're right." Horror filled Slade's eyes. "If Niall Kavanagh has perfected a weapon of that sort, it could start a plague!"

It hardly bore imagining. "What should we do?"

"*We* aren't going to do anything. You're going home. I—" Slade paused.

"What?"

He put his finger to his lips. Now I heard the sound of footsteps approaching the house, and the gate creaking. Slade blew out the lamp. We hastened to the window and saw, far below us, three men coming up the front walk.

"Who in the devil?" Slade muttered.

They carried lanterns, but we couldn't see their faces. They mounted the stairs and disappeared under the roof of the porch. A moment later there came a loud knocking.

"Kavanagh!" one of the men called. "If you're in there, open up!"

"It's Lord Eastbourne," I whispered. "I recognize his voice."

"Lord Eastbourne!" Slade's profile, illuminated by the moonlight, showed surprise. "What is he doing here?"

Now was the time to fill Slade in on the remainder of what I'd learned in Whitechapel. I told him about the letter written by Lord Eastbourne. "He furnished the laboratory. Dr. Kavanagh is working for him."

"My, my, you're just full of surprises." Slade regarded me with amusement.

"But I still don't understand why, if Kavanagh is working for the British government, Lord Palmerston didn't know about him and the invention."

"Lord Eastbourne is an ambitious man," Slade said. "He must have learned about the invention and gone behind Palmerston's back to hire Kavanagh."

"But why?" I heard shuffling and muttered conversation from Lord Eastbourne and his men on the porch.

"Maybe he didn't know whether the weapon would work, and he wanted to wait until Kavanagh came up with a successful model, and then reveal it to Lord Palmerston and the Queen. That would have done wonders for his career." Slade thought a moment. "He may even be planning to encourage a war between Britain and Russia. That would give him a chance to demonstrate Kavanagh's weapon, and a victory for Britain would make him a hero."

"Now I understand why he left me in Newgate Prison. He didn't want me to tell anyone about Dr. Kavanagh and the invention and have it come out that he'd hired Kavanagh without official sanction."

"Now I understand what became of the letter I wrote to Palmerston," Slade said grimly. "Lord Eastbourne must have intercepted it. When he read it, he had a choice: show it to Palmerston, warn him about Wilhelm Stieber, and come to my defense; or protect his secret."

Outside, Lord Eastbourne called, "Kavanagh!" and pounded on the door. I heard a key rattling in the lock, and the door opening.

"They're coming in!" I whispered.

Footsteps clattered in the entryway. Lord Eastbourne said, "Search the house." I heard him and his companions mounting the stairs.

"We can't let him find us," Slade whispered.

He urged me under Niall Kavanagh's bed and slid in after me. We lay facedown, side by side, while the footsteps marched through the house. Despite my terror, I was intensely attuned to Slade—his breathing, his scent, the warmth of his body. I felt an almost overpowering impulse to touch his hand. He lay still and rigid. Light spread across the floor of the tower as one of the men entered. Slade and I held our breath. The man muttered, "Filthy pig," then left. His footsteps hurried down the stairs, and he called, "Kavanagh's not here. The house is empty."

Slade and I exhaled.

"Then we'll proceed," Lord Eastbourne said.

His voice came from the direction of the kitchen. I heard him moving around, and splashing noises; then he and his men exited the house. Slade scrambled out from under the bed. I followed. As we peered out the window, we heard rustling noises in the bushes alongside the house, then more splashes. Through the window drifted a sharp, pungent, oily odor.

"I smell kerosene," I whispered.

Slade turned to face the door and sniffed. "I smell gas. Lord Eastbourne must have opened the taps."

We looked at each other in sudden, appalled realization. A loud *whump* came from outside the house; then a roaring, crackling noise. An orange glow of flames lit the night. Slade grabbed my hand. We ran for the stairs, only to find them blocked by flames that coiled along the floor like a dragon and leaped up the walls where Lord Eastbourne and his men had poured kerosene. Slade said, "We'll have to climb out a window."

"Why would Lord Eastbourne want to burn down the house?" I asked as we sped from room to room. Flames licked at all the windows; the outside of the building was on fire.

"To destroy the evidence of Niall Kavanagh's work and anything that could tie it to him," Slade said.

"Maybe he knows Kavanagh killed those women in Whitechapel. If his relationship with Kavanagh became public, what a scandal there would be!"

"Here's another possible reason," Slade said, hurrying me up the stairs. "What if Lord Eastbourne realized that the weapon was too dangerous to use? He wouldn't want to be associated with it."

"If he knew that he'd managed to trap two witnesses in the fire, he would be delighted."

"This is what you get for refusing to leave when you had the chance!"

Smoke pervaded the house; we coughed and choked. We reached an attic, and Slade threw open a window. The air that poured in was hot and smoky, and I could hear the flames roaring louder. Slade climbed out the window and dropped some ten feet to the roof of a cupola. "Jump!" he shouted, arms raised.

I offered up a silent prayer and jumped. For a brief, terrifying moment I fell, my skirts ballooning, my heart in my mouth. Then Slade's arms were tight around me. He set me on the roof. We looked down, in dismay. The ground was more than thirty feet beneath us, and there were no trees near enough to climb down. The entire main story of the house was ablaze. I heard bells ringing in the distance, calling out the fire brigades, but they surely wouldn't arrive soon enough. We were doomed.

"Miss Brontë!" a voice called from below.

I had heard that voice too often for my liking. Astonished, I peered down. "Mr. Heald?"

"Yes, it's me!"

"Who?" Slade said.

"Oliver Heald," I said. "An acquaintance of mine."

Accompanied by scraping, bumping sounds, Mr. Heald appeared amid the trees and smoke. "At your service, Miss Brontë." He looked up at me with his usual, cheery smile. He was dragging a ladder.

"What's he doing here?" Slade asked.

"He must have followed me. Again." Once again I hadn't spotted him, even though he must have trailed me all the way from Haworth to the Lake District to London to Tonbridge, as unlikely as it sounds. And Slade had been too distracted to notice Mr. Heald lurking in our vicinity. I laughed, because once I could have smacked Mr. Heald for his nerve, but now I could have kissed him.

"Is there anything else you want to tell me?" Slade said.

Mr. Heald positioned the ladder against the cupola. Slade made me go first. Mr. Heald held the ladder steady while I descended. Its base was so close to the flaming wall of the house that my skirts were singed. But I landed safely, and so did Slade, a moment later.

"Thank you," I said to Mr. Heald.

"Anything for my favorite author," he said with a little bow.

"Run!" shouted Slade.

He hurried us away from the house. As we ran across the weedy grass, the gas ignited and the house exploded. The boom was louder than the loudest thunder. A great wave of force rose up under me, lifted me off my feet, and slammed against my back. We crashed flat on the ground. I looked over my shoulder. The house was a mass of flames. They roared and spewed; they stained the night sky orange. Black smoke writhed around the chimneys, which toppled as the roof caved in. Windows shattered. Glass fragments blew out. Flying debris pelted us.

Slade was on his feet, pulling Mr. Heald and me to ours. "Come on!"

We hastened toward the edge of the property. My right knee had hit the ground hard when I fell. Supported by Slade and Mr. Heald, I limped. Trees loomed between us and the wall that enclosed the workhouse. I heard a series of smaller booms. At first I thought they were more explosions inside the house. Then something hit the ground in front of me. Dirt flew up.

"Gunfire!" Slade said. "Take cover!"

"Who's shooting?" Mr. Heald said as we raced toward the trees. He looked terrified. I felt sorry for him because all he'd wanted was to be near me, and he hadn't bargained on this.

"It's Lord Eastbourne and his men," I said. "They must have stayed to make sure the house was destroyed. They saw us. They can't allow us to live."

"Who is Lord Eastbourne?" Mr. Heald said.

"I'll explain later."

The trees seemed miles away. I hobbled as fast as I could. More shots boomed, kicking up more dirt around us. They came from our left. I looked that way, and so did Slade. He said, "It's not Lord Eastbourne."

A man was running toward us, a pistol raised in his hand. His blond hair gleamed in the firelight. He was Wilhelm Stieber's minion, the athletic one. Just before we reached the trees, he fired again. Slade knocked me down on the ground. The bullet hissed over us. Another shot blared from our right. Mr. Heald shrieked, spun in a circle, and stumbled.

"He's been shot!" I cried.

"Get inside the woods!" Slade ordered. He caught Mr. Heald before he could fall. "Go!"

As I crawled beneath the trees, I glimpsed a man near the barn. He stood in darkness, the barn screening him from the fire. The moonlight silvered the barrel of his gun, reflected in his pale eyes. It was Wilhelm Stieber.

That glimpse lasted only a second, but I knew Stieber had seen me and recognized me. I burrowed into the woods like a rabbit hiding from a hawk. Slade followed, dragging Mr. Heald. We stopped by the wall. Slade laid Mr. Heald on the ground.

I bent over Mr. Heald. I called his name. "Where were you shot?"

He groaned. Moonlight sifted through the foliage, and I saw that his face was deathly gray, his eyes and mouth wide open as he gasped for air. The front of his shirt was drenched with blood.

"Stay calm," I urged. "We're going to help you."

Slade ripped open Mr. Heald's shirt. His chest was awash in blood that flowed from a hole at his right breast. The hole made a sucking, gurgling sound every time he breathed.

"The bullet went in his lung," Slade said. "There's nothing we can do."

"Then we must take him to a physician!"

Mr. Heald's gasps weakened. I seized his hand. It gripped mine in a convulsive spasm. He stared pleadingly up at me. His lips formed my name. Then his breaths ceased; his hand went limp, his gaze vacant.

"He's dead," Slade said.

"No!" I cried. Sorrow magnified all the gratitude and guilt I felt toward Mr. Heald. He'd saved my life, and I'd never even signed his beloved copy of *Jane Eyre*.

In the distance, the fire still roared; crashes came from the house as it collapsed. Footsteps crunched through the woods toward us. Slade dragged me away from Mr. Heald. "Stieber and his men are coming. We have to go."

31

>≻⊰

WE MADE OUR WAY INTO TOWN ALONG A CIRCUITOUS ROUTE. When we reached the high street, it must have been near nine o'clock; no other people were about. The buildings were dark, although the sky glowed orange from the burning workhouse. Slade stopped short of the Rose and Crown. "We'll say goodbye here."

I felt a panic as strong as when we'd been trapped in the fire. "Where are you going?"

"Back to the laboratory," Slade said, "to find Stieber. He wants me more than he wants you. I'll lure him and his men away from Tonbridge and deliver him to justice. You'll be safe."

"What am I supposed to do?"

"Stay here," Slade said. "I'll deal with Stieber. I'll exonerate us. You needn't worry about anything."

It was so like him to try to take on the world single-handedly. I loved him for his valor. But he'd placed me on a pedestal because he thought I was too good for him, and I was finding it most uncomfortable. I chafed at sitting idle while he fought on my behalf, and the past had shown that we could accomplish more together than separately.

I sought an excuse to prevent Slade from leaving. "There's blood on your shirt. "You're injured."

Slade glanced down at his shoulder. "It's only a scratch."

I walked around him, inspected him, and gasped. "Your back is covered with blood!"

Indeed, his shirt looked as if it had been dyed crimson and ripped to shreds. He twisted around to see. "I must have been hit by debris from the explosion. I didn't even notice."

"You had better see a physician," I said.

"There's no time. I'll be all right."

"At least let me examine the cuts."

"Never mind." Slade's expression repelled the very idea of my seeing him undressed, hurt, vulnerable, and weak.

"You can't go around bleeding like this," I said. "The wounds may fester. Besides, you'll attract attention."

Slade couldn't argue with that. He let me take him into the Rose and Crown. I was glad I'd registered under a false name, as a married woman. Anyone who saw us would assume Slade was my husband. They wouldn't suspect that the famous spinster author Currer Bell was up to no good. I sneaked Slade into my room, which was luxuriously furnished with a four-poster canopied bed. The impropriety of the situation embarrassed me; the intimacy excited me as well as disturbed me. But I could not have done otherwise; Slade needed help.

While he removed his shirt, I went in search of the housekeeper, from whom I obtained washcloths, bandages, and a bottle of alcohol. I told her my husband had been injured in a minor accident and his shirt ruined. She gave me a clean shirt left behind by another guest. When I returned, Slade was sitting in a chair, stripped to the waist. Even as I felt a shameful thrill at the sight of his nakedness, I winced because his back was a gory mess of cuts, blood, and embedded glass fragments. As I poured water from the jug on the washstand into the basin, neither of us spoke. We didn't look at each other. I carefully picked the glass out of his flesh. Luckily, I'd had some experience with nursing while caring for my sisters and brother, and the cuts weren't deep. As I cleaned them, I tried not to notice his lean, strong muscles or the heat from his skin, or to glance over his shoulders at his bare chest, but I couldn't help wanting to caress him; I couldn't stop the molten, heavy sensation that spread through my body. Dabbing the cuts with alcohol, I tried to think of myself as a nurse and Slade as my patient.

I failed miserably.

"The bleeding's stopped," I said, bandaging the wounds. "You should heal just fine."

He put on the clean shirt. His expression was cold, hard; he'd sealed himself off from me. He stood, ready to leave, and I knew it was unfair to keep him with me. I knew the agony of being in the presence of someone who had rejected me; I should let Slade go. But suddenly I was overpowered by emotion. His confession, Lord Eastbourne, the fire, Wilhelm Stieber, the death of Oliver Heald, and our own narrow escape—it was all too much, after Katerina's murder, my arrest, and my ordeal in Bedlam. I began to cry.

Slade acted as remote as if he were a million miles away. "You'll feel better when you're home with your family."

"My family is gone," I said between sobs. "While you were in Russia, Emily, Anne, and Branwell died of consumption."

"My God." Slade was shocked, mortified. "I'm sorry. I didn't know."

He put his arms around me, but I cried harder because, even though Slade was still with me, I had lost him, too.

Slade spoke hesitantly: "You must be upset about Oliver Heald. Was he a close friend?"

I perceived that Slade wanted to know if I had been romantically involved with Mr. Heald. I wondered if Slade was jealous; but if so, what did it matter? I had enough other proof of his love, and I had rejected it. Once I might have been tempted to say I'd been in love with Mr. Heald to pay Slade back for his charade with Katerina, but that would have been disrespectful to Mr. Heald as well as untrue, and I hadn't the heart for petty games.

"No," I said. "He was just an admirer of my work. I'd only met him a few times." I gave an incoherent explanation of how Mr. Heald had followed me around. "But he was a good man. I was mean to him. I wish I could take it back, but I can't. He saved my life, and he died because of me."

I wept, my face buried against Slade's chest. Slade was as rigid as if I were a bereaved stranger who'd thrown herself at him. My requited love for him was as hopeless as every unrequited love I'd ever experienced. But sometimes the body does not accept what the mind knows. My face involuntarily lifted to Slade's. Our eyes met. Mine streamed with tears. His were alarmed. I sensed him wishing to recoil—but he didn't. I felt a rush of the euphoria that one feels when one has survived a disaster. With it came an instinctive hunger to celebrate life. And I knew Slade felt the same. The rigidness of his body yielded. He bent his head. His mouth met mine with a force as cataclysmic as the explosion at the workhouse. He kissed me with a need and passion that equaled mine.

I have always scorned novels in which the heroine sees stars or hears music when she and the hero kiss, but now I understood the truth in the cliché. Stars and music there were none, but flashes like lightning seared my closed eyes. Thundering sensation rocked us both. Longing vanquished my modesty and sense of propriety. I drank Slade like a woman dying of thirst gulps water; I tasted blood and smoke and fire. My body melted against him. The hardness at his loins pressed urgently against me. I then learned that when a man and a woman who are former lovers become lovers anew, they cannot start at the beginning, with chaste kisses on the hand or cheek. They plunge straight into the depth of engagement they once shared. I wanted more than what I'd done with Slade in the forest in Scotland three years ago. Shame and sin be damned—I wanted us to join in the ultimate fulfillment that I'd never experienced but always craved.

We moved toward the bed, until Slade suddenly wrenched away from me. Breathing hard, his face suffused with desire and horror, he said, "I shouldn't have done that." Either he didn't realize that I'd instigated the kiss or he'd decided to take the blame himself. "I'm sorry."

I was appalled at my rash behavior and frightened by the thought of the consequences that might have befallen me if Slade had been a weaker, less noble man. I stood there in an agony of helpless longing as he headed for the door.

"Please don't leave me!" I cried.

"I would have to go even if we hadn't almost—" Slade shook his head. "I have to deal with Stieber, then Niall Kavanagh. When I'm finished with them, I'm going after Lord Eastbourne."

"You're not going without me." I hurried to the door and stood with my back against it.

Impatient, and angered by frustrated desire, Slade said, "We agreed that going in the workhouse would be the last thing you did."

"That was then. Things are different now." I tried to forget my own desire, calm myself, and speak rationally. "I want revenge against Stieber, too. Not only did he torture me in Bedlam; he killed my most loyal admirer, a man who saved my life. I owe justice to Mr. Heald. Besides, I have my own quarrel with Lord Eastbourne. I have to make both of those villains pay."

"And how, pray tell, are you going to do that?" Slade deployed scorn as his shield against me.

"I'll think of something. How are you going to find Niall Kavanagh?"

"I'll think of something."

"I can save you the trouble."

Suspicion narrowed Slade's eyes. "What are you talking about?"

"When Mr. Heald came to rescue us, you asked me if I had anything else to tell you. I didn't get a chance to answer."

"What is it?"

"I know of a place Niall Kavanagh might have gone," I said.

"Where?" Slade demanded.

I folded my arms. "I'm not telling you unless you take me with you."

Slade groaned. "Blackmail again! Why am I not surprised? All right, tell me where you think Niall Kavanagh went. I'll go to my lodgings and retrieve my bag. We'll meet at the train station in an hour."

I could imagine arriving at the station and finding him long gone. "No. I won't tell you where we're going until we're on our way."

Slade's expression turned ominous, but he realized that I

wouldn't back down. "Very well. But this will be our last venture together. And—" He paused, searched for words, then said, "About what happened in here: I promise it won't happen again."

I half expected Slade not to show up at the train station, but he was waiting there, his valise in hand. "Now are you going to tell me where we're going?" he asked me at the ticket booth.

I told the clerk, "Two tickets to London."

"Why?" Slade said. "Haven't we already searched it thoroughly enough to be sure that Niall Kavanagh isn't there?"

"London is only our first stop."

"May I ask what our final destination is?"

If he knew, he might escape me along the way. "You may ask, but I'll tell you only this: be prepared for a long journey."

Slade demonstrated his powers of deduction. "We're going to Ireland, aren't we? To hunt Dr. Kavanagh in his native territory."

I finally admitted as much.

"We shouldn't just hope to run across him by wandering around blindly," Slade said. "I suppose you have a notion of where to look?"

"I do."

Upon arriving in London, we transferred to a northbound train and rode all night. I slept through the Snowdonia mountain range and awoke as the train rattled over the Britannia Bridge across the Menai Strait. The sunrise turned the water into shimmering gold. Soon we were in Anglesey, a large island off the Welsh coast. We glided past green cornfields to Holyhead, the port for travel across the Irish Sea. After we left the train and breakfasted in the refreshment room at the station, we walked to the jetty where the steam packets took on passengers. We'd hardly spoken during our journey, and we did not speak now. Neither of us was eager to address the concerns that we must address eventually. We purchased our tickets for passage on a steamer bound for Dublin. I paid for them out of the funds given me by Lord Palmerston; Slade had very little money left from a cache he'd hidden somewhere in England before he went to Russia and retrieved sometime after he'd returned.

The weather turned stormy while we were at sea. A journey that should have taken four hours extended to eight. I am prone to seasickness, and I could not bear to go below deck, where the ship's tossing was most strongly felt and other passengers ailed. Only by sitting still in a deck chair, in the rain, with my eyes closed, could I keep from being sick. To my relief, the sea calmed as we drew near land. I felt better as I stood at the railing and watched Ireland appear, its green hills obscured by mist.

Here was a place comprised of two different worlds. One was the land of myth and imagination, of haunting airs played on fiddles, harps, and pipes; of leprechauns, changelings and magic spells; of Celtic warriors, roving bards, and strong whiskey. The other world was my own family's homeland. Papa had grown up on a modest farm in County Down, one of ten children. His brothers had stayed there, but Papa had left Ireland in 1802 to study at St. John's College, Cambridge. After he was ordained, he made a trip to Ireland to visit his relations. He never went back again.

I had never been to Ireland; I believed I was English to the core. But when the ship docked at Kingstown, I felt an affinity for Ireland, even though my first sight of it was less than pleasing. The afternoon was gray, the piers deserted, the amusement park drab in the rain. The only Irish I saw were laborers offloading cargo from ships. But their shouts rang with inflections that sounded like Papa, who'd never entirely lost his accent. When we reached the railway station and I negotiated for tickets to Dublin, Slade turned to me in surprise.

"I do believe I hear Ireland in your voice." His own brogue was perfect; adept at languages and disguises, he seemed the quintessential Irishman.

"When I was a child I spoke with an Irish accent," I recalled. "I picked it up from Papa. It's coming back."

While riding the five miles north to Dublin, past the rain-soaked tenements on the outskirts of the city, I reflected that there was a third Ireland—the world shaped by the English. In 1541, Henry VIII declared himself King of Ireland and seized lands from the Irish lords. Elizabeth I and James I completed the conquest. Protestant Englishmen colonized Ireland and formed a new ruling class. In 1641, Irish Catholics rebelled. The Catholic gentry briefly regained control of the country until Oliver Cromwell reconquered Ireland in 1653. There followed the bloodiest period in Irish history. A third of Catholic Irish were killed. Much of their land was given to British settlers. The Penal Laws banned Catholics from public office, excluded them from many professions, deprived them of the right to own property and vote, and restricted the practice of the Catholic religion.

The French Revolution fueled the spirit of revolt in Ireland. In 1791, the Society of United Irishmen rose up against the English. Papa's brother fought with the rebels. But the rebellion was crushed, rebels and civilians tortured, massacred, burned alive, and hanged. Some fifty thousand people died in the Irish Rebellion of 1798. The result was the Act of Union, which in 1801 abolished Ireland's parliament and made Ireland a part of the United Kingdom. In July of 1848, the year that revolution swept through Europe, a nationalist group called Young Ireland attempted an uprising at Tipperary. The rebellion was easily put down by police. England still held Ireland firmly under its thumb.

I am a staunch English patriot, but I couldn't help sympathizing with Ireland, the underdog. Half of my heritage originated from this wet, misty landscape that I saw passing by the carriage window. Here on Irish soil, two bloodlines warred within me.

At the station in Dublin, I said, "It's too late to go to Niall Kavanagh's family home tonight. We must find lodgings."

"I have friends here," Slade said. Indeed, he had friends in all corners of the world, people he'd met during his espionage-related travels. "They'll lend me a bed. And I know the perfect place for you."

Although I didn't want to be separated from him, I didn't object. I didn't think he would abandon me now that we'd come so far. I also doubted that Wilhelm Stieber could have tracked us here yet. Moreover, staying together posed greater dangers than spending the night apart.

Slade hired a carriage, and we traveled through the old city. The evening was thick with peat smoke that immersed the gray stone buildings and cloaked the spires of cathedrals. My first impression of Dublin was one of emptiness, quiet, and desolation. Gas lamps burned along the main thoroughfares, in public houses, and in elegant mansions on fashionable squares; but all around were wastelands of darkness. When I remarked upon my observations, Slade said, "It's because of the famine."

The Great Famine had started in 1845, when Ireland's potato crop had failed. A recurring blight turned acres upon acres of potatoes into foul black mush. The potato was Ireland's staple food, and people all across the country suffered. I had seen nothing about this in the press, but Papa had gleaned shocking accounts from correspondence with Irish clergymen. People crawled along the highways, begging for food, their mouths stained green from eating grass. They died in ditches. Mothers ate the flesh of their dead children. Every town was overrun by walking skeletons. An outcry went up because vast quantities of grain and livestock were shipped out, for the benefit of Irish landlords and English consumers, while the Irish starved, and the English government had provided little relief. Now, six years later, the blight had passed and good harvests resumed, but too late for the million people who had died of starvation and disease. A million others had emigrated, leaving towns half vacant. Dark shapes huddled in the alleys, homeless families sleeping outdoors. Beggars dressed in rags accosted our carriage. I heard glass shatter and saw three men breaking into a shop. Whistles shrilled, and constables raced to stop the looting.

We stopped at a small building with whitewashed walls, in a cobbled courtyard where a statue of the Virgin Mary stood. Slade helped me out of the carriage, lifted down my bag, and told the driver to wait. He escorted me to the door and knocked. A panel in the door slid open, revealing an iron grille, behind which appeared an old woman's face, framed in a starched white wimple.

"Good evening, Mother Agnes," Slade said with a smile and bow.

"Why, if it isn't John Slade as I live!" Glad surprise brightened her stern visage. "What in heaven brings ye here?"

"I've a guest for you." Slade introduced me. "Could you put her up for the night?"

"With pleasure." The nun opened the door, smiled at me, and beckoned.

Slade was installing me in a Roman Catholic convent!

"I'll see you in the morning," he said.

32

MOTHER AGNES PUT ME IN A VACANT CELL WHERE A FIGURE of Jesus on the cross hung over an iron cot. I felt as if I had entered forbidden territory; yet I slept well. In the morning I breakfasted with the nuns. They were kind and asked no questions. The soda bread, black pudding, and stewed coffee restored my energy. When Slade came to fetch me, I felt strong enough to face the day.

"Good morning, Miss Brontë." He was clean-shaven, and his color had turned healthier. "Are you ready to tell me where we're going?"

He didn't say where he'd been, and I didn't ask. "To Clare House, in County Wicklow. It belongs to Sir William Kavanagh, Niall's father, head of the family's whiskey brewery."

"Ah. Let us hope our man has gone to ground there."

We boarded yet another hired carriage. As it took us out of the city, Slade cleared his throat. "There are matters we need to discuss."

Apprehension clenched my hands in my lap. "I suppose so."

"We can't just gad about like this together."

Embarrassment warmed my cheeks. I knew how improper it was for a single woman to travel with a single man not related to her. That I'd done so before with Slade didn't excuse my behavior. Then he had posed as my cousin. Then I'd been certain that nothing regrettable would happen, but now things were dangerously different. Furthermore, I had to protect Currer Bell's reputation as well as Charlotte Brontë's.

But I said, "I can't afford to care what people will think. To save Britain from Niall Kavanagh, Wilhelm Stieber, and Russia, I must risk my respectability."

Although Slade nodded in resignation, he frowned. "Someone is bound to wonder what our relationship is. The Kavanagh family, for example. How will we introduce ourselves?"

That was a good question. I knew the only answer. "We must say that I am your wife."

"My *wife*." Slade sounded sobered and chastened. I could tell what he was thinking: if things had been different, I would be his wife now. The same knowledge saddened me. He didn't like the idea of the pretense, which made a mockery of our past; nor did I. "Well, I suppose there's no alternative."

I took from my pocket the cheap, imitation-gold band I'd bought in London, and I put it on my ring finger. "There. That makes it official."

We looked at the ring on my hand, then away from each other. Instead of speaking, we looked out the window as the carriage rattled through Dublin. The city was filled with coaches and omnibuses. I studied the people on the streets. Rich and poor, some were red-haired and freckled; others blond and Norse; others dark-haired with pale skin and eyes. Some chatted and laughed as they went about their business; others brooded darkly. Yet they all seemed to share a stalwart endurance of misfortune and suffering.

We drove along a rural highway south into County Wicklow. The air was fresh, mild, and spring-like, the sky a bright blue filled with billowy white clouds over a landscape colored every shade of green—emerald, chartreuse, jade, moss, and viridian. Ancient stone towers and pillars studded fields divided by walls, hedgerows, and patches of woodland. Sheep and cattle grazed. Thatched cottages sported flowers in window boxes. We passed farmers in long-tailed jackets and tall hats, smoking pipes and driving carts pulled by shaggy-maned ponies. The Wicklow Mountains faded into azure in the distance. But even this natural beauty was scarred by the Great Famine. Villages lay in ruins, abandoned by peasants who'd left Ireland in search of food and work. Many fields were rocky and barren, the churches surrounded by gravestones. We passed wagons overloaded with grim, shabbily dressed families headed to ships bound for the New World. I felt a terrible pity for these people forced to leave their homes, and a burning anger toward those who had not helped them or had worsened their plight.

My first glimpse of Clare House predisposed me to hate the Kavanagh family.

Their estate had a vast park with lawns and woods, terraces and gardens. We drove along a formal avenue lined with beeches, to a huge eighteenth-century Palladian mansion built of silvery gray granite. Its hundreds of windows surely kept an army of maids occupied.

"That one family should live in such luxury in a country so poor! It's outrageous!" I exclaimed. "Have the Kavanaghs no shame?"

"Probably none," Slade said, "but take care not to show what you think of them. We need their cooperation."

We got out of the carriage on the driveway that circled a fountain, near the bottom of the wide front steps where twin stone lions displayed the family crests. The main door opened. Three men met us. The one in the middle was white-haired, dignified, dressed in black. His comrades wore country tweeds, and each carried a rifle. He looked down his haughty nose at us. "Good morning. May I be of service?"

I took him for the Kavanagh's butler and his companions the groundskeepers, protecting the house from the outlaws that the famine had created. Slade introduced himself, then said, "I'm a commissioner of the Metropolitan Police in London." He produced a badge that identified him as such. "My wife and I are here to see Sir William Kavanagh."

The butler studied Slade. I could see his distrust battling his fear of angering a representative of English officialdom. "I'm afraid Sir William is busy."

"Tell him it's about his son Niall," Slade said.

"Ah. Just a moment." The butler marched into the mansion, while the groundskeepers stood guard over us. In a moment he returned. "Sir William is in the ballroom. Come with me, please."

The lord of the manor was merrymaking while the commoners suffered! Slade and I followed the butler into an enormous room whose high, white ceiling was encrusted with plaster rosettes and ivy borders; gold-framed mirrors reflected enormous crystal chandeliers. French doors overlooked a terrace, a fountain in which stone dolphins spouted, and a sweep of lawn and gardens. But except for these features, the scene in the ballroom was not what I'd expected.

Rows of cots contained pale, haggard, emaciated people. A physician ministered to them. Three women in white aprons distributed food. The two young ones pushed a trolley laden with a tureen and served bowls of soup to the patients. The older woman was small and delicate, the dark hair under her cap streaked with gray. She sat down by the bed of a child and spooned soup into his mouth. A man was unloading stacks of clean linens from a cart. When he saw Slade and me, he stopped his work and approached us.

"My apologies for the informal reception, Commissioner." He extended his hand to Slade. "William Kavanagh, at your service."

He was in his sixties, broad across the shoulders, with thick, bowed legs and unruly red hair turning white. His genial face was rosy and sweating from exertion. With his shirtsleeves rolled up, he hardly matched the elegance of his manor, but he had confidence grounded in wealth and status. He indicated the older woman. "This is my wife Kathleen."

She came to his side and curtseyed, shyly polite. Her immense, clear blue eyes were fringed by black lashes. She must have been a beauty in her youth, and she was lovely still.

"Since the famine started, the county's been rife with consumption, cholera, and typhoid," Sir William said. "We've set up a sick ward here."

"I see," Slade said. I could tell from his tone of voice that he, too, had changed his prejudiced ill opinion of the Kavanaghs.

Sir William noted our chagrin; he smiled. "Life's been good to us. Helping others less fortunate is the least we can do. But you came to talk about Niall. What's he done this time?"

His tone bespoke a long history of hearing bad news about his son. So did the worry that creased Lady Kathleen's forehead. Slade said, "Is he here?"

"No," Sir William said.

I detected no hesitation or falseness in his reply.

"When was the last time you saw him?" Slade asked.

"Three, four years ago," Sir William said. "He's our black sheep."

I heard a soft sound from Lady Kathleen. When I looked at her, she averted her gaze.

"What's he done?" Sir William repeated. "It must be serious if you came all the way from London."

Slade glanced at the patients in the beds; those awake were listening avidly. "We should discuss this elsewhere."

It was obvious that although Sir William knew about Niall's bad character, blood was blood and he saw Slade as a threat to his family. But he said, "All right." He stalked toward the French doors, beckoning Slade. I went, too. Lady Kathleen started after us, but Sir William told her, "Stay here, I'll handle this."

Outside on the terrace, Sir William bade us sit in wrought-iron chairs at a table under a striped umbrella, but he remained standing. His unfriendly gaze commanded Slade to state his business.

Slade spoke gently, and I remembered that he'd been ordained as a clergyman before he'd become a spy. He must have been schooled on how best to deliver upsetting news, but his manner couldn't lessen the horror of what he said: Niall Kavanagh had formulated the theory that diseases are caused by animalcules, then tested his theory on women of the streets and killed and dissected them; he'd been hired by Lord Eastbourne to build a weapon based on his theory; and his work had come to the attention of Wilhelm Stieber, the Tsar's chief spy. After Slade reported that Niall had disappeared and Stieber was hunting him, Sir William shook his head violently.

"I won't listen to any more of this!" The ruddy color had drained from his face. "Niall's always been a troublemaker, to be sure, but he's not the monster you've made him out to be!"

I heard a strangled cry, from Lady Kathleen. She stood partially hidden by a potted shrub, her hand clapped over her mouth, appalled by what she'd overheard.

"Damn you for coming here and telling awful lies about my son to his mother!" Sir Kavanagh burst out at Slade.

Lady Kathleen stumbled blindly down the steps to the lawn. I followed her. The lawn was uncut and weed-choked, probably due to the servants fleeing the famine. The rose garden into which Lady Kathleen hurried was similarly ill-maintained, the bushes overgrown, the dead blossoms left shriveled alongside the new blooms, the odor funereal. Lady Kathleen wandered aimlessly, wringing her hands. I pitied her, but I couldn't pass up a chance to further Slade's and my investigation.

"I'm sorry," I said, ashamed of my readiness to take advantage of her. "I wish you hadn't had to hear that."

"It's all right." Lady Kathleen's voice was quiet, with a melodious Irish lilt. "I've been dreading this day. Now that it's come, it's a relief."

"You knew what Niall has done?"

"Not the specifics. Nor how bad they were. But Niall is my son." Lady Kathleen stopped wandering and turned to me. "Do you have children, Mrs. Slade?"

This was the first time anyone had addressed me by my fraudulent name and title. Disconcerted, I said, "No."

"Maybe you will someday," Lady Kathleen said kindly. "Then you'll understand. I carried Niall, I gave birth to him. I know him better than anyone else can. And I knew, from the start, that he was . . . different."

I resisted the urge to force the issue of Niall's whereabouts. "Different in what way?"

"I have five children. None of the others were as curious about the world as Niall was. As soon as he could walk, he would go into the fields and dig holes to find out what was under the ground, and

234 → L A U R A   J O H   R O W L A N D

rip plants up by their roots to look at them. One day he tore open all the rosebuds in this garden to see how the flowers looked before they bloomed. He would climb trees, take baby birds out of their nests, and handle them so much they died." Her face showed alarm at his ignorant destruction of beauty and life. "When he was seven, he killed a cat that was expecting kittens, and he cut open her stomach to see what was inside!"

I felt the horror that I heard in her voice. I began to understand how his curiosity had compelled Niall Kavanagh to do the terrible things he'd done.

"Niall was just as careless with people," Lady Kathleen said. "He drowned a shepherd's little girl because he wanted to see how long she could stay under water." Lady Kavanagh shook her head, unable to fathom how her child could have behaved so cruelly. "He held her head down until she stopped breathing."

Curiosity must be an essential trait for a scientist, but Niall Kavanagh had clearly been over-endowed with it, and lacking in conscience and compassion.

"Sir William told the girl's family that it was an accident," Lady Kathleen said. "He gave them money. He talked to the authorities, and they excused Niall because he was just a child."

He'd used his wealth and influence to protect a murderer. "Wasn't Niall ever punished?" I asked. "Wasn't he ever taught that it's wrong to hurt people?"

"Of course." Lady Kathleen's tone sharpened at my implication that her negligence was to blame. "I talked to him again and again. But he never seemed to understand that what he'd done was wrong. I made him stay in his room and go without supper; I took away his toys; I spanked him. But it only made him angry because *I* didn't understand *him*." Baffled, she said, "He was so excited whenever he discovered something new. He thought he should be praised for whatever he did."

I wondered if he'd later thought he deserved praise for stealing his mentor's work, for his affairs with his colleagues' wives, for airing his controversial views, and then taken offense because he'd been criticized and cast out instead.

"He was the same way at school," Lady Kathleen said. "Instead of doing the homework that was assigned, he would read books and write reports on subjects he'd chosen himself. When he was punished, he would fly into a rage. He was expelled from several schools because he attacked his teachers. We had to bring him home and hire a tutor for him. But he would go into the village and drink, and start brawls. And he got several girls with child."

"Did Sir William know about all this?"

"I tried to tell him," Lady Kathleen said, "but he didn't really listen."

I could hear the murmur of Slade's voice telling Sir William about the evidence against Niall. Sir William's voice replied, loud and angry: "Scribbles in notebooks. Scientific paraphernalia. That doesn't prove my son is guilty of murder. You're twisting everything around to make him a criminal!"

A spasm of pain tightened Lady Kathleen's delicate features. "He's never wanted to believe there was anything wrong with Niall."

"So he did nothing?"

"Not until Niall was sixteen. There was a riot in Dublin, when some Catholic students protested against the English government. Niall marched with them even though we aren't Catholic."

"You aren't?" I was surprised; I'd assumed the Kavanaghs were Catholic, like most Irish.

"No. Our family is Protestant."

I now recalled that many Irish nobles were. "But I understood that when Niall went to England, he was a devout Roman. He agitated for Catholic rights and even joined a branch of Young Ireland during the revolutions of 1848."

"He converted to Catholicism," Lady Kathleen said. "His father was furious."

Maybe he'd done it to infuriate his father. Maybe he had an inherent need to set himself in opposition to authority; maybe he perversely craved the punishment that angered him so. By styling himself an Irish Catholic in England, he'd certainly courted disapproval. "What happened to him during the riot?"

"He stabbed a constable," Lady Kathleen said. "The police arrested him and put him in jail. Sir William blamed Niall's friends, and the troubles in Ireland, and everybody but Niall."

In the background, Slade's voice continued, low and relentless. Sir William declared, "Someone must have planted the evidence."

"Who?" Slade asked.

"Maybe your government," Sir William said. "There are plenty of folks in it who'd like to silence anyone who agitates for Irish rights."

"Sir William thought Niall just needed a change of scene," Lady Kathleen said. "He used his influence to get the charges dismissed, and to get Niall admitted to Oxford. We thought Niall could get a proper education and put his mind to better use. But while he was there . . ."

"I know," I said, sparing her the pain of describing her son's career in England.

"I prayed that he would see the error of his ways and mend them," Lady Kathleen said sadly. "But I knew in my heart that something was missing in him from the start. A moral sense, the ability to care about other people. When I saw him this last time, I gave up hope."

"When was that?" I spoke quietly, controlling my eagerness.

"In early May. He hadn't been home in three years, and he'd changed so much I barely recognized him. He was skin and bones. His hair was long, and he'd grown a shaggy beard. He looked and smelled as if he hadn't washed or slept in days. And his eyes were wild, like a madman's. He said he was in trouble. When we asked him what kind, he wouldn't explain. He just begged us to protect him. Sir William said he could stay here. We thought that was what he wanted. He'd brought his trunks, and some packages."

An internal thunder reverberated through me. Niall apparently hadn't left everything behind in his house in Whitechapel or his secret laboratory. Did he have with him the makings of his weapon?

"But Niall said that people were after him, dangerous people, and he couldn't stay here because they would find him." Lady

Kathleen sounded as perplexed and frightened as she must have been that day. "So Sir William sent Niall . . ."

"Where?" I asked urgently.

Lady Kathleen compressed her lips. We listened to Slade say, "Your son is a danger to himself as well as to others. I'll ask you again: Where is he?"

"If he's a problem, I'll deal with him myself," Sir William said.

Lady Kathleen's face twitched, responding to the tug of the conflict inside her. "Sir William doesn't want me to tell."

"There really are people after Niall," I said. "Your best hope of keeping him safe is to help Mr. Slade find him first."

"I've never gone against Sir William's wishes."

I could see that she longed to place the heavy weight of her son's troubles in other hands. "This time you must. For Niall's own good."

She exhaled a tremulous, forlorn sigh. "I can't."

"Then you must help Mr. Slade persuade Sir William to change his mind. Come."

When I brought her to the terrace, I was shocked by the transformation that Sir William had undergone. He looked older and shrunken, his confidence diminished. In his heart he knew the worst about Niall despite his lifelong effort not to believe it, but he raised his fist to Slade and said, "Get off my property, or I'll have you shot!"

Lady Kathleen hastened to him. "Mr. and Mrs. Slade are right. You must tell them where Niall is."

He turned his anger on her. "Don't tell me what to do!"

She persisted bravely. "We can't protect Niall anymore. We need help."

"You're no match for Wilhelm Stieber," Slade interjected. The force of his personality held Sir William captive as if he had the man by the throat. "Let me save Niall." Compassion mellowed his clear, hard gaze as he glanced at Lady Kathleen. "For his mother's sake."

Sir William stared at us in wounded fury, as though we'd all conspired against him. Then he lowered himself into a chair and spoke to his wife in a quavering voice. "Our son is a criminal. He's gone mad. He killed those women. I'm to blame because I didn't help him when I could have."

The sight of a strong, proud man breaking is terrible. I could hardly bear to watch.

Lady Kathleen laid her hand on her husband's. "Help him now," she urged softly.

Sir William turned to Slade. "I lied when I said I hadn't seen Niall in years. He came home a few weeks ago."

"In early May." Lady Kathleen repeated the words she'd spoken to me.

"I sent Niall to France the next day. A distant cousin of mine owns a château in Normandy. Niall is there—as far as I know."

33

>-<

I HAVE NOTICED AN INTERESTING PHENOMENON IN FICTION: When-ever the author tells the reader what his characters are planning to do, it does not happen. Something else occurs to render their care-ful forethought useless, to foil their hopes and the reader's anticipa-tions. Whether or not this is always true in books, it is in the case of the story that I am now telling.

Before we left Ireland, Slade and I formulated a plan to travel to London, where I would stay with his sister while he went on to Paris. There he had friends who would accompany him to Normandy and help him capture Niall Kavanagh. Afterward, he would deter-mine what to do with Niall Kavanagh and the weapon and how to take his revenge on Wilhelm Stieber. I couldn't like this plan. Not only was it vague, but I dreaded sitting idle and waiting for news of what had happened.

Would Wilhelm Stieber kill Slade? Or would Slade prevail, but abide by his stubborn intention to leave me because he didn't want me tainted by his sins?

But I could not follow Slade where he was going. Impro-priety aside, I would only be in the way, and the danger was too great. I therefore reluctantly agreed to the plan. We had no idea that unexpected complications would force us to change course.

We arrived in London early the next morning. I was exhausted and disoriented from crossing the kingdom so many times that I'd lost count. The trains roaring in and out of Euston Station, the hurrying crowds, and the smoke and heat of the city all dazed me. I didn't notice anything amiss until Slade said, "There are more police than usual."

I blinked and saw the constables patrolling the platform. "What are they looking for?"

"Your guess is as good as mine," Slade said. "But I have a bad feeling about this."

When we entered the station, his instincts proved correct. Two large posters hung on the wall. One showed a black-and-white reproduction of my portrait by the artist George Richmond, which I'd sat for last year. Beneath it were printed the bold words, "Have you seen this woman?" Smaller print gave my name, description, and words to the effect that I was wanted by the police. The other poster bore a crude drawing of Slade, with a similar legend.

Slade cursed under his breath. I said, "This is surely Lord Eastbourne's doing." The few days' grace that Lord Palmerston had obtained for me were over. Now I, and Slade, were the objects of what appeared to be a massive manhunt.

"We'd better make ourselves scarce." Slade took my arm and we hurried but did not run outside, lest we draw attention. He waved down a carriage, flung our bags on top, and bundled me inside, shouting an address to the driver as he jumped in with me. Fortunately the driver didn't recognize us. Slade shut the windows, to keep us hidden while we rode through London. "You'll be safe at my sister's house."

"When shall you leave for France?"

"Today. The sooner I get out of England, the better."

The carriage eventually turned onto the fashionable street in Mayfair where Slade's widowed sister, Mrs. Katherine Abbott, lived. Slade pulled his hat low over his eyes and looked out the window. He called to the driver, "Don't stop! Go around the block."

"What's the matter?" I asked.

"There's a constable standing in the square. He's watching

Kate's house. Lord Eastbourne must have ordered surveillance on my associates."

I trembled with fear. As we rattled down the alley behind the house, Slade peeked out the window again and said, "Good. They didn't think to station a man here. Come on."

We jumped from the carriage. Slade hauled down our baggage and paid the driver. The alley was lined with brick walls that enclosed the back gardens of elegant Georgian houses. When we hurried through the gate, I recognized the pretty garden—I'd stayed here before, during my adventures of 1848. Slade sneaked us in the back door. We stole through the kitchen and up the stairs. The house was quiet. We saw no one until we entered the morning room. There, a woman dressed in a pale green silk gown sat at a desk, writing a letter.

"Kate," Slade said.

She started, exclaimed in surprise, and turned. Her hand clutched her throat.

"John! And Charlotte! Good Lord, what a fright you gave me!" Katherine Abbott bore a strong resemblance to her brother. She had his black hair and striking gray eyes, but her figure was small, slim, and graceful, her features prettier. "If I were the kind of woman who gets the vapors, I'd have fainted dead away!"

"I'm sorry," Slade said. "We didn't mean to scare you."

"Then you shouldn't have sneaked into my house like thieves." Kate's anger turned to relief. She embraced Slade, then me. "Thank God you're all right! Do you know that the police are after you? Do you know what they think you've done?"

"Yes," I said.

"How do you know, Kate?" Slade asked.

"They were here," she said, "not an hour ago. Two of the most arrogant, menacing fellows I've ever had the bad luck to meet. John, they said you went insane and murdered two nurses in Bedlam. As for you, Charlotte, they said you murdered a Russian actress and three women of the streets in Whitechapel. Of course I didn't believe it. It's utter hogwash!"

I was so thankful for her loyalty that tears momentarily blinded me.

"What in the world is going on?" Kate demanded.

Slade said, "We'd better sit down."

We sat in the parlor. Slade told Kate about his travails in Russia, Wilhelm Stieber, Niall Kavanagh and the invention, his arrest, and his incarceration and torture in Bedlam. "I killed those nurses in self-defense. Had I not, we wouldn't be having this conversation. I'm sorry, Kate."

"Well, I'm not," she said staunchly. "I won't have a Prussian mercenary spy murdering my brother."

I took up the story, telling Kate how I'd spotted Slade in Bedlam and all that had led up to my finding Katerina and being arrested for multiple murders and thrown in Newgate Prison.

"Oh, you poor dear!" she exclaimed, hugging me. "If only I'd known! I'd have rescued you."

Her sympathy was balm to my spirit, which had suffered from too much cruel treatment of late. "Fortunately, the Queen intervened." I detailed my search for Niall Kavanagh. Slade and I took turns describing Kavanagh's secret laboratory in Tonbridge, what we'd found there, and what had happened—except for our personal matters.

Slade finished our tale with an account of what we'd learned in Ireland. "I'm going to France," he told Kate. "I brought Charlotte to stay with you while I'm gone, until this whole business is cleared up."

I expected that Kate would readily agree, for she'd helped me before, during Slade's and my collaboration in 1848. She had liked me and encouraged my relationship with her brother. But instead she looked stricken. "John, I'm afraid that's not possible."

"Why not?" Slade asked.

"Do you know that the police are watching this house?"

"Yes. That's why we had to sneak in."

Kate shook her head, twisted her hands. "You can't get out of the country."

"Of course I can," Slade said. "The policeman outside didn't see us arrive, and he won't catch me when I leave."

"No, you don't understand!" Kate explained, "You're the most wanted criminal in the kingdom. The army has troops stationed at the ports, watching for you. They have orders to capture you alive or dead."

"What?" Slade said as I gasped in dismay. "How do you know?"

"Your former superior told me," Kate said.

"Lord Eastbourne?" Slade said. "He was here?"

"With the police," Kate said. "He's questioning everybody connected with you. He knows you'll try to leave England. He told me that if I saw you, I should persuade you to turn yourself in—if I wanted you to live."

Slade and I exchanged a look of horror. Lord Eastbourne had anticipated our moves all too well.

"He's also looking for Charlotte," Kate told us. "He suspects you're together."

"Don't worry," Slade said. "I've sneaked out of England unnoticed before; I can do it again. And Charlotte should be safe here as long as she stays out of sight."

"No. She won't. Lord Eastbourne and his men searched the house. Even though you weren't here, he thinks you'll show up eventually. He said he'll come and search it again." Kate turned to me, regretful. "I want more than anything in the world to help you, but you mustn't be here when he comes back."

"She's right," Slade said.

I was dismayed that our plan had foundered, and Slade's voice troubled me because it sounded so forlorn. Exhaustion and pain had caught up with him; he hunched over in his seat, arms resting on his knees, hands dangling. I was frightened because I'd counted on him to know what to do next, and he didn't. But he quickly rallied and got to his feet.

"There must be some trustworthy friend I can lodge you with," he said, pacing the floor. "Just let me think."

"No," I said, for I saw the only solution. "I must go to France with you."

Kate exclaimed in astonishment. Slade stopped pacing, his expression grim rather than surprised: he had been expecting my suggestion.

"A woman has no place in such business," Kate told me. "Think of the danger!"

"My work will be harder if I have to worry about you," Slade said bluntly.

"I'll be safer away from England. You won't have to worry about Lord Eastbourne finding me." I added, "I've been useful so far. I can be again."

"Very well." Slade turned to Kate, who gamely accepted our decision. "Our first challenge is to get away from this house without being caught. Sister, dear, we need your help."

Kate insisted that Slade and I must eat before we departed. After breakfast, I hurriedly washed myself; then she helped me dress in a teal silk gown and frilled bonnet she'd lent me. When I rode off in her carriage with her driver, the police constable tipped his hat to me; he'd mistaken me for Kate. He didn't see Slade crouched on the carriage floor with our bags. We traveled across the Thames to Southwark.

Southwark is populated by dock laborers, boatmen, and other folk who make their living on the water. Their disreputable lodging houses and taverns stood amid shops stocked with ropes and sails, quadrants and brass sextants, chronometers and compasses, and preserved meat and biscuits guaranteed to keep during long voyages. We proceeded to the wharves that had existed long before the new walled docks on the other side of the river had been built to accommodate large modern steamships. The wharves handled London's coastal trade, and international trade in goods that didn't need guarding. Here, the river was crowded with passenger steamers, lighters, and barges. Stevedores loaded grain, coal, tea, wool, produce, and timber onto ships that looked rundown, blackened by the smoke that puffed from their stacks. Laborers pushed wine casks in handcarts to the warehouses. The fragrance of coffee and spices competed with the stench of hides. When we alit from the carriage, Slade's eyes scanned the scene.

"What are you looking for?" I asked.

"A friend who owes me a favor."

While we trudged along the wharves, I heard loud swearing near a particularly disreputable hulk of a steamship. Discolored sails furled around its masts. Its hull was scuffed, patched, and stained with algae. The captain stood on the dock, shouting orders peppered with curses to a crew comprised of turbaned lascars and a Jamaican with skin as black as ebony, who were fixing the paddle-wheels.

Slade called, "Francis Arnold! Why don't you junk that crippled wreck of yours?"

The captain turned and scowled. He had a long torso and short legs; he wore a threadbare military coat and cap. Fierce blue eyes blazed under shaggy brows and tousled, sun-bleached yellow hair. "The *Gipsy* is as seaworthy as any ship in the world." His accent was unexpectedly cultured. His complexion was a weathered red-brown, lined and freckled, with a tracery of white scars on his left cheek. "Who in hell are you to say—" He stared in wonder and recognition. "No! My eyes deceive me!" His face broke into a grin full of white teeth. "It can't be John Slade!"

"In the flesh," Slade said.

They exchanged greetings, which involved punches, backslapping, and jokes in different languages. Captain Arnold said, "What have you been doing all these years?"

"Working for the Foreign Office, among other things."

"Ah." Captain Arnold raised a bushy eyebrow. He obviously knew Slade was a spy.

Slade declined to elaborate. "What have you been up to?"

"Carrying cargo to and from America and the West Indies," Arnold said. Slade later told me that Arnold belonged to a breed of ship captains who had no fixed schedule and no regular ports of call. They took on cargo wherever they could find it and transported it anywhere. Their vessels were often built of junk from marine yards, and they sometimes had space for passengers. "I just returned from Antigua." That explained why he didn't know that Slade was the most wanted man in England. Now he noticed me hovering uneasily in the background.

Slade drew me forward. "May I introduce Captain Francis Arnold. He and I served together in the East India Company army."

"He saved my life during a brawl in a tavern in Lisbon." Captain Arnold touched his scarred cheek. He bowed to me, said, "It's an honor to make your acquaintance, um—?" and looked questioningly at Slade.

Slade swallowed. "This is my wife, Charlotte." He seemed as abashed as I felt. To appear before strangers as a married couple was one thing; to lie to a friend was embarrassing; but the truth about our lack of a legal relationship would have disgraced me worse.

"Your wife, eh?" Captain Arnold punched Slade's shoulder. "Well done, man! My congratulations. I never thought you'd settle down. You did right to wait. You've found yourself a lovely woman." He smiled at me.

I blushed hotly.

"What brings you here, Slade?" Captain Arnold said. "Are you taking your bride on a tour of your old comrades in hell-raising?"

"I need a favor," Slade said.

"Just ask."

"We need to go to Cherbourg. Can you take us?"

"I'd be glad to, but why not take the packet? It would be much more comfortable for your wife."

"We've run into some trouble. We can't leave England in the usual manner."

Captain Arnold asked no questions. "I can get you to Cherbourg." Later Slade told me that Arnold had a sideline: he smuggled people out of countries in which they had enemies after them or were wanted by the law. "There's just one problem. Business hasn't been good lately. The big ships undercut the small operators like me. I don't have the money to take my ship out without payment up front."

He and Slade put their heads together and figured the cost of the journey. The price they settled on would use up almost all the money Lord Palmerston had given me. How Slade and I would manage later, I knew not; but we paid, gladly. We were on our way to France, and that was all that mattered.

34

❧❦

CAPTAIN ARNOLD LED US UP THE *GIPSY*'S GANGPLANK. THE Jamaican carried our bags aboard. He and the lascar crewmen wore sharp knives. They were alien and frightening. As we went below deck, Captain Arnold said, "You'll have to hide down here while we travel out of England. I apologize for the accommodations. They aren't very pleasant."

That was the understatement of the century. The room was a compartment inside the empty cargo hold, its door a panel cleverly designed to look like part of a solid wall. Not much larger than a closet, it smelled of the tea, spices, coffee, and wool that the ship had carried. It contained a washstand and basin, a chamber pot—and a single mattress covered with an old blanket. I tried to hide my dismay.

"I've slept in worse places," Slade said, affecting a light tone. "And my wife can put up with it for a short time."

"I'll leave you to settle in, then," Captain Arnold said, "while I get the ship ready for the journey."

Alone, we stood in awkward silence on either side of the bed, which nearly covered the grimy floor. Slade said, "We'll take turns sleeping. You can have yours first. I'll go up and help Captain Arnold."

Hidden behind the sliding panel, I felt as if I'd been sealed into my coffin. I examined the bed, which smelled stale, as if it had been used by people who didn't wash. I spread the shawl Kate had lent me over it before I lay down. Exhausted, I promptly fell asleep.

I dreamed that I was hurrying through the criminal lunatics' ward in Bedlam. I carried the dying Oliver Heald cradled in my arms. Drenched with blood, he looked up at me, smiled a ghastly smile, and said, "Anything for my favorite author." Ellen Nussey and Arthur Nicholls trailed us, arguing about whether I had gone mad and should be committed. Julia Garrs stood by an open door and beckoned me. Entering, I found Niall Kavanagh's secret laboratory. The mutilated corpses of three women hung from hooks like sides of beef. They sizzled in the fire that Lord Eastbourne had set. I lay strapped to a table. Gas hissed as Wilhelm Stieber bent over me, fixed clamps around my head, and turned the crank on his torture machine. A jolt of lightning seared my mind and ignited the gas in a white, thunderous, rattling explosion.

I awakened with a scream caught in my throat. I sat up, and the nightmare faded, but the rattling continued. The panel opened, and Slade entered the compartment. He carried a tray laden with bread, cold meat, and cheese, a teapot and cup. "I've brought your dinner."

"What's that noise?" I said.

"They're hauling up the anchor." Slade set down the tray and crouched beside me. "What's the matter?"

"Just a bad dream. What time is it?"

"About ten o'clock at night."

I'd slept the whole day. Now I heard the *Gipsy*'s steam engines roar. The ship began to move, plowing through the river. In spite of my nightmare, I felt refreshed and alert; dreaming often purges the emotions. I realized, more clearly than before, what had happened.

I was no longer Charlotte Brontë, the respectable spinster daughter of Haworth's vicar, or Currer Bell, the toast of literary London. I was a fugitive on the run, a criminal in the eyes of the law. Cut off from society, from my friends and family, I was leaving my homeland, perhaps for good. Surely I would never write another book. My name would sink into infamy, then obscurity. Yet I didn't collapse into tears and sickness and utter helplessness as I had at other times when disaster struck. I felt as if a storm had swept through my life, cleared everything away, and left me calm. If the worst had already happened, what more had I to fear?

I didn't foresee the dangers that lay ahead. I had a sense of lightness, a great relief despite my sorrow. I felt more alive than I ever had. Suddenly I was famished. I gobbled the food that Slade had brought. It seemed the best I'd ever tasted. But when I'd finished eating, how alarmed I was by Slade's appearance! He was unshaven, his clothes dirty from working on the ship, the skin under his eyes shadowed. He looked tired to death.

"When will we be at sea?" I asked.

"Early tomorrow morning."

"Then you'd better sit down. You'll be more comfortable."

Slade reluctantly eased himself onto the bed and sat beside me. Neither of us spoke as the paddlewheels churned and the ship steamed down the Thames. After a while I felt him relax: he'd fallen asleep.

When one is in love, each new discovery about the beloved is miraculous. I'd never seen Slade sleeping, and I gazed upon him with fascination. Slumber erased his usual guarded expression, drained the tension from his muscles. He looked young, innocent, and vulnerable. My desire to touch his face had nothing to do with lust. I felt a new, purer affection toward Slade. Yet it was wrong for me to be in bed with a man to whom I wasn't married.

That undercut my happiness only for an instant. Ideas I'd never entertained before argued with my sense of propriety. Who said I was doing wrong? Society did. But society had already turned against me because it believed I'd broken the rules. Why should I be obligated to obey them any longer? Why hold myself to society's standards of honor? I experienced an elating sensation of recklessness. Perhaps I was now free to live as I pleased.

During our journey down the river, troops stopped and boarded the *Gipsy*. I remained calm as they tramped through the ship. Slade slept on, and I didn't wake him when I heard them outside our compartment. I fancied myself his protector. When they were gone, I congratulated myself on my newfound bravery. Little did I know how severely it would soon be tested.

Hours passed. The engines began to roar at full throttle. A rapping on the panel awakened Slade. Captain Arnold called, "You can come out now."

As we emerged up on the deck, my eyes were dazzled by the sun, a brilliant beacon that had just risen above the horizon where sky met ocean. The sea was calm, colored violet, rippled like shirred silk. The coast of England was a mere smudge behind us, France not yet visible in the distance. Other ships rode the waters, but none near. The *Gipsy* blazed a steady course, paddlewheels splashing, smoke billowing from her stacks. The light had a strange, animated quality; it glinted and danced; whatever it touched shimmered with radiance. I was conscious of each breath of fresh salt air that swelled my lungs, of my heart's rhythm, of the blood swiftly flowing in my veins—and of Slade, who stood in the bow beside me.

I exclaimed, "We've lived to see another day, and I am truly thankful!"

"As am I," Slade said. "Better alive than dead, has always been my philosophy." Sleep had knit the raveled fabric of his health; his color was good. But the eyes he turned to me were clouded by dark thoughts. "Now that we have a moment's leisure, I must tell you how sorry I am for involving you in such bad business."

I couldn't let him shoulder the entire weight of guilt. "It was my own choice to become involved." I could have walked away from him in Bedlam, and I had not. That I had pursued him was wholly my fault.

"I'm not talking about what's happened these past two weeks," Slade said. "I mean the first time I saw you three years ago, when I struck up an acquaintance with you to further the investigation I was conducting. It was selfish of me. I should have left you alone."

"Do you regret knowing me?" I said, hurt by the idea.

Slade said with passion, "Never! My only regret is that you must regret knowing me, and that I have destroyed your love for me and ruined your life. I promise to make things right for you and set you free of me."

"But I don't!" My passion more than equaled his. "You haven't! To be free of you is not what I want!"

Incomprehension rendered his face blank. "But when we were at the laboratory, you indicated that you didn't want anything to do with me except to find Niall Kavanagh and get us out of trouble."

"I didn't mean to." Now was the time to correct his mistake under which I'd allowed him to labor because I couldn't express myself honestly. "I'm in love with you still. That's why I'm here." Slade's company was as important to me as finding Niall Kavanagh and saving England. "I wanted to be with you then. I do now."

Slade shook his head. Gladness tugged his mouth into a smile even as he frowned in disbelief. "Can this be true? Surely I hear you wrong."

I hurried to sweep away his conviction that he was a pariah and that I thought myself too good for him. "I didn't declare my feelings for you because they seemed so hopeless. But things have changed."

"Not all things. There's still blood on my hands. I'm still a fugitive."

"So am I." I endeavored to share the thoughts I'd had while he was sleeping. "We've gone beyond ordinary law and morality. The past is over; we can only go forward. And if I am to be alone in the world but for one companion, I thank Heaven that my companion is you." This was the most fervent, unguarded, and audacious speech I'd ever made to a man; yet I felt neither hesitation nor shame. Some force within me had overpowered the shy, convention-bound woman I once was. I flung my arms open wide. "I will be with you on any terms."

Slade leaned back from me, alarmed. "You are too generous."

"It isn't generosity that compels me, it is pure selfishness. I want you. I mean to have you if you still want me." Even though my brazenness astonished me, I said, "Whatever time I have left on this earth, I want us to live it to the fullest together, and if you refuse me this, then God damn you, John Slade!"

I was shocked by my profanity, and further shocked when Slade threw back his head and let loose a boisterous laugh that carried across the water. "Well spoken for a parson's daughter, Charlotte Brontë! You've just made me the happiest man alive!"

He lifted me off my feet and spun around. I laughed, too, with the same joyous, reckless abandon. Sea and sky whirled past me. Giddy and lightheaded, I exulted. Then Slade's expression sobered. He stopped whirling and lowered me to the deck. I felt the smile vanish from my face. The sun struck his at an angle so that all the light of the day seemed to emanate from his eyes. Never had I so wanted him to kiss me; but he did not. Instead, we gazed at each other in full, awed realization of the pact we'd made. I heard myself utter words I'd never imagined speaking.

"I don't care if we can't marry. I'll be your wife in fact if not in name or law."

I was dizzied by the thought of the physical intimacy that my proposition implied. Slade was visibly shaken by the heat that flared between us. Then his eyes crinkled with sly humor. "I'm pleased to tell you that the sacrifice of your virtue won't be necessary."

Contrary to a popular fallacy, ship captains are not permitted to officiate at weddings while at sea. Any marriages thus created are not recognized by the law. But circumstances had favored Slade and me. Captain Arnold was an ordained clergyman who'd served as a chaplain for the East India Company's army, who preached Sunday sermons aboard his own ship. Indeed, he had converted his entire crew to Christianity. I know not what reason Slade gave him as to why we wanted him to marry us after telling him we were already married. Maybe Slade explained; maybe Captain Arnold was bound by loyalty to take his old comrade's request in stride; at any rate, he agreed.

Slade and I took turns washing in cold seawater in a shower bath that the crew had rigged up in a shed on deck. I dressed in a lilac-colored gown I'd bought in London, Slade in a clean set of spare clothes from his valise. That very morning Captain Arnold performed the ceremony. Slade and I stood side by side in the bow, with the crew for witnesses. I had no veil or flowers. Our music was the sound of the ship's engines and churning wheels. It wasn't the wedding I'd envisioned. In fact, I'd been so certain I would never marry that I'd avoided trying to imagine the impossible. Now I could hardly believe I wasn't dreaming.

"If anyone present knows any reason why this couple may not be joined together in holy matrimony," Captain Arnold said, "speak now or forever hold your peace."

I thought of Jane Eyre and her first, ill-fated wedding to Mr. Rochester. I almost expected a stranger to materialize and declare the existence of an impediment. But none did.

Captain Arnold said, "Do you, John Slade, take this woman to be your lawfully wedded wife, to have and to hold, from this day forward, for better and for worse, for richer or poorer, in sickness and in health, to love and to cherish until death do you part?"

Slade turned to me. I doubt that any other bridegroom had ever looked so serious and ardent. He said in a quiet, firm voice, "I do."

I looked into his eyes, and I began trembling violently; I felt hot, then cold, as realization sank in: I had gained the man I loved, but with what consequence? My happiness would be dependent on Slade, our fates entwined. I felt my separate identity dissolving. In another moment, Charlotte Brontë—and Currer Bell—must give way to Mrs. John Slade. What a solemn, strange, and perilous thing was marriage! Yet my attachment to Slade never faltered. When Captain Arnold repeated the ritual question to me, I answered, "I do," without hesitation. Triumph swelled inside me. Slade smiled as if he'd read my last-minute doubts but never believed they would prevent our marriage. It seemed predestined, a step along a course from which neither of us could deviate.

"Have you a ring?" Captain Arnold asked.

Slade took from his pocket the ring I'd bought for myself. I proffered my hand, which was steady now. He slipped the gold band on my finger. My eyes filled with tears, through which the ring sparkled as brightly as if set with diamonds.

"I pronounce you man and wife." Captain Arnold said to Slade, "You may kiss your bride."

The crew grinned as Slade drew me into his arms. Our kiss was brief, possessive, and fierce. Captain Arnold offered his congratulations. The crew cheered. They improvised a wedding breakfast of bread and cheese enlivened with rum. Afterward, they played wild, exotic music on drums and peculiar stringed instruments. Imagining what Papa and Ellen and my other friends would say if they could see me, I felt a stab of sorrow because they were absent. But I would not ruin this day by dwelling on what I'd lost instead of on what I had. Slade and I danced, exhilarated and laughing.

After the celebration, the captain and crew went back to work, but we lingered on the deck. We were both impatient for what necessarily followed a wedding, yet anxious because it might not live up to our expectations. At last Slade said, "You can go in first."

"All right." Quaking, I went to the cabin where Captain Arnold had said we could stay now that we didn't need to hide anymore. It was small, but the linens on the berth were clean, and it had a porthole that admitted the sunlight and sea wind. I undressed, then put on my plain white nightgown. My reflection in the mirror over the washstand looked less like a bride than a nun, I thought ruefully. I sat on the berth, pulling the sheets up to my chin.

Soon Slade entered the room and shut the door. He looked as nervous as I felt. I watched him undress. Although I blushed, I did not turn away. We were married; I could know him as well as I wished. Slade stripped off his shoes, socks, shirt, and trousers, his motions clumsy and self-conscious. Wonder filled me as I saw him completely naked, his muscles lean and strong, his skin sleek with black hairs. The only nude males I'd ever seen before were Greek statues, and these had not prepared me for my first full sight of my husband. Slade's aroused manhood moved me profoundly. I burned with need for him. Forgetting modesty, I undid my nightdress and let it fall around my waist.

Such delight I took in the sharp breath that I heard Slade draw; what pride in the desire I saw in his eyes!

He slid under the sheets with me. The press of his body against mine as we embraced was shockingly personal. There is no warmth like the warmth of bare flesh touching bare flesh. It consumed me as flames consume dry kindling. This physical part of marriage seemed an ordeal by fire. At first we were awkward together. His hand caught in my hair when he stroked it; when we kissed, our noses bumped; knees and elbows jarred as we attempted to meld ourselves together. I didn't mind the awkwardness; it made our lovemaking seem real, rather than a fantasy of the sort I'd had during lonely nights. Nor did I fear what must happen, even though I'd heard married women speak in whispers about how painful it was. Rather, I feared that I would fail to please Slade, that he would find me lacking or offensive.

But the fervor with which he kissed me soon convinced me that he found me as desirable as I could hope. And my own desire banished my inhibitions. When he caressed my breasts, I shamelessly moaned with pleasure. I eagerly caressed him, greedy to acquaint myself with his body, smug in my wifely right to enjoy him. I gloried in the exclamations of pleasure that I provoked from him. Between us we conjured up the ancient magic that all lovers do. We moved in graceful rhythm on the bed, turning and entwining and arching together, as if in a dance. I heard the ocean, and we became one with it. I smelled the sea on Slade, tasted salt on his skin. When I stroked his manhood, it pulsed with the swift current of blood inside. An urgent tide of desire rose in my own loins. I grew wet and slick with it. I gasped out, "I am ready."

Slade hesitated. "I fear I'll hurt you."

"I don't care!" I lay on my back, opening myself to him.

He mounted me. The instant his manhood touched between my legs, my excitement leaped too high. I could not wait for Slade. I cried out as I soared to the crest of the ecstasy that I'd experienced for the first time, with him, three years ago in the forest in Scotland. As I rode the waves of pleasure, he entered me. I felt a resistance within, then a tearing sensation. My pleasure numbed the pain. Slade thrust, his breath coming faster, his eyes closed, his face and muscles straining. I held him tight, savoring his pleasure as much as my own. He arched his back and shouted. I felt his hardness break, then the warm flood of his release. As he lay against me, panting and exhausted, drenched in our perspiration, I clasped him as if he were a drowning man I'd pulled from the sea.

We spent most of the next two days in our cabin. The crew tactfully left us alone. They set food and drink outside the door. Slade and I were lost to the world, occupied with mutual exploration. Our first lovemaking had dissolved the boundaries between us. My natural reserve was gone. Marriage negated the fact that Slade and I had known each other for but a short time. There was no intimacy in which we did not engage. I grew as familiar with Slade's body as my own. But our discoveries were not confined to the physical. We talked for hours, sharing the most private details of our lives. I learned about Slade's family and childhood, his years in the East India Company's army, and his greatest experiences as a spy. He was surprised to hear about my newfound fame as an author and the literary friends I'd made. Everything we said and did had a serious, urgent significance, as if we were trying to cram a life's worth of experience into these few brief hours.

Perhaps they were all we would have.

Two days after we'd left London, the ship neared the high cliffs, long beaches, and jagged rocks of the Normandy coast. Slade and I stood on the deck, ready to resume our search for Niall Kavanagh.

35

CAPTAIN ARNOLD LET US OFF AT
THE DOCK IN CHERBOURG. THE
afternoon was cloudy, with a damp, chill wind that rocked the ships
in the harbor and chilled me to the bone. Cherbourg was a
medieval town no more remarkable than any English port village.
Slade and I walked through drab, malodorous streets so narrow
that one could almost touch the gray buildings on either side. The
people spoke French in a dialect I found hard to understand. This
was not the France I'd always yearned to visit. If Cherbourg had
any fine museums or monuments, I did not see them. We were a
hundred and seventy miles from Paris, that great capital of fashion,
art, and literature, but I didn't care. I was living a miracle.

I had boarded the ship a spinster and disembarked a married
woman. I looked at Slade and thought, "That is my husband." No
other man was as handsome, strong, or dashing as mine. Glowing
with pride, I wanted the whole world to see us together. I felt more
confident about the future than I ever had, as if our marriage rendered us invincible.

That was an illusion, as I would too soon discover.

Slade scrutinized the scene for threats. "France seems quiet.
There shouldn't be any revolutions to bother us."

During the revolutions of 1848, the French populace had
rebelled against government corruption and repression, high food
prices, and unemployment. Radical societies staged public demon-

strations in Paris. The government sent in the army, which fired on the mobs. Violent insurrection spread. King Louis-Philippe abdicated. The radicals formed a new government, but their haphazard reforms dissatisfied workers all over France. Three days of civil war against the army ensued. The streets of Paris ran with blood. Some fifteen hundred people were killed. The revolution was eventually suppressed by the military dictatorship that took power. From the turmoil rose Louis Napoleon Bonaparte, purported nephew of the first Napoleon. He symbolized revolution and authority, tradition and social reform; he promised everything to everybody. Elected President of France in December 1848, he spearheaded the formation of a new republic. I understood that it was a severe, oppressive regime, but it had indeed calmed down the country.

"We'd better find lodgings," Slade said.

His French was better than mine; I marveled at his facility with foreign languages as he quickly obtained a room in a modest inn. To fortify ourselves before we assailed Niall Kavanagh, we ate a good luncheon of chicken cooked in a sauce of cider and cream, fish stew with shrimp and mussels, cinnamon rice pudding, and a strong apple brandy. Then we set out for the château.

Following the directions given us by Sir William, we walked east out of town. The château was a sixteenth-century miniature castle, built of gray stone in hybrid Gothic and Renaissance style, whose two round towers with pointed roofs rose above woods surrounded by orchards. On this gloomy late afternoon it had a foreboding, sinister aspect; but I, in my high spirits, thought it romantic.

"What is our plan?" I asked Slade.

"To hell with plans," he said. "Little good they've done us. We'll play it by ear this time."

He rang the bell attached to the locked iron gate. No one answered our summons. A cold, thin rain began to fall. Slade said, "You could slide between the wall and the gate. I can climb over the top."

We did. Inside, we walked up a short road, beneath dense foliage. The owner liked privacy, Sir William had mentioned. He was a wealthy amateur wild game hunter who collected animals for zoos and specimens for scientists. He was presently away on an expedition in India. An expanse of paving stones encircled the château and separated it from the forest. We marched up to the front door, an iron-banded affair recessed in an arch. Slade employed the brass knocker.

"Niall Kavanagh?" he called.

There was no sound except the rain pelting leaves. I backed out of the arch, looked up at the château, and saw a movement in an upstairs window—a curtain lifted and hastily dropped. "He's here."

Repeated knocking and calling did no good. Slade tested the door; it was locked. We circled the house, unsuccessfully trying other entrances. At the back we came upon mews and storage buildings. By the wall Slade found a square structure with a stone base, built on a slant, perhaps two feet tall on its high side, covered by two iron doors.

"It must be the entrance to the cellar." He cautiously lifted open one door, then the other. Inside, wooden stairs descended, vanishing into darkness.

I have an instinctive fear of dark places underground. "We aren't going down there, are we?"

"*We* aren't," Slade said. "You stay here."

Marriage hadn't changed his high-handed way of ordering me about. Vexed, I said, "I won't let you go. It can't be safe."

"We didn't come all this way to be safe. And this appears to be the only way to get to Niall Kavanagh. Don't worry—I'll be careful."

Marriage hadn't given me any power to control him, either. I could only watch nervously as Slade reached in his pocket and produced matches and a candle. Holding the lit candle in front of him, he cautiously descended the stairs, whose shaft had walls made of earth, stones, and timbers. The stairs were steep, their end too far underground to see. Suddenly he yelled, plunged downward, and vanished. I heard a series of bumps, then silence.

"John!" Terrified, I bent over the entrance and peered down. Did Slade lie unconscious at the bottom of the stairs? I tried not to think that he might be dead. I saw nothing. What should I do?

I had read enough novels to know that the heroine who ventures into dark cellars inevitably meets with disaster, but I could not abandon Slade. There was no one to rescue him except me. I crawled backward down the stairs, clinging to the risers above me as my feet groped for the ones below. The daylight framed by the doors overhead did not illuminate my way very far. I was soon engulfed in darkness, blind. Reaching the point where Slade had disappeared, I called his name; I received no answer. I tested the step with my foot. It seemed as intact and level as any of the others. Thinking that Slade must have slipped and fallen, I lowered my weight onto it.

It gave way as I let go of the upper step to which I'd been holding. I fell screaming through a distance that seemed like miles. My feet hit a hard surface; then I tumbled head over heels down a steep, slippery ramp. My screams echoed in the utter blackness that surrounded me. The ground leveled out, and I stopped in mid-tumble when my feet struck something. It grunted and said, "Bloody hell!"

"John?" Glad I was to hear his voice, but terrified that I'd hurt him. "Are you all right?"

"I was until you kicked me in the back. Are you?"

Sitting up, I moved my arms and legs. "Yes." I ached all over, but nothing seemed broken.

"What are you doing down here? I told you to stay outside."

"I followed you because I was worried about you."

"Well, now we're both trapped," Slade said glumly.

My hand found his; we held onto each other in silence for a moment. "At least we're together."

"For better or worse." Slade chuckled. He withdrew his hands from mine. "Now where did that candle go?" There were fumbling noises. "Ah."

I heard a scrape, and a flame flared; Slade relit the candle. We stood, and he held the candle aloft. I saw ancient stone walls slick with moisture and became conscious of the dank, earthen, and animal smells in the chilly air. The flagstone floor was littered with dirt, straw, and rodent droppings. The light didn't penetrate the farthest reaches of the cavernous room. We could barely see the rafters some twenty feet above.

Slade shone the candlelight on the ramp down which we'd tumbled. "I'm ready to leave this pit, aren't you?"

We crawled up the ramp. At the top, we stood and looked up at the trapdoor through which we'd fallen. Slade raised his hands, but there was at least three feet of space between his fingertips and the door. "Climb on my back," he said.

I obeyed, clutching at him while he swayed. Kneeling awkwardly on his shoulders, I pushed up on the door. "I can't move it."

Slade lowered me. "There must be another way out of here."

We slid down the ramp, then explored the cellar. The candle's flame elongated. "That draft must be coming from a door," I said.

As we forged onward, a large square object came into view. It was a cage with thick iron bars that looked big enough to contain the Minotaur.

"The owner must use this for the wild animals he brings home," Slade said.

A creaking sound came from overhead. We looked up as a rectangle of brightness opened in the ceiling. A shaft of daylight beamed upon us. An object came hurtling down. It crashed on the floor with the sound of glass breaking. It was a large bottle, now in fragments. The liquid it had contained spread over the floor. From the liquid rose fumes that smelled of chemicals, pungent and sickly sweet, disturbingly familiar.

"It's ether!" I'd had an unfortunate and unforgettable experience with ether in 1848.

Slade and I dodged more bottles that shattered. We covered our noses and mouths with our sleeves and hurried toward the far end of the cellar, but the fumes overtook us. Slade said, "I have to put out the candle or they'll ignite the fumes." He blew on the candle. Above us, the trapdoor slammed shut. We were plunged into darkness. The fumes filled the cellar. I couldn't help breathing them. Lightheaded and drowsy, I collapsed, then fell into deep, impenetrable unconsciousness.

A throbbing headache awakened me. I opened my eyes to dim, hazy, yellow-tinged light. My body was stiff from lying on the hard surface under me. Slowly the world gained definition. I saw a ceiling made of rusty metal a few feet above my face. When I turned my head to my left, fuzzy vertical stripes, crossed at wider intervals by horizontal ones, emerged from the haze. I blinked, and the stripes turned into iron bars. My wits came back in a cold rush of dread. I remembered the cellar, the cage, the breaking bottles, and the ether fumes, which I no longer smelled. But where was Slade?

I turned my head toward my right. He lay near me, flat on his back. His eyes were closed, but his chest rose and fell with even breaths. He was unconscious but alive. My sigh of relief caught in my throat as I realized that we were inside the cage . . . and that there was someone else in the cellar with us. I could hear breathing that had the ragged, wheezy sound of bad lungs. Paper rustled; a pen scratched. I smelled liquor and a fetid, sour human scent. A man sat on a stool some ten paces from the cage, a lamp on the floor beside him. He hunched over a notebook propped on his knees, writing furiously. His white shirt and dark trousers hung on his thin body. Tousled, shaggy red hair partially concealed his face; I could only see a beaked nose and the glint of gold-rimmed spectacles. He lifted a wine bottle, his hand trembling as he gulped a thirsty draught. His visage struck such a bolt of dreadful recognition into my heart that I sat up and stared.

During the earlier part of the adventures I describe herein, I had encountered the ghosts of persons beloved to me, and now it was happening again. Many times had I seen the man before me in just such an attitude, on nights when drink and drugs tormented his mind and he scribbled poems until he collapsed from exhaustion. Many times had I heard him laboring to breathe while the consumption ravaged his lungs. Three years ago I had stood by his deathbed. And here he was, resurrected.

"Branwell," I said, my voice raspy from the ether, cracking in disbelief.

He started, dropped his pen, and turned to me. Now I realized that this apparition was not my brother. His nose was not as long or sharp as Branwell's, his face not as gaunt. Branwell had died at age thirty-one; this man was at least a decade older. Yet the resemblance was still astounding. He had the same coloring, the same flush of liquor on his cheeks. He, too, had once been handsome. He had a similar loose, sensual mouth, and brown eyes that were sunken and bloodshot, fevered by madness. He rose and walked toward me with Branwell's unsteady gait. Stopping short of the cage, he glared at me.

"Who are you?" Although his voice was deeper than Branwell's, it had a familiar inflection—an Irish accent not quite erased by an English education.

Addled by the ether, shocked by the sight of him, I couldn't speak.

"Who is he?" The man pointed at Slade.

Slade stirred, groaned, and propped himself up on his elbows. "Charlotte?" His voice was furred with sleep. He gazed in bleary confusion at the man before us. "Who—?"

Now I realized who the man was. "This is Niall Kavanagh."

Slade rubbed his eyes. "Well," he said, at once bewildered and gratified. "Dr. Kavanagh. At last."

"How do you know who I am?" Fear joined suspicion in Kavanagh's manner. "Who are you people?"

"My name is John Slade, and this is Charlotte Brontë." Slade added, "My wife," as though he'd momentarily forgotten we were married. He dragged himself over to Kavanagh. "Pleased to make your acquaintance." He extended his hand through the cage's bars.

Kavanagh recoiled. Slade noticed the cage and the fact that we were inside it. His gaze moved to the stout iron padlock that held the door shut. He frowned. "Did you put us in here?"

"Yes." Kavanagh grinned.

"Did you throw the bottles of ether at us?"

"I did."

"Why?"

"Because you were trespassing." Kavanagh uttered a giggle tinged with hysteria. It raised a chill on my skin, for I had often heard it from Branwell. My dead brother truly seemed to live inside Niall Kavanagh, whose humor abruptly turned to angry belligerence. "Why did you come?"

"Let us out of the cage," Slade said, "and we'll explain."

"No!" Kavanagh faltered backward. "If I let you out, it's all over for me." Again I heard the echo of Branwell in his voice. *It's all over for me*, Branwell had often said during fits of black despair. "You want to destroy me and steal my work—just like everybody else!"

I remembered Branwell claiming that the world was against him, that everybody was in league to plagiarize his poems, wring all the artistic talent from him, and toss him aside like a dry husk. "We don't want to hurt you," I assured Niall Kavanagh in the soothing voice I'd employed with my brother. "We came to help you."

"Why should you want to help me? I don't know you. How do you know me? Who are you?"

I opened my mouth to speak. Slade said, "Charlotte." His tone warned me that our captor might react badly to the truth about ourselves or our motives. I turned to Slade. "We owe him an explanation." I then told Kavanagh, "I'm an authoress. My husband is a former espionage agent for the British crown. We've learned that Lord Eastbourne at the Foreign Office employed you to build a device based on your research on animalcules."

Kavanagh pounced on this news with all the temper that Slade had anticipated. "Lord Eastbourne said my invention was worthless. He ordered me to cease working on it. He reneged on our contract, the bastard!" Kavanagh's expression turned sly. "But he didn't fool me. Lord Eastbourne wanted to steal my invention and take credit for it himself." He didn't seem to have considered the possibility that Lord Eastbourne had realized that the weapon worked far too well and was far too dangerous to be built and deployed.

Now Kavanagh regarded us with heightened suspicion. "Are you working with Lord Eastbourne?"

"Far from it," Slade said. "He did me a bad turn, too."

"Any enemy of Lord Eastbourne's is a friend of mine," Kavanagh said, although he sounded less than amicable. "But I don't need help. I'm quite all right on my own."

"No, you aren't," Slade said. "You're in a lot of trouble."

"How would you know?"

"You were in such a hurry to quit the British Isles that you left your things behind," Slade said. "Not to mention that you look like a wreck."

Kavanagh's distrust deepened. "How did you find me?"

"We spoke with your parents," Slade said. "They told us you were here."

Kavanagh huffed out angry breaths; he clawed his hair. "They promised to keep it secret! The traitors!"

"They're concerned about you," I hastened to say. "You told them that someone is after you. They said you were terrified."

"Not anymore." Kavanagh's quaking body and the haunted look in his eyes belied his words. "I ran away from Lord Eastbourne. Surely he's stopped looking for me by now."

"He hasn't," Slade said. "A few days ago he went to your laboratory in Tonbridge. He burned the place down. What do you think he'll do when he catches up with you?"

Kavanagh wobbled. Fear paled the flush in his cheeks. "He'll never find me here."

"Don't count on it," Slade said. "Lord Eastbourne will go through the same channels that my wife and I did. But he's not your only problem."

"What are you talking about?"

I took up the story. "Lord Eastbourne isn't the only person who's after you. There's a man named Wilhelm Stieber. He's the chief spy for Tsar Nicholas of Russia. He has two Prussian soldiers—"

I stopped because Kavanagh's face had turned so ghastly white that I thought he would faint. He dropped onto his stool and whispered, "It's true, then. I wasn't just imagining them. They were snooping around my house in Whitechapel. I saw them when I went back to look for some things I thought I'd left there. I hoped it was just a hallucination." Hunched in fear, he asked, "What do they want with me?"

"Stieber knows about your invention," Slade said. "He wants it for the Tsar."

Kavanagh stared, his mouth open, astonished. "He believes my invention works?"

"Yes. That's why he traveled all the way from Russia to find you," Slade said.

"At last!" Kavanagh's mood altered yet again; a gleeful smile crept across his face. "Somebody important believes in me. He doesn't think I'm deluded. At last, my genius is recognized!" Kavanagh dropped to his knees, clasped his hands. "Thank God!"

Slade and I exchanged troubled glances. Kavanagh didn't seem to understand that being wanted by Russia wasn't the boon he craved. Slade said, "Stieber believes so strongly in your invention that he has tortured people to obtain information on your whereabouts. He wants it so badly that he has killed twice in an attempt to get it."

I watched trepidation erase Kavanagh's smile.

"Stieber and the Tsar are even less trustworthy than Lord Eastbourne, and they're far more dangerous," Slade continued. "They mean to use your weapon in a war against England. Thousands of people will die."

"So be it," Kavanagh said, shaken yet defiant. "The way England has treated me, and my people, it deserves to be punished."

"Should a plague start in England, it will spread to Ireland. Your own people will be killed," Slade said.

Kavanagh sniffed.

Reader, I do not mean to give the impression that Branwell was as unreasonable, self-centered, or destructive as Niall Kavanagh. My brother started out a generous, considerate, loving person. Despite his weaknesses and passions to which he succumbed, he never had the dire, inborn flaw that afflicted Kavanagh. But Branwell and Kavanagh were points along the same spectrum of bad character. Even though my experience with Branwell had been miserable, it gave me insight into Niall Kavanagh. Perhaps I could gain command over the man.

"I understand how you feel," I said. "You want to be valued for your genius. You want to be remembered. You want your name written into the history of great men of the world."

Such had been Branwell's fondest wishes. Now Niall Kavanagh nodded eagerly. "Yes! That's right! It's what I've been working toward all my life!"

"But that won't happen if you fall in with Wilhelm Stieber," I said.

"Oh?" Kavanagh thrust out his lip and folded his arms, like a boy who's been denied a sweet. "Why not?"

Slade quickly caught on to my aims. "Stieber will steal your invention. He'll kill you and dump your body in a ditch."

"No one else will know what happened to you," I said. "It will be as if you never existed."

The conceit leaked out of Kavanagh like air from a balloon. At last he realized that he'd gotten in trouble over his head, and he dissolved into trembling fright, misery, and despair. He looked worse than Branwell had when most plagued by the aftereffects of liquor and opium. Crawling up to the cage, he implored, "What should I do? Help me! Please!"

I heard Slade expel a breath of satisfaction. I, too, was glad that we had Niall Kavanagh ready to cooperate with us; but I pitied him as I had pitied Branwell. Such another sorry waste of talent!

"Everything will be all right," Slade assured Kavanagh. "We'll take you back to England. We'll protect you."

"You'll be safe," I said. "You can work in peace, and be rewarded handsomely."

Slade and I avoided looking at each other while we spoke; we felt guilty for deceiving a sick, vulnerable man. Kavanagh didn't know that we intended to turn him over to the British government, which would likely make sure he quit his dangerous research and never built any more destructive devices.

"Oh, yes!" He sobbed in relief; delight shone through his tears while he envisioned a rosy future. "Thank you!"

"All you have to do is let us out of this cage and come with us," Slade said.

"Very well." Kavanagh sprang up. "Now what did I do with the key?" We held our breath, fearing that he'd lost it. Kavanagh began hunting in his pockets. "Oh, no!"

"Maybe you dropped it." I'd enacted such a scene many times with Branwell, when he'd misplaced his valuables. Now I endeavored to stay calm. "Look everywhere you've been since you used the key. Retrace your steps."

Kavanagh crawled along the floor, peering through his spectacles, his hands scrabbling in the dirt. "Ah!" He triumphantly held up the key, scurried to us—then halted. "Why should I trust you to do what you say you will?" His suspicion flared anew.

"Because we have your best interests at heart," I said.

"Because we're the only people who can help you," Slade added. "Unlock the cage, and we'll show you that we're on your side."

Kavanagh frowned, torn between his wish to believe us and the fear engendered by drink, disease, natural inclination, and ill treatment from other folk. "How do I even know that you're who you say you are? Have you any proof?"

"In my pocketbook." It lay on the floor some fifteen feet away, where I'd fallen when I'd lost consciousness. "There," I said, pointing.

Kavanagh set the key on the stool on his way to fetch my pocketbook. He rummaged inside the pocketbook and found the paper I always carried, the only identification I'd brought. He read, "'I am Charlotte Brontë. In case of an emergency, please contact my father, the Reverend Patrick Brontë, at the parsonage in Haworth, Yorkshire.'" He looked askance at me, tossed the paper and pocketbook on the floor, and turned to Slade. "What about you?"

Slade reached inside his pocket and removed a card. As he handed it to Kavanagh, I saw that all it said was, "John Slade." Kavanagh took the card, glanced at it, then snorted and threw it onto my pocketbook. "It doesn't say you ever worked for the Foreign Office."

"Agents don't carry documents that identify them as such," Slade said. "That would be dangerous, should we fall into the hands of our enemies."

"That's a convenient explanation," Kavanagh said scornfully. "Who are you really?"

Although we tried to convince him that we were telling the truth, we couldn't overcome his suspicion. Kavanagh jabbed his finger at us. "Ah! I know who you are. You're agents for the Tsar. You're trying to trick me into giving you my invention and telling you my secret techniques for building it!"

We could only deny it; alas, we had no proof to offer. Kavanagh grew more agitated. He ambled in circles, muttering to himself. "If they found me here, so will their accomplices, so will Lord Eastbourne. They'll kill me. They'll steal my invention and my secrets. I'll never have the fame or glory I dreamed of. What shall I do?"

Slade and I tried to reason with him, but he wouldn't listen. He gulped wine from his bottle. "I must leave this place. I must find somewhere else to hide."

I despaired because the liquor would only make him less tractable. Now he flew into a rage, tearing at his hair and clothes. "How unjust it is that I should be a fugitive, when I am the greatest scientist who ever lived!" Kavanagh wept and blubbered. "How terrible that I should have to hide the most spectacular invention of all time or die!" He turned on us in fury. "Damn you! You've brought me to this!" Like Branwell, he blamed others for his woes. "If I must die, then so must you!"

But Branwell had never physically harmed anyone but himself. Kavanagh scrambled away, snatched up something that lay in the shadows beyond his lamp. He returned, brandishing an axe.

"No!" I fled to the far end of the cage and cringed.

"Pull yourself together, man," Slade ordered, and I heard the desperation beneath the authority in his voice. "Think rationally. You know Lord Eastbourne has treated you ill. You've seen Stieber's spies sniffing around, trying to nab your invention. But what harm have we ever done you? None! We shouldn't be punished for everyone else's sins."

"If you kill us, you'll just make things worse for yourself," I said. "You're already wanted in connection with the deaths of Mary Chandler, Catherine Meadows, and Jane Anderson. Two more murders, and you'll surely hang."

Kavanagh gaped, stricken. "You know about my experiments?" Then he giggled. "You won't live long enough to tell."

He swung the axe. Slade ducked. I screamed. The blade struck a bar of the cage with an ear-splitting, echoing clang. Kavanagh reeled, off balance. He hauled back for another swing.

"For your own good, don't!" Slade shouted. "Cooperating with us is your only hope of surviving, let alone getting the recognition you want."

Kavanagh's mood shifted yet again, with lightning speed. Mischievous cunning gleamed in his bloodshot eyes. "Maybe you're right: you can do me more good alive than dead."

36

✦

KAVANAGH ABRUPTLY TURNED AND DEPARTED. HIS FIGURE vanished into the darkness of the dungeon. His shuffling footsteps receded down a passage; then a door slammed shut. Slade and I looked at each other in bewildered surprise.

"What can he intend?" I asked.

"I haven't the foggiest idea," Slade said, "but we'd best get out of this cage."

He yanked on the lock, but it held firm. I tested the bars, which were too sturdy to break. Slade stretched his arm through them, but it reached a fraction of the distance to the footstool. The key glittered there like fool's gold, bright and mocking. We then tried to move the cage, but it was bolted to the floor. Slade removed his coat, grasped one sleeve, and flung the garment at the key. He only managed to knock the key off the footstool. It bounced on the floor and landed farther out of reach. Slade said, "Damnation!"

"Maybe we can pick the lock." I lifted my hands to my hair and was about to remove a pin, when we heard wheels rattling. Slade signaled me to desist. He hurriedly donned his coat. We stood and waited, endeavoring to look innocent. I hoped Kavanagh wouldn't notice that the key had been moved.

He reappeared, pushing a cart laden with boxes, casks, and various tools. "This is my invention. I've made up my mind that people must know what I've accomplished before I die. You shall have the honor of being the first." Kavanagh bent over a box on the cart and removed the top. Inside, cushioned by straw, were a dozen glass jars with metal lids. "Look!" He held a jar aloft on his palm, displaying its powdery, brownish contents; he beamed with pride. "The culmination of my scientific research."

"That's the disease-producing material you used to infect those women in Whitechapel?" Slade said.

As we gazed upon the jar with repugnance, Kavanagh laughed. "No, no. Those experiments were but an early stage in my work." He shook the jar; the powder swirled inside. "This is a culture of something far more serious. Have you ever heard of woolsorter's disease?"

I nodded. Woolsorter's disease was an ailment of cattle, sheep, and goats, also of farm folk who handled animal products; hence, its name. In the cities it was known as ragpicker's disease, afflicting people who manufactured buttons from animal horns and brushes made from bristles, worked in the leather industry, or handled cloth that had touched persons suffering from the disease. The symptoms were a cough, sore throat, fatigue, and severe difficulty in breathing. Woolsorter's disease was usually fatal within days. There was no cure, and no prevention except to boil the victims' clothes and bedding, wash down their rooms with lye, and cremate their dead bodies. The disease was one of the oldest and most dreaded in history, believed by some to be the sixth plague mentioned in the Bible. Outbreaks had frequently ravaged Europe. Now Slade and I were horrified to realize what Niall Kavanagh's invention was.

"This one jar contains enough animalcules to infect an entire city." Kavanagh tossed the jar up into the air and barely managed to catch it. He giggled at our fright. "Would you like to know how I cultured them?"

"First we would like you to put that jar down," Slade said. "Then we would like to come out of the cage."

"Never mind what you want," Kavanagh said, although he did set the jar in the box. "I want you to know the details of my research, so I will tell you, and you will listen."

He assumed the pedantic manner of a professor lecturing. "I traveled to the countryside, talked to farmers, and located a field where some cows that had died of the disease were buried. I dug them up."

I had heard that the disease could afflict people or animals who disturbed such gravesites, even decades after the burial. The disease was commonly thought to arise from a curse put on the fields. Niall Kavanagh had proven this theory wrong.

"I wore protective garments like these." Kavanagh delved into a box and removed a rubber suit with a hood, boots, and gloves attached, and a cloth mask. "That's how I avoided contracting the disease.

"I collected samples of the remains. I took them back to my laboratory and exposed some live sheep to them. When the sheep became ill, I drew their blood. I put it under the microscope and saw the animalcules—tiny, wormlike creatures. I found the same creatures in fluid from the lungs of the sheep after they died. I experimented with cultivating the animalcules. First I grew them on plates of blood, meat broth, and gelatin. Then I discovered that the best medium is the aqueous humor from cows' eyes, which I obtained from a slaughterhouse. I incubated them at the same temperature as the human body. When I had achieved the purest cultures I could, I introduced them into the nostrils of healthy sheep. They all contracted the disease." Kavanagh's voice rang with the excitement he must have felt at the time. "I had discovered its true cause!"

Now we knew what purpose the sheep, the glass plates, and the equipment at the laboratory had served. The glass box with the gloves had protected Kavanagh while he worked with his cultures.

"I discovered that the animalcules could be heated, dried, and ground into powder, yet retain their disease-causing properties. I have made the greatest breakthrough in the history of science!" Grandiosity sparkled all over Kavanagh. I was sadly reminded of Branwell during his rare moments of triumph, when he'd managed to publish a poem.

"At first I thought to report it to the Royal Society," Kavanagh said. "I hoped it would regain me the honor I'd lost when I was expelled by those fools who dare to call themselves scientists. But they were so set against me that they might not believe I had accomplished something so tremendous. My discovery contradicted all the accepted theories about disease. No, I told myself; I mustn't hand it over to the Society men to reject and ridicule. Why should I? Why did I need their esteem any longer?"

Spreading his arms, laughing exultantly, he whirled about the room. "I had outshone them. I was like a god above mortals. I need not curry the favor of small, inferior men anymore." Kavanagh stopped whirling, swayed dizzily. "But I couldn't bear to keep my discovery to myself, to marvel at alone. What should I do with my knowledge? How could I use it to gain the recognition I'd craved all my life?" That it might endanger mankind didn't seem to have occurred to him. "One day I was sitting in my laboratory, wondering what to do next, when suddenly my mind made a dazzling leap to a higher plane of intuition. Suddenly I realized that my discovery was even greater than I'd first thought. Whoever has this—" He gestured at his jars of deadly cultures "—owns the very power of life and death!"

Even though I was appalled by the fact of such power in Kavanagh's irresponsible hands, I was spellbound by it; I couldn't speak. Slade, too, was dumbstruck.

"I had a vision of a plague spreading across the world as in Biblical times," Kavanagh said, "created not by God, but by man. A plague so deadly and so relentless that the combined power of all the nations in the world couldn't stop it. That was when I conceived the idea of inventing a weapon of war, based on my discovery."

Nor had it occurred to him that he might use his knowledge for the benefit of his fellow humans. Their welfare had never meant anything to him, as his mother had explained.

"From a jar of dust to a weapon of war. That is quite a big leap," Slade said.

Kavanagh appeared not to notice Slade's sarcastic tone. "Too big a leap for small minds to follow," he said smugly. "I became aware of that when I tried to interest the British government in my invention. I'd run out of money to develop my weapon, and I thought that the government would be glad to provide it." A scowl darkened his face. "None of the officials I approached was interested. Everyone thought I was a crackpot."

"Not everyone," Slade murmured to me. "I gather that Wilhelm Stieber has spies inside the government who heard about the weapon. That must be how he caught wind of Kavanagh."

"All except for Lord Eastbourne," Kavanagh said. "He advanced me the funds. *He* was willing to take a chance on me. But he turned out to be a deceitful, dishonorable villain."

"Just how do you plan to disperse your cultures widely enough to infect large populations?" Slade said. "By riding around on a bicycle equipped with a bellows, like a circus clown? You would be stopped before you got very far."

Kavanagh waved his hand, dismissing the contraption we'd seen at his laboratory. "That was an early concept. I've devised a much more effective system. I'll show you."

He crouched by his cart and placed a funnel inside a cylindrical metal canister that was perhaps ten inches tall and six in diameter, with a narrow opening. Then he pried up the lid of a small wooden cask. The odor that wafted from it was smoky, acrid, and sulfurous.

"That's gunpowder," Slade said in dismay as Kavanagh poured it into the funnel and black dust hazed the air. "For God's sake, man, keep it away from the lamp!"

"Don't worry," Kavanagh said. "I know what I'm doing."

Awful realization struck me. "He's building a bomb!"

He pointed a blackened finger at me and grinned; his teeth were stained with wine and decay. "The lady is absolutely right." He removed the funnel and wiped his hands on his trousers. "All it needs is an igniting device and a fuse."

He took up a short copper tube, crimped one end shut with a pliers, then filled it with a substance that looked like salt, from a glass jar. Some spilled on the floor. Slade said, "Be careful. Those chemicals are dangerous."

"They won't explode until I'm ready." Kavanagh threw a pinch of gunpowder into the tube, which he jammed inside the mouth of the canister. He mixed a paste of water and gunpowder and coated it onto a length of thick cotton twine. He stuck this fuse into the tube, then unpacked four jars of his culture, positioned them closely around the container, and secured them with a buckled leather strap. He proudly surveyed his handiwork. "There!"

Slade and I stared, aghast.

"When the bomb is detonated, the jars will shatter," Kavanagh explained. "The blast will disperse the powdered culture. The wind will spread it far, far abroad."

"It won't work," Slade said, but he looked as shaken as I was.

"It will," Kavanagh said, all preening confidence. "The world will see."

"What are you talking about?" Deepening horror pervaded Slade's voice. "How will the world see?"

"At my demonstration," Kavanagh said.

"You mean to set off the bomb?" I said, shocked beyond shock.

"Yes, in a public place where many people are gathered, where many can witness its effects firsthand." Kavanagh rubbed his hands together and smiled with gleeful anticipation. "It will be the biggest experiment ever conducted in the history of science!"

"But the bomb will kill hundreds of innocent people," I said, even though I knew Kavanagh wouldn't care. "Hundreds more will become infected with the disease and die."

"Thousands, most likely." Kavanagh was nonchalant. "That's an inevitable consequence of scientific research—experimental subjects must be sacrificed."

There was that chilling word again, which had made me shiver when I'd read it in his journal. Slade said, "You'll die, too. If the bomb doesn't blow up in your face, the disease will kill you. You're not immune to it, even though you think you're a god."

"That's all right. I'm willing to be a martyr." The hubris suddenly drained from Kavanagh; he turned sorrowful and resigned. "I haven't long to live, anyway. This morning I woke up feeling more unwell than usual." He drew a deep, wheezing breath, then coughed so hard that his face reddened and he held his ribs. "I must have inhaled some of the culture." He shrugged. "I'm as good as dead right now."

Slade and I looked at each other with fresh consternation. Kavanagh might have infected us!

"Don't worry," Kavanagh said. "You haven't been exposed to the culture, and the disease doesn't spread from person to person. You'll live to tell the world everything I've told you, after I'm gone."

This, then, was the role he intended Slade and me to fill: he needed his story publicized, his genius revealed, and we were to be his spokesmen.

Kavanagh tenderly placed the bomb on the cart. "I'll say good-bye now." His burning eyes had the farsighted look of a soldier going to the battlefield. He grasped the cart's handles.

"Wait," Slade protested. "You can't leave us in this cage. How are we going to tell anyone anything while we're locked up? You have to let us out!"

"Oh. I almost forgot. Here." Kavanagh tossed a long, slender object into the cage, at our feet. It was a metal file. "Use that to saw through the bars. By the time you get out, my demonstration will have taken place already."

"When?" Slade demanded. "Where?"

"Within two or three days," Kavanagh said. "That's how much time I have before I'm too ill to do it. As to where—" His parting glance at us was mischievous and chilling. "You'll know soon enough."

Then he shuffled away, pushing the cart laden with death.

37

>‒<

"DR. KAVANAGH!" I CALLED. "PLEASE COME BACK!"

"Come back, damn you!" Slade shouted, rattling the bars of the cage.

Kavanagh did not heed our pleas. After their echoes faded, all we heard was the draft sighing through the dungeon.

We looked at each other, and in spite of our dismay, my heart lifted. Even though Slade and I were trapped in this dire predicament, we were together. Our marriage had multiplied our individual powers. If anyone could escape this prison, Slade and I would.

Slade smiled; he'd read my thoughts. "It may be all over for Niall Kavanagh, but it isn't for us."

"Not yet, at any rate." I gave Slade my hairpin.

He set to work on the lock, but the mechanism was stiff; the hairpin broke. So did the others I gave him. Slade took up the file that Kavanagh had left us. He sawed a few strokes on a bar of the cage, then on the shank of the lock. "The lock seems to be made of a softer alloy, and there's only one piece we need to cut in order to get out."

He filed two scratches on opposite sides of the shank, indicating where we should cut. We took turns filing. It was slow, tedious work. The file was dull, and soon became duller. After some three hours we'd barely managed to nick the lock. We developed sore, running blisters on our fingers. The oil in the lamp burned down;

the flame went out. Slade and I continued working in pitch darkness. We blindly passed the file to each other. My ears rang with the rasp of metal against metal. The lock seemed to grow thicker as I labored. We must have continued all day, or night, or around the clock—I knew not which. We grew hungry, thirsty, and tired. After an eternity, we stopped to rest.

"If you have any new ideas about how to free ourselves, let's hear them," Slade said.

I started to say I did not, when a faint noise stopped me. "Did you hear that?"

We listened to the quiet sound of a door creaking open, somewhere above us, then soft, stealthy footsteps descending. "Dr. Kavanagh is coming back!" I whispered.

"It's not him," Slade said. "That's not his gait. And there are several people coming."

I was so weary, my mind so disoriented by the darkness, that it took me a moment to think who they might be. "Lord Eastbourne and his men?"

Then I heard low, masculine voices with a foreign accent. Slade tensed beside me as a current of dread ran through both of us. He said, "I would prefer Lord Eastbourne."

We stood up in the cage and waited helplessly. A yellow glare burst like a sun in the darkness. All I could see was that brilliant, radiating spot. Slade and I raised our hands to shield our eyes as it drew nearer. Squinting, I perceived three figures approaching. One man held the lantern from which the light emanated. Another walked by his side. Each held a pistol aimed at Slade and me. The third man followed. My eyes adjusted as the two men in the lead stopped at the cage. I recognized their blond hair, their military bearing, the cold, classical handsomeness of one and the puffy, unwholesome face of the other. They moved apart, and the third man came to stand between them. Dressed in black, he seemed made of the same darkness as the shadows in the dungeon. His silver hair, his pale, hooded eyes, and his gold-rimmed spectacles gleamed with a light of their own.

It was Wilhelm Stieber and his two Prussian soldiers.

Terror stabbed deep into my heart, which pounded so hard that my ears filled with the sound of my blood roaring. My bowels turned to water; my lungs contracted; I felt weak with cold, sickening despair. All our running to keep one step ahead of Stieber had been futile. He had caught up with us at the worst possible time.

A smile of gratification curved his cruel, sensual mouth. "Ivan Zubov," he said to Slade. "But of course that is not your real name. The time for pretenses is long past. John Slade, what a pleasure to meet you again."

I sensed the animosity Stieber bore toward Slade, a malicious presence that consumed the air, as threatening as the pistols that his men aimed at us. Slade stood firm, his shoulders squared, his head high. His own hatred for Stieber radiated like a hot, fierce energy from him toward his foe. The space around the two men crackled, as if two bolts of lightning had met.

"Wilhelm Stieber," Slade said. "I could say that it's a pleasure to see you, but that would be a lie."

Stieber peered at me. "Ah, Miss Charlotte Brontë. How convenient to find you with Mr. Slade. You have spared me the trouble of tracking you down." Evil cheer crinkled his smooth skin as he noticed the file lying on the floor of the cage and the lock with the two tiny notches we'd worked so long to make. "Did Dr. Kavanagh imprison you in this cage?"

"Yes," Slade said.

Stieber chuckled. "He did me a favor."

"Indeed. How did you find this place? You couldn't have gotten any clues from Dr. Kavanagh's laboratory. It was already burning when you arrived."

At first I did not understand why Slade would converse so civilly with Stieber when he wanted to lunge at the man's throat. Then I realized that he wanted to keep Stieber talking, to delay the violence that Stieber surely meant to do us, and give himself time to think of a way to escape.

"I consulted some members of the Royal Society in London." Stieber smiled, smug and condescending: he'd seen through Slade's ploy but he couldn't resist the chance to show off his cleverness.

"Dr. Kavanagh has many enemies among them. When I told them that I was an Austrian police official and Dr. Kavanagh was wanted for a murder in Vienna, they were glad to furnish me with information about his family. I then traveled to Ireland. Imagine my chagrin when his mother and father informed me that you—and your wife—had already been there." Stieber brimmed with sly humor. "Congratulations on your marriage."

"Many thanks," Slade said evenly.

"Sir William and Lady Kavanagh were under the impression that you work for the British government," Stieber continued. "I corrected their mistake. I told them that you were a mercenary hired by the Russians to kill their son. I said that I could save him if they told me where he was. They were more than eager to cooperate."

I was horrified that he'd tricked the Kavanaghs. I felt anger flare in Slade, but all he said was, "You're too late. Kavanagh is gone."

"I know." Stieber's eyes narrowed with hostility, as if he blamed Slade and me for Kavanagh's departure. "Where is his invention?"

"He took it with him," Slade said.

I had gathered that Stieber was a man of rare intelligence and perception; now I watched him review the news about Dr. Kavanagh, combine it with facts already in his possession, and swiftly grasp the situation. "Kavanagh intends to deploy his invention."

"Bull's-eye," Slade said, pointing at Stieber.

For the first time I saw Stieber confounded. He turned away, attempting to hide the fact that he'd suffered a devastating blow. For once he appeared fully human.

Slade hurried to take advantage of Stieber's weakness. "Kavanagh is going to demonstrate his weapon in public. It will be seen by hundreds of people. It won't be a secret anymore. And he's sure to be caught. Too bad for Russia."

I'd not thought of how Kavanagh's actions would affect Stieber. Now I realized that Kavanagh had put himself beyond the grasp of Stieber and the Tsar. But that was small consolation.

Stieber faced us. He'd regained his smoothest, hardest, most imperious countenance, but the blood showed through his pale complexion. A vein pulsed at his temple; the sinews in his neck tensed like cords of steel. His rage was frightening, and Slade and I were captive scapegoats.

"Where did Kavanagh go?" Stieber demanded.

"He refused to tell us," Slade said, "but he went not long ago. Maybe you can catch up with him, if you leave at once."

I prayed that his attempt to send Stieber away would work, but Stieber glared, his rage magnified by contempt. "Do you think I'm so stupid? That I would let you go? After hunting you for so long? After you and your woman have caused me so much trouble?" His laugh flared his nostrils. "Dr. Kavanagh has evidently decided to let you live because he wants you to tell his story in case he can't." His intuition amazed me yet again. "But I won't repeat his mistake."

He gestured at the soldiers. The ugly one moved closer to the cage, his gun leveled at Slade's chest. The other aimed his weapon at me. Stieber said, "Tell me where Kavanagh went."

"I already told you, we don't know." Slade's voice was steady, but I knew his thoughts were racing as fast as my own. Staring at the pistol trained on me, I wondered if all my life's labors, all my striving toward publication, fame, and love, would soon end with a single gunshot. Would my remains never come to light? Would no one ever know what had become of me?

"I don't believe you." Stieber shouted, "Tell me!"

"All right, I do know," Slade said in a startling about-face. "But you'll have to torture the information out of me. Wouldn't you like to finish what you started in Bedlam?"

He wanted Stieber to open the cage, I deduced; he wanted to lure Stieber within fighting reach.

"It would be my pleasure," Stieber said. "You have sixty seconds to tell me where Kavanagh went. If you don't, then my comrade will begin firing bullets into your wife. You will watch her die slowly and painfully. Then we'll do the same to you."

He began counting in a measured, ominous cadence. I was mute, paralyzed by terror. That Slade and I would die together was little comfort.

"Go ahead. Kill us if you like." Slade's brazenness didn't hide his desperation. "But you'll be making a fatal mistake. You need us to find Kavanagh."

Stieber stopped counting. He regarded Slade with sudden, disappointed comprehension. "You really don't know where Kavanagh is. In that case, you're just wasting my time. You and your wife have outlived your usefulness."

"You're wrong," Slade hurried to say. "Haven't you noticed that we've always been one step ahead of you, one step closer to Kavanagh? Let us out, and we'll help you catch him before he demonstrates his invention."

Stieber laughed, a short burst of anger and hatred. "How? When you don't have any more notion as to his whereabouts than I do?" He ordered, "Shoot the woman."

The soldier cocked the pistol. Slade jumped between me and the gun and shouted, "No!" I looked around to see the other soldier take aim at my back. Slade wrapped me in his arms and held me against him as we stumbled about the cage, like dancers trapped in a shooting gallery. Now that all his ploys had failed, I tried desperately to think of a way to save us.

Our situation was akin to one I'd encountered while writing novels. I would reach an impasse where I'd created problems with the plot that I couldn't resolve. I'd learned that the only solution was to relinquish logic and conscious rumination and let my mind float free. I had also learned to attain this state under circumstances not conducive to rational thought. I'd begun writing *Jane Eyre* in rented quarters while my father lay recuperating from delicate, painful eye surgery and I had a toothache. I had finished it at the parsonage while Branwell raved drunkenly. Those distractions had barely impinged on me. Now I closed my eyes. The sounds of Stieber's threats and Slade's protests faded. My mind spun backward through memories of the house in Whitechapel and the laboratory in Tonbridge. They swam around an image of Niall Kavanagh's face. Time seemed to stop, my fate suspended.

Sometimes the solution to my problem strikes me like a stingray harpooning a whale. It did now, with such speed that I couldn't reconstruct the line of intuition that snapped my eyes open and my mind back to the present. I blurted, "Mr. Stieber! What does Niall Kavanagh look like?"

Stieber glanced at me in surprise. I felt Slade inhale a sharp breath. Confusion spread across Stieber's gaze. Slade laughed softly as he exhaled. He knew that I had found the coin with which to buy our lives.

"Describe Dr. Kavanagh," Slade said.

Stieber glared instead of replying.

"You can't, can you?" Slade said. "Because you don't know what he looks like. You've never laid eyes on him. Or his invention."

It was true; I could tell from the frustrated rage in Stieber's eyes, the compression of his mouth. The fearful, suspicious, unbalanced Kavanagh had completely managed to evade Stieber.

"You couldn't pick him out of a crowd," Slade mocked Stieber.

"No matter," Stieber said. "You've seen Kavanagh. You will describe him and his invention for me before you die."

"Certainly. Niall Kavanagh is about forty years old, not very tall, with spectacles. His invention is a bomb." Slade said, "Of course there are many men who fit his description. And the bomb is small enough to hide in a box."

Stieber was silent. He regained his machine-like aspect, cold and calculating. His men stood immobile, their fingers on the triggers while he weighed his need to find Kavanagh against the likelihood that Slade and I would foil him. I knew he longed to kill us as punishment for Slade's trickery and betrayal of the Tsar. All the air seemed to leak from the dungeon, leaving us in a vacuum that reeked of decay and nerves. My heart thudded against Slade's while our suspense mounted to agonizing heights and our fate hinged on Stieber's decision.

At last Stieber motioned to his men. They lowered their guns. He said, "I only need one of you to identify Kavanagh. Mr. Slade, you are coming with me. Your wife will stay behind. If you cooperate, she won't die."

As I stammered in horrified protest, Slade said, "Two pairs of eyes are better than one. If something happens to one of us, you'll have the other. Either we both go, or you can kill us now."

Either Stieber didn't want to waste time arguing, or he saw the wisdom of Slade's words. "All right. You both shall accompany me."

My breath came in rapid, dizzying gasps. Slade held me up, but his knees buckled under his own relief.

"Be warned," Stieber said. "If you should attempt any tricks, I will kill you. If we do not find Niall Kavanagh, I will kill you."

He didn't say that he would kill us even if we did find Kavanagh for him. We all knew that after we had served our purpose, he couldn't let us live because he didn't want to gamble on the outcome of another round with Slade. But neither Slade nor I objected. We'd been granted a chance to save ourselves, catch Niall Kavanagh, and confiscate his bombs and his cultures before he set off a plague that would kill millions of innocent people.

"Fair enough," Slade said, and I nodded.

Our adventure had taken a turn that I could not have predicted: we were now in league with the devil.

38

"THE KEY IS OVER THERE," SLADE SAID, POINTING AT THE FLOOR where it had fallen.

Stieber turned to the handsome soldier. "Get it, Friedrich."

Friedrich fetched the key. Stieber ordered Slade and me to move away from the lock. "Wagner, cover them," he said to the ugly soldier.

Wagner trained his pistol on us while Friedrich opened the cage. "Mrs. Slade, you'll come out first," Stieber said. "Stand over there." He pointed at a spot some ten feet from the cage. I complied. "Wagner, guard Mrs. Slade. Friedrich, cover Mr. Slade."

Wagner shambled up to me. He stood too close, his gun almost touching my bosom.

"Behave yourself, or your wife dies," Stieber told Slade. "Put your hands up and walk out of the cage. Slowly."

Slade raised his hands and moved toward the door. As he crossed the threshold, Stieber said, "Stop." Slade obeyed, his face set in wary lines. "Friedrich, search him."

Friedrich ran his hand over Slade. He discovered the file that had found its way inside Slade's coat. Stieber said, "We'd better search Mrs. Slade for hidden weapons, too. Wagner, you may do the honors."

Wagner's hands touched every part of my body and lingered

upon the most intimate places. I cringed. A lewd smile curved his thick lips. Slade seethed, but there was nothing else he could do. When Wagner finished, I felt as dirty as if I'd been smeared with excrement.

"We are ready now." Stieber took up the lantern. "Friedrich, you escort Mr. Slade and go first. Keep your hands up, Mr. Slade. Wagner, you'll follow me, with Mrs. Slade." He glanced at me and added, "I will give you the same warning I gave your husband: Be on your best behavior, or I will have him shot."

Friedrich marched Slade across the dungeon. Stieber went next, lighting the way. Wagner poked the gun against my back as he and I followed the others along a passage that had stone walls and a low, arched stone ceiling. When we ascended an uneven stone staircase, I felt as if I were Eurydice climbing up from the depths of hell. When we emerged into daylight at the top of the stairs, I was overcome by relief and gratitude. I exulted in the sun shining in a corridor with a tiled floor and tapestries hanging on the walls. I had been resurrected, by Hades incarnate. Stieber moved toward a door at the end of the corridor, but Slade said, "Wait."

"Why?" Stieber said, brusque with impatience. "We must hurry to catch up with Dr. Kavanagh."

"That will be difficult without knowing his destination," Slade said. "He's been gone more than twenty-four hours. He'll have traveled quite far already."

"You said he'd just left."

Slade shrugged. "I lied."

"Do not lie to me again," Stieber said. "Locate Dr. Kavanagh."

Although I had faith in Slade, he was not a magician who could pull a rabbit out of a hat that contained no rabbit. How could he locate Kavanagh, who'd breathed not a word of his destination to us?

"I will," Slade said, "if you'll let Charlotte and me search this house."

"We have already searched it," Friedrich said. It was the first time I'd heard him speak. His English was stilted, his voice reedy for a man of such masculine appearance.

"We found nothing." Wagner's voice had a guttural, growling quality.

"We may recognize a clue that you missed," Slade said.

"Very well," Stieber said, "but be quick about it."

Guarded by the soldiers, Slade and I explored the château. The first-floor rooms contained furniture covered with dust sheets. The ancient kitchen was cluttered with dirty dishes and stank of rotten food. I feared that Dr. Kavanagh had left traces of his cultures and we would be infected; but we found none, and no scientific equipment. We proceeded upstairs.

"The only room he used up here is that one," Stieber said, pointing to a door.

Slade and I stepped into a rat's nest similar to the one in Tonbridge. Here, too, were the unmade bed, the liquor bottles, and the soiled chamber pot. Kavanagh had left his clothes strewn around the room; with only a few days to live, he didn't need them. He'd also left canisters of different shapes and sizes, rolled twine, wire, and copper tubing, and jars dusted with chemicals.

"You mentioned that Dr. Kavanagh's invention is a bomb," Stieber said as Slade opened the drawers of the dresser and I looked in the cupboard for papers. "What kind of new bomb can kill more people than the bombs already in use?"

Slade had no choice but to share Kavanagh's dangerous secrets with Stieber. The cupboard was empty; I turned to the desk. My fingers trembled with urgency. We couldn't afford to vex Stieber by taking too long at our task, and we must catch Dr. Kavanagh before he staged his demonstration. I desperately hoped that whatever I found would give us some advantage over Stieber, some idea of how to keep him from Kavanagh and the weapon.

"*Ach, mein Gott!*" Stieber exclaimed in response to what Slade had said about woolsorter's disease, animalcules, and cultures. "Kavanagh is right. Whoever possesses his knowledge and his cultures will rule the world!" He sounded gratified by the news, rather than horror-stricken as Slade and I had been. "The Tsar will be very pleased."

The desk drawers contained crumpled scraps of paper that bore Niall Kavanagh's familiar, incomprehensible scribblings. Then I came upon a neat ink drawing of a thick, crooked, elongated cross with one arm shorter than the other. The space inside it was filled with lines, squares, and illegible notations. Arrows and X's marked various spots. Kavanagh had drawn a little picture—a tapered column arising from an oval, with lines flowing down like hair from the top—at the center of the cross. A strange sense of familiarity gripped me. This drawing represented no figment of Kavanagh's fevered imagination, but something real, a place I knew. But where?

A shadow fell across the page. Stieber looked over my shoulder. "What is that?"

"I think it's a map," I said.

Slade joined me. "A map of what?"

"I don't know." But I was suddenly certain that Kavanagh had fantasized about demonstrating his weapon long before he'd sprung the idea on us. This map was proof, and a clue to his destination.

Studying my face, Slade read my thoughts. His eyes sharpened. "You do know." He tapped his finger against the paper. "What is this?"

The shock of meeting Niall Kavanagh, the fatigue from my ordeal in the dungeon, and my terror of Wilhelm Stieber all impaired my mental faculties. "I can't remember!" I said in frustration.

"Think!" Slade pleaded.

I let my vision blur; the map went hazy before my eyes. From deep in my memory came the roar of voices, the tinkle of water falling, and George Smith's voice: *The transept was offset to accommodate the trees that were on the site. The building isn't completely symmetrical.* As I refocused my gaze on the lopsided cross drawn on the paper, I saw the lines turn into corridors and the squares into fantastic displays of art and machinery surrounded by chattering crowds. The column set on an oval became a glass fountain that weighed four tons.

"It's the Crystal Palace!" I cried. "The Great Exhibition. In London. That's where Niall Kavanagh plans to demonstrate his weapon!"

39

>—<

"THE GREAT EXHIBITION IS THE IDEAL SITE FOR KAVANAGH'S demonstration," Slade said.

"Thousands of people attend every day," I said, "and many prominent citizens."

"Politicians, courtiers, foreign royalty and dignitaries. Kavanagh couldn't hope to find a bigger or more illustrious audience anywhere else."

I felt sick as I contemplated the scope of the impending disaster. "They'll scatter to their homes all over England, Europe, and America. They'll spread the disease everywhere."

"Kavanagh must have visited the Great Exhibition before he left England," Slade said. "These spots he marked on the floor plan must be the places he's decided to plant his bombs."

Stieber snatched the map of the Crystal Palace from my hand, folded it, and tucked it in his pocket. "We must hurry to London. Friedrich, escort our prisoners outside."

Friedrich hesitated. "What if they are wrong? What if the Great Exhibition is not where Dr. Kavanagh is going?"

"It has to be," Slade said. I nodded, convinced by my intuition as well as by the fact that we'd found no evidence to indicate otherwise.

We hastened out of the château in single file, Slade leading, Friedrich close behind with the pistol aimed at his back, Stieber next, and Wagner guarding me. Outside the gates, a carriage, horses, and driver waited. Stieber said, "Take us to the ferry dock as fast as you can."

The journey back to England was frightful, the ocean rough. Despite my state of starvation, I ate and drank little because I was seasick. The next morning we reached Portsmouth. As Friedrich and Wagner walked Slade and me down the gangplank, my sickness abated, but I trembled with anxiety. If we found Niall Kavanagh before he staged his demonstration, what further purpose would we serve for Stieber? If we didn't, the Crystal Palace would become the starting point of the worst catastrophe in history. Either way, Slade and I hadn't long to live.

At the railway station, we found a huge, noisy crowd in the waiting area. Trains stood motionless by the platforms. People sat on benches, trunks, bundles, and boxes. Women rocked crying babies and scolded fractious children. Men flocked around the ticket booths; they shouted questions, argued, and threw up their hands in vexation. Stieber elbowed his way toward a ticket booth while his men watched Slade and me. A railway guard stood near us, and Slade called to him, "Excuse me—what's the problem?"

"There's been a wreck on the track," the guard said. "There won't be any trains moving from here toward London until it's cleared."

A little boy ran about the room, spinning a toy top. He bumped into Friedrich's leg. Friedrich lost his balance and staggered, away from Slade. Wagner turned from me to catch his comrade. While the two Prussians were distracted, Slade grabbed my hand and we ran.

Friedrich and Wagner yelled, "Stop!"

Slade towed me through the station, pushing people aside. I heard Friedrich and Wagner calling Stieber. I saw Stieber among the crowd, fighting his way toward us. We reached the front door, but a group of travelers entering the station blocked our exit. We turned. Friedrich, Wagner, and Stieber came charging after us as Slade and I raced for the rear door. We burst out the door onto the platform. More people waited there. We wove between them to a train and rushed up its steps. In the empty compartment, Slade flung open the door on the other side. We jumped down to the tracks. As we ran across them, a spike caught my hem. Before Slade and I could tear my skirt free, our pursuers arrived. Friedrich and Wagner pointed their pistols at us. Stieber demanded, "Where do you think you are going?"

He'd deduced what I hadn't realized until now—that Slade had fled for another reason besides escaping Stieber. Slade had a destination in mind, a plan for getting us to London. Stieber had read Slade's thoughts even though I hadn't. Perhaps enemies were even more attuned to one another than lovers were.

Slade hesitated, torn between his reluctance to tip his hand and the knowledge that Stieber wouldn't let us get away again and we could go nowhere without the man. He said reluctantly, "I've a friend who can take us to London. He lives nearby."

Friedrich and Wagner looked skeptical. Stieber considered: he suspected a trick, but he had a choice between cooling his heels in Portsmouth or gambling on Slade. He said, "Take us there."

We traveled in a hired carriage a few miles to the countryside, and arrived at a gray-brick mansion three stories high, capped by a mansard roof, that stood amid spacious grounds. When we disembarked on the driveway, the sound of voices and laughter and the roar of machinery greeted us, although I saw no one. Black smoke wafted over the treetops, from the back of the house. Slade led the way there. We came upon a crowd gathered on a lawn that extended toward open fields. The women were dressed in long smocks and hats with veils, the men in coveralls. Chattering and excited, they faced the end of the lawn. At first I thought we'd interrupted a strange sort of garden party. Then my gaze followed theirs, and I realized what Slade's plan was.

"Dear God," I said.

There was a gigantic, inflated balloon, made from panels of gray cloth, shaped like a fat sausage that tapered to a point at each end, more than a hundred feet long. A net of ropes encased the balloon. Some tethered the balloon to pegs in the ground. Others suspended a pole horizontally below and parallel to its long axis. From the pole hung a large wicker basket that contained a bulky machine with a huge propeller. Three men worked on the contraption. One stood in the basket, tinkering with a triangular cloth that resembled a sail and was attached to the ropes below the balloon. A second shoveled coal into the machine, which belched smoke and roared. The third man adjusted the boiler, which puffed clouds of steam.

It was an airship, similar to the model I'd seen at the Crystal Palace.

Stieber, Friedrich, and Wagner were as stunned as I. "We are going to London in *that*?" Stieber said.

"Unless you have a better idea," Slade said.

Hot air balloons had been invented long ago, and they were common enough that I'd seen them at fairs, but the steam-powered airship was a recent innovation. The one based on the model at the Crystal Palace had never yet flown. I could hardly believe that I might get a ride in this one. My heart fluttered with excitement, then quailed. Would it not be dangerous?

We approached the airship. Stieber and his men stopped me a few paces from it. He told Slade, "We'll wait here." While they held me hostage to his good behavior, Slade moved forward and called to the man in the basket, "Dr. Crick!"

The man wore a helmet over gray, frizzled hair. His lean, stooped figure was clad in a blue coverall. He peered at us through dark-tinted spectacles perched on his beaked nose. "Hello?"

"I don't know if you remember me," Slade said, "but I'm—"

"John Slade. Of course." The man had a toothy grin and a fluty, cultured accent. "I never forget a face, even though I haven't seen yours since you attended my class in physics at Cambridge. Wasn't it you who demonstrated Newton's principles of gravity by dropping an apple and a bathtub off Magdalen Tower?"

Slade laughed. "It was, I'm sorry to say."

"Boys will be boys," Dr. Crick fluted. "To what do I owe your sudden reappearance?"

"I ran into a former classmate some time ago. He told me you'd retired from teaching and made great progress in developing a steam-powered airship."

"Voila!" Dr. Crick spread his arms, made an exaggerated bow, and said, "I'm giving rides. Would you like one?"

"Yes, and so would my friends," Slade said, indicating Stieber, the soldiers, and me.

"It would be my pleasure. Those ladies and gentlemen are next, but if you can wait—"

"I can't," Slade said. "We must go to London, and we must go now."

"London?" Dr. Crick hunched his shoulders. "But I've never flown that far. I don't know whether my airship can make it."

"Could you try? It's urgent." Slade added, "I'm on official business."

"Official business, oh, well, then." Dr. Crick's look said he was privileged to know that Slade was, or had been, an agent for the Crown. "In that case, we'll give it our best shot."

Slade turned and beckoned. Stieber, his men, and I hurried forward. Slade introduced me as his wife, and Stieber and the soldiers as friends visiting from Prussia. Dr. Crick said, "It's a pleasure to meet you." He was oblivious to our companions' menacing air. "But I'm afraid I can only accommodate three of you, plus myself and my assistants. Any extra weight will drag the balloon down, and the basket only holds six."

"Leave your men behind," Slade told Stieber.

I knew what he was thinking: their absence would much improve our chances of thwarting Stieber. But Stieber said, "We all go or no one goes."

"My friends and I will take the place of your assistants," Slade said to Dr. Crick. "Just teach us what to do."

"Very well." Dr. Crick was glad to cooperate for the sake of crown and country. A speedy but complicated lecture on operating the airship ensued. Then he said, "You should use the conveniences before we take off. All we have on board is a pail."

We took his advice. Stieber made sure that Slade and I had no chance to escape in the airship without him and his men. Dr. Crick's assistants helped us climb into the basket. It was crowded with the engine, a coal bucket, and sundry equipment. I gazed nervously up at the balloon, which resembled a levitating whale caught in a net. Could it really carry us aloft?

The assistants shoveled a last load of fuel into the engine. They spun the propeller, whose three blades began to turn lazily. Smoke puffed out of the engine's funnel, which was pointed downward so that sparks from it wouldn't ignite the hydrogen gas in the balloon. Dr. Crick and Slade hauled up the anchor. The assistants untied the balloon's tethers. The airship began to rise.

"Bon Voyage!" Dr. Crick said cheerfully.

"How fast does this go?" Slade shouted above the roar from the engine and propeller and the hiss of the boiler.

"I clocked it at ten miles per hour last time."

"It's about seventy miles from Portsmouth to London," Slade said. "That should take us at least seven hours."

He sounded disappointed, but Dr. Crick said, "Maybe less, depending on the wind. And unlike a train, we needn't stop for passengers or follow a track. We'll go as the crow flies."

The lawn fell away beneath us. The floor of the basket pressed up against my feet as the balloon lifted my weight. My stomach plunged while I rose. My heart pounded; I grew giddy. As the airship gained altitude, the people and the mansion below shrank until they were as small as dolls and a dollhouse. Dr. Crick worked the controls on the engine. The propeller blades accelerated into a whir. The funnel discharged smoke that streamed behind us as the airship moved forward. I felt a wave of something akin to seasickness, but I was too thrilled to care.

Ever since I was a little girl, I have wished for wings, for the ability to soar above the earth. Now I floated through thin air, looking down at the treetops, free from the shackles of gravity. I would have jumped up and down with glee had I not been afraid to upset the basket, which rocked gently in the wind. Airborne by the miracle of science, I gazed up at the sky and marveled that I was in it. The billowy white clouds seemed close enough to touch. I clapped my hands and laughed.

"Isn't this wonderful?" I exclaimed.

"It certainly is," Dr. Crick said, pleased and proud. "We've got a good tailwind."

Friedrich sat in a rear corner of the basket, his knees drawn up to his chest, his arms and hands clasped over his head. Wagner's ugly face was pale and dripping sweat. I gathered that both men were afraid of heights.

Slade stood beside me, gazing at Stieber, who stood in the opposite side of the basket. They wore the same hard, calculating expression, and I knew what they were each thinking: *If I attack him, what are my chances of throwing him off the airship before he throws me?* Neither moved. Fighting was too dangerous hundreds of feet above the ground. Stieber wouldn't risk his life before he'd completed his mission, and Slade wouldn't risk dying and leaving me with Stieber. Their stalemate allowed me to enjoy my first flight in peace.

We soon left the city, which resembled a toy village. We motored over fields, pastures, and woodland—a patchwork of different shades of green, like a quilt, that rippled over hills. Tiny people on the roads looked up, pointed, and waved. How small, how petty, did the tribulations of the world seem from my lofty perspective! Could mankind not forget them and enjoy the God-given miracles of life?

I glanced at Slade. He and Stieber kept watch on each other while viewing the scene below us. Slade flashed me a smile, sharing my delight. Stieber seemed impressed against his will. I think he resented being at the mercy of nature and science, hated anything he couldn't control. I could almost pity him, but not quite.

Dr. Crick yanked on a rope, adjusting the sail, which functioned as a rudder. Friedrich remained huddled on the floor. Wagner sat next to him, green and rigid as a corpse. We floated over sparkling streams crossed by miniature bridges, and farmhouses suitable for Tom Thumb. Hours passed, during which I was so enchanted that I didn't notice when Slade left me to stand beside Stieber. Then I happened to glance up and see them facing out the other side of the basket, talking. I moved next to Slade, to listen.

"It's invariably fatal. There's no antidote." Slade was speaking about woolsorter's disease. "If Russia uses Kavanagh's bomb in a war against Britain, it won't only destroy Britain. The plague will spread everywhere."

"That may be the case, but I am not concerned about it," Stieber said.

"You can't stop it outside Russia's borders," Slade persisted. "Millions of Russians will die, too. Even the Tsar isn't immune."

"I have my orders to capture Dr. Kavanagh and the weapon and deliver them to His Highness. I will do so."

"If you explained to the Tsar, he would understand that the weapon is too dangerous ever to use. He's ambitious, but not stupid."

"It's not my place to explain."

Slade stared at Stieber in disbelief and repugnance. "How can you be so blindly obedient? Have you no conscience?"

"What you call conscience, I call a luxury in which I do not indulge," Stieber said calmly.

"Why?" Slade said, vexed and bewildered. "Why does someone as intelligent as you not want to think for himself and do what's right?"

"Because I bow to the authority of those I serve," Stieber said. "That is my calling."

The engine thundered; the boiler shrieked; the propeller beat the air. Slade regarded Stieber with the air of a scientist studying a poisonous snake because he wants to know what is in its venom before it bites him and he dies. Stieber contemplated a village on the ground, the minute spire of its church glinting in the sunlight. Perhaps he was more affected by the miracle of flying than I'd thought, and it relaxed his discretion, for he began to talk.

"I was born in Merseburg, Saxony. My father was a government official. My mother was from a family of wealthy English landowners."

I was surprised to hear that Stieber had English blood; he seemed so foreign. Slade and I listened with interest as he went on, "My family moved to Berlin." We both abided by the saying, *Know thine enemy.* "My father wanted me to enter the church, and so I studied theology at the University of Berlin."

Nor had I imagined Stieber as a former clergyman. Slade raised his eyebrows in surprise that he and his foe had that much in common.

"There, I had an experience that changed my life," Stieber said. "A young friend of mine was accused of theft. I believed he was innocent. I argued for him in court, and he was acquitted. I realized that I wasn't meant to be a cleric. I left the divinity school to study law. I kept it a secret from my father because he wouldn't approve. I had to pretend to be continuing my theology studies. I even preached a sermon.

"As I spoke, I felt ashamed because I was an impostor who proclaimed the word of God in order to procure tuition money from the father I was deceiving. There was then a stir among the crowd. His Highness Friedrich Wilhelm, King of Prussia, walked into the church." Nostalgia brought a smile to Stieber's face. "His presence inspired me. My words rolled through the arches like thunder: 'Divine forgiveness will not be accorded you on the flaming day of the Last Judgment—unless you bow to the earth in penitence!'"

Had his character been as holy as his preaching was dramatic, he might have made as good a vicar as Papa.

"The King was impressed," Stieber said. "As he left the church, he gave me a most gracious bow. I experienced the glory of approval from on high. From that moment, I desired to experience it again."

That desire was what drove Stieber, I realized. It was more seductive than the wish to achieve power, wealth, and fame for himself. I began to understand why he'd made service to the high and mighty his calling.

"But I was not so free of conscience then as now," Stieber said. "I felt guilty for deceiving my father, so that night I confessed. My father was furious. He drove me out of his house and refused to pay for my studies. I then had to earn my own tuition and living. This I did by working as a secretary to the Berlin police department. I met police inspectors, who took me along when they investigated crimes and arrested criminals. I found much more satisfaction in that than in the courtroom, even after I was appointed a junior barrister. I instead became a police inspector in the criminal division.

"I solved a murder that the police had been investigating

unsuccessfully for eighteen months. I also traced a band of robbers who'd been hiding in the woods, after the army had searched in vain. I heard them snoring in a cave." Pride radiated from Stieber even as he smiled wryly. "Then came the Tomascheck case. A tailor named Franz Tomascheck had insured his life for one hundred thousand talers. When he died a year later, the insurance company paid the money to his widow, who left Berlin for parts unknown. I arrested a Hungarian swindler who said he'd recently met Tomascheck in Bohemia. Acting on this evidence that Tomascheck was alive, I had his grave opened. The coffin contained only his old flatiron and a load of bricks. I then traveled incognito to Bohemia, where I found Tomascheck living with his wife. I also found the physician they'd paid to sign a fraudulent death certificate. I arrested them all."

Stieber fell silent. We watched the landscape passing below us. A miniature waterwheel paddled in a creek as narrow as a ribbon. Tiny men fished in the stream. As Stieber contemplated them, I sensed his thoughts: he was fancying himself as God, from whom no human sins could remain secret, who could dispense justice as he saw fit.

"Not long afterward, a privy councilor in the Ministry of the Interior asked me to come and see him," Stieber said. "He told me that the authorities in Silesia had uncovered a conspiracy to overthrow the government. He ordered me to conduct a secret investigation. I traveled to Silesia in disguise. Upon arriving I contacted a man named Hermann, who'd supplied the tip about the conspiracy. Hermann said the conspirators planned to seize property from the rich and distribute it to the poor. I discovered their identities and arrested them. They were charged with treason and sentenced to prison. The case caused a scandal. Politicians excoriated me for illegal 'secret police' work. But I was just following orders. I didn't reveal who gave them because I'd been sworn to secrecy."

In addition to his desire to please his superiors, he had such a strong sense of loyalty that he would rather bear the brunt of public censure than betray them. His loyalty transcended the law and the fact that they were mere mortals with human failings. Slade and I were amazed that such an evil man was motivated by such a noble trait.

"In 1848, I was drawn into the turmoil of the revolutions that plagued Europe," Stieber continued. "The King had made himself unpopular by dissolving a new constitutional convention formed by his people. He rode through the city alone, hoping that his boldness would prevent a rebellion. Instead, he was assailed by a violent mob. I happened to be there. I single-handedly cleared a path for him and pulled him to safety inside the palace gates."

Stieber clearly relished his heroism. "The King fainted. I carried him into the palace, where I was surprised to discover that he was an actor impersonating the King. The real King thanked me for my brave service. He actually took my hands in his and squeezed them," Stieber marveled. "And he recognized me from my sermon that he'd heard. I informed him that I was now a police inspector and secret agent. I took the opportunity to tell him about my accomplishments. He rewarded me with a promotion to chief of the Berlin police force. It was the proudest day of my life."

I suspected that the King's esteem had compensated Stieber for his father's disapproval, but not entirely. Perhaps Stieber had never recovered from being cast off by his father, and he continued to seek approval from his superiors out of a need to heal the wound that would never heal. That need was the vulnerable human core in Stieber.

"I investigated and thwarted many conspiracies against the King's regime," Stieber said. "Word of my expertise spread. Other heads of state applied for my assistance in unmasking members of secret societies in their kingdoms. One of them was the Tsar."

"That explains how a Prussian agent became the Tsar's chief spy," Slade said. "I was wondering. But how do you justify working for the Tsar? Doesn't that interfere with your loyalty to your King?"

"Not at all," Stieber said. "The King loaned me to the Tsar in exchange for certain favors."

"Favors such as military support from Russia, I suppose," Slade said. "But how can you serve the King while you're chasing Dr.

Kavanagh and his weapon for the Tsar? Aren't you spreading yourself a bit thin?"

"I am killing two birds with one stone. The King ordered me to
travel to England to track down the Communist League, a revolutionary society that has established its headquarters in London. I
infiltrated it and befriended its leader. He suffers from painful hem-
orrhoids. I posed as a physician and obtained a remedy for him.
When I brought it to his house, I stole the register of the Communist
League. The members will soon be arrested." Stieber added, "In
case you are interested, the leader's name is Karl Marx."

Slade said with incredulity and contempt, "How can you do it?
Have you no sympathy for the people that your masters oppress?"

"I have much sympathy," Stieber said. "I believe that the soil
that nourishes their grievances is poverty, and eliminating poverty
is the only truly effective weapon against subversion. Poverty can
only be eliminated by providing better education, better pay, and a
better standard of living for workers. But I disapprove of secret
plots and attempts to overthrow governments. Changes in society
must be implemented within the framework of law and order,
rather than by rebellion and violence."

His views were more liberal and humane than I'd assumed, but
I could not approve of his actions, and neither could Slade.

"That's a pretty speech," Slade said, "but instead of acting on
your beliefs, you abdicated your personal responsibility."

"I have stated my ideas to the Prussian court, and it has made
me many enemies there."

"According to you, you have access to European heads of state.
You could have influenced them and worked to eliminate poverty.
Instead, you became a running dog for corrupt dictatorships."

Anger rekindled in Stieber's eyes. "I'm no different from you.
You've done things that you think are wrong, because you followed
orders. There must be as much blood on your hands as mine. Your
conscience can't be any more free of guilt."

Slade gazed straight ahead at the clouds in the distant sky, his
jaw tight. I knew that Stieber's words had stung him because there
was truth in them. But he said, "I'm not like you. I'll prove it by

making a proposition that you never would: Let's put our loyalty to our superiors aside and join forces to put Niall Kavanagh out of commission and protect the world."

Stieber didn't hesitate for an instant before saying, "I cannot do that."

Slade looked at me, smiled ruefully, and shrugged; he hadn't expected Stieber to agree, but he'd thought the deal worth a try. Now he and Stieber were at an impasse. They could never reconcile their different ideas of duty and honor.

During the next few hours, the novelty of flying wore off, and I grew tired of standing in the basket and sitting on its hard floor. I was exhausted due to the terrible toll that the past few harrowing days had taken from me. The constant noise from the engine frayed my nerves; the sun burned my skin and made my eyes ache. Using the pail was an embarrassing necessity. Friedrich and Wagner remained immobilized by fear. Slade and Stieber spoke no more while they helped Dr. Kavanagh operate the airship, but their mutual hostility was palpable. Learning that they had much in common didn't make Slade like Stieber any better. One always hates most in others what one hates most about oneself. And there was too much bad blood between Slade and Stieber, too many offenses that neither could forgive.

My own spirits rose during a spectacular sunset. Floating through a sky colored orange and red, beneath lavender clouds, I felt as if I were experiencing the glory of God at close hand. But night came fast, and we were engulfed in darkness. We traveled by compass and the faint light from the stars, the moon, and the lamps twinkling on earth. At about eight o'clock we finally neared London.

The city was unrecognizable, its vast spread almost hidden beneath a pall of smoke tinged yellow by the thousands of lights in buildings and along streets. I glimpsed a few tall towers and church spires, but the only familiar landmark I could make out was the Thames, a black curve that divided the city and glittered in the moonlight.

"Where is the Great Exhibition?" Stieber asked.

"In Hyde Park," I said.

"But which way is that?" Dr. Crick said.

As he and Slade took turns peering through binoculars, trying to get their bearings, the wind picked up. The balloon blew back and forth. The basket swayed. I clung to the edge.

"We'll have to land soon," Dr. Crick said. "If the wind gets any stronger, I won't be able to steer the airship."

A loud boom rocked the night. Everyone started.

"Someone is shooting at us!" Wagner cried. He threw himself on the floor beside Friedrich.

Slade, Stieber, Dr. Crick, and I watched a red fountain of stars burst in the sky. More booms preceded fountains, cartwheels, and sprays of red, green, and white lights.

"It's fireworks," Slade said.

Now I saw, beneath them, a structure that glittered and reflected like a long, cross-shaped block of ice. "There," I said, pointing. "The Crystal Palace!"

40

GETTING TO THE CRYSTAL PALACE WAS NOT EASY. THE WIND BUF-feted the airship, sending us off course. Dr. Crick set the engine on full power. He and Slade and Stieber hauled on the rudder line, straining to turn the balloon. The basket swung violently while I hung on for dear life. Wagner clasped his hands, closed his eyes, and prayed aloud in German. Friedrich moaned. Somehow we managed to regain our course. The Crystal Palace grew larger as we approached. The rockets boomed louder, exploded closer. I could see streamers of smoke trailing the colored stars as they fell.

The engine clattered, coughed, and died. The propeller slowed, then ceased.

"We've lost power." Dr. Crick tried to restart the engine, but couldn't. "We have to land now, or I'm afraid we'll be blown out over the ocean."

He opened the vent on the balloon's underside. Gas hissed out. The airship began to descend. We dropped through a dimly glowing, acrid veil of smoke. Then we were below it, above the great expanse of Hyde Park. There, people milled about; gaslights burned along roads full of carriages. The Crystal Palace glittered in the distance. Treetops rushed up to meet us. My heart was in my throat; my lungs constricted with fear.

"Pull!" Dr. Crick shouted.

Slade and Stieber heaved on the rudder line. We veered away

from the trees, over a broad lawn. People below us spotted the airship descending. They scattered. When we were some ten feet above ground, a gust of wind rolled the balloon sideways. The basket tipped. We tumbled out, screaming. I landed so hard on my hands and knees that my teeth slammed together and my spectacles were knocked askew. I righted them and saw Wagner facedown beneath me. I heard Slade calling, "Charlotte! Are you all right?"

I struggled to my feet. "Yes."

Slade was standing, too. But Friedrich lay groaning and clutching his thigh. "My leg is broken!" Wagner didn't move; he was either unconscious or dead. Even though I disliked him, I was horrified to think I'd accidentally killed him. Stieber sat, dazed. He rubbed his head. People surrounded us, staring and exclaiming.

Dr. Crick knelt, his watch in his hand; he chortled with glee. "I flew the first steam-powered airship from Portsmouth to London in five hours and thirty-nine minutes! I've made history!" Then he looked up and said, "Oh, dear!"

Without passengers to weigh it down, the airship rose into the sky, just as the fireworks began their grand finale. Rocket after rocket launched. The balloon soared straight through the booming cascades of colored sparks. They burned through its fabric. The gas inside ignited with a cataclysmic blast.

A mass of orange flames shot through by the fireworks roiled over Hyde Park. It lit the sky as brightly as the sun. My horrified cry joined the uproar from the crowd. Burning cloth fragments flew apart. They glowed and fluttered, like fiery birds. The ropes curled like flaming snakes as they fell. The basket crashed to the earth, engulfed in fire, like Icarus's chariot.

Dr. Crick burst into tears. "My airship!"

The crowds ran from the burning debris that drifted down from the sky. A police constable sped toward us. "Hey! You weren't authorized to land a balloon here. This is quite a serious offense!"

Slade and I backed away. The constable fixed on Stieber, grabbed him by the collar, and said, "You're under arrest."

Slade caught up my hand. We bolted. I heard Stieber say, "Let me go!" and the constable say, "Ah, you're a foreigner. What's your name? Was this an attack on England?"

We ran through the crowds and the smoking wreckage of the airship, toward the Crystal Palace. So did many other people. To take shelter in a glass house might have seemed absurd, but the Crystal Palace was the only building nearby. Mobs jostled us, trampled on my feet. We joined a huge crush at the door. Elbows jabbed me as Slade muscled our way past a tight pack of angry men, crying women, and frightened children, through the odor of hot, sweaty flesh and the shrill of frantic voices. Inside the building, the Great Exhibition was even more crowded than it had been on the day I'd visited it with the Smith family, and night had transformed the place.

Thousands of burning lamps reflected in the glass walls and ceiling. The air smelled of gas fumes and shimmered with heat. Flickering shadows distorted the faces of the people that Slade and I passed as we fought our way along the main aisle down the transept. The Great Exhibition had become an inferno populated by ghouls.

"If Niall Kavanagh is here, how will we find him?" I asked.

"It's too bad Stieber has the map," Slade said. "Can you remember the places Kavanagh marked?"

"I'll try."

Guided by my faint memory of the map and the Great Exhibition, I led Slade down the west nave, where I thought I'd seen an X. We entered the display from Turkey. Beneath swags of red drapery, glass cases held hookahs, knives and swords with curved blades, and a camel saddle. A party of foreign gentlemen had taken refuge there. They spoke excitedly in French, discussing the explosion of the airship. But we didn't see Niall Kavanagh.

Slade hurried me away, saying, "I remember an arrow pointing in the vicinity of that exhibit."

It was the China Court, which contained ceramic vases, painted lanterns, embroidered screens, and jade figurines. These were surrounded by frightened, sobbing women—a church group from a country parish. Again we found no Niall Kavanagh and no bomb, but when we left the court, Stieber came striding down the aisle. He'd escaped the constable. He carried a pistol. Spying us, he broke into a run.

Slade and I turned and fled. Hand in hand, we ran past the towering zinc Amazon on horseback and a mob gathered around the Koh-i-noor, the biggest diamond in the world. We hid in the machinery exhibit, behind a cotton-spinning machine. Stieber did not reappear.

"I think we've shaken him off," Slade said.

A man wandered down a nearby aisle. He was so nondescript that I might not have noticed him, except that he had with him a brown leather suitcase mounted on wheels, which he was pulling by a long handle. It was a clever invention, more useful than many items in the Great Exhibition. I took a second look at the man. He was short and slight, dressed in a long coat, its collar turned up; a cap hid his hair and face. He walked with a familiar, shuffling gait.

"There," I whispered excitedly, and pointed. "It's Dr. Kavanagh!"

As Slade and I started toward him, Kavanagh saw us. Alarm widened his eyes behind his spectacles. He pivoted, then scurried off.

"Stop!" Slade yelled.

Kavanagh sped through the crowd, bumping into people, his suitcase rolling over their feet. We lost sight of him, but we followed the protests he left in his wake. Veering around a corner, we found ourselves in the transept again. People were massed around the fountain, which gleamed orange as if the gaslight had alchemized its glass structure and its spilling water into molten fire. They gazed up at a dais covered with red velvet. There stood a small, dumpy woman resplendent in peacock-blue silk and a man in white breeches, shiny black boots, and a coat decorated with epaulets and brass buttons. Soldiers, ladies, and gentlemen flanked the dais. Niall Kavanagh skirted the audience, and we chased him while the woman spoke. I was too far away to get a good look at her, and the Crystal Palace echoed with noise, so I could only hear scattered phrases of what she said: ". . . my dear husband's pride and joy . . .

had to visit it again . . . can't stay away . . ." But her voice was instantly recognizable.

"It's Queen Victoria," I said. "And Prince Albert."

"What damnable bad luck!" Slade said. "They would have to pick tonight of all nights to drop in. We have to catch that madman before he blows them to kingdom come!"

As we gained on Kavanagh, I spied George Smith at the edge of the audience. Beside him was William Thackeray. They were drinking glasses of lemonade, smiling and making comments to each other as they watched the royal public appearance. Near them were George's mother and Mr. Thackeray's fair, buxom mistress. I was horrified to see my friends in danger.

"Stop!" I begged Slade.

He didn't hear me. I wrenched my hand out of his. While he pursued Kavanagh, I hastened to my friends, calling, "Mr. Smith!"

George turned to me in surprise. "Charlotte?" A smile of pleasure brightened his handsome face. "What are you doing here?"

His mother stared at me with an annoyance so sudden that she couldn't hide it. "I didn't know you were back in London, Miss Brontë."

"I must warn you," I said, and fumbled for the words to tell them about Niall Kavanagh and the bomb.

"Well, if it isn't Jane Eyre," Mr. Thackeray said, all sly delight. He drew his mistress forward. "Do you remember Mrs. Brookfield?"

She murmured a polite greeting and looked askance at my disheveled clothes and hair. I was so distraught that all I could think of to say was, "You must leave at once!"

"Why?" George said, perplexed.

"But you just got here. The fun has only just begun," Mr. Thackeray said. "Would you like some lemonade?" He offered me his glass.

"Something terrible is going to happen," I said.

"What nonsense are you talking?" Mrs. Smith demanded.

I saw, beyond her to my left, Stieber rushing toward me. To my right I saw Slade tackle Kavanagh, who fell. With my attention split between those sights, I was unable to react to either. Then Stieber was upon me. He seized my arm.

"I beg your pardon," Mr. Smith said indignantly. "What do you think you're doing?"

"Where is Slade?" Stieber demanded. "Where is Dr. Kavanagh?"

"Unhand the lady," Mr. Thackeray ordered.

He put his hand on Stieber's chest and shoved. Stieber lost his grip on me. He took a few steps backward, raised his pistol, and aimed it at Mr. Thackeray.

"He's got a gun!" Mrs. Brookfield cried. "William, look out!"

I heard Kavanagh screaming. Stieber turned toward the sound. Slade hung onto Kavanagh's leg with one hand and grabbed the suitcase with the other. Kavanagh clung to the suitcase's handle. He kicked Slade in the chin, yanked the suitcase away from Slade, and went stumbling away.

"Dr. Kavanagh!" Stieber shouted. "Stop!" He pointed his gun up at the ceiling and fired.

There was a bang that reverberated through the Crystal Palace, then the sound of glass shattering. George flung his arm over my head to shield me; we ducked as splinters rained down. On the dais, Queen Victoria and Prince Albert looked around in confusion. The crowd dissolved into screaming, swirling chaos. People bleeding from cuts and hysterical with fright ran toward the exits at either end of the transept. The mob followed in a blind stampede. Soldiers hurried the Queen and Prince down from the dais. Pandemonium swallowed up the entire royal party. I heard the Queen shriek; I saw the diamond tiara she wore sink below the bobbing heads of the people in the fleeing crowd. I saw Kavanagh running.

Stieber ran after him, called, "Stop!" and fired another shot.

The bullet pinged off the floor near Kavanagh. He screamed, tripped, and fell. He twisted around to see who'd shot at him. His spectacles were crooked on his face, his mouth open. Slade picked himself up and started after Kavanagh.

"Don't move!" Stieber swung the pistol around, aiming at

Slade, at me, and the space cleared by the audience's flight. "Everyone stay where you are, or I'll shoot again!"

Crowds surged in both directions along the transept, ignoring Stieber, growing as other folks joined the rush from the Crystal Palace. Only a few people were left. George Smith had his arm protectively around me. Mr. Thackeray stood at my other side, clutching his glass of lemonade, the sardonic expression wiped off his face by shock. His mistress and George's mother were gone, carried off by the crowd. But Queen Victoria sat in a tangle of her peacock-blue skirts, by the crystal fountain, where she'd fallen. Prince Albert knelt at her right. A lone gentleman from her entourage stood at her left. It was Lord Eastbourne.

I was alarmed to see him. He stared, equally alarmed, at me, Slade, and Dr. Kavanagh. Perverse fate had brought us all together!

The Queen spied me, and her face darkened with ire. "Miss Brontë. I might have known. Whenever there is trouble, you are right at its center." She struggled to rise. Prince Albert gave her his hand and hauled her up. "Pray tell, what is going on here?"

I was dumbfounded and tongue-tied.

She observed Stieber holding the gun and said, "Who are you?"

Slade stepped forward and bowed. "Your Majesty, please allow me to introduce Wilhelm Stieber, chief spy to Tsar Nicholas."

"Mr. Slade? Is that you?" Her mouth opened in amazement as she saw the gun that Stieber had slewed in her direction. Stieber's expression went blank, so flabbergasted was he to meet the Queen of England under such circumstances. She quickly recovered her regal demeanor. "I can't say I'm happy about making your acquaintance, Mr. Stieber, but I would like it much better if you would please not point your firearm at me."

Confounded, Stieber aimed the gun at Niall Kavanagh instead. Kavanagh clutched his suitcase and gazed at the Queen, so awed by her presence that he'd forgotten to escape when he'd had his chance. The Queen said, "Mr. Slade. I am glad to see that you have risen from the dead. Perhaps you would be so good as to explain this."

"Mr. Stieber has been plotting with the Tsar to arm Russia for a war against England," Slade said. "He's in London to capture a scientist who has invented a weapon that's capable of killing millions of people." Slade indicated Kavanagh. "This is Dr. Niall Kavanagh, the scientist. That suitcase contains his weapon. I came back from Russia to keep it, and him, out of Stieber's hands."

The Queen sputtered in bewilderment. Prince Albert said, "That is what Miss Brontë told us at Osborne House. Don't you remember? It seems to be true."

She glared at her husband, then at Slade and Stieber. "If it is true, then why bring this bad business here, of all places? How dare you disrupt our beloved Great Exhibition?"

"I beg your forgiveness, Your Majesty," Slade said. "Dr. Kavanagh wants to demonstrate his bomb. This is the place he chose. Miss Brontë, Mr. Stieber, and I merely followed him here."

Uncomprehending and irate, the Queen turned on Kavanagh. "Why would you do such a thing? Dr. Kavanagh, you are a British subject. If you have invented such a weapon, you should have presented it to me, through official channels, and let me be the judge of when and where to test it. Why did you not?"

Kavanagh wasn't listening. He'd noticed Lord Eastbourne. Anger and hatred enflamed his bloodshot eyes. "We had a deal," he said, lurching to his feet and pointing at Lord Eastbourne. Lord Eastbourne recoiled as if from a leper's touch. "You agreed to help me build my weapon, but then you changed your mind. You called me a fraud. You cut me off."

Slade said, "Perhaps Lord Eastbourne could answer Your Majesty's questions."

41

>‹

"**D**O YOU KNOW DR. KAVANAGH?"
THE QUEEN ASKED LORD EAST-
bourne in surprise. "Is what he says true?"

"Your Majesty, I've never seen this man before," Lord
Eastbourne said calmly. "He's lying."

"You forbade me to tell anyone about our arrangement. You
said that if I did, no one would believe me." Kavanagh fixed
an accusing stare on Lord Eastbourne. "You burned down my
laboratory."

"I haven't the slightest idea what he's talking about." Lord
Eastbourne's face was a placid, urbane mask. "Pay him no attention, Your Majesty."

I found my voice. "Lord Eastbourne did burn down the laboratory. Mr. Slade and I were there." I moved out of George Smith's
embrace, to stand beside Slade. "We saw him."

Slade nodded. "We were almost killed."

Surprise jarred the mask of innocence off Lord Eastbourne's
face. As he turned to Slade and me, his lips pursed; then his features
tightened with vexation. I knew what he was thinking: he hadn't
known we were at the laboratory; he'd believed there had been no
witnesses to his act of arson; and he heartily wished we had died.

"Miss Brontë is lying, too, Your Majesty," Lord Eastbourne said.
"She's a murderess, and a fugitive. And Mr. Slade, well, Mr. Slade is
a traitor." His voice was unnaturally thin. "Don't believe them.

They're trying to . . . to incriminate me to save their own skins."

Neither the Queen nor the Prince was fooled. They regarded Lord Eastbourne with hurt, reproachful expressions. She clasped a hand to her chest as though his betrayal of her trust had pierced her heart and said, "Why?"

Lord Eastbourne seemed to realize that there was no use denying what he'd done, but he hurried to provide an explanation that put him in a good light. "I didn't tell you about Dr. Kavanagh because I wasn't sure that he could really deliver what he promised, a weapon with destructive powers such as the world has never known. But I felt duty-bound to investigate his claim, in case it had validity. I entered into a private arrangement with Dr. Kavanagh because I didn't want to bother Your Majesty about a project that might come to nothing. I paid for his research myself, in order to spare your treasury the expense. As it turned out, my misgivings about Dr. Kavanagh were justified. He is a fraud."

The Queen shook her head. Lord Eastbourne couldn't hide his fear now, but he blustered on. "The laboratory was in a building that I had purchased. Dr. Kavanagh had left it in such bad condition that it was beyond repair. I was within my rights to burn it down. I didn't know that Mr. Slade and Miss Brontë were there."

"That's not why you burned it down," Niall Kavanagh said. "You wanted to get rid of anything that could connect me with you. You wanted to destroy me and my work. But here I am." He bowed to the Queen, wobbled, and righted himself. "Your Majesty, I have the weapon here."

He fumbled with the latches on the suitcase. He opened it and lifted out the bomb. It had appeared more impressive in the dungeon than it did here, surrounded by splendid inventions. Queen Victoria, Prince Albert, Lord Eastbourne, and Stieber gazed dubiously at the glass jars strapped to the canister of gunpowder, the limp fuse. "That is the weapon?" Stieber said.

"See, Your Majesty?" Lord Eastbourne said, jubilant. "It's not a new miraculous weapon of war. It's an ordinary bomb that an idiot could build. This fellow is clearly mad."

"Please don't let appearances deceive you, Your Majesty," I

found the courage to say. "The bomb isn't the innovation. The innovation is the powder in the jars."

Slade quickly and concisely explained that Dr. Kavanagh had discovered that animalcules caused disease and had learned how to cultivate them. "Those jars contain enough culture to infect thousands of people with woolsorter's disease, which is fatal. The bomb is only the mechanism of spreading the culture through the air."

"It will work," Dr. Kavanagh insisted eagerly.

"Bosh and nonsense," Lord Eastbourne said. "Everyone knows that diseases are caused by bad air. Whom are you going to believe, Your Majesty? A madman, a murderess and traitor, or me? I have served the Crown long and faithfully. My record is unimpeachable."

"Not anymore," Slade said. "You blotted it when you succumbed to your ambitions. You didn't keep Kavanagh and his research under wraps for Her Majesty's sake. Rather, you wanted the weapon for yourself. You wanted the power that it would give the man who owned it. You wanted a place in history as much as Dr. Kavanagh does, at the price of your loyalty to your sovereign. You're the traitor, not I."

With a visible effort Lord Eastbourne ignored Slade. "I advise you to judge for yourself, Your Majesty." He flung his hand toward the bomb in a gesture of disdain. "Is this a weapon that will revolutionize warfare, or a joke?"

"It's not a joke!" Kavanagh wailed.

The Queen looked uncertain, although she liked Slade and I saw her incline toward taking him at his word. Slade said, "Let's try a test. Dr. Kavanagh, open one of those jars. Lord Eastbourne, you breathe the culture and show Her Majesty that it's harmless."

Lord Eastbourne took a step backward, his expression filling with alarm.

"Just as I thought," Slade said. "He's afraid to take the test. He knows Dr. Kavanagh has succeeded in creating the weapon he paid for. He reneged on their contract because he realized that the weapon is too powerful for him to control, too dangerous to use. And he had another reason for burning down the laboratory besides covering up his involvement: he knew it was rife with disease."

"That is proof enough for me," the Queen said. Indeed, it was obvious from Lord Eastbourne's face that everything Slade had said was true. "Lord Eastbourne, you have committed such serious breaches of protocol and crimes against the state that it will require a court to determine—"

Lord Eastbourne's eyes glazed with panic. He'd changed from a suave, confident gentleman into a cornered animal. He shuffled a few quick steps backward, then turned and ran into the receding horde.

"Wait!" called the Queen. "How dare you leave while I'm speaking to you?" She saw four soldiers hurrying to her aid. She ordered them, "Go arrest that man!"

Two of them hurried off; the others remained to guard her. Prince Albert said, "Don't worry; he won't get far."

"In the meantime, I have business with Dr. Kavanagh," the Queen said, turning to the scientist. "I am declaring your invention the property of the Crown and the British government. If you would be so good as to hand it over."

Kavanagh looked startled. "No." He knelt and flung his arms around the bomb.

"My dear sir, that was an order from the Queen," Mr. Thackeray said, regaining his eloquence, even though fear blanched his big, florid face.

"You have to obey," George Smith said. He, too, was pale and shaken. I saw him glance from me to Slade, trying to discern our relationship.

"I won't," Kavanagh said.

"Take it," the Queen told the two soldiers.

They started forward. Stieber pointed his gun at them and said, "I claim the weapon in the name of Russia," then started toward Kavanagh. "Put it in the suitcase and give it to me."

"Don't move!" the soldiers ordered, aiming their rifles at Stieber.

He froze. Kavanagh took a loose jar of culture from the suitcase and cried, "Nobody come near me, or I'll drop this." Everyone stood still, terrified. "There's no use fighting over my invention." Kavanagh gloated because two such powerful heads of state wanted it. "I'm not giving it away to anyone. I'm going to stage my demonstration. You can all watch."

He fumbled in his pocket and brought out a box of matches. I gasped with horror. That the Queen herself, and Prince Albert, would be among Kavanagh's first victims!

"Your Majesty and Your Highness should leave," Slade said urgently. "Go somewhere far away." He told George Smith, Mr. Thackeray, and me, "You should leave, too."

"I'm staying." I would not abandon my husband.

"I won't leave Charlotte," George declared. Not only did he wish to protect me, I observed; he'd figured out that Slade was his rival for my affections and he wouldn't let Slade be a hero while he decamped like a coward.

"Nor will I," Mr. Thackeray said. "A proper Englishman doesn't desert the battleground."

Prince Albert took his wife by the hand. Her expression was anxious, conflicted. Stieber said, "Everyone will stay," but he sounded uncertain. Events were moving too fast, too unpredictably. The Queen and the Prince, George Smith, and Thackeray were wild cards that he'd not had time to figure into his game. He moved the gun back and forth, as if he couldn't decide whom it would be best to shoot.

"Let the Queen and the Prince Consort go," Slade said. "If you hurt them, you'll be shot dead the next moment. You won't be able to do your duty to the Tsar."

I watched Stieber realize the truth in Slade's words, even though he was clearly loath to cooperate with Slade and wondered what tricks he might have up his sleeve. "Very well."

Prince Albert said, "Come, along, dearest." ·

"I will not." The Queen tore her hand free. "Britain is in danger. I can't run off like a ninny and hide. I must defend my kingdom."

I heard Slade stifle a groan. The Queen's contrary nature had asserted itself at the worst possible time. Dr. Kavanagh frowned because attention had shifted away from him.

"It's not necessary for you to be here," Prince Albert said. "I will help Mr. Slade resolve the situation peacefully."

The Queen swelled with wrath. "Are you saying that you and Mr. Slade can accomplish that better than I can?"

Prince Albert winced; he realized he'd touched a sore point. "Of course not. But you're the Queen. If anything happens to you, what will become of Britain?"

"Why should anything happen to me?" the Queen said, in high dudgeon now. "Why do you assume that I'll fail?"

"Think of the children," Prince Albert pleaded. "Do not put their mother in danger."

The Queen hesitated, torn between her duty as a monarch and her love for her children. Then her plump, girlish face hardened into mature lines. "There are times for being a mother and times for being a soldier. This is the latter sort of time. I will stay." She embodied the spirit of her ancestors who'd ridden into battle at the forefront of their armies. At that moment she looked like Henry VIII. "You go."

"I can't leave you." The prince was aghast.

"You will take care of the children. That's an order."

Prince Albert was stunned; evidently his wife had never pulled rank on him so harshly before. "Well, then . . ."

Dr. Kavanagh interrupted: "I'm going ahead with my demonstration. Stay and watch it or not."

"Go!" the Queen urged Prince Albert. "Now!"

He lumbered away, casting a worried look over his shoulder. The Queen turned to Dr. Kavanagh. "There's no need for a demonstration. I believe your theory about diseases. I believe that your invention is as wonderful as you claim. Your scientific achievement is duly recognized."

Even as I admired her for her courage and her astute assessment of what to say to placate him, Kavanagh said, "Your recognition isn't good enough."

Her eyebrows went up. "Why not? I am the highest authority in the land."

"Lord Eastbourne tried to sweep me and my discovery under the rug." Kavanagh bent an accusing stare on the Queen. "What's to say that you won't?"

Drawing herself up, her head high, she said. "I swear on the throne."

Her oath rang with the full augustness of her royal blood, but Kavanagh only frowned, toying with his matches. He absently set down the jar.

The soldiers rushed at him. Slade said, "No! Don't!"

Kavanagh screamed, gathered up his bomb, and clasped it to his chest.

"If you break the jars, we'll be infected and the entire Crystal Palace will be contaminated," Slade said.

Even as the soldiers skidded to a halt, Stieber fired his gun. The Queen shrieked. One soldier spun, fell, and lay still. A wet patch spread on his uniform jacket. The other soldier gaped with shock. He was a middle-aged man who'd probably spent years guarding the royal family but never experienced a crisis like this. Confused, he aimed the rifle at Kavanagh.

"Do not shoot him," Stieber said. "Drop your weapon and walk away." He needed Kavanagh alive, for the Tsar. He aimed his gun at the Queen. "Do as I say, or I'll shoot Her Majesty."

She gasped. The soldier let his rifle fall and reluctantly departed. Stieber said to Kavanagh, "If you give me the bomb and come with me to Russia, the Tsar will give you your own laboratory."

Awe, disbelief, and yearning combined in Kavanagh's expression. "He would do that?"

"Yes," Stieber said.

"I'll top that offer," Slade said, and looked to the Queen. "With Your Majesty's permission."

"You have it," she said. "Proceed."

"Not only will we give you a laboratory," Slade told Kavanagh, "you'll have unlimited funds for your research."

Kavanagh listened, as rapt and wishful as a little boy at Christmas, looking at toys in a shop window. Setting his bomb on the floor, he glanced from Slade to Stieber. I wished I could do something to sway his decision, to avert disaster.

"Oh, don't be so stingy!" the Queen scolded Slade. She said to Kavanagh, "I'll put Britain's best scientists at your disposal, to assist you with your work. I'll create a new Royal Scientific Society and appoint you head of it." She seemed to understand better than anyone Kavanagh's need for affirmation of his importance. "And you'll give lectures about your discoveries to Parliament."

Emotion choked Kavanagh. "Such riches are laid before me. But it's too late." He burst into tears. He smiled a sickly smile filled with pain. "I'm dying."

Stieber blinked as enlightenment struck him. "He has the disease?"

"Yes," Slade said.

George Smith, Mr. Thackeray, and the Queen shrank away from Kavanagh, fearing contagion. Stieber cut his eyes at Slade. "Why didn't you tell me?"

"Would it have made any difference if I had?" Slade said.

Stieber didn't bother answering. "Come with me, Dr. Kavanagh. Share your knowledge with the Russian scientists before you die. The Tsar will give you a state funeral, with your body embalmed in a glass coffin and the Russian army parading you through the streets of Moscow."

Kavanagh sobbed. "I have two more days to live, at most. I wouldn't make it to Russia in time."

"Give us the bomb," Slade said, "and we'll have your state funeral here in England."

"Miss Brontë and I will write your life story together," Mr. Thackeray said. "She's a famous authoress, I'm a famous author, and everyone will read about your great scientific breakthrough."

"I'll publish your biography," George chimed in. "I own a major publishing house, I should mention. I'll flood the country with copies of the book. Your face will be on the covers, in every bookstore in Britain."

"You'll be immortalized," Slade said.

"Immortalized." Kavanagh's voice was hushed; his eyes shone with tears and rapture. "It's what I always wanted." For a moment

I thought he would capitulate. We were all paralyzed by suspense. I felt hope in the air. We waited . . . until Kavanagh's habitual distrust returned. "But when I'm dead, I won't know whether you kept your word. Instead of giving me the honors I deserve, you might just relegate me to obscurity." His ghastly expression showed how much he dreaded that fate. "No. I won't be bought by promises. I must go ahead with my original plan. Then I can die happy, because everyone will know what I've done."

He struck a match. With trembling hands he applied the flame to the fuse.

42

THE FUSE CAUGHT FIRE. IT BEGAN TO BURN. THE FLAME REFLECTED in Niall Kavanagh's spectacles. Kneeling before his bomb, he had the reverent look of a saint witnessing a divine visitation. For an instant, the rest of us watched in motionless, horrified silence. The next instant, everything happened so fast that I barely had time to register who did what and when.

Slade exclaimed, "Your Majesty! Run!"

She tried to, but stumbled on her skirts. George Smith rushed to help her. Supported on his arm, she ran with him, but tripped again and fell, bringing George down with her. Slade charged toward the bomb. So did Stieber. He didn't want the bomb to explode, kill him, and foil the Tsar's plot against England, but neither did he want Slade to gain possession of the device. Before Slade could throw himself on the fuse and smother the flame, Stieber rashly gave in to his desire to destroy Slade. He fired the pistol.

I screamed, "Look out!" But I was too late. Slade dropped as if the bullet had cut his legs out from under him. A shout of pain burst from him as he landed with a heavy thud, on his side, before he reached Kavanagh. He tried to raise himself, his hands slipping in blood that spread on the floor beneath his body. Stieber aimed the gun down at Slade. I rushed to him and grabbed his arm. He threw me off and pulled the trigger.

The gun clicked. It had run out of bullets.

As I sighed with relief, he tossed the gun aside and took another from his coat pocket. He'd taken the extra weapon from one of his men before he'd left them. Now he saw, as I did, that the fuse had burned down to a mere inch. The flame flared and sputtered. Stieber dove at it while he fired on Slade again. Slade rolled away from the shot. He kicked out at Stieber with his left leg. His right leg was bleeding from the wound in his thigh. His foot struck Stieber's knee. Stieber flailed his arms and lost his grip on the gun as he tried to rebalance himself. It flew out of his hand, skittered across the floor, and stopped near the glass fountain. Stieber fell on his buttocks. Slade crawled toward the fuse. I hurried to help him, but Stieber raced up behind me and shoved me away. He and Slade lunged for the bomb. They collided in midair.

Kavanagh smiled beatifically, as if nothing that was happening could affect him. He seemed ready to die a martyr to his own genius, at peace at last.

Mr. Thackeray stood by, shifting his weight from one foot to the other, as if he couldn't decide whether to join the melee or run. His face had the expression of a stray dog I'd once seen wander into Euston Station, panicked by the roaring locomotives and the crowds. He still clutched his glass of lemonade.

The burning end of the fuse had almost reached the igniting device on the bomb. The flame burned brighter. It crackled and sizzled as it consumed the gunpowder that coated the twine. Slade and Stieber crashed to the floor together, their hands outstretched inches from the fuse. I grabbed the glass from Mr. Thackeray's hand and dashed the lemonade onto the fuse.

Sometimes we act best when we act unthinkingly. Sometimes the body takes the initiative when the mind is too fraught with confusion to guide us. I didn't pause to remember that liquid extinguishes fire. I instinctively put the ancient knowledge to work.

The fuse hissed and fizzled out. Lemonade splashed Niall Kavanagh. Uttering a startled grunt, he looked from the wet fuse to me. Slade and Stieber were struggling to untangle themselves from each other. Kavanagh giggled, took another match out of the box, and struck it. But the match was drenched. It wouldn't light. Neither would the next one he struck. Rendered impotent by common sense, the scientific genius wailed.

Mr. Thackeray and I were so surprised that we stood gaping. Kavanagh flung the matches on the floor. Then he hurled himself, shrieking and sobbing, at me. I was caught off guard. He grabbed me by the front of my dress and shouted, "You spoiled everything!" He shook me so hard that my neck snapped back and forth and my teeth jarred.

His face was purple with fury, bleared with mucus, his blood-shot eyes burning through his tears. At the corners of his mouth, saliva frothed. He reminded me of Branwell during one of his rages, desperate for opium and liquor. But Branwell had never laid a hand on any of us. I had never feared that he would hurt me except inadvertently. Niall Kavanagh punched my left ear. I cried out as pain shot through my jaw, cheekbone, and temple. The lights in the Crystal Palace shimmied and fragmented, as if behind a pane of shattering glass. Noises echoed weirdly. Through them I heard Slade calling, "Charlotte!"

My vision cleared, but I was so dizzy that that the world spun. Niall Kavanagh was yelling at me, calling me profane, ugly names. His angry face whirled before me. Nauseated by vertigo, fearing contagion, I turned my head away. I seized his wrists and tried to break his grip on me, but although he was skin and bone, weakened by disease and dissipation, his temper lent him strength. I could not break free.

Near us, Slade was on the floor with Stieber. Hands gripping each other's throats, they grunted, shouted, and kicked. Slade rolled on top of his enemy. He lifted Stieber's head up, then banged it against the floor. He thrashed free of Stieber and sped toward me.

"I'm all right," the Queen told George Smith, who hesitated between his duty to assist her and his desire to save me. "Go fetch help."

Although clearly reluctant to abandon her and me, George went running. I saw Stieber raise himself to a sitting position.

Gasping and coughing, one hand at his throat, he pushed himself onto his knees. He walked on them toward the bomb.

"Never mind me!" I cried to Slade as I grappled with Kavanagh. "Stop Stieber!"

Mr. Thackeray recovered his wits. "Go ahead," he told Slade. "I'll take care of Miss Brontë."

Slade wheeled around and charged at Stieber. Mr. Thackeray took hold of Kavanagh's collar, said, "Desist, or I'll be forced to hurt you," and pulled.

With one hand still twisted in the folds of my dress, Kavanagh flung his other arm up and behind him. His fist hit Mr. Thackeray's face. Mr. Thackeray yelped and released Kavanagh. I struck out at Kavanagh, pummeling his face. He seemed not to care, even though blood poured from his nose. He shook me, cursing while I fended off slaps and punches. My vertigo upset my balance; I fell. He crashed upon me, just as Slade tackled Stieber and brought him down.

Flat on my back, I kicked, but my legs were entwined in my skirts. I struggled to push Kavanagh away, but his weight held me down. He caught my wrists, pinned them to the floor. Mr. Thackeray seized Kavanagh by the arms and heaved. Kavanagh lifted off me like a tiger ripped from its prey. The ruffle on my dress tore off in his hands. He shrieked; his body arched and flailed. As Mr. Thackeray tried to grip him in a headlock, Kavanagh snarled and bit. He assailed Mr. Thackeray like a dervish made of kicks, swings, and punches. He was so consumed by violent urges that he forgot who'd angered him; he didn't care whom he attacked. Mr. Thackeray clumsily dodged and parried blows. They landed everywhere. His legs caved. I snatched at Kavanagh, but he swerved out of my reach. He lowered his head and rammed it into Mr. Thackeray's stomach. Mr. Thackeray doubled over, dropped to his knees, and fainted.

I tried to stand, but my dizziness tilted the floor up at a sickening angle. My ear rang and my head ached from Kavanagh's blow. I saw the bomb, sitting in a puddle of lemonade, ignored by everyone. I heard the Queen shout, "Miss Brontë, get the bomb! The bomb, you idiot!"

I dragged myself toward it while Kavanagh hobbled to a standstill. The Queen's words had penetrated his tantrum; he saw me and realized that he was about to lose his precious invention. He bellowed, ran ahead of me, and snatched up the bomb. He crammed it into the suitcase and secured the lid. The room pitched like the deck of a ship in a storm, but I managed to reach him. I grabbed the suitcase.

"You can't have it!" Kavanagh shrilled. "It's mine!"

We fought a tug-of-war. He had hold of the handle and I, the wheels. I hung on even though I was sweating and sick. The jars inside the suitcase rattled dangerously. I prayed that shaking the bomb wouldn't set off the gunpowder.

Slade wrestled Stieber by the fountain. Stieber's movements had grown feeble; his strength was waning. Slade straddled his stomach and punched his face again and again. Slade's expression was merciless as he administered the brutal beating. It seemed as if he dealt Stieber one blow for each of the Russian radicals and British agents executed, one for Katerina's death, one for his torture in Bedlam, one for mine. Stieber wriggled helplessly, his face a mass of blood.

I yanked on the suitcase with all my might. At the same moment Kavanagh shoved the suitcase at me. I fell backward. The ceiling undulated; lights twirled. Kavanagh pulled on the suitcase. An attack of retching weakened my grip on the wheels.

Stieber flung out his hand and groped for the pistol he'd dropped. His fingers grazed it, but it slid out of his reach. Slade saw. Delivering another punch to Stieber's face, he snatched up the pistol. Stieber pounded his fist against the bullet wound in Slade's thigh. Slade yelled and convulsed with pain. Stieber grabbed the wrist of Slade's hand that held the pistol. He and Slade grappled for control of the weapon. It discharged with loud bangs, spewing bullets that ricocheted off the floor

Kavanagh ripped the suitcase out of my hands. Exhaustion and dizziness overcame me. I collapsed. Kavanagh absconded, the suitcase in tow. He wheezed and coughed, his steps slowed by exhaustion, his strength sapped by disease: a dead man on his last, desperate flight.

Slade wrenched the pistol and himself away from Stieber. He rose on his good leg, teetered on his injured one. Stieber sat up, bleeding from his nose and mouth. Slade aimed the pistol at his foe and cocked the trigger. His raw, battered face wore an expression of triumph so unholy that it was frightening. At last he would have his revenge.

The Queen shouted, "Kavanagh is getting away!" She started after him, hobbled on a sprained ankle, and stopped. "Mr. Slade!" She pointed at Kavanagh, who'd progressed some ten feet down the transept. "Shoot him!"

Jolted out of his private obsession, Slade looked from Stieber to Kavanagh. His face went momentarily blank as he observed Kavanagh lugging the suitcase that contained the bomb, which needed only a new fuse and new matches to explode. He aimed the pistol at Kavanagh.

"There's one bullet left," Stieber said, his words muffled by cut, bloody lips. "You can shoot him or me. It's your choice."

"Him!" The Queen jabbed her finger at Kavanagh.

Slade gritted his teeth against the pain of his wound. His trousers were drenched with blood. I watched him realize that if he shot Kavanagh, he would have to kill Stieber with his bare hands, and he hadn't enough strength left. He swung the pistol around to Stieber.

"Don't! That's an order!" the Queen shouted.

"You'd better shoot Kavanagh before he's out of range." Amusement gleamed through the blood running into Stieber's swollen eyes.

Although he knew that Kavanagh and the bomb posed a greater immediate threat than Stieber did, Slade hesitated. I saw his thirst for revenge battling his duty to the Queen and his need to save the world. I was so much in sympathy with my husband that I couldn't speak, even though my own life hung in the balance. The decision must be Slade's.

"Well?" Stieber said with a malicious smile. "Which will it be?"

Despair shone in Slade's eyes.

They met mine.

Love obliterated the anguish and indecision in his gaze.

As Kavanagh hobbled farther away, Slade clasped the gun in both hands to steady it, sighted on Kavanagh, and fired. The gun kicked in his hands as it boomed. The force knocked Slade to his knees. Kavanagh twisted, then crumpled. He lay beside the suitcase, writhed, and squalled. Slade had sacrificed his revenge, for my sake.

Stieber pushed himself to his hands and knees. He crawled, then walked on all fours, then stood up and ran with a lurching, unsteady gait.

George Smith returned, accompanied by a horde of policemen. The Queen directed them to Kavanagh. The police surrounded the scientist. She said, "Take that suitcase, and be careful with it!"

Mr. Thackeray awoke and said dazedly, "What happened?"

I gathered myself up. Still battling dizziness, I faltered over to Slade.

"Are you all right?" I asked. The sight of all the blood on him horrified me. Could he lose so much and survive? I wrung my hands, not knowing what to do. I embraced him and kissed his cut, bruised face.

"I'm fine," Slade gasped out.

He limped after Stieber, fell, and cursed. Helpless, he aimed the gun at his retreating enemy. He pulled the trigger, and I knew he hoped Stieber had lied about the number of bullets left in the gun. But the gun only clicked. Stieber had spoken the truth. With a roar of enraged frustration, Slade threw the gun at Stieber. It landed on the floor inches short of its target. Stieber reached the crowds still massed at the distant end of the Crystal Palace.

"Stop him!" I cried.

No one did.

43

Aweek after the scene at the Crystal Palace, I returned to Bedlam. It was a rare, fine summer morning in London, shortly before eight o'clock. The sky was blue, the air freshened by a cool wind. Pigeons fluttered, their wings flashing white in the sun, above the dome of the insane asylum. The horrors that I'd experienced there still gave me nightmares, but today I felt no fear as I entered Bedlam. Slade was beside me. He limped from the gunshot wound in his thigh and leaned on a cane, but fortunately the bullet had gone straight through, causing no serious damage besides an alarming loss of blood. That he hadn't died was a testament to his strong constitution and will to live.

We walked together beneath the shade trees on the grounds of Bedlam. I carried a gift- wrapped box from a confectionary store. We climbed the wide staircase with the other visitors, then proceeded to the criminal lunatics' wing. I hesitated, my heart suddenly pounding, outside the iron door, that portal to hell.

"Don't be afraid," Slade said, his hand closing warmly around mine. "Everyone who worked for Wilhelm Stieber is gone."

"I know." The police had arrested the doctor who'd tortured us. Wagner was dead, accidentally killed by me. Friedrich had hanged himself in Newgate Prison. We had learned this from a Foreign Office agent who'd come to see us at the hotel where we were staying. But I had to steel my nerves as the matron admitted us to the criminal lunatics' wing and led us down those dismal corridors. She unlocked a door, put her head in, and said, "You've a visitor."

While Slade waited outside, I entered the cell. Julia Garrs sat primly on her bed. She smiled, and her violet-gray eyes sparkled with pleasure. "Charlotte! You've come back to see me! They said you wouldn't, but I knew you would."

"Hello, Julia." Tears stung my eyes because she again reminded me so painfully of Anne. "I brought you a present."

She tore open the wrappings. "Oh, I love candy! Thank you so much."

"I wanted to thank you," I said. "You saved my life."

When Lord Palmerston had sent his troops to Bedlam, Julia had guided them to me. If not for her, I would have been murdered by Stieber.

She nodded as if she understood, even though I couldn't tell her what had happened. I said, "If there's anything I can do for you, please let me know."

"Could you find my baby?" she asked. "And tell him that I'll be with him soon?"

All I could say was that I promised I would. I pitied her, and I thanked God that Anne was at peace. I bid goodbye to Julia, then joined Slade in the corridor. He said, "Are you sure you want to do this?"

"Yes." I had set off a chain of events, and I felt obligated to witness all the consequences.

The matron led us to another cell. Slade and I peered in the window. Niall Kavanagh crouched on the floor, dressed in pajamas, his red hair tousled; his spectacles had slipped down his nose. Pen in hand, he scribbled frantically on sheets of paper. His writings and diagrams looked like utter nonsense.

"He's been doing that every day," the matron said. The army had taken Kavanagh straight from the Crystal Palace to Bedlam. The doctors had removed the bullet that Slade had fired into his shoulder and stitched up the wound. They'd also discovered that he was suffering from pneumonia, not woolsorter's disease. He wasn't going to die yet. "His ma and pa came to see him yesterday, and he got so violent we had to tie him up in a blanket gown."

I pitied Sir William and Lady Kavanagh. As I wondered what terrible new ideas he was formulating, Kavanagh looked up. His face was puffy, his gaze blurred. He didn't seem aware of me. Then he bent his head over his papers and continued scribbling. My heart ached because I saw Branwell in him. But I took comfort from the fact that my brother had come to his senses and repented of his sins in the end, while Kavanagh had not.

"What will become of him?" I asked Slade.

"He'll probably spend the rest of his life here."

"But shouldn't he be tried in court and punished for what he's done?" After all, he'd murdered the three women in Whitechapel, and he'd almost killed the Queen, not to mention millions of other people.

"Imprisonment in Bedlam will have to be punishment enough," Slade said. "Kavanagh can't be put on trial. He can't go out in public, not even to be hanged. God only knows what he might say. He has to stay in Bedlam, where his ravings won't be taken seriously and the doctors can control him with drugs. Otherwise, the whole story might come out. And the government does not want the story to come out."

Queen Victoria had cleaned up after the fiasco at the Crystal Palace with admirable if not gentle efficiency. She sent for the army to restore peace at the Great Exhibition, then ordered Slade, George Smith, Mr. Thackeray, and me to accompany her, Prince Albert, and the royal entourage back to Buckingham Palace. When we arrived, we were given rooms in the guest quarters. The Queen's personal physician removed the bullet from Slade's leg and dressed the wound. I kept vigil by his bedside while Slade slept.

In the morning, after breakfast, a servant escorted me to a

chamber where I found George and Mr. Thackeray sitting at a vast, highly polished table beneath a crystal chandelier. They didn't appear to have slept any more than I had. They had dark shadows under their eyes and the stunned look of people who had wandered into strange territory and didn't know if they could ever go home. They rose when I joined them. We remained standing while the Queen and Lord Palmerston entered.

We made our bows; the Queen acknowledged them with a brisk nod. She seated herself across the table from us, motioned us to sit, and said, "I've summoned you here to talk about the sorry business at the Great Exhibition."

Standing beside her, Palmerston smiled, but with less humor than usual. "We must ask you not to discuss it with anyone, not even among yourselves."

I suspected he was sorry to have missed out on the excitement. Perhaps he also thought he could have handled the situation better than we had.

"Oh, don't mince words," the Queen said impatiently. "We're not asking. It's an order."

"My apologies, Your Majesty," Palmerston said.

"It would serve no good purpose for the British people to learn what almost happened," the Queen said. "It would only frighten them and destroy their confidence in the government."

Neither George, Mr. Thackeray, nor I dared to suggest that since the threat to Britain had been engineered by one of its own officials, perhaps the government deserved to lose some of its citizens' faith in it. When the Queen said, "Do you swear to keep the events of last night a secret?" we each solemnly said, "I do."

"You are free to go," Palmerston said. "Unless you have questions you'd like to ask."

"I hope Dr. Crick is not in trouble?" I said.

"Fortunately for him, no one was hurt when his airship exploded," Palmerston said. "I've had him sent home. He won't be punished."

"The only thing he's guilty of is having the bad judgment to fall in with you, Miss Brontë," the Queen said, cutting her eyes at me.

Mr. Thackeray spoke up. "What's to become of Dr. Kavanagh?"

"That is yet to be determined," the Queen said.

"What about his research?" George asked.

"Her Majesty has declared it a state secret," Palmerston said. I understood that it was his idea. "We'll collect Kavanagh's papers and equipment and put them in a secure place."

"Shouldn't his work be continued?" Mr. Thackeray asked.

"It could be used for the good of mankind," George said. "Why, it could revolutionize science."

"Possibly," the Queen said, "but his theory about the cause of disease is too extreme to be sprung on the world all of a sudden."

"His techniques for culturing the animalcules are too dangerous to let fall into the hands of our enemies during this troubled age," Palmerston said. "His work must be suppressed until the time is right to make it public."

I couldn't imagine when that would be. "But Wilhelm Stieber knows about Dr. Kavanagh's research. He'll tell the Tsar."

Palmerston's smile thinned. "Not if we can help it."

"Your Majesty, may I ask how Mr. Slade is?" George said, looking at me.

"My physician tells me that Mr. Slade is expected to make a full recovery. But you could have asked Miss Brontë." The Queen gave me an unpleasant, insinuating smile. "I daresay she knows more about Mr. Slade than anyone else does."

I covered my embarrassment by asking, "Is there any news of Lord Eastbourne?"

"He was caught this morning at his home, where he'd gone to pack his things and fetch money to leave the country," Palmerston said.

"What will become of him?" Mr. Thackeray asked.

"He will get his comeuppance," the Queen said, "never fear."

"In the meantime, we would like to thank you for your service to the Crown," Palmerston said to George, Mr. Thackeray, and me. "I'm sorry that because of the need for discretion, we can't give you any medals, but please know that you are held in the highest honor."

"Yes," the Queen said. "Mr. Smith and Mr. Thackeray, you are heroes. And you, Miss Brontë, are a heroine." She pronounced the last word as if she'd had another one in mind.

We thanked her and Lord Palmerston. After she had dismissed us, George and Mr. Thackeray and I were escorted out of the palace to a carriage that waited to take us home. Mr. Thackeray said, "That was certainly a hullabaloo, wasn't it, Miss Brontë?" I noticed that he didn't call me Jane Eyre. I suspected he never would again. "I could have dined out on it for the next ten years if I hadn't been sworn to secrecy."

George held out his hand to help me into the carriage. "May I?"

"Thank you, but I'm not going yet." I wanted to wait for Slade.

George dropped his hand. "I understand." He sounded dejected. I recalled that he'd seen me kissing Slade last night. He'd deduced that there was no place in my heart for him. "Well, then," he said with an attempt at a smile. "I hope to see you the next time you're in London."

As I bade goodbye to my friends, I felt a distance between us. Last night they'd seen a new side of me, and it had frightened them. Because of me they'd become involved in a near disaster. Our friendship would never be the same, I regretted as I watched the carriage roll out the palace gate. But although I had lost something valuable, I had found what I had set my heart on that day I'd visited Bedlam. I turned and went back inside the palace, to Slade.

Now the bells at St. Sepulchre's Church tolled eight o'clock. A huge crowd massed outside Newgate Prison to watch justice served. Men, women, and children pressed against the railings that surrounded the scaffold, a platform some ten feet high and ten feet long, which abutted the wall of the prison. Upon the scaffold, the gibbet consisted of two parallel beams supported on two wooden pillars. A roof sheltered a pair of benches. Slade and I sat in the gallery provided for privileged spectators, amid government and court officials and their guests. I felt sick to my stomach with anticipation and dread.

I had never witnessed a hanging before, although public executions were a popular form of entertainment in London.

"You don't have to watch," Slade said, uneasy for my sake. "We can leave now."

"I must. We'll stay."

I knew he wanted to see his investigation through to its end, and I felt a duty to witness the consequences brought about in part by my actions. It was my duty as a writer to look straight at them, so that I would be able to tell the story with firsthand authenticity. Gazing at the gentlemen and ladies seated with us and the people in the crowd below, I was startled by their gay conversation and laughter. They showed none of the sorrow, fear, or sobriety that befitted the occasion; only ribaldry, humor, and drunken debauchery did I observe.

"It's like a carnival," I said.

"Or like Romans come to watch the gladiators fight," Slade said. "This is blood sport in the name of the law."

Two sheriffs emerged from the prison. As they sat on the benches on the scaffold, the crowd's noise quieted to an expectant hum. The hangman came out next and stood by the gibbet. Then the pastor appeared, escorting Lord Eastbourne.

Men cheered and booed, boys whistled; they doffed and waved their hats. Ladies and girls applauded. My attention riveted upon Lord Eastbourne. He wore a formal black suit; his wrists were tied behind his back. His jaw was tight; his ruddy complexion had gone pale. His eyes looked straight ahead as he mounted the steps to the gallows. He seemed unaware of the crowds, their jeers. I shrank from him, afraid that our gazes would meet, that I would see the hatred and anger he must feel toward me because I had played a role in his downfall.

Lord Eastbourne ignored the galleries. If he knew that Slade and I were there, he gave no indication. He stoically took his place on a trapdoor set into the platform, under the gibbet.

The crowd fell almost silent. Only a few coughs, a crying child, and the faraway sounds of the city disturbed the hush that engulfed the execution ground. My heart raced; I could hardly breathe. The pastor asked Lord Eastbourne if he had any final words.

Lord Eastbourne could have said that he was guilty of nothing except rash ambition and going behind the Queen's back. He could have pointed out that he'd tried to put Niall Kavanagh out of action and undo the damage he'd done. He could have added that letting me rot in jail and letting the government think Slade was a traitor were not capital crimes. He could have protested that he'd been sentenced to die only because someone had to pay for the fiasco at the Great Exhibition. All these statements would have been true. But nothing he said could alter his fate.

Lord Eastbourne shook his head. He didn't lower himself by pleading his case to the riffraff. He stood tall and proud while the pastor intoned prayers for him, but I was close enough to see him trembling. The hangman drew a white cotton nightcap over his head, bound a muslin handkerchief over his face. I saw his breath suck and puff at the cloth over his mouth. The hangman placed the rope around Lord Eastbourne's neck and tightened the noose. He bent and withdrew the pin that held the trapdoor in place.

The trapdoor fell, opening a rectangular hole beneath Lord Eastbourne.

He dropped some two feet into the hole.

I winced as the rope pulled taut. I heard him grunt, his neck snap.

With his white-shrouded head canted at an angle, Lord Eastbourne writhed for a terrible moment. Then he was still. His clothes were limp and loose, as if the man had gone out of them. A corpse swung from the gibbet.

The crowd went wild. People cheered, stamped their feet, and howled. Police forced the mob away from the scaffold. I felt so faint that the riotous scene wavered before me.

Slade took my hand. "Let's get out of here."

When we were inside a carriage, riding through the crowds that streamed away from Newgate Prison, I recovered enough to say, "I thought I would feel that Lord Eastbourne got what he deserved and justice had been done. But I don't." There was a hollow in my heart, a sense of unfinished business rather than vindication. "It's as if his death wasn't punishment enough. And I feel evil because I participated in the taking of a human life, which I am beginning to doubt anyone has the right to do, even in the case of traitors or murderers."

"I know," Slade said. "Those have been my thoughts, too, at every execution I've seen. Hanging is an eye for an eye, but it doesn't always satisfy the need for vengeance. That can persist even after the criminal is dead, when he's beyond our reach." A frown darkened his features, which were thin and drawn from the hardships he'd suffered. "And in this case, Lord Eastbourne wasn't the only guilty party, or the one who most deserved punishment."

I nodded, equally distressed. Wilhelm Stieber was still at large.

"That reminds me. I may have some news of Stieber." Slade took from his pocket a letter that he'd received this morning. He opened the envelope and unfolded the letter. "It's from the Foreign Office. They've been searching for Stieber, canvassing Whitechapel, questioning the European refugees. One of their informants sighted Stieber aboard a ship that was bound for Casablanca." Slade added bitterly, "He's given us the slip."

I murmured in disappointment, but I wasn't surprised. Slade exclaimed, "I wish I could have killed the bastard!"

"You were faced with a difficult choice," I reminded him. He had loved me enough to sacrifice his revenge, and he'd put the good of the many ahead of his own momentary, long-desired satisfaction. "You made the right one."

". . . Yes," Slade said.

I knew he was thinking over the events of that night, wondering what he might have done differently. I told him a deep-seated belief of mine: "If one thing had turned out differently, so might everything else. If you had killed Stieber, perhaps you couldn't have saved us all."

Slade looked skeptical, then resigned. "Perhaps I could have. But there's not much use in debating; we'll never know. It's over."

"It is," I said, relieved. "If England and Russia go to war someday, we can be glad that Niall Kavanagh's weapon won't be used by either side. Perhaps Stieber will get his just desserts. But for now we can think about our future." We had discussed it this past week, and we'd agreed that the first thing we must do was break the news of our marriage to my father, in person. Furthermore, I wanted a real wedding, in our church at home. "Shall we leave for Haworth today?"

Slade wasn't listening. He continued reading his letter, and a strange expression of gladness mixed with dismay came over his face.

"What is it?" I asked.

"I've been reinstated. I am an agent of the Foreign Office once again."

"But that's good news." I was delighted for him, because I knew this was what he wanted, his honor and the Crown's trust in him restored. "Isn't it?"

He put aside the letter and took my hands in his. The anguish in his eyes told me everything. Tears welled up in my eyes. "Oh, no."

"Oh, yes, I hate to say. The bad news is that I'm being sent out on an assignment."

I clung to him in a futile attempt to keep him with me, but duty had called; he must answer, and I knew he wanted to go. His work was in his blood, as writing was in mine. I would not ask him to give up his vocation. He'd offered to do so when he'd proposed to me three years ago, but I had refused because I couldn't let him make the sacrifice and I couldn't leave Haworth. The only compromise would have been to live apart, which neither of us had wanted. Now that we were married, I must brave the separation.

"An assignment where?" I asked faintly. "To do what?"

"I can't tell you," Slade said. "It's supposed to be kept secret. In fact, I won't know myself until I board the ship."

"When is that?"

Slade exhaled in sad regret. "Tomorrow morning."

I was alarmed. "But you're wounded. How can they put you back to work so soon?"

"My wound isn't serious. It'll heal while I'm en route to wherever I'm going."

"After everything you've been through for the sake of England, don't you deserve a respite?" I said, indignant. "Couldn't you ask for one?"

"I'm afraid not," Slade said.

"Perhaps if we told your superiors at the Foreign Office that we are newly married, they would grant us a little time together."

"They wouldn't." Slade explained, "The Queen herself ordered that I should go on this mission."

I remembered the Queen's barbed references to my vigil at Slade's bedside during our night at Buckingham Palace. She was aware that we were lovers, even though she didn't know we'd married. I also remembered her anger at me for bringing the business with Niall Kavanagh, Wilhelm Stieber, and Lord Eastbourne to a head, even though I'd done it inadvertently and things would have been worse if I hadn't. A part of her blamed me for the near disaster at the Great Exhibition. She couldn't forgive me, and she still couldn't forget that I had been involved in the endangerment of her children three years ago. She'd been forced, once again, to declare me a heroine, but she had found a most personal way to punish me.

"She's sending you abroad to separate us!" I was so infuriated that I forgot all the respect I owed the Queen. "That cruel, petty, hateful, diabolical harpy!"

Slade drew back, shocked by my outburst. "I don't believe she would do that."

"Of course you don't. You're a man. I'm a woman, and I know what women are capable of doing to other women they don't like."

"All right, if you say so." Slade clearly wanted to avoid an argument. "But be that as it may, I can't defy Her Majesty."

Nor could I. I had thwarted Wilhelm Stieber, defeated Lord Eastbourne, and sabotaged Niall Kavanagh's bomb, but I was helpless against the Queen. I wept with all the rage, despair, and heartache that I'd accumulated during my adventures. "I've found you and now I'm losing you again!"

"I won't be gone forever," Slade said, although he looked as miserable as I felt.

"What if you don't come back?" That was the fear I'd harbored during his three years of absence.

"I will. I promise." Slade enfolded me in his arms, held my head against his chest. He spoke with tenderness and passion. "We're husband and wife. Not even fate can separate us forever." He kissed my hair while our carriage bore us on our last journey through London and I sobbed. "And I'm here now. We'll make our last day and night together count."

EPILOGUE

R EADER, I RETURNED TO
HAWORTH ALONE.

Slade and I did endeavor to make our brief time together happy.
The memory of it would sustain us in the future. But we knew
how thin those memories might have to stretch—over years, perhaps. The strain of our imminent parting infused every hour that
passed, everything we said. Our last lovemaking had a feverish, desperate quality. Neither of us slept that night. In the morning, we
dallied over breakfast so long that we were late to Euston Station.
We had but a moment for last words on the platform before my
train left.

"When will you return?" I had forbidden myself to cry.

"As soon as I can," Slade said.

"Will you write to me?"

"If it's possible."

After a hasty kiss and embrace, I boarded the train. As it huffed
out of the station, I put my head out the window and waved to
Slade. He stood on the platform and waved back, his figure growing smaller with the distance until I could see him no more.

I wept all during that journey, and when I arrived at Keighley
Station that evening, my eyes burned, my face was swollen, and my
head ached. I hired a wagon to take my bag to Haworth, but I
decided to walk the four miles. The evening was warm, mellowed
by a golden sunset. The air vibrated with the songs of birds that
winged from tree to tree as I plodded along the road. The moors

exuded the fresh, sweet scents of grasses and flowers. At first the loveliness around me was a torment. Nature's indifference to my pain seemed cruel. But soon my familiar, beloved landscape began to work its healing magic. By the time I reached the parsonage, I was calm enough to face Papa.

I found him at the dinner table with Mr. Nicholls. I was dismayed to see Mr. Nicholls, for I had wanted a quiet homecoming and no guests to complicate matters. At least Ellen wasn't there, as I'd feared she would be. My father and his curate rose to greet me with exclamations of surprise and relief.

"Charlotte, where have you been?" Papa asked. "I was so worried about you."

"So was I," Mr. Nicholls seemed truly concerned about my welfare, not angry that I'd rudely left him in the Lake District. "Are you all right?"

"Yes." I was glad that Papa had apparently put aside his anger at Mr. Nicholls and they were united in their concern for me. But their solicitude dissolved my frail composure. Exhausted, I dropped into a chair, gave in to despair, and wept anew.

"What happened?" Papa asked as he and Mr. Nicholls hovered awkwardly near me.

"I can't tell you." I couldn't break my silence and risk the Queen's displeasure.

"I see." Papa's expression said he was envisioning a scenario as disastrous as the one in which we'd found ourselves three years ago. He summoned Martha Brown, who brought me tea, and waited until I had regained my self-control. Then he said, "Can you at least say whether matters have been resolved?"

I assured him that they had.

"What has become of John Slade?" Papa asked.

Mr. Nicholls frowned at the unfamiliar name. "Who is John Slade?"

Now was the time to announce that Slade and I were married, but I could not. Papa didn't want me to marry at all, and he would be furious because I hadn't notified him first or sought his permission, even though he liked and admired Slade. He would also be horrified by my makeshift nuptials, especially since Slade and I couldn't legitimize them with a proper wedding in church. Mr. Nicholls would surely heap his disapproval on top of Papa's, which was more than I could face. Furthermore, they would think ill of Slade for leaving me, and worse of me for entering into such a reckless union. They wouldn't understand the circumstances or believe that love should outweigh propriety.

"Mr. Slade is just a friend," I said, even though I hated to lie and deny my husband. "He's gone abroad for the foreseeable future."

Papa received this news with relief. "It's for the best, Charlotte. I like the fellow, but he brings trouble whenever he comes around."

Mr. Nicholls observed me closely, his heavy brow furrowing. I colored because I sensed that he had deduced something of my feelings for Slade. I feared a scene that would reveal my secrets. But all Mr. Nicholls said was, "If you ever need a friend, I'm here." And I was comforted, even though he wasn't Slade.

13 June 1852. I finish my tale on my first anniversary. When Slade and I wed on board the *Gipsy*, we didn't realize that it was Friday the thirteenth. Those were such tumultuous times that I had lost track of the calendar and failed to notice that we'd chosen a most inauspicious day. Now a year has passed, and I still have not told anyone that Slade and I are married. Without Slade by my side, I cannot bear to face the questions, the censure, and the scandal that would surely arise if I did tell. Furthermore, there were no physical consequences of our marriage that would have necessitated making it public. I keep it as close a secret as the events involving Niall Kavanagh and Wilhelm Stieber.

In the meantime, I go about my business. Although plagued by low spirits, ill health, and loneliness, I have enjoyed visits with Ellen Nussey and other friends. I have made a pilgrimage to Anne's grave in Scarborough. Papa had a stroke, which paralyzed him for a few days, but he has recovered. I correspond with Mr. Thackeray and George Smith, who have generously forgiven me for that night at the Crystal Palace. Indeed, George and I have resumed our friendly flirtation through the mail. On paper we can be as we were, if not in person. I am presently working on a new novel, entitled *Villette*. Arthur Nicholls has been a constant, sympathetic presence in my life.

I have not heard from Slade. I do not know where he is. I do not know whether he is alive or dead, whether I am his wife or his widow. When Slade returns, we shall announce our marriage. If he does not . . .

That is a possibility too awful to contemplate. I will not heed superstition and believe that because we wed on an unlucky day, our marriage is doomed. I have more faith in Slade than to think his enemies will defeat him or that he will forsake me. He *will* return. Of that I am certain.

AUTHOR'S NOTE

*B*EDLAM: The Further Secret *Adventures of Charlotte Brontë*
is a novel in which I have combined fiction with actual historical
characters and events. Charlotte Brontë was the real-life author of
Jane Eyre. In 1851, she was a literary celebrity, much sought after,
the subject of speculation and gossip. She enjoyed friendships with
other literary figures, including George Smith (her publisher), and
William Makepeace Thackeray, who appear in this book. She and
Mr. Smith had a close personal relationship, and they carried on a
flirtation through the mail, as evidenced by her letters to him. Mr.
Thackeray really did introduce Charlotte as "Jane Eyre" at his lecture. He did have an insane wife, and the fact that Charlotte dedicated the second edition of her book to him fueled the rumor that
she had been a governess in his house, had an affair with him, and
based the heroine and hero of *Jane Eyre* on herself and Mr.
Thackeray. (That rumor wasn't true.)

The Reverend Bronte, Ellen Nussey, Arthur Nicholls, Lord
Palmerston, Queen Victoria, Prince Albert, the royal children, Tsar
Nicholas, and Prince Orlov were also real people. So was George
Smith's friend, Dr. John Forbes, whom Charlotte did consult about
her sister Anne. Wilhelm Stieber was in fact a super-spy of his
time. He had a remarkable career, which he described in his mem-
oir, *The Chancellor's Spy*, and according to him, he really did travel

to London in 1851 to roust Karl Marx. He died in 1882. Oliver Heald is a fictional character inspired by Charlotte Brontë's actual fans, who did sometimes show up at her house uninvited. Katerina the Great is based on the actress Rachel, whose stunning performance Charlotte saw at the French Theatre. Niall Kavanagh is a composite of various scientific geniuses with character flaws (see *The Scientists* by John Gribbin), plus a big dash of Branwell Brontë and Dr. Frankenstein.

Real historical settings are featured in this book. They include Newgate Prison and Bethlem Royal Hospital, popularly known as Bedlam. Charlotte actually visited both institutions, although it happened in 1853 and not 1851, and she wasn't an inmate in either place. She also attended the Great Exhibition. Bethlem Royal Hospital still exists today, in modernized form. Osborne, Queen Victoria's retreat, still graces the Isle of Wight. The London district of Whitechapel is the same place where Jack the Ripper began his reign of terror in 1888. During Victorian times, Whitechapel was so rife with violent crime that some Jack the Ripper experts disagree on how many of the women murdered were Jack's victims and how many were killed by other people. A serial killer in Whitechapel in 1851 was entirely possible.

The scenes in Russia take place in real historical settings (Butyrka Prison, the Kremlin, and areas of Moscow). I have portrayed Russia's atmosphere, people, and social conditions as accurately I could within the bounds of my story. The Third Section was the Russian secret police organization. In the nineteenth century, Russia did have a political rivalry with England, which led to the Crimean War in 1853.

Victorian science is one of my favorite elements in the book. Galvanism, mesmerism, and the treatments administered to the patients in Bedlam were all methods in use during the period. Phrenology was indeed the rage, and Charlotte and George Smith did pay a visit to Dr. Browne the phrenologist. (Those are the actual results of Dr. Browne's analysis.) The airship is based on the first engine-powered airship, built by Henri Giffard, which he flew in 1852. Woolsorter's disease is now known as anthrax. The germ theory of disease—the idea that infectious illnesses are caused by microorganisms—was developed in 1862, by Louis Pasteur. In 1851, the general public and most scientists would have scorned the theory. But the existence of microorganisms had been discovered (during the seventeenth century), and multiple scientists can have the same idea; the credit generally goes to the one who publishes first. I believe it's possible that the cause of anthrax and other diseases could have been discovered earlier. And although germ warfare is a twentieth century invention, the means to build a simple biological weapon existed at the time that *Bedlam* takes place.

I must emphasize that *Bedlam* is fiction. Reality and imagination are intertwined in it. Characters and plot have roots in fact, but the major events in the story never happened.